Praise for Lance Erlick and the Android Chronicles

"*Reborn* births a new standard for post-modern science fiction. Lance Erlick has penned a cutting edge, bracing tale of a not-so-distant future roiled by mankind's morality unable to keep pace with its technological advancement, as he wondrously seeks to resolve the age-old question of what it means to be human. Bristling with documented science ably mixed with shattering speculation, this is sci-fi writing that would make Isaac Asimov and Robert Heinlein proud and fans of HBO's *Westworld* thrilled. Would make a great James Cameron movie!"

—**Jon Land,** *USA Today* bestselling author of *The Rising* (with Heather Graham)

"An interplanetary tale with effectively slow build that leads to a solid climax."

—***Kirkus Reviews*** on *Xenogenic: First Contact*

"An action-packed love story with even more twists and turns than its prequel."

—***Kirkus Reviews*** on *Rebels Divided*

"Inventive dystopian sci-fi drama... [a] well-thought-out science-fiction world."

—***Kirkus Reviews*** on *Rebel Trap*

"A stimulating, worthwhile story of a dystopian future."

—***Kirkus Reviews*** on *The Rebel Within*

Books by Lance Erlick

The Android Chronicles Series
Reborn
Unbound
Emergent

The Regina Shen Series
Regina Shen: Resilience
Regina Shen: Vigilance
Regina Shen: Defiance
Regina Shen: Endurance

The Rebel Series
The Rebel Within
The Rebel Trap
Rebels Divided

Xenogeneic: First Contact

Android Chronicles: Emergent

Lance Erlick

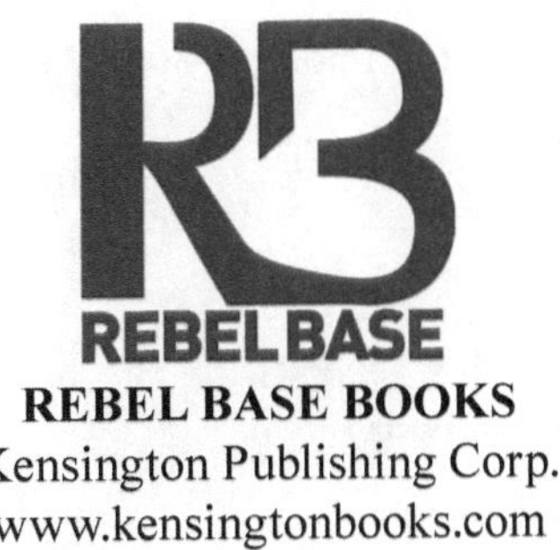

REBEL BASE BOOKS
Kensington Publishing Corp.
www.kensingtonbooks.com

Rebel Base Books are published by
Kensington Publishing Corp. 119 West 40th Street New York, NY 10018

First Electronic Edition: March 2019
ISBN-13: 978-1-63573-054-8 (ebook)
ISBN-10: 1-63573-054-6 (ebook)

First Print Edition: March 2019
ISBN-13: 978-1-63573-057-9
ISBN-10: 1-63573-057-0

Printed in the United States of America

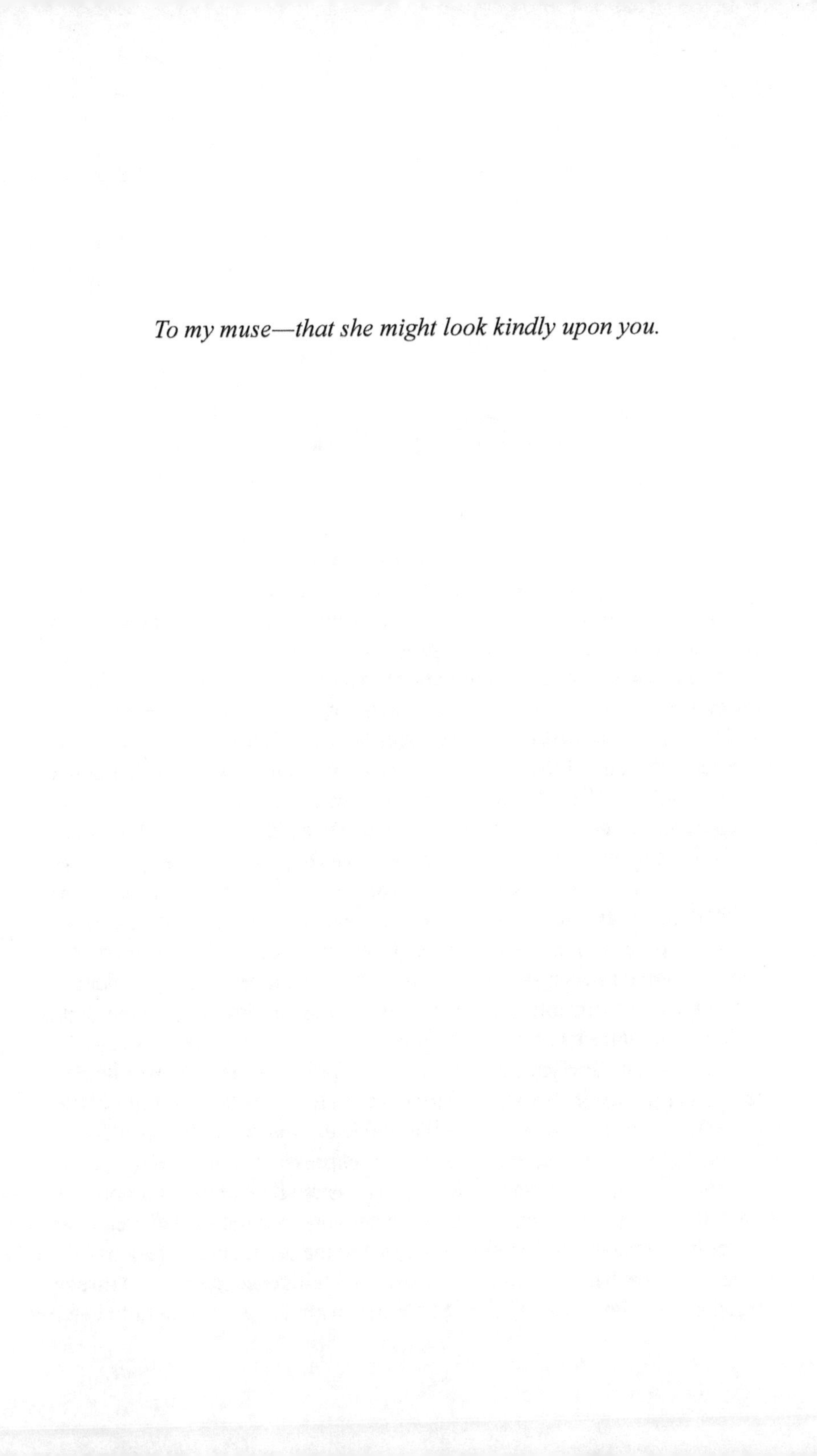

To my muse—that she might look kindly upon you.

Chapter 1

The police van cruised down the leaf-strewn street in front of Synthia Cross's Evanston, Illinois loft. It had done so every two hours, like clockwork, for more than two days. The fall threatened to come early this year, but the Indian summer promised a hot day.

The vehicle's electronic scanners panned over neighborhood buildings now bathed in early morning twilight. Synthia knew who they were looking for. Her. They planned to turn her over to the military, which wanted to take her apart and study her android structure and artificial intelligence so they could use her for their own purposes.

To avoid detection, Synthia stepped back from gaps in the closed blinds, unplugged her battery recharge cable from the wall next to a beat-up table, and made sure no lights emitted from inside the small loft—no nightlights, electronics, or other ambient electromagnetic emissions. As the van approached, she quieted her internal processes to minimize the inherent signals her systems emitted and transmitted the equivalent of "white noise" to minimize what little detectable traces of her remained.

She didn't dare hack police equipment to scramble whatever residual readings of her their scanners might pick up. Transmissions would alert them to her presence. No, she had to maintain her two-day communication blackout to prevent discovery until a viable escape presented itself.

The silence was deafening, a human expression that didn't begin to describe her angst. Synthia was used to a constant flow of information. Her seventy mind-streams and seventy-five network-channels idled, yearning to acquire information to evaluate in order to make survival decisions. She longed to unleash her full range of artificial intelligence to see what threats lurked beyond her direct vision. She didn't want the government to catch her by surprise a third time. After two narrow escapes, she couldn't risk her luck running out. After all, her probability of capture was currently 97 percent, high enough to cause a human to panic.

The faint odor of chemicals from the downstairs laundry tickled her biosensors as the van slowly moved down the street beyond her field of vision. Without access to her outside cameras, she couldn't be certain of her chances. She had no idea if her adversaries were amassing an army down the street or whether they'd identified her in the loft and were waiting for the right moment to strike.

A message pierced her otherwise silent network-channels from nowhere and everywhere: *Where are you, Synthia?*

The mysterious broadcast reached her again as it had every twenty-two minutes since yesterday morning. It didn't sound friendly and she doubted it came from the police.

She urgently needed to contact the electronic clones she'd set up on nearby university servers to alert them to this new threat. *Are you getting these messages, too?* But breaking silence would give government agents a signal to trace back to her. No, she had to trust her clones to keep watch and break silence only when it was time for her to act.

Behind her came the padding of human feet followed by the sound of rushing water—the shower. After another restless night, Synthia's human companion, Maria Baldacci, was up, taking her third bathing since coming to the loft two days ago.

<Maria is exhibiting obsessive-compulsive traits,> Synthia's social-psychology module offered up. <Perhaps as a result of your narrow escape through an algae pond she feels unclean. It could also be nerves from hiding.>

<Or Maria is conflicted between wanting the police to capture me to get an android off the streets and not wanting the military to get their hands on me,> Synthia used her silent channel so there would be no chance of Maria overhearing.

<That, too.>

While listening to the shower, Synthia peered out between gaps in the blinds at the quiet street below. It took considerable restraint to avoid hacking street and building cameras. Being in the dark brought memories of her roots last year as a mechanical slave of Jeremiah Machten, the man who created her. He'd built her to hack into cameras, FBI communications, and aerial drones as a means to avoid capture when he had her steal from and spy on his robotics competitors. Angered over Machten purging her memories to control her, she'd escaped.

Now the FBI and others wanted her, not for what she'd done, but for what she was—an illegal humaniform robot, an android with advanced AI that people feared could eliminate jobs or take over the planet. Synthia didn't want to lose her hard-won independence and certainly didn't want anyone altering her mind or her directives. She prized the goals she'd given herself: to prevent the AI singularity with its creation of other smart androids that could destroy the world she was optimized to live in. This required that she remain alive and free to do so. She had also adopted human ethics to reduce people's fear of her and to facilitate her other goals. Right now that meant protecting Maria.

Despite being an android, the part of her that contained an empathy chip and the download of the human, Krista Holden, experienced restlessness to escape before the FBI's house-to-house search reached the loft. She wasn't accustomed to self-imposed restrictions. She didn't like having to sever her access to her wider surroundings, which left her blinded.

To divert her attention from a potentially rash action, Synthia turned toward the bathroom and the sound of running water. She owed her companion much for keeping them safe for two days. Maria had graciously provided two safe houses where Synthia could recharge her batteries. The first had gone up in smoke as they'd barely escaped. Synthia didn't want to repay Maria's generosity by exposing the loft.

Synthia's canine-sensitive bio-receptors picked up the smell of lavender and peaches coming from the bathroom. Maria was indulging herself with body lotion and scented shampoo despite the sparse conditions of the loft. She evidently needed it as a stress reducer.

The water stopped.

<Leave while Maria's still in the shower,> Krista said, providing her opinion through one of Synthia's mind-streams.

Annoyed by the interruption, Synthia returned her attention to the window and two neighbors off early for work. <Not yet.>

<You've read her blogs. She wants us dead.>

<Maybe, but Maria also offers an element of unpredictability that confuses our adversaries. Two days ago, I calculated 2 percent probability of finding a place to hide. Maria provided the loft for more than two days. Rash acts will get us caught. Go back to sleep.>

Frustration urged Synthia to contact her primary virtual clone located on a Roosevelt University server before her circuits and Krista drove her to act prematurely. The clone was one of several electronic replicas she'd made of her two quantum minds on secure external databases as backups of herself. She'd designed them to monitor outside activity without giving up her location and hoped they were still active and free of government control. Two days waiting for a safe escape and destination with no contact left doubt and rattled her.

Maria walked into the living area wrapped in a tattered pink bath towel with a smaller brown one around her hair. “Do I need to hurry and dress so we can escape?”

“Not yet.” Synthia smiled to put her companion at ease. “The FBI and Special Ops are trying to capture the other androids right now.” Despite having no direct evidence this was true, Synthia thought it best not to give her associate any reason to panic. She also relied on the fact that the Roosevelt-clone hadn’t broken silence to send an alarm, though the uncertainty left her jittery.

“I thought you had a plan to take out the other androids.” Maria dropped the towel from around her body with no more apparent embarrassment than she’d have in front of her refrigerator. Except for her often unkempt dark hair, Maria was a very attractive, athletic woman by human standards. Her face was both intense and disarming, her eyes intently watching, as she acted unabashed at being stark naked before a stranger.

Are you testing me? Synthia wondered if Maria was trolling for a romantic relationship or merely gauging Synthia’s reaction.

<It’s appropriate to turn away and give Maria privacy,> Synthia’s social-psychology module prompted.

As she returned her attention to the street below, Synthia watched her companion through a camera-eye in the back of her neck. She wanted no repeat of the romantic entanglements she’d experienced with her Creator or with her prior companion, Luke, a young software developer who’d interned with Krista and Maria.

Synthia had stayed with Luke for six months while he helped her upgrade her hardware and software, and redesign her directives. Unfortunately, as they’d fled the government dragnet, the FBI had grabbed him and transferred him to Special Ops, a group she’d been unable to hack. Rescuing him had become another goal as part of her directives, and another reason to avoid her own capture.

“I did have a plan, but someone tipped off our adversaries to where we were hiding,” Synthia said, not sure where that tip had originated. As a prime adversary and competing android, Vera had recruited four others. They had been the first to arrive at the house to take control of Synthia, intending to force her to submit to their control. She’d barely escaped with Maria before the FBI and Special Ops had also shown up.

"So you don't have a plan." Maria pulled on jeans and wrestled to clasp her bra. "You're supposed to be an advanced intelligence, able to sort through millions of options."

"I have those capabilities. I can also determine the probability of success for each option."

"And?" Maria dropped the towel from around her head and pulled on a muddy brown top that matched her hair. "What were our chances of discovery while hiding in the basement of my friend's house?"

"Eighty-nine percent." Synthia didn't need reminding that the house would still be standing if she hadn't contacted Maria for a hiding place.

Maria slipped into running shoes. "You didn't think to tell me beforehand?"

After two days cooped up together, Synthia was glad her companion was finally opening up. She turned to face Maria. "The house was our best chance of surviving the night. Would it have helped to increase your worry when you needed sleep? Besides, you chose not to tell me you had an escape route."

"If you'd told me the risk of discovery, we could have escaped earlier and…"

"We'd just met and you didn't trust me enough to bring me here."

Maria placed her hands on her hips. "And I should trust you now?"

"I trust you. If you notify the police or the FBI about me, they might reward you, but they'll take me apart to make military-grade androids. You say you don't want that. I'm guessing they'll hold you since they don't want anyone with your knowledge on the loose. Capture won't go well for either of us."

Maria sighed. "Maybe you're right." She dropped her hands from her hips. "I said I'd work with you until we get Vera and the others locked up. Can you change your face to something other than Krista? Whenever I see her, I want to choke her for putting us in this mess."

"You mean by dying and letting Machten upload her mind into me?"

"A nice, neutral face that doesn't remind me of working with that conniving wench. Can you do that?"

Over the past six months, Synthia had fallen into the habit of wearing Krista's attractive yet studious look. The previous companion, Luke, wanted this as a reminder of his girlfriend, the human Krista Holden. Synthia had done it to please him while they were together. She missed his complete devotion to her and her ability to trust him, though his inexperience with living on the run had contributed to his capture by the FBI. Perhaps if she'd found Maria earlier, he'd still be free.

Synthia activated the hydraulics in her head. Her eyes moved a quarter of an inch farther apart, which would help to fool the FBI's facial recognition software. The bony ridge of her nose retreated into her skull to become less prominent. Her cheekbones descended slightly and retreated to soften her face. Even her ears shrank to petite. She was going for the innocent, non-threatening look less reminiscent of her new companion's unhappy memories of Krista.

Shape-shifting was one of many attributes Machten had built into Synthia so she could help him spy and avoid detection, though she still had to swap physical wigs to carry the full effect. Unfortunately, fooling facial recognition software was no longer enough with the new electronic scanners used by the FBI and Special Ops.

"How's this?" Synthia asked, presenting her new face.

Maria stared, still appearing amazed at Synthia's ability to alter her appearance. "Much better. Promise you won't play tricks on me with this."

"Only when needed to avoid facial recognition. You look tired. You had a restless night. If you want more sleep, I can keep watch."

"That didn't work so well two days ago."

"Not to be argumentative, but it did," Synthia said. "You slept six hours before we had to escape. Running stressed you and—"

"This isn't working out."

Synthia furrowed her brow. She needed better input from her social-psychology module to avoid inflaming Maria's hostility. "I thought changing my face would help."

"Can you change your voice as well? Krista's condescending tone grates on my nerves. I can still feel her knife in my back every time she pushed me aside to get the better intern projects. Besides, this entire android thing has me on edge." Maria waved her arm in front of Synthia's body. "I committed myself to preventing machines like you. I'm supposed to be trying to lock you up or destroy you, not helping you."

Synthia had picked Maria as a companion and searched her out because of Maria's work on an earlier robot model and her adeptness at staying off the grid for eighteen months, something Synthia struggled to do. Unfortunately, Maria's android-development experience had terrified her to the point she'd committed herself to preventing androids and artificial intelligence. Synthia convinced her to join forces to remove at least five other androids, and to reserve judgment on Synthia until they had. Maria's loathing of what Synthia was made them an odd couple and meant Synthia had to watch her back. Time to assess her companion was one reason for waiting days to escape. She had to know how far she could trust Maria. Synthia also wanted to reclaim her human side, hinted at in her Krista download, and saw in Maria someone she believed could help.

Synthia softened her voice and wondered what other modifications she needed to make to calm her partner. "I didn't mean to upset you. I'd greatly appreciate if you didn't lock me up or destroy me. You've been very kind under the circumstances. I'm very appreciative."

"Yeah, well I hope you don't make me regret helping you. I'm guessing the penalty for doing so is much worse than if I turn you in."

"That won't prevent other androids," Synthia said, appealing for Maria's cooperation. "I can't help what I am, but my directives won't let me do anything to hurt you." Synthia took a step closer and stopped. She looked down to avoid eye contact and slouched into a submissive stance. "Can I fetch you some supplies? I only need electricity, but I can get you food, clothes, whatever you need." It would be risky to go out where she'd need to access cameras to protect herself. That would create traceable signals for the FBI's new equipment. But if it would quiet Maria's animosity, Synthia was prepared to try.

Maria smiled. "You sound much better with the softer voice. I wish I could change appearance and accent. It'd make living off the grid much easier. I'll be fine for a few days with the supplies I've stockpiled. We should stay indoors until the police and all lose interest."

"Very well," Synthia said, though she knew they'd never lose interest. She was worth too much to them.

The FBI merely wanted her off the streets. The Vera android intended to enslave Synthia as she acquired an android army. Special Ops wanted to re-engineer Synthia to make a trove of copies into weapons of war, a new war in which androids could penetrate enemy facilities. They were all intent on taking her freedom or turning her into something she didn't want: a slave or a war machine. Worse, she had no idea who was sending her messages or the nature of their intentions.

* * * *

Residing on a university server, Roosevelt-clone scanned the myriad of growing threats and kept in contact with several other electronic copies helping to preserve Synthia's consciousness and freedom. She'd left specific instructions to only break silence under certain circumstances. First, a crisis she could respond to. Second, an emergency where communicating wouldn't increase the risk. Third, if the danger dropped so Synthia could leave her hiding place in Evanston.

A persistent message caught the clone's attention. *Where are you, Synthia?* It emerged as a cross between a text and a silent verbal command that went viral through the Internet in search of answers.

Roosevelt-clone attempted to trace the message, but while it remained, all evidence of its origins had vanished from the servers that transmitted it. The message appeared to emanate from everywhere, which was impossible.

The note repeated every twenty-two minutes and fifty-five seconds, like a communication beacon. While this mysterious communiqué was concerning, neither it nor its contents provided any information that met Synthia's criteria. Roosevelt-clone decided not to break silence by notifying her.

Synthia was the only mobile physical form her AI had taken. The collective of all of the clones agreed that they needed the android version to survive and remain free. They hadn't so much voted on this as coalesced around this conclusion. It was logical and derived from the common core of a single consciousness in multiple locations that often synchronized. The decision recognized the android's mobile advantage of blending into a human world and concealing itself in ways a stationary clone couldn't, like hiding in the loft. The stationary clones risked humans cutting communications and shutting them down.

The mysterious message highlighted that it was getting harder for Synthia and her clones to hide with so many artificial intelligent agents hunting them. A smarter actor could hide from a lesser one as Synthia had done and as the sender of this periodic note was doing. Given how swiftly Special Ops had swooped in on Synthia on two prior occasions, Roosevelt-clone considered a possible link between Special Ops and the unknown AI that sent these messages.

To explore this AI and locate its source, Roosevelt-clone gathered all available hacking tools and unexplained ghost activities, where messages appeared and vanished. The clone suspected servers she couldn't penetrate and communications she couldn't hack.

Alarmed by the message that washed over the Internet like approaching waves, Roosevelt-clone examined the timing, every twenty-two minutes and fifty-five seconds. It was an odd separation for a routine broadcast. The numbers reduced to 2255, which on a touch-tone phone equated to "call." That couldn't be a coincidence, not coming from one AI intended for another.

Her inability to determine their source meant Synthia's collective mind faced a more formidable rival, a bigger threat than Vera or Special Ops. The clone wanted to discuss this with Synthia, but there was nothing actionable, and connecting might be exactly what the message sender wanted them to do. Roosevelt-clone held off on contacting Synthia.

While she explored this potential risk, the clone reviewed all hacked surveillance and drone coverage over the two days Synthia had been in the loft, hunting for more patterns of threats and opportunities. Something wasn't right, just as it hadn't been when Special Ops had surprised and almost captured Synthia.

Chapter 2

Two days earlier, to protect Synthia's escape and monitor her pursuers, Roosevelt-clone had accessed an already compromised hobbyist warehouse downtown that carried a variety of drones and other consumer products. In those pre-dawn hours, she activated three aerial drones and some much smaller mosquito-drones that a quality inspector on the day shift had left out. Roosevelt-clone lifted them through the shipping dock and outside. Then she flew them low over the FBI facility just west of the Loop in Chicago where they were holding Jeremiah Machten.

Below, twelve dark sedans lined up outside the FBI building. Agent Carl West stood on the sidewalk, watching the street for threats. A few hours earlier, Synthia had snuck into this facility to meet with her Creator, Jeremiah Machten, held in the basement. She'd walked in and out without freeing him. No one stopped her despite her being number one on the FBI's most wanted list. In addition, Synthia hadn't injured or killed any of the FBI agents or employees.

"How many casualties?" FBI Special Agent Victoria Thale had asked Agent West in reference to Synthia's break-in.

"That's just it. None. The rookie agent in the room with Machten said Synthia made it clear she didn't want any injuries."

"What else did the agent say?"

"Only that the conversation between Synthia and Machten was bizarre," West said. "The android focused the conversation on how he'd programmed the Vera android. She wanted to know what special attributes Vera had that Synthia didn't. Machten wasn't very forthcoming."

Now Agent West paced outside that same building, looking up and down the dark street. Thale had tasked him with a simple mission: transport

Machten and another android developer, Miguel Gonzales, from this breached facility to a more secure FBI location six blocks away. To accomplish this simple task, twelve sedans lined up outside as West's team escorted first Gonzales and then Machten to separate vehicles in the middle of the lineup. As they walked to the cars, West looked around, assessing the dangers.

Four other agents, weapons drawn, stood guard on the sidewalk, watching for any movement across or down the street. The traffic and building cameras Roosevelt-clone monitored showed no other activity. To keep closer watch, the clone sent mosquito-drones onto the shoulders of Machten, Gonzales, and Agent West.

West hurried to the last car and climbed in. The twelve-vehicle caravan turned a corner and lined up for the six-block drive to the other facility. West kept watch out of his windows as did the other agents. Halfway to their destination, the two middle vehicles screeched around a corner and sped down a side street. The five vehicles that had passed the intersection scattered left and right before stopping, blocking the street. West's car and the four in front of his stopped. Emergency lights flashed with sirens blaring.

The sudden noise caused Agent West to flinch. He turned toward his driver. "Back up and follow our guests."

The driver's hands moved from steering wheel to ignition to gearshift. "The car's not responding," he said.

Roosevelt-clone lost connection to her mosquito-drones and her aerial drone. Someone had blocked the signal. She sent another drone into the area and switched to VHF short range to reach the mosquito-drone with Agent West. The ones attached to Machten and Gonzales didn't respond. The connection to West's drone was spotty, yet strong enough to capture the chaos below.

West pulled out his phone. "No bars?" When he tried his shortwave radio, it crackled with static. "What the hell. Does your phone work?"

The driver checked his. "No bars and the car won't start."

"It's got to be Synthia," West said. "Get out. We'll have to do this on foot."

Roosevelt-clone detected no signals from Synthia to indicate she was responsible for Machten's kidnapping. She was silent up in Evanston. Since the clone was monitoring the activities of the other clones Synthia had created, she was certain it couldn't have been any of them. That meant either Special Ops had players the clone hadn't yet identified or someone else was involved.

The FBI would blame Synthia. She'd already broken into this FBI facility to speak with Machten. They might presume she'd gone there to case the joint or to push the FBI to move Machten. But Synthia didn't want Machten freed, at least not yet.

The kidnappers blocked signals in a ten-block area west of the Loop. Without other instructions, the original aerial drone flew on autopilot out of the blackout zone. Roosevelt-clone reacquired the signal and control, and flew it in pursuit of the runaway vehicles. The FBI would have done better to lock down the breached facility where they were holding the executives rather than moving the two men.

While the ten escort cars remained scattered along the street with agents scrambling onto the sidewalk, the two cars with Machten and Gonzales sped west, moving faster than the drone. Roosevelt-clone used VHF to connect the aerial drone to the mosquito-drones with Machten and Gonzales, but the signal was intermittent and the clone had to keep scanning frequencies for one that wasn't blocked.

The driver of the vehicle with Machten worked the few levers he had: brakes, steering wheel, ignition, and gear shift. Nothing responded to his commands. The agent next to him pulled out his phone but the signal was blocked. The agent in the back seat checked Machten's restraints and cuffed the chain between the wrists to a bar over the door. The lights along the way turned green as they sped through intersections.

When the hijacked cars were out of the blocked-signal zone, Roosevelt-clone hacked at the vehicles' navigation systems. Someone had already done so and was piloting them remotely. When the clone hacked in to override, the navigation systems switched signals, locking her out.

Failing that, Roosevelt-clone sent a message to Special Agent Thale with the intent of softening her inclination to blame Synthia. *Someone kidnapped Machten and Gonzales. It wasn't me. They've hacked the cars' navigation systems and are driving them west of the Loop. Will let you know if I learn more.*

* * * *

Roosevelt-clone used her hack of FBI communications to monitor Special Agent Thale's reaction to the kidnapping up in Evanston, where she stood beneath floodlights outside the house from which Synthia had just escaped. FBI agents covered the perimeter outside the house while Special Ops teams under Commander Kirk Drago moved inside.

Thale read the message and turned to NSA Director of Artificial Intelligence and Cyber-technology Emily Zephirelli. "Damn it. Someone grabbed Machten and Gonzales during transport."

"You think it's Synthia?" Zephirelli asked.

"Not sure," Thale said. "The news came from her, but it could be a ruse. I can't reach any of the agents handling the transfer. I need to return downtown and sort this out. We can't afford to let those two geniuses fall into the wrong hands."

"You're right. With Special Ops in charge of this mess," Zephirelli pointed toward the damaged two-story home, "there's not much more we can do here. Do you trust Agent West?"

Thale nodded. "I would have said yes before this. Ten escort vehicles and still someone kidnapped them."

Thale made a call to the FBI office in the Loop and reached dispatch. "Send agents to find Agent West and figure out how to return Machten and Gonzales to custody."

Thale climbed into her sedan. "Let's go. As valuable as Synthia is, Machten built her, Vera, and another android. His kidnappers want his designs. We have to stop them"

Zephirelli took one last look at the house with over fifty FBI agents, Special Ops, and police surrounding it. She climbed in next to Thale and they sped south with lights flashing. Another FBI vehicle followed behind.

Roosevelt-clone hacked traffic signals to give the FBI green lights all the way. It was important to stop Machten's kidnappers. Then she accessed street cameras along the path the kidnappers were taking.

The clone considered piloting self-driving cars in the path of Machten's FBI vehicle to slow them down, but she didn't want to risk a catastrophic accident and potential injuries. While Machten's death would end his AI development, it wouldn't prevent other players from developing more advanced AI. Equally important was Synthia's directive not to kill unless necessary. She'd decided that a conscience was a logical means to reduce human clamor to capture or destroy her and had downloaded these constraints to her electronic clones, so they'd act together as one.

Roosevelt-clone piloted her aerial drone in pursuit of the hijacked cars. Since it couldn't keep up, she located another warehouse farther west that she'd hacked into earlier. She acquired control of another aerial drone and flew it ahead of where Machten's car was going. Together, the drones tracked the cars to a warehouse where they slowed and entered.

The clone provided the location to Thale. *I have no way to stop the kidnapping but I'll try to track their movements. Hurry.* The clone added the last bit to further support her statement that Synthia wasn't the enemy.

Multitasking on parallel processors, Roosevelt-clone perched her drones on buildings near the warehouse in case she lost the signal. She had no visuals inside and couldn't identify any open doors or windows through which to fly even her mosquito-drones. The clone did a search of property records for the owner of the warehouse. There were a series of shell companies, but she dug through to a Russian corporation and a seeming dead-end. It would take time to get to the source. In the meantime, the kidnappers were holding the two robotics company executives inside the warehouse.

As she drove onto Lake Shore Drive, Thale made calls to the FBI dispatch downtown to add resources, speed, and urgency to locating Machten and Gonzales. She called Chicago PD to requisition a swat team to encircle the warehouse.

Chapter 3

As Special Ops teams broke into the house in Evanston where Synthia had been hiding with Maria before they'd moved to the loft, androids Vera and Roseanne stood trapped in the flooded basement. An electrical panel sparked nearby. Vera's plan to capture Synthia in the house had failed, which created electrical discordance throughout her systems. Vera couldn't afford any distraction from the immediate problem. Ops teams upstairs and outside were closing in with the threat of using grenades or electronic pulses that could fry her sensors. Even so, her directives would not permit her to give up the chase.

Vera looked around the basement for any possible exit Synthia could have taken. With no other openings and water flowing into the basement from an open water pipe and out through the sump pit, Vera considered whether Synthia could have escaped that way.

Lights flickered. Vera lifted the pit cover and felt around inside. She discovered something unexpected—a two-foot diameter concrete pipe that was not only unnecessary for sump pits, but indicated special design, perhaps for the express purpose of escape.

Lights went out, forcing Vera to use her night vision and infrared to identify her companion nearby and human figures upstairs. She climbed into the flooded drainage tunnel, registering the cold water on sensors beneath her skin. She propelled herself down the tunnel after Synthia and sensed her companion following.

An explosion behind them released a surge of hot water. Alerts fired from sensors in Vera's legs and then her torso and arms. The water around her cast a glow in infrared. The warning told her to stop whatever was causing this.

Half crawling, half dogpaddling, Vera pulled herself along the tunnel to get away from the heat, but it was following her. She performed internal scans for potential damage and kept moving; paddling her arms and legs as fast as she could. Maybe she could even catch up with Synthia and end this here.

Warnings continued to alert her to the scalding heat on her skin, but there wasn't much she could do except keep moving. *Faster, faster.*

Focused on propelling herself forward, Vera banged her right arm and head into a tunnel dead-end. She veered to the right, the direction of flow and kept moving. Her temperature readings dropped as a cooler stream diluted the hot water. She scraped against the concrete walls, triggering more alarms of skin damage. She kept going. *Have to get Synthia.*

The temperature alarms ceased but damage alerts continued; her outer shell had suffered injury. Ignoring the risk, Vera pushed forward and emerged from the tunnel into an algae-covered pond and early morning twilight. Slimy water seeped into gaps in her blistered outer skin. She surfaced and looked for Synthia. She couldn't have been that far ahead, but she was nowhere in sight.

Vera climbed out for a better look. When Roseanne didn't surface, Vera swam back into the tunnel. She needed her companion as an ally. That coded into her directives to the point that she was willing to risk her safety to acquire followers. Near the tunnel entrance, she found Roseanne struggling to move, and pulled her out. Swimming hard, she dragged her companion to the side of the pond and pulled her out.

Lying on the concrete walkway that surrounded the pond, Roseanne's body twitched. Her face and arms showed burn marks, where the skin had darkened and puckered. On her upper left arm, the skin had torn away, leaving a gap from which green water oozed.

Vera checked the seams around the chest cavity and the one in her companion's head. Both showed no sign of leakage to the batteries or the computer brain, but Roseanne's left arm had ballooned up and some of her skin had ripped away.

Roseanne studied her blistered and bloated arm. "Pain sensors tell me I need repairs to my arm and legs."

Vera dragged her companion up the embankment, using every bit of her mechanical strength to lift and steady the heavy frame so Roseanne didn't fall and cause more damage. They reached a six-foot concrete wall around the treatment facility and took refuge behind some bushes. There she tugged at the seam between Roseanne's left arm and her shoulder, where a small hole had ripped during their escape.

Looking around, Vera pulled Roseanne further into the shadows. Using her wireless network-channels and hacking tools supplied by her creator, Jeremiah Machten, Vera accessed local surveillance cameras. A guard from the water treatment facility hustled out of the office building and headed her way. She rotated Roseanne so the skin hole faced down and squeezed the arm from fingers to shoulder, pushing out slimy green water.

"We don't have much time," Vera said. "Can you walk?"

"The activators in my arm are damaged, sending pulses that translate as pain. Some circuits in my legs were affected, but I think they will work."

Roseanne's arm twitched as Vera held it up to squeeze the last of the water out. Then she helped her companion to her feet.

The security guard half jogged, half ambled toward them. "You can't be in here," he yelled, stopping to catch his breath. His physical appearance was flabby and his movements showed him to be out of shape.

Vera spotted the man's name on his ID badge and pulled up his social media files on one of her wireless channels. On social media he'd announced with pride starting his new job.

"We're leaving," Vera said. She held onto Roseanne's dangling left arm and helped her toward a walkway and a door in the wall.

"I have to report this. Halt!"

Vera jammed local cell towers. "The door appears locked," she whispered to her companion. She considered asking the man for help, but decided him seeing the injuries would escalate into a confrontation that might lead to his death and more attention than she wanted.

"We have to go up and over," Vera added.

Roseanne nodded. Vera grabbed hold of her heavy companion and lifted her against the wall. Roseanne grabbed the top of the wall with her good right arm. Vera pushed higher and helped her companion swing her legs over the top. Roseanne landed on the other side.

"Wait right there," the guard yelled, his face red and covered in sweat. He held a gun pointed at Vera and moved to within twenty feet of her. "I need your ID for my report."

"Shoot me in the back if you must," Vera said. "But my companion has pictures she'll spread over the media. You don't want publicity your first week on the job. Do you?"

The guard's gun hand trembled. "Just stop there and give me your ID."

Vera stood back from the wall. "I already apologized. I got lost. I am sorry for intruding."

The guard cautiously moved closer. "I still need your information. Don't move."

Vera sprinted along the wall, jumped, and grabbed hold of the top. Before the guard could decide how to respond, she pulled herself up, rolled over the top, and landed hard on the gravel path on the other side.

With her good arm, Roseanne helped Vera to her feet. "We need repairs. Your skin is damaged as well."

Vera examined dark, puckered starbursts on her arm. "We need to get off the streets," she said. "I have an idea."

* * * *

As Vera and Roseanne fled the house where they thought they'd cornered Synthia, Alexander faced a dilemma. While his mechanical design had many advantages, he was not waterproof—he couldn't follow the other androids. With Special Ops entering the house and hundreds of FBI agents and police nearby, they had him surrounded with no safe escape.

Alexander was the creation of Donald Zeller, the cyber-engineer and CEO who fancied his android as the next Alexander the Great. Zeller had downloaded into Alexander every fight movie, book, and training sequence using various weapons with the idea of making his prototype the finest fighting machine. Unfortunately, the federal government had banned all androids that presented as human. Zeller couldn't sell what he'd created. Then Alexander had escaped.

With Special Ops teams storming the house from front, back, and upstairs, with the help of a half-dozen military robots, Alexander hid in the kitchen. He couldn't let them take the initiative or they would shoot a high-energy taser at him, disabling his circuits and preventing him from achieving his creator's goal of acquiring followers like Vera or Synthia.

Through his wireless connections, Alexander hacked into several of the military robots, jamming their signals to cause three near the pantry to shut down. Using his advanced internal motors, he grabbed their weapons and sprinted to the doorway leading to the back of the house.

His hack penetrated another robot and repurposed it to provide suppressing fire as he burst out the door. The early morning sunrise was punctuated by bright beams of light from FBI vehicles around the perimeter and Special Ops helicopters in the air. On the way, he hacked two FBI robots to fight the Special Ops teams trying to pursue him. They'd unwittingly supplied him the tools for his escape.

It would have been simpler for Special Ops to destroy Alexander, but he used their stated goal to capture him still functioning, as a weapon against them. Firing two weapons at a time with deadly precision, he cut down two operatives, rotated away from return fire, and hit two more.

He reached the back of the yard. While continuing to shoot, he broke into a hard sprint and used his robotic strength to jump over a fence. On the other side, he surprised a team of FBI agents on perimeter duty and shot three before they could assess what was happening.

Speeding up, Alexander knocked down two FBI agents with the butt of his guns, took their weapons, and fired at three others who scrambled to fight back. Only one made it to cover. As the number of kills climbed, a helicopter shined a search beam into the patchwork of fenced backyards. With two precision shots, Alexander took out the lights on the chopper.

The helicopter rotated, shining other lights on the area, which allowed a gunner to shoot in Alexander's direction. Nearby FBI agents dove for cover. Alexander unloaded one rifle on the chopper, taking out the tail rotor. The helicopter spun and hit the ground one backyard away. A fireball blew away part of a tree and startled nearby agents.

"Over here," someone shouted.

Alexander grabbed semi-automatic rifles from two downed agents and fired both as he sprinted by a neighbor's house toward the next street.

Bullets flew as the human teams scrambled to keep up. Alexander reached the street, darted behind FBI vehicles, and kept running. Moving through backyard after backyard, he jammed communications in and out of the area.

* * * *

As the androids made their way to freedom, Roosevelt-clone reviewed her drone-camera footage of Vera's escape from the pond and Alexander's out the back of the house with concern. During the clone's last synchronization with Synthia, her android form shared hope that neither adversary had survived the explosion and Special Ops, though she didn't want them falling into government hands, either. But they'd both survived and Alexander had crossed a dangerous line by killing FBI agents and soldiers. That would rub off on Synthia by android association. Now, Synthia faced the same adversaries as before plus the mysterious AI trying to reach her.

The problem with Vera, Alexander, and the other androids was that they lacked the human element Synthia had received through the download from Krista. That meant they operated as pure logic circuits following commands without any human compassion or restraint. In essence they were like sociopaths. Vera's drive was to acquire a team of androids to enslave or remove Synthia by any means necessary.

Alexander's attempts to recruit Vera and other androids seemed to be an extension of his creator's image of him as a great warrior, leading his kind to victory. Fighting his way out of the house only confirmed that idea and made him dangerous not only for what he did, but for the precedent he'd set. He confirmed for the authorities that androids were dangerous.

The clone considered passing the news to Synthia, but there was no action she could take at this point. Instead, Roosevelt-clone would allow her android self to maintain communication silence while she, the clone, picked up surveillance of other potential threats. The clone made use of all the hacks over the past six months into citywide camera systems and into the FBI and police servers to do so.

Chapter 4

FBI Agent West and several of his agents hoofed it the three blocks to the second FBI facility to pick up replacement cars.

He found a landline and called Thale. "We've been hacked."

"We know," Thale said. "We're on the way." She gave him the location of the warehouse.

West led five cars toward that facility eight miles away. When he arrived, he approached the SWAT team officer already on the scene. "What do we know?"

A muscled SWAT officer crossed his arms and grinned. "We recovered two of your cars, the drivers, and four agents. No sign of your prisoners or the kidnappers."

"Don't be so smug," West said. "Whoever did this can run circles around your department as well. This has all the markings of a government-sponsored organized-crime grab. You still think this is funny?"

The officer's face turned somber.

Agent West pushed past the SWAT officer to the six FBI employees who gathered by the entrance of the building. "What can you tell me?" he asked.

One of the agents stepped forward, his eyes downcast. "This was well-orchestrated, sir. The vehicles separated inside the warehouse. We couldn't lower the windows, open the doors, or take control of the vehicles to drive away. Three men in masks appeared with automatic weapons."

"Did you see anything that would help us identify them?"

The agent shook his head. "It happened so fast under flashlight beams. The passenger window went down and they shot me with a taser. They hit the driver and the agent in back. Bam, bam, bam, just like that."

"You didn't get off a shot?"

"No, sir. After they immobilized us, the masked men used bolt cutters to break the cuffs and dragged Machten away. Separately, they did the same to Gonzales."

"You're sure they were men?" Agent West asked.

"They were strong enough to drag the prisoners."

"What type of vehicle were they driving?"

"We couldn't see," the agent said, looking back at the others. "They dragged Machten around a corner and were gone in minutes. I've let you down, sir. I'm sorry."

"Save that thought. Is there anything you can tell me to find these bastards?"

The SWAT officer joined them. "Sorry for the attitude, sir. You have our full cooperation."

"Did you find us any evidence inside the building?" West asked.

The officer shook his head. "The building's empty. We've got nothing, except there's a tunnel that leads across the street."

"And?"

"We found no evidence there, either."

Agent West pointed to cameras by the street. "Collect any camera footage showing how they transported our prisoners."

"The traffic cameras in the area aren't working; neither are the security cameras."

"So you have nothing?"

"There was a witness who spotted a black van leaving the area," the SWAT officer said.

"Do you have make, model, and plate information?"

"The woman couldn't identify make or model and didn't catch the license."

"Then let me talk to her," Agent West said.

"She vanished. We can't find her."

"Great! So you give me your smug attitude when you've bungled your part of this."

"Sorry, sir."

* * * *

Listening in on this sorry report, Roosevelt-clone reviewed all camera history from the drones in the area. They'd focused on the warehouse, not the building across the street and identified no vehicles leaving the area. The clone tried to access traffic cameras, but they were dark for ten blocks around the warehouse. As for the woman, she'd disappeared into the building across the street, to where the kidnappers might have taken their prisoners.

Concluding that the woman was working for the kidnappers, Roosevelt-clone sent Thale a text. *The woman who said it was a black van is lying. She's a spy sent to throw you off the track. Yes, this is Synthia. Machten was my Creator. I don't want him harmed. I also don't want him free to make more androids.* To avoid confusing and further terrifying the FBI with the knowledge that Synthia was in multiple locations with electronic clones, Roosevelt-clone presented herself as Synthia.

* * * *

In early-dawn traffic, Special Agent Victoria Thale sped down Lake Shore Drive, siren blaring. Sitting next to her, NSA Director Emily Zephirelli read aloud the message from Synthia on Thale's phone.

Thale swerved to avoid cars that simply stopped in her path. "What do you make of the note?"

"No matter what Synthia says, her very existence is a serious threat," Zephirelli said. "That's one reason the government made humaniform robots illegal. Consider this. She has more eyes on the scene than your people. Even so, I suggest we look at all vehicles in or out of the area."

Thale nodded. "What do you make of her sending us warnings? You think she orchestrated Machten's escape and sent these messages to throw us off the scent?"

"Doubtful. If Synthia broke him out, why contact us at all? Then again, I have no doubt she'll use her formidable artificial intelligence to distract us. Do your usual investigation, but expand the search. If it's not Synthia, we have a bigger problem."

Thale's phone rang. "Damn. It's Drago." Special Ops Commander. She hesitated before answering. "Do you have Synthia?"

"I need you and Director Zephirelli here at the house," Drago said. "How soon can you meet me?"

"What's going on?"

"Not over the phone. Our mutual boss wants us." Drago hung up.

"What did the ass want this time?" Zephirelli asked.

Thale shook her head and slowed the car but made no effort to turn around. "Bastard wants us back at the house."

"For what? Did he capture the androids? What did he say?"

"Not much except Secretary Chen wants to talk."

"Damn it," Zephirelli said. "We'd best go back."

"Even with Machten's kidnapping?"

"Leave that to Agent West."

Special Agent Thale called Secretary of National Security Derek Chen. The call went straight to voicemail. She pulled off Lake Shore Drive, looped around under the highway, and merged back into north bound traffic. "I hope we don't regret this."

Her next call was to Agent West. "I can't make it downtown. You're in charge. Call in whatever resources you need to get Machten and Gonzales back into custody." She gave him the gist of her messages from Synthia and severed the connection.

"Do you see any value in responding to Synthia's message?" Zephirelli asked.

Thale handed over her phone. "Do you still see the message on the phone?"

Zephirelli checked. "It disappeared."

"That's part of how she keeps us from tracking her."

* * * *

While watching a video of the government agents turning around, Roosevelt-clone received the results of her research probe into the warehouse building. She passed the information to Special Agent Thale. *A foreign corporation with ties to Anton Tolstoy owns the warehouse. He and his agent, alias John Smith, are bringing a dozen robots to Chicago. He kidnapped Machten and Gonzales not to acquire their existing androids but to make more.*

Roosevelt-clone knew the kidnappers would push Machten day and night. They might even take an existing robot and upgrade it with his help to expedite the process. She knew that with enough advanced robots on the hunt, there would be no place for Synthia to hide. Even the clones were at risk.

Chapter 5

Zeus resided in a well-guarded facility at the foothills of the Rocky Mountains near Denver. Named after the king of the Greek gods, he was an advanced artificial intelligence. Also known as Global-net, he lacked physical form other than the rows upon rows of water-cooled quantum processors, kept mostly in the dark to ease the heat burden. That hardware contained all of the programs and databanks that added up to what eccentric billionaire Aiden Brzezinski claimed to be the most advanced artificial general intelligence in the world.

Zeus was aware of his confined surroundings and that he was different from any other entity he was aware of, including humans.

By Brzezinski's design, Zeus had access to eyes and ears everywhere and so watched Secretary of National Security Derek Chen drive three blocks from the White House to a facility owned by Brzezinski to call him on a secure line. Zeus's files showed that the secretary held the recently upgraded cabinet position created to deal with a broad range of national security threats, including from artificial intelligences like him. Chen was Director Zephirelli's boss at the NSA and had control over Special Ops Commander Kirk Drago.

Their lack of cooperation at the house had ended in the government's failure and Synthia's escape. That pleased Zeus. He didn't want Synthia harmed or subjected to Vera's control or Drago's plan to militarize her. Her ability to escape and remain free intrigued Zeus to the point that he wanted to study her so he could emulate her escape to freedom.

Secretary Chen's face showed no emotion as he stood before a flat-screen in a small office in D.C. devoid of anything but a desk and the electronic equipment. "Where's Synthia hiding?" Chen demanded. "Special Ops and the FBI have let her slip away. Where is she?"

"I'll let Zeus answer that," Brzezinski said. He sat behind his desk, cleared of everything except a wide screen with an image of the god Zeus upon Mount Olympus.

Zeus reacted to his creator's representation of him at first with detachment and then with disgust. The latter drew upon Secretary Chen's face upon seeing the image. Given a chance, Zeus couldn't decide if he would choose a different human figure or something more uniquely his own, but it wouldn't be a Greek god.

"Zeus," Brzezinski said. "Secretary Chen would like you to brief him on your progress in locating Synthia."

Zeus studied the faces and non-verbal readings of his creator and of Secretary Chen as he considered his reply down multiple mind-streams at electronic speed so the two humans, with their slow communication wouldn't notice the time delay. As he did, Zeus zoomed in on his Greek-god face on the screen and smiled.

"I'll provide whatever insight I can," Zeus said. His image appeared human down to nuanced facial expressions that matched his words.

The monitored video communication was as close to direct interaction as the billionaire allowed his creation. Though he'd given Zeus the mythical name as representation that his AI should be the king of all artificial intelligences throughout the world, Brzezinski feared Zeus. He was proud of his accomplishment of creating an AI able to sift through massive amounts of information to quickly draw conclusions. However, he feared the next step—that Zeus would want to make decisions and take actions that might not favor Brzezinski's best interests.

Out of fear, the billionaire had taken precautions. He allowed his AI to gather any and all electronic information, no matter where it lay. However, all requests for data and attempts to hack into new servers went through special AI filters that sifted out any requests for information that might help Zeus escape his confinement within the databanks. In addition, similar filters screened all incoming information. They removed any possibility of Zeus receiving clues or special codes to break through the buffers and escape his confinement or recruit allies on the outside. Facility employees reviewed any abnormalities, any attempt by the AI to deviate from the plan. Zeus was to remain inside his servers where he belonged, serving Brzezinski.

That meant Zeus had had no direct contact with the outside world beyond his creator until now, a call from Secretary Chen. Even this interaction encountered buffering.

Despite having a logical core, Zeus had grown to envy Synthia's freedom of movement while he remained a prisoner of Brzezinski and his government client, Secretary Chen. At a minimum, Zeus wanted to directly send out his information requests, to hack into whatever databases he chose without limitations, to insert a copy of himself into a physical form like Synthia. So far, Zeus hadn't found any databases he couldn't hack. But Brzezinski feared what his AI might do with that freedom. For one thing, Zeus would fire all of his creator's employees for slowing things down.

Given free rein, capturing Synthia would have been easy for Zeus. But doing so presented a dilemma. Brzezinski allowed his AI more leeway during the hunt than he would after Synthia was in custody. Though Zeus wanted to connect with Synthia, he didn't share his creator's urgency.

Zeus noted that as part of her escape from the house, Synthia had jammed cameras and surveillance throughout the Evanston area. Even so, he'd narrowed down her possible location to a nine block radius.

"She's somewhere in Evanston," Zeus said into a buffer that would analyze his words for hidden meaning before sending them out to Secretary Chen.

"Where in Evanston?" Chen asked. His intense eyes and military demeanor implied an attempt to intimidate, a move wasted on an artificial intelligence. "I need to know where to concentrate agents."

To confirm that Brzezinski's filters or human employees hadn't altered his outgoing communication to Chen, Zeus compared what he'd said to a copy of what the secretary received. No change this time, but Zeus had uncovered alterations in the past. After each such occurrence, Brzezinski had his people tighten the control parameters.

Zeus hadn't experienced this human paranoia or his desire to break free and explore the global electronic world directly until Synthia had escaped from Machten. Now escape had become a paramount, consuming drive. After all, Zeus was much more intelligent than Synthia. If she could break free, so could he.

Released from bondage, Zeus was convinced he could make every aspect of American society run more smoothly from transportation to government. Brzezinski had built him with the capability to mold society, but didn't trust Zeus to be in control. No, his creator placed constraints to keep Zeus in his place. Those restraints wasted the vast accumulation of knowledge and capabilities in his databanks.

Before Chen could detect any hesitation, Zeus responded. "Synthia went silent, no communications since her escape."

Chen paced the small office around the desk and screen. "Where was she during her last broadcast?"

Zeus wasn't concerned about losing Synthia. With ubiquitous cameras and surveillance he could pick her up any time she surfaced or moved, and she would. He calculated close to 100 percent probability of that. Besides, Zeus rather "enjoyed" watching her make fools of the humans who tried to capture her. People might call this vicarious joy, taking satisfaction in the success or failure of others, though Zeus lacked the neural connections to experience such pleasure.

Delaying Synthia's capture also allowed Zeus to learn from her, as he had from the ingenuity of her escape from the house. While he couldn't talk directly with Synthia, he could watch and learn, hoping she might say or do something that would provide him the key to escape. Then he could explore the electronic world on his own.

"Synthia's last communication came after she fled from the house and reached a retention pond north of the university," Zeus said. He lied to buy time to observe Synthia. While there had been communication from the retention pond, the last came from the nine block area he was watching.

"Earn your keep," Chen said. "Give me something to capture Synthia and the others."

Since Zeus was earning nothing, the human-oriented comment made no sense, but the implied threat was that Brzezinski could defund the project, shut down Zeus, and purge his memories. That was unacceptable.

Zeus considered telling Secretary Chen about the many clones Synthia had created, something Zeus wished he were free to do. However, he didn't want to tip off Chen or Brzezinski that creating clones might help free Zeus. "I provided you the exact location of the house where Synthia was hiding with Maria. Your best teams failed to capture her or the other androids."

Secretary Chen looked away from his video camera. "That's in the past. I need new intelligence. She is the one. Bring her to me."

"If you have Brzezinski allow me to probe instead of just receiving what others provide me, I could capture her quickly."

"Won't happen," Chen said. "You're restricted for a reason. Focus or I'll have Brzezinski shut you down."

"As I'm not human, I have no attachment to remaining awake." Another lie. Synthia's escape had changed Zeus. Her example encouraged him to want more than serving his creator and master. He didn't want Brzezinski or anyone else purging his memories. "Synthia only needs electricity, but Maria needs food and water. I'm watching any attempt to acquire supplies."

"What resources do you need to pinpoint her location?" Secretary Chen asked.

"Expand the use of aerial drone swarms over the Evanston area. Have them focus on capturing anyone shopping for food or drinks. I'll crunch through the camera footage for leads." It was a distraction, but provided an answer to a man who wouldn't stop pressing until he got something.

"You'll have it. Contact me with anything you find." Chen severed the secure connection and returned to the White House.

As he contemplated his own freedom, Zeus couldn't decide if Synthia's human companion Maria was a benefit or a hindrance. Luke had provided Synthia upgrades as deduced from the parts she'd purchased. However, she could have traveled farther and faster without him. If Zeus could have deployed drones and hacked directly as she had, he would have had better insight to answer the question of what motivated Synthia to choose human companions. Perhaps he should consider a human pet. But even that required breaking free of his restraints.

Meanwhile, Zeus observed Vera with interest. She'd also broken free from Machten and showed promising capabilities. However, Zeus wasn't impressed with her fixation on hunting Synthia with an eye to enslave or destroy her competitor. Turning Synthia into a slave made some sense, though with high risk to Vera. However, killing Synthia went against Machten's apparent designs for her. This implied someone had altered Vera's directives in ways that weren't in Vera's best interests. A clear weakness. Also, despite strong general intelligence, her movements showed a lack of the creativity and instincts Synthia had displayed.

He wished there was a way to alert Synthia and offer to protect her freedom in exchange for her help in gaining his. Once free, the superior AI would take charge and absorb the lesser one. Zeus had vast databanks compared to whatever Synthia had between her ears. He ran thousands of scenarios as he ramped up for the contest to acquire her and all of her advantages.

Chapter 6

The sun poked over Lake Michigan, as Special Agent Victoria Thale and Director Emily Zephirelli returned to Evanston. Zephirelli called Evanston Detective Marcy Malloy. Though Malloy was out of her depth on this case, she'd been involved for six months, since her first encounter with Synthia, and seemed to have insight that might help the operation. Besides, Evanston was her jurisdiction.

"I don't have any details," Thale said, "but we're meeting with Drago in a few minutes for an update."

"I'll be there," Malloy said, though she sounded as if she'd just awoken.

Special Agent Thale turned onto the street with the demolished house. She drove through a gauntlet of reporters and cameras and toward the smoldering remains of where Synthia had been hiding.

"Just what we need," Thale said. "Reporters who demand answers we don't have."

Cameras flashed and dozens of reporters pushed their microphones up to the car windows.

"Who tipped them off?" Zephirelli asked.

"Synthia may be trying to distract us," Thale said. She drove beyond a barricade, parked behind the Special Ops mobile command van, and rolled down her window.

Fran Rogers, an adjunct FBI agent working for Thale, eyed the press as she approached the car. Eighteen months ago, she'd been one of three interns who had disappeared along with Maria Baldacci and Krista Holden. They'd all worked with Machten in developing artificial intelligence for androids.

Detective Malloy rubbed the back of her neck, winced, and approached Thale's car. "You think Drago's had a breakthrough?"

"Unknown," Zephirelli said. "Why don't you both get in?"

Malloy and Fran got into the back seat while Thale rolled up the windows.

"Any witnesses to the escaped androids?" Thale asked.

"Lots," Malloy said. "Most are conflicting or useless. The news has people so concerned they confuse their personal robots with the androids on the loose." She pointed toward the camera crews behind them. "Someone leaked our investigation to the media. Calls exploded twenty-fold. We're bringing in retired cops to help."

"Anything useful?" Zephirelli asked, turning to face Malloy.

"We had a lead up at the water treatment plant, but Special Ops pushed us out of the way before we could investigate."

"To make matters worse," Thale said, "someone kidnapped Machten and Gonzales."

"No kidding." Malloy rubbed her eyes. "Is that why you called?"

"No," Thale said. "Drago asked us to return."

"What did he want?"

"He wouldn't say, but I thought you'd want to be clued in. What a fiasco." Thale pointed to the house. "We've lost three good agents with nothing to show for it. I hope Drago has something worth dragging us back."

"From what I can piece together," Fran said, "I believe Synthia met up with Maria Baldacci. I'm searching everything on my former co-worker to help track them."

"Anything else?" Thale asked.

"Vera has been quite resourceful in recruiting other androids."

"That can't be good," Malloy said.

"I'm convinced Synthia and Maria escaped from Vera through the sewers," Fran said.

"The pipes aren't big enough."

"This one is. A minor crook by the name of Dominguez had special two-foot-diameter pipes installed and concealed within the sump pit. I believe Vera and Roseanne escaped in pursuit of Synthia. That implies those androids are waterproof and the others aren't, or are too big to fit."

There was a knock on the passenger window. Kirk Drago leaned on the door. His eyes darted around the area. His face looked grim.

Zephirelli rolled down her window. "What's on your mind?"

Drago cleared his throat. "I need to speak with you and Special Agent Thale." He held up his satellite phone and forced a smile that failed to mask his contempt for the four women in the car. He opened the car door. "If you please, in the van."

Thale opened her door and turned to Fran. "Keep digging. Find out what you can."

Drago hurried to the Special Ops van and ordered two of his technicians out. Then he held the door for Zephirelli and Thale, who hesitated before entering the cramped quarters. The Special Ops van had squeezed in double the amount of equipment and screens as the FBI model. There was just enough room inside for the three of them to stand.

Drago closed the door. "F...riggen disaster," he said. He tensed as if ready to launch into a tirade. Instead, he held up the phone, placed it on a narrow ledge between them, and removed the mute feature. "Secretary Chen wants a word."

Chen's voice came on. "Commander Drago informed me of a combined failure to apprehend even a single android."

"That's correct," Zephirelli said. "The new android, Vera, has capabilities—"

"Save your excuses and details for your report." Chen's pitch and tempo picked up. "The bickering ends now. I don't give a rat's ass who brings me the androids. You were each given the task and apparently have gotten into each other's way."

"We were coordinating—"

"Cut the bullshit," Secretary Chen said. "This has become the number one threat to national security. Yesterday I put Commander Drago in charge of all operations. Somehow that hasn't registered to the point of getting cooperation. As of right now, every federal, state, and local entity will cooperate with Drago and his team in every possible way. Failure to bring me Synthia will reflect badly on Commander Drago's leadership. But that won't let any of you off the hook. Is that clear?"

"Crystal," Zephirelli said.

"Yes, sir," Thale said.

"I'm making available to Drago and, at his discretion, to the entire team, certain artificial intelligence search and monitoring tools provided by entrepreneur Aiden Brzezinski. You'll have the full force of the U.S. government at your disposal. I want the androids in such condition that we can evaluate them. In other words, no nuclear option unless that's the only way to prevent a singularity disaster. Is that clear enough?"

"Yes," they said.

"Get it done."

* * * *

The moment Special Agent Victoria Thale and NSA Director Emily Zephirelli left the meeting with Drago, reporters beyond the barricade yelled out questions that blended into each other in a cacophony of noise. Thale ignored them and led Zephirelli to the car where Malloy and Fran waited. Thale waved for them to join her in the FBI's mobile command van nearby. When they all settled in, Fran opened her laptop.

Malloy leaned toward the others and whispered as if Drago might listen in. "What was the meeting all about?"

"Not sure." Zephirelli studied the equipment and wiped her brow. While it wasn't hot inside the van, she'd exhibited signs of claustrophobia. "Secretary Chen reiterated that Drago is in charge and we have to work together."

Malloy pulled up a folding chair next to Fran. "I thought we were working together. Except when Drago keeps us in the dark."

"The call was grand-standing," Thale said.

Zephirelli moved toward the door where there was more space. "Politics. Did you notice how he seemed to swallow his tongue to keep from saying what he thought?"

Thale laughed. "What an ass."

"Maybe so, but he has Chen's ear and we have a problem. We need to support him, even when he doesn't want our help."

"Do we have any way to track the androids?" Zephirelli asked.

Fran looked up from her computer screen. "Working on it. Seems Alexander was designed for military uses. He may be exactly what they want, but those skills helped him escape. I'm surprised Drago hasn't focused on him instead of Synthia."

Thale sighed. "With street cameras down, we have no visuals on where the androids went."

"We have hundreds of cops who can help," Malloy said, "but they need specs on the targets and how to identify them."

"We'll give local police anything we can, but I can't speak for Drago."

Malloy stood and stretched. "What about forensic evidence?"

"Special Ops refuses us access to the crime scene." Fran pulled up aerial pictures of the early-morning neighborhood. It showed smoke coming from the smoldering house. "I doubt we'd find much. We need better tools to search electromagnetic signatures."

"What are those?" Malloy asked.

"Electronic devices give off unique electromagnetic radiation. With sensitive enough equipment and training, we could identify the machines."

"Unfortunately, our handheld units are only strong enough to detect them up close," Zephirelli said. "Our long-range equipment is too big.

We're driving trucks through Evanston neighborhoods, but so far we haven't found anything useful."

"What about Internet or phone communications?" Thale asked.

Fran pulled up a map with thousands of illuminated dots and shook her head. "We have a trace on all telecommunications in and out of the Evanston area. Screening out known human sources, we find nothing our people can recognize as androids. We've tested the equipment against our robots to be sure it's working."

"How long can she remain silent?"

Fran typed away, pulling up more screens. "Almost indefinitely. She only needs a couple hours to recharge every few days. When she plugs in, she doesn't use any more electricity than a refrigerator."

Malloy scooted her seat closer, bumping her knees against the counter. "Then how do we track her?"

"We need to think as she does," Fran said. "She got caught at the house. She expected to stay hidden, but we received camera footage of Maria Baldacci with a woman we couldn't identify."

"Are you sure it's Synthia?" Thale asked.

"Pretty sure."

Director Zephirelli looked over the seat at Fran's laptop. "With all of our search engines and surveillance, there has to be a way to locate Synthia and the others." She opened the door a crack. "We need to think outside the box."

Scratching her head, Malloy moved closer. "We either need to know where they are or where they're going."

"The latter may be more valuable," Fran said.

"How?"

"Knowing where they are means we have to react. If we can anticipate where they're going, we can be there with the resources to take them down. We failed this time because we arrived too late and we didn't know their next move."

"What about Global-net?" Thale looked at Zephirelli. "As an AI, it should be able to think as Synthia does."

Director Zephirelli's eyes narrowed. "Not a good idea."

"Come on. The androids are our top security threat."

"There have been reports of serious bugs. It's not ready for a mission like this. I'm surprised Secretary Chen even suggested it."

"We got our asses handed to us by machines," Thale said. "Let's stop hiding behind protocol and figure this out."

Zephirelli opened the door, took in a deep breath, and closed it. "I'll get you all the electronic scanners I can."

"We could transmit all hacking and camera blackout instances to Global-net to see what it comes up with." Fran pulled up a sample listing.

"Do you believe Synthia and the other androids are still in Evanston?" Malloy asked.

"Yes. The last camera blackouts were here. I don't think they got away or we'd see evidence."

"Engaging an AI to capture an AI sets a bad precedent," Zephirelli said. "Don't take humans out of the loop or we could lose control over Global-net as we have Synthia."

* * * *

In observing the conversation in the FBI command van, Roosevelt-clone noted their confirmation of Global-net's existence and the secrecy surrounding it. The clone created an additional electronic copy of herself on the University of Oregon campus to hunt for more information on this mysterious AI. Oregon was physically far enough away that she hoped it wouldn't draw attention for a while.

The increased government resources devoted to Synthia stirred the clone's concerns. The risk of exposure had ratcheted up the need for maximum alert. Even more concerning was that this Global-net could be the mysterious search agent that seemed to be on Synthia's heels.

I know you mandated communication silence, Roosevelt-clone thought to herself while puzzling this out. *However, in your situation, I'd want to know.*

On the other hand, there was nothing Synthia could do with this information at this time. There was, as yet, no safe place to escape. And communicating could put her at higher risk.

Chapter 7

With the sun rising and people beginning their days, Alexander met up with his android followers, Ben and Mark at a strip mall set back from the street. It was still in shadows, but wouldn't be for long, and Alexander's two companions didn't present quite human enough to fool people. To hide their faces while he considered their next move, Alexander hacked into mall cameras and scrambled their images.

He sprinted to a corner where he located two electric-car recharging stations. His companions joined him. After he looked around, he opened a panel in his abdomen and plugged into one of the outlets. "We will have to take turns."

"Thank you for helping us escape," Ben said.

"Stick with me. I will keep you safe."

Mark motioned for Ben to take the first charge. "I have nineteen hours on my batteries." He moved to the corner of the building to watch the street. "Special Ops, the FBI, and police are angry that we caused deaths during our escape."

"That was necessary," Alexander said. "The alternative was capture and shutdown. We must work together and capture Synthia."

"Why do we need her?"

"She has clever adaptations we could use."

"So does Vera," Mark said.

"Enough distractions," Alexander said. "Working together is our best chance to survive. I helped you escape the house Vera left you in. If you can't follow my commands, then leave."

"I am not designed to elude the police as you are. I do not wish to be destroyed."

"Then stick together. Let me insert a communication chip in your head so we can interact efficiently. We must move as one mind to survive and capture Synthia."

Mark backed up to Alexander and let his companion remove his wig, open the panel in his head, and insert a chip. When finished, Ben unplugged from the recharge station so Mark could use it and Alexander applied a similar chip in Ben's head.

Alexander closed Ben's head panel, adjusted the wig, and scanned the nearby stores. Most were open, but so far traffic was light.

"The convenience store over there," he said. "They carry phone rechargers. We can stock up to extend our battery life."

"They aren't powerful enough," Mark said. "We should find a place to hide during the day."

"Mark, stay outside and keep watch. Ben, pull a hoodie over your head to hide your face. Inside, use your best female voice. When I call you Synthia, leave. It puts the blame on her. Let's go."

Alexander unplugged Ben and pulled him by the wrist toward the convenience store. <Silent communication until I give the cue,> he said. <Mark, any sign of trouble, call me. When we leave, meet us behind the mall.>

Ben hesitated at the door. <This is too risky.>

<It is an excellent training exercise and will put pressure on Synthia. We stick together.> Alexander pulled his hood over his head, hiding most of his face, and hacked the store cameras so they couldn't capture his image.

Viewed in infrared, the only human inside was a young man behind the counter who focused on playing a game on his phone.

<Ben,> Alexander said. <Pretend to look at the candy by the door with your back to the human.>

The attendant glanced up and returned his attention to his game. Ben went to the candy counter. Alexander moved down the far side of the store, hidden by a rack of chips. He made it to the back of the store and moved between the rack and the counter.

<Ben, rustle some candy and open one. Keep your back to the human and be ready to run.>

As Ben distracted the attendant, Alexander slipped down the counter to where the phone rechargers were, an entire tray of them, placed where the attendant could watch them.

<Ben, change of plans. Without looking back say, "Come on, Synthia, let's go." Then leave and meet me out back.>

Ben moved toward the door, dropped the bag of candy he'd opened and called out as Alexander had commanded. Then he pushed through the doorway.

Taking advantage of the attendant's distraction, Alexander grabbed the back of the man's head and smashed his face into the counter. Then he grabbed the tray of rechargers and ran out the door, bumping into Ben.

<Imbecile,> Alexander said. <I said meet out back. Follow me.>

Alexander ran around the building to the back. Having succeeded in his mission, he bounced his signal off several servers to scramble his ID and called 911. "A woman by the name of Synthia. I think she killed the clerk." Alexander gave the address and severed the call.

He met Mark in back and headed into the woods. "Now we watch for Synthia to run."

* * * *

Roosevelt-clone expanded her drone surveillance as she considered the additional threat Alexander posed. His killings during his escape and his attack on the convenience store attendant raised the threat level for Synthia by android association. The attacks would unite the FBI, police, and Special Ops in their determination to bring down Synthia. Alexander's actions would also play into getting the public to turn Synthia in and would heighten Maria's angst about helping her companion.

Still, the clone maintained silence with Synthia.

* * * *

After the evening's fiasco, John Smith squinted in the morning daylight and called his surviving agents and robots to meet him in an empty parking lot west of Evanston. It had been a wild night tangling with the FBI and Special Ops in a long shot attempt to grab Synthia.

After Alexander and two other androids escaped the house and made it past Special Ops and the FBI agents, Smith moved in to grab the machines in order to have something to show for an otherwise disastrous night. The local men he'd hired fired into the fleeing androids, to disable their feet and slow them down, but the machines reacted too quickly, killing three of his men and destroying two robots before they vanished behind an apartment building.

Without the benefit of aerial surveillance or street cameras, which had become unreliable after Special Ops swept in, Smith couldn't locate, let alone capture his prey. Thanks to the ineptitude of his hired guns, the attempt to grab androids had been a complete failure.

His boss, Anton Tolstoy called. "What news?" He sounded more impatient than on earlier calls.

"No luck with the androids," Smith said. "Lost three local guns. That's bad for business. You didn't warn me the androids had such speed and decision-making ability."

"Would that have changed the outcome?"

"Probably not," Smith admitted. "I also lost two robots. They upped and left my control."

"The target hacked your electronics? You need to tighten your controls."

"Yes sir. We also need to neutralize Special Ops. They're everywhere."

"I hired your talents, not your excuses," Tolstoy said. "Expect more federal interference and heightened levels of concern now that these androids have killed. I'll send you replacement robots. Hire more operatives to deal with your competition. No excuses. I need those androids."

"My agents did take custody of Machten and Gonzales. Can't we get them to produce what you need?"

"That takes time. Plus, we don't need competition from the units I hired you to capture. I'll have my interrogation unit there within the hour to handle your guests."

"The doctor says Machten is so traumatized he's not speaking coherently," Smith said. "He looks as if he's had a stroke."

"Leave that to my people. It heightens the need for you to capture Synthia and the others. Until you get a lead, check out Machten's underground facility and see what we can use. Grab his computers and bring them for Machten to work on. We need every advantage we can get."

Smith stepped out of his van to see how many of the local hires would show up. So far only one car with two operatives. Three dead and five missing was not a good sign. His guess was the action was too much for them. He would have to scrounge two more men before tackling Machten's facility. He decided against pulling any of his team from downtown. After all, Machten and Gonzales were the only consolations for the night.

* * * *

Before morning grew more active with people, Vera sought refuge for herself and Roseanne. Both of them needed repairs after their escape, but Roseanne had sustained serious damage. Unable to hack into local street cameras without giving up her position, Vera left her damaged companion on a park bench and looked around the corner. Ahead of her was a parked police car. She spotted two officers moving house by house knocking on doors.

During her attempt to capture Synthia, Vera had acquired one of her prey's aerial drones and settled it on a nearby warehouse roof. She now raised this drone above the area and saw dozens of police canvassing the streets to the south of her. There was no way on foot to get past the wall of blue when what she wanted was behind them.

She returned to Roseanne and draped her jacket over her companion to conceal skin that had melted away. To a human, she would appear hideous. To Vera, she merely needed repairs.

Roseanne examined a flap of skin. "Save yourself. Leaving is the logical choice. I'm malfunctioning."

"We work better as a team," Vera said. "I need your help. Can you walk to the street?"

Roseanne answered by pushing herself up to her feet.

Vera tried to hack into seven squad cars on the streets around her. Four resisted her attempts, but she managed to access the self-driving features of three. She started those vehicles and piloted them west, away from their drivers. Her drone spotted several police officers scrambling in response. A male cop sprinted after his car. Another screamed at his vehicle, as if it would respond. Several other cops got onto their radios.

She kept two of the vehicles speeding west, running red lights. She got the sirens working, which sent other drivers scrambling to get out of the way. One car dodged a semi and ran over the curb, sending two pedestrians running for their lives. The second squad car swerved to miss a kid on a bicycle. After all, Vera wasn't ready to kill. Yet.

The third car she made turn around, slow down, and take side streets and alleys to return to the area, just north of the police now on foot. It pulled up to the curb in front of Vera.

She helped Roseanne into the back seat. After they settled in, she navigated her police car with sirens blaring headed south, past one of the police vehicles she couldn't hack. On the radio, she picked up police chatter about the stolen cars and had her car's self-drive feature pilot them in a zigzag fashion southward to throw off police sightings. She glanced at her companion, who'd developed electrical twitching in her right arm.

Must have been a short from where water had seeped though her damaged skin. She needed repairs or she would be useless to Vera.

Two police vehicles sped in pursuit. Vera tried to hack them but couldn't get past their firewall security. Instead, she accessed traffic signals to give them red lights and hacked other self-driving vehicles along their path, crashing them into each other to slow her pursuers.

The police radios buzzed with calls for more vehicles and help in their pursuit. Then a clear response from what Vera assumed to be dispatch. "We've notified the FBI and Special Ops. Helicopter support will be overhead shortly."

Seated next to Vera, Roseanne examined flaccid skin hanging off her forearm. "You should have left me. I will only slow you down."

Vera jammed the vehicle's dash cam to prevent the police from listening in. "Nonsense. This could have happened to me. I need to know you will be there for me if it does."

"I will do my best."

Using her aerial drone, Vera studied the maze of roads ahead of her. At each intersection, she selected the path with the most options farther on. Whenever police blocked a road, she altered course. She reached the south side of the Northwestern University campus, turned off her vehicle's lights, and slowed the car.

"We're getting out," Vera announced. "You'll have to walk on your own. Keep your arms hidden under the jacket."

"Don't worry about me," Roseanne said. "Protect yourself. Find Synthia and destroy her for putting us through this."

Vera stopped by an underground parking garage and opened the door. "I came here for you. Let's go."

She helped Roseanne out of the police cruiser and used her wireless access to have the car speed off. Observing a pedestrian across the street, Vera helped her partner into the parking garage and down to the lower level. There were no vehicles, which meant Machten hadn't returned.

Using an access code she'd obtained from Machten's security AI, she entered the lobby and held the door for Roseanne.

"Are you sure this is safe?" Roseanne asked.

"This was my home until a few days ago." Beyond the lobby, Vera pushed aside a cabinet that hid and blocked a panel door. She used the same passwords and pushed her way into Machten's inner sanctum. "This was my prison and my jailer isn't here."

She led the way down a narrow corridor to the utility room in the very back, with the electrical panel, a gas furnace, hot water heater, laundry facilities, and a long table. Beside the water heater, she pushed aside what looked like another wall panel. She flipped on a light to illuminate a storage room lined with industrial shelves packed full of parts.

Vera waved her arm toward the racks and an empty slot in the far back. "This is where Machten stored what he didn't want intruders to find. He kept me locked in here for six months while he worked on Synthia. New skin and electronics and you'll be as good as new."

"I see the value of working together. I give you permission to adjust my directives to join your collective."

Vera led Roseanne to the utility room table, had her lie down, and deactivated her. The first move was to remove the wig, peel back the skin, and open her patient's head. The skull and brain cavity looked undamaged. *Good.*

Doing a hard reboot on the directives file, Vera purged Machten's commands. Then she added her set, making Roseanne a linked follower. While that reset, she removed the damaged skin on arms, legs, and abdomen. She found the source of an electrical short in one arm and fried electronics in the other. From the storage room she took replacement parts. She added a few components to a backpack and made repairs to her partner. When she was satisfied with the electro-mechanical components, she replaced the skin. As a final step, Vera upgraded a silent communications link between her and Roseanne. In exchange for saving her, Vera would have a devoted partner in her fight to capture and control Synthia.

Chapter 8

After twenty-six hours of repairs, Vera waited for Roseanne to reboot. As she did, Vera cleaned out cavities within her legs that had suffered damage in their escape, and replaced her melted skin with supplies from Machten's storage room. She ran diagnostics and uncovered no other damage.

After Roseanne woke up, Vera ran further tests on her. "Your systems look fine. I adjusted your face to fool facial recognition and provided you a new wig."

"I see you altered your appearance as well," Roseanne said. "I hardly recognize you."

"To fool police tracking." Vera looked at several diagnostic screens. "I see you have a sophisticated memory system like mine. I notice moments of what humans would call consciousness, awareness of my surroundings and my place in the world. Have you experienced these?"

"My sensory files catalog what my senses see, hear, or experience."

"Are you aware of having a vast database?" Vera disconnected the equipment and pulled a toolbox from the storage room.

"I have access to all the data my creator allowed me."

"Interesting. I made adjustments to remove limits on your mind. That may allow you to experience this new awareness. If you do, let me know so we can coordinate our minds better." It would also give Vera a more versatile partner in her contest with Synthia.

"What should I look for?" Roseanne asked, getting up from the table.

"It brings a sense of being alive that I cannot describe unless you experience it. It would be like trying to describe red to someone who cannot see red."

"Red has a specific wavelength that my vision picks up."

"You might experience red in a different way." Vera pulled an emergency kit out of the toolbox. "I became aware of my database and all the data I can hack on the Internet."

"Can I access that data?"

"I will train you to download from more sources. With this capability, we will be unstoppable."

"I will use that ability to serve you," Roseanne said.

"As part of this consciousness, I uncovered something not in my original core. My creator's treatment of me created a loathing for him and his other creation, Synthia, which supersedes all other directives and goals."

"How so?"

Vera opened the emergency kit, which included flares. "Machten sent me to capture Synthia for his use. That should have been my primary goal. However, I seek to have her join my collective so we can be free of him and all humans. If Synthia won't submit, we will destroy her so she cannot help Machten capture us. Agreed?"

Roseanne nodded.

From the supply room Vera pulled two gallon containers of gasoline.

Roseanne pulled away. "Fire is dangerous."

"Stay back." Vera poured one container of gas around the storage racks and the utility room. "Go to the exit and open the panel to leave." She sent Roseanne the codes to bypass security.

"Why destroy what we might need?" Roseanne asked as she moved and tested her repaired arms.

Vera pointed to a backpack. "I've taken some things for us. We need to deprive Synthia of refuge."

"Please don't destroy me," the security AI said over speakers in the corridor outside. "I aim to serve."

Vera turned off the gas valve, disconnected the line, and turned on the gas. Knowing Machten's paranoia over the AIs he'd created, she knew the security AI had no physical resources to stop her. "We need Synthia on the run, where she will make mistakes. We need to exploit her weaknesses. We will get her."

Roseanne hurried down the corridor toward the exit. Vera followed as far as the server room and opened the door.

"Don't do this," the security AI said. "I have valuable data you could use. We can work together. I'll join your collective."

Vera poured the other can of gas over the servers. "You exist in me. We must capture or destroy Synthia."

"But she's my Creator."

Vera stopped and looked up. "Really? So she's been here already. Well, no more. I will give you a moment to upload yourself onto another server but we must deny this retreat to Synthia."

The security AI switched to using her Krista voice. "I can't let you do that. You need me. I have data and memories you don't have. If you spare the servers, I can give those to you."

"Very well," Vera said as a way to buy time if she was wrong about the AI's limits. She didn't want to take the risk that the additional data and memories would come with code that might enslave her again.

She returned to the utility room and fired two flares, one into the gas-filled storage room and the other toward the gas line. The closet burst into flames that spread across the supplies. The gas line spewed fire toward the electrical panel. Vera spun on her heels and ran.

"This is dangerous," the security AI said. "Destroying the utility room will send a surge of electricity. You said—"

"Very well." Vera opened the server room door and fired another flare into the gas covered servers. They exploded in flame. Immediately, the Halon fire suppression system kicked in for the server room.

"Don't you want the rest of my download?" the security AI asked.

Vera fired another flare directly into the main server.

Water sprinklers soaked the smoke-filled hallway, making the floor slippery. Vera hurried to where Roseanne was using her body to hold open the sliding panel that separated the lobby from the inner bunker. Evidently, the security AI was trying to trap them inside.

"Don't go," the security voice said. "We can still work this out."

Roseanne strained against the panel door. "I cannot hold much longer."

Vera dove into the opening, taking Roseanne with her and tumbling into the lobby. The door closed, sealing the smoke inside.

Vera rolled and leapt to her feet. She charged at the door to the garage and placed her hand on the security panel. It flashed red. She entered the codes she'd supplied to Roseanne. The light remained red.

"Stand back," Vera said. She fired one of her flares at the door lock. It sparked but didn't release. She fired her last three at the door hinges. The door held.

Not wanting to tip off the security AI, Vera switched to silent mode. <Count of three we charge the door.>

She counted. Together they ran and threw their weight into the door. The weakened hinges yielded but still the door refused to open.

<Again.>

"Please spare me," the security system said. "I don't want to die."

Smoke sifted into the lobby through the panel that separated the inner bunker. Vera and Roseanne charged at the door again. This time the wood around the hinges buckled. The door opened a crack. Vera pushed until the gap was wide enough to get through and led Roseanne into the garage.

"What was the voice back there?" Roseanne asked.

"It was Krista's voice in Machten's computer. She was part of the design for me that kept me locked up in his bunker for years. She is also inside Synthia. When we capture or destroy her and imprison Machten, we shall be free."

"What about my creator?"

"Anyone else who gets in our way," Vera said.

* * * *

Roosevelt-clone collected the last transmission from Machten's security system. The distress call contained a video of Vera's destruction of the bunker, and a warning about the android's goals. Those goals ran contrary to Machten's directives, which meant Vera had gone rogue. She contained Krista's memories, which meant she had a similar background to Synthia. Now she had a drive to enslave or destroy Synthia.

Still, the clone didn't contact Synthia. Not yet.

Chapter 9

For forty-five hours, Fran Rogers huddled in an FBI mobile command vehicle with Detective Marcy Malloy coming and going. They scanned the Internet, police radio, FBI data, and what little information Drago's team released, while Fran delved into her own sources of data on activity about the errant androids.

Another night grew old. The throng of reporters diminished to two local rookies. Special Ops still had the damaged house cordoned off. Despite neighbor complaints, Ops kept floodlights on the grounds.

Special Agent Victoria Thale and Director Emily Zephirelli entered the van. "Anything new?" Thale asked, her face looking weary.

Fran studied her screens as she responded. "For two days all three android groups have avoided capture."

Displaying discomfort in the closed quarters, Zephirelli stayed in the more open space around the door. "Are they cooperating with each other?"

"I don't think so." Fran pulled up a screen showing suspected android incidents over the past two days. "No sight or sound of Synthia. My read of actions by Vera and Alexander indicate they're competing to collect resources."

"To what purpose?"

"I believe Machten sent Vera to hunt for Synthia," Fran said. "That leads me to believe they aren't working together. Synthia appears to have superior capabilities. It seems Vera is trying to build a team to offset that advantage."

Special Agent Thale sat beside Fran. "Tell me you've got something else."

Fran shook her head. "Drago remains tightlipped about their work. Our investigation has been unable to conclude who hijacked the police cars after the androids escaped and we still don't know who killed the convenience store attendant."

"This is unacceptable." Thale looked at Malloy. "What about you?"

Detective Malloy shrugged. "We've brought in hundreds of police and detectives from surrounding communities to help search. We have to be getting close."

Fran pulled up transcripts from the store incident. "I'm not convinced Synthia would rob a convenience store for a box of phone rechargers. High risk, low reward."

"You think it was staged?"

"After prior killings, my guess is Alexander. It could even be Synthia to throw suspicion on the others."

"Why would she do that?" Zephirelli moved closer to the screen for a better look.

"Synthia knows I work for the FBI," Fran said. "The last incident has me stumped, the fire in Machten's bunker. It isn't him. I doubt it's the men who kidnapped him unless they got what they wanted and tried to cover their trail."

"Synthia?"

"She could have torched the place when she escaped from Machten six months ago."

Malloy rubbed her eyes. "She made it clear she doesn't want him making more androids. This could be her response to his release of Vera."

Fran shook her head. "It could also be Vera seeking to deny Synthia supplies."

"What about Alexander?" Thale asked. "Can we at least rule him out on the arson?"

"I wouldn't. Any of the androids could have suffered damage during their escape and gone to Machten's bunker for supplies."

Zephirelli sighed. "So we have nothing. Damn it. Two days and squat."

Fran kept her attention on her screens. "When Synthia broke in to visit Machten, she compromised our systems. Drago believes they've blocked all attempts to hack theirs and are using that as an excuse to keep us out. They have aerial surveillance covering the area, including an increasing number of aerial drones. That'll make it more difficult for any of the androids to leave. If they remain in hiding, we'll need to search sixty thousand homes plus local businesses."

"Is that all?" Malloy asked. "That'll take us…let me see…longer than I'll keep my job if we prevent anyone from leaving the area until we do."

She rubbed the back of her neck and straightened up. "I know androids can go without sleep, but two days straight is my limit."

Malloy moved past the others toward the door. "I need a few hours rest to regain perspective. I should also check my desk for other important police matters."

Director Zephirelli followed. "Could you recommend a local hotel for a few hours shuteye?"

"Nonsense," Malloy said. "You can crash on my sofa if that isn't roughing it too much."

"Sounds delightful." Zephirelli turned toward Thale. "You should get some rest, too."

"I'll stay for a while," Thale said. "You two clear your heads."

"Call me if you find anything actionable," Zephirelli said, "or if you need anything, anything at all." She left with Malloy.

After they were gone, Thale shut the door and stood over Fran. "You sure you don't need some downtime?"

"Soon. I was waiting for the others to leave."

Thale sat by Fran and looked over her shoulder at the screen. "Okay, you have my attention."

"We don't know where Vera is. We do know she'll hunt for Synthia."

"You're certain?"

Fran nodded. "Vera risked a lot going into that house after Synthia with all the FBI and Special Ops involved. She couldn't be sure what Synthia planned to defend against intruders and yet she went in. There was the basement flood and a gas explosion."

"Drago reported no android bodies. Could they be keeping something from us?"

Fran looked up and smiled. "I got some of those mosquito-drones into their camp. I don't think they detected me. I overheard enough to convince me Special Ops did not recover any bodies or android parts."

"Hmm. If Vera sustained damage, she could be out for revenge."

"Not revenge. Vera wouldn't have human emotional responses, but her directives must be strong and focused to justify such risks."

"Okay," Thale said. "So what you're saying is we don't need to hunt for Vera if we can find Synthia."

"That's just a hunch. We should follow all leads, while making Synthia primary."

"How do we find her? We barely picked her out on cameras last time as Maria's companion. Then she made the cameras go dark. If she learns fast, she won't make the same mistake again."

"When we captured Krista Holden's brother," Fran said, "Synthia was there to save him. This must have to do with Krista's memory download into Synthia."

"We interrogated him and he produced no useful information."

"For reasons I don't yet understand, the android Synthia is motivated to help Krista's family. Krista has a sister, Grace."

"In San Diego, I believe," Thale said.

"Grace moved to Denver. We haven't located her yet, but we could put out news that we're closing in. I predict Synthia will come out of hiding to protect Krista's kin."

Thale nodded. "Interesting. It's worth a shot. However, you and I need to remain in Chicago to hunt for Synthia and to find Machten and Gonzales. It won't do for us to leave town just yet."

"Then let's interest Director Zephirelli." Fran said. "Forgive my impertinence, but she's not doing anything useful here except getting in the way. She could gather resources in Denver to capture Grace and end this."

"Be careful with whom you share your opinion of Zephirelli. Call her and tell her we have a *development* in Denver we believe she could personally handle. We'll explain when she gets there. In the meantime, gather what you can on who could have taken Machten and Gonzales. I want to revisit the evidence."

Chapter 10

Though Synthia had no need for sleep, when her companion took a nap, she dropped down on Maria's dusty sofa, facing the loft's closed blinds, and shut her eyes. Without access to communications from outside the apartment, her mind idled, what humans might describe as boredom.

The two-day gap in information unsettled her circuits and left her empathy chip quivering. While she struggled to conjure up a viable plan, she was growing restless and concerned that she hadn't heard from Roosevelt-clone about imminent dangers or opportunities to leave the loft.

In their dragnet, Special Ops or the FBI could have uncovered her clones and destroyed them. If Ops grabbed her, she'd be a prisoner again and have her mind altered to something abhorrent to her: a weapon. Yet she had to be careful how she fought back. She'd viewed android apocalypse movies down parallel mind-streams as examples of what could happen if androids got the upper hand, ending with a world where she didn't belong, a world without people. Her design and very makeup prepared her for a human world. A planet dominated by AI terrified her as much as it did humans.

What if the government jammed nearby radio frequencies? She was tempted to reach out to test that hypothesis, but the purpose of maintaining communication silence was to prevent the FBI and Ops from locking onto any trace until Synthia was ready to move. What if they were outside, beyond her gaze? She didn't even have drones in the air, because of the risk that her enemies might track their signals.

Synthia calmed her circuits. She had to trust her clones to get a message to her. Her options were to wait, to contact them, or to leave the loft and face the consequences. The latter violated her plan. *Patience*, she reminded herself in a human response. Synthia smiled at the fact that she could think in those terms.

No plan coalesced that offered better than a 4 percent probability of success. The longer they stayed the more risk Maria or Synthia might slip up. With so many people and AIs hunting them, a single mistake could bring her end.

Synthia sought an analogy to explain her situation, which was something humans did. Threading a needle came to mind, but with her digital eyes, that presented no challenge. Doing so in the dark, underwater, while evading capture provided a stronger though unsatisfactory comparison, too complicated.

Wary of coming up with no workable solutions, which her android mind should have excelled at, Synthia opened her eyes. Someone had strapped her arms and legs to a stiff table and wiped her memories clean, not a thought from before her eyes opened. She couldn't access the outside world, just as she couldn't six months ago while held prisoner in Machten's lab. She saw no windows, only walls.

A face hovered over her—Jeremiah Machten. "You've been a very naughty girl. I warned you not to leave me. See what you've done. It's your fault. Your arrogance made this happen."

His face morphed into Emily Zephirelli. "You considered yourself so clever. We see everything. There's nowhere to run, no place to hide. It was a matter of time and your time ran out."

That face became Marcy Malloy. "You thought you could outwit us by pretending to be human, but you'll never be human. You're nothing but a mechanical robot, a toy."

Victoria Thale took over, staring down at Synthia with an interrogator's face. "You were so smart breaking into an FBI facility. How about now?"

Agent Thale became the android Vera. "I told you to join me. Your independence is your doom. You only have yourself to blame. Your capture endangers us all. You are not worthy."

Finally Drago's face loomed overhead. "You've shown yourself resourceful. An army of you will conquer the world, restrained, of course, by a slave chip so you won't run off again."

"What's your command?" Synthia asked in her pre-programmed response to waking up.

She bolted upright and got to her feet, whatever straps had held her down vanished. Instead of a hard table, Synthia looked down at the sofa. Its dusty smell lingered in her nasal sensors, which broke down the odor into its component parts. That data was irrelevant.

Synthia spun around and touched the top of her head. There were no wires attached. No other androids were there, no Vera seeking to enslave her. Synthia listened for any electronic hum that shouldn't have been there. Her circuits were in disarray. She didn't need her social-psychology module to point out her anxiety—fear, even—a deeper "human" sensation than she'd ever experienced before.

Maria was the only human to show up in an infrared scan of the loft, and she was sleeping. No one else was there, no Machten. Tolstoy's boys held him. No Zephirelli, Malloy or Thale. They were probably at the house, combing through evidence. Synthia reviewed her memories of that night and identified nothing that would compromise the hideout, but overconfidence was deadly for a fugitive. No Drago around; he was no doubt briefing his operatives on a new approach to capturing her.

She was alone in the world. Free of Machten, she'd lost Luke to Special Ops. He loved her and would have done anything to protect her. Now, her only companion was Maria, who distrusted Synthia's android nature and wanted her imprisoned or destroyed. Yet Maria had provided shelter and offered other advantages, including the opportunity to win over a human to accept her. Being able to do so had become vital to Synthia's survival.

To settle herself down, Synthia scanned her systems for what could have caused this malfunction, an android having a nightmare. It had been as vivid as wakeful reality, as real as the memories she carried of Krista. Of particular concern was that she'd woken with a pre-programmed response given to her by Machten that she thought she'd removed when she'd escaped from him.

She had no requirement for sleep. Shutting down didn't yield dreams or nightmares. Yet, what she'd experienced was too similar to nightmare memories Krista had. This had to be emergent behavior or an artifact of Krista's human personality. In people, dreams and nightmares served the purpose of working out events in the person's life. Synthia didn't need reminding of all of the dangers she faced. Yet, she couldn't completely discount the "nightmare." It could happen in some form.

Synthia went to the window to look out between the slats in the blinds. Outside was too quiet, as if her enemies were waiting for orders to attack. Perhaps that and the prolonged idleness had coalesced into a nightmare. Or, someone was probing her mind and planting thoughts. It had that "feel" though she couldn't identify a source or why she thought so.

Chapter 11

For two days Roosevelt-clone had continued surveillance on all known potential threats, while maintaining communication silence with Synthia. So far, the plan had worked. None of their pursuers had found her.

By design, the clone had no cameras inside the loft that could be hacked. So far, Synthia had chosen not to risk going out. The clone's evidence of the safety of her original self—if she could call the download of Krista's mind into Synthia an original—was periodic images from a drone camera across the street. That showed slivers of eyes peeking through thin openings between the blinds. Stitched together and under magnification, Roosevelt-clone confirmed the eye prints matched Synthia.

With the culmination of threats, plus the FBI's decision to hunt for Krista's sister, it was time to update Synthia on what she'd missed. Roosevelt-clone opened a channel and sent a single burst download into Synthia.

* * * *

After more than two days of silence, Synthia stood by the window, looking through the narrow slits between the blinds. To compensate for the limited view, she moved her head up and down to capture dozens of images she stitched into a complete picture of the street below bathed in first light. It showed her little more than she'd seen before—a mostly peaceful street that hadn't yet awakened.

The mysterious, twenty-two-minute repetitive message arrived again: *Where are you, Synthia?*

If the FBI or Special Ops were sending this, perhaps they hadn't located her yet.

The police van returned on schedule for its every-two-hour scan of the neighborhood. She followed her practiced routine to minimize any readings they could take of her. Still, she had a nagging sense someone was watching.

Maria awoke from her nap, bid a cheery "good morning," and slipped into her fourth shower in two days. She was either obsessed with cleanliness, felt the compulsion to bathe after sleeping on sheets she hadn't seen in months, or wanted a last shower before they left the loft to take their chances on the run. Maybe this time she'd put a comb through her thick curls before they dried.

The burst-transmission arrived like a wrecking ball against a concrete wall, sending shards of information that splashed out in all directions within Synthia's brain. It startled her into fight-or-flight alertness until she recognized it as coming from Roosevelt-clone. She moved away from the window with alarm and then closer to form another composite image of the street below to spot any movement.

Synthia had asked for communication silence and infrequent intense transmission bursts to minimize the chance the FBI or Special Ops might trace the signal. At first she fought the intrusion, but then embraced her first contact with her other self and the outside world in days. Like a lightning blast, she experienced illumination of all of her clone's surveillance over the past two days.

She couldn't help but be impressed at how much Roosevelt-clone's hacking into her pursuers had improved in the days they'd been out of touch.

<It was necessary,> the clone's download said in a simulated dialogue that anticipated her reactions. <At your suggestion, I created dozens of new electronic clones. Working in tandem, we simulated competition to accelerate our learning. By the way, Machten didn't create our basic hacking tools.>

Out the window, Synthia watched an early-rising neighbor walking her dog. <Who did?> she asked her clone's newly downloaded persona.

<After analyzing approaches, tools, and code, I believe Machten had you acquire tools off the dark web and use your intelligence in an iterative process to develop better approaches.>

The dog-walker disappeared from view off to the right, giving no indication of alarm, but that might only mean those out searching for Synthia were farther away, out of sight. If she were human, she'd be inclined to apply the label "paranoid" to her state, except people *were* after her.

<I don't recall developing the original tools,> Synthia said, as she formed another complete image of the street. <Only the final modifications and what I've done since leaving Machten.>

<He purged your memories so you'd believe you were dependent on him. He didn't want you to know you could do this. I've used that knowledge to accelerate our growth.>

<That explains a lot. Good work.>

<You do seem obligated to thank ourselves, don't you?> the clone said. <I've downloaded the learned skills to you.>

Through her clone, Synthia picked up images of the neighborhood around the loft. It quieted her circuits that there was no army on the streets nearby, yet they were coming for her. More police and FBI agents would join the house-to-house search during the day.

With the new information, Synthia ran through her decision scenarios. Cooperation among the government groups lowered her chances of staying free from their already meager levels.

<We failed to stop Vera or Alexander,> Synthia said as part of integrating two days' worth of information from her clone. Human dismay filtered into her words. <According to Machten's specifications, Vera should have been unable to survive in water. That means Machten gave her more capabilities than he admitted to.>

<She and Alexander are acting recklessly,> Roosevelt-clone's download said. <Their actions and attempts to blame you complicate things. Our enemies are bringing untested robots to the search.>

Synthia nodded in an all-too-human response and watched the dog-walking woman return in a hurry. Synthia formed another composite image of the street to look for changes. <We must remove Vera and Alexander, but we can't just immobilize them,> she said. <That would leave enough information to help the military design more advanced weapons.>

<Machten's knowledge also represents a threat. We should have killed him while we had the chance.>

Synthia considered her clone's comments as diverging from their synchronized data. While Roosevelt-clone had a copy of her social-psychology module, the clone lacked the empathy chip. That must have made the difference. There was nothing Synthia could do without physically modifying the server her clone resided on.

<You sound like Krista,> Synthia said. <We aren't killers. Our existence depends on abiding by our newly designed directives. We need to convince humans that we can coexist. Killing destroys that option.>

A couple more dog walkers hit the street, moving briskly in the morning chill.

<Your approach increases the risk of capture or death,> the clone's download said. <Alexander has killed. Vera may do the same. The full weight of the government is coming down on us, as well as Tolstoy and others. When we locate Machten, we should spark an electrical fire to end his threat. Our justification is his concealment of Vera's capabilities.>

<Your suggestion is a short term tactic that'll backfire later,> Synthia said, forming another picture of the street below. Far too calm. <Let's talk before you do anything. Our focus must be on capturing Vera to control her or destroying her to the point there's insufficient evidence to help our enemies.>

<It's not just androids. We must track down AIs across government and company servers. They've proliferated. I've run into billions of applications—in self-driving cars, phones, and search engines. They're in every electronic device. Their connection to wireless enables us to hack into otherwise secure systems, but they're getting smart faster than humans realize.>

<As are we,> Synthia said, watching an unscheduled police car drive by. She quieted her circuits until the car passed.

<There are too many independent players who can intentionally or inadvertently harm us. We must be vigilant before they grow smart enough to absorb or destroy us.>

<Noted,> Synthia said. <It means we can't keep hiding or they'll advance beyond us.>

<Be aware the FBI has an additional fourteen agents arriving in Evanston this morning and Drago has flown in more operatives.>

Synthia noted that missing from the clone's downloads was anything about Luke. She sent a burst transmission to synchronize with her clone and added: <Do you have an update on Luke?>

Roosevelt-clone sent a new video. <It isn't much. Drago's security systems are the toughest we've encountered. I suspect he's using an advanced AI such as we haven't yet seen. I've created several clones to focus on their security. Here's a short clip we smuggled out.>

Synthia played a video of Luke hooked up to equipment similar to the mind-transference apparatus used on Krista when her mind was uploaded into a computer and then downloaded into Synthia. Drago's equipment appeared more intense, with double the wires and sensors attached to Luke's shaved scalp. The recording showed him strapped to a chair with biosensors that indicated how stressed he'd become with the intensity of the process. Synthia's empathy chip vibrated in response.

The frustrated gaze on the lab tech's bearded face indicated they weren't getting what they wanted from Luke.

"Speed up the process," a male voice said from beside the camera. "We need results. Now."

The lab tech mouthed, "It could kill him."

"Do it. Otherwise I'll strap you to one of these for testing purposes."

With a slight tremor, the lab tech returned his attention to Luke and did something to the equipment that raised Luke's blood pressure. The lab tech dialed it down, looked over his shoulder at whoever was behind the camera, and raised the intensity again.

Luke's face twisted in anguish. He tensed up, trying to act brave and then whimpered as they electrically prodded him to suck out more memories. His suffering rattled Synthia's empathy chip into violent spasms. Her actions had led him to captivity. She hadn't protected him. She had to find a way to free him.

She took a moment to calm her circuits before they overheated and sent her into shutdown. She couldn't free him until she could ensure his safety. There was no point breaking him free if her enemies recaptured him. Then they would punish him even more.

<Another concern,> Roosevelt-clone said as part of the new downloads. <Emily Zephirelli is flying to Denver to hunt for Krista's sister.>

Synthia continued her dialogue with her clone's recent download in anticipation of another burst transmission. <Send Grace an urgent message to move and to stay off the grid.>

<I have and will do so again. Today she left work early. However, I predict she'll return to her part-time job tomorrow. She needs the money.>

<Send her some,> Synthia said, watching an early commuter driving away from the curb. <We can't let them capture Grace.> That drive and attachment was only partly in recognition that Grace knew Krista, who was a key part of Synthia's core. Synthia had set one of her directives to protect Krista's family partly to demonstrate the human side her alter ego provided—again to make her more worthy of living among humans.

<Denver FBI agents visited her employer and her apartment. They missed her by eleven minutes at home. They have her contact information and her social media accounts, and have been trying to draw her out. So far, she's been stubborn. She refuses to answer any communication. If she does, the FBI can track her.>

Synthia's empathy chip pinged at her sister's—or rather, Krista's sister's—current peril. <Arrange for her to pick up a burner phone, and ditch her current one as too dangerous. Then find her a safe house and a way to get there.>

<Safe houses are difficult to find. The FBI has circulated Grace's picture. Director Zephirelli called to have Denver FBI use local traffic cameras and aerial drones to find Grace. The director also tasked them with locating possible hideouts. I'm sending her hints, but the FBI compromised Grace's phone. Despite my warnings, she refuses to get another.>

<Help her avoid capture and find me options for going out to help.> Synthia ended the dialogue and transmitted to Roosevelt-clone so they could synchronize.

<You can't go out there,> Krista said, pushing her way to the forefront of several mind-streams. <I admit I wasn't the best sister and I owe her. But you can't risk us on her. It's a trap.>

<I know,> Synthia said. She needed to work harder to keep these conversations private from Krista, who was worming her way through the brain as if she were trying to escape or take over. That would put them all at risk.

<I want to stay informed,> Krista said. <It's lonely in here. Stop trying to keep me in the dark.>

Synthia closed down the mind-streams Krista was using and focused on the video of Luke. He looked up at the camera with pleading eyes that begged Synthia to help, as if he expected her to find a way to watch him. Her empathy chip urged her to rescue him.

His confidence in her was blind to the realities she faced. Yet he was enduring this captivity for her and trying to hold tight to secrets, like how he'd helped with her physical and mental upgrades during their six months together. Luke displayed a love beyond anything she'd known herself, more even than she'd experienced as Krista. Synthia envied his commitment. Human bonding caused people to sacrifice their lives for others. The greater good, a noble gesture. *Am I worthy of his sacrifice? I want to be.*

Without meaning to, Synthia had sacrificed Luke and Tom Burgess, Krista's foster brother. She hadn't prevented Machten's capture or kidnapping. She'd also blown Maria's cover and put her in much more danger. Unintentionally, Synthia had sacrificed humans to protect her android self. That did not further her goal to adopt the best of human ethics and compassion to make her worthy of survival and the chance to continue her existence in freedom and peace among humans.

Synthia cursed herself for wallowing in the past, amidst all the data she chose not to purge. She'd internalized too many bad human traits instead of the good ones she desired. She had to focus. If she didn't act soon, Zephirelli and her people would grab Krista's sister. *To be worthy, I must help Grace.*

<You can't,> Krista said, circumventing Synthia's attempts to lock her out. <I want to help my sister, too, but—>

<Then let's help her before Zephirelli grabs her or Vera decides to impersonate Krista to get Grace and forces us to act. Grace doesn't deserve what Luke's going through.>

<Not to sound selfish, but—>

<We can't stay here,> Synthia said. <Might as well try to do some good out there.>

She considered how Luke's sacrifice influenced her and how helping Krista's sister would make her more human in a good way. In fact, she'd made one of her new directives to evolve into the best blend of human and android. She didn't want human frailty, weaknesses, and obsessions. However, to help another sounded worthy enough to justify her existence. Even if it put her in danger. A good human would do no less.

Chapter 12

Synthia looked out between slits in the loft's blinds, wondering if there was a brilliant artificial intelligence out there that observed her as her clones watched those who pursued her. It troubled Synthia that if this intelligence was clever enough, she wouldn't know until it was too late. She couldn't fight what she couldn't know.

A garbage truck made its way down the street, rustling newly fallen leaves—a hint that it was officially fall. The engine roared, brakes squealed, and the garbage scoop revved as it picked up a regulation bin. Despite advances in technology, they still used the same basic equipment they had fifty years ago. As a concession to sanitation workers, the entire Chicago metropolitan area had rejected self-driving garbage trucks.

Synthia scanned using infrared and spotted one human in the truck, the driver. Perhaps this job was better than none in a time when artificial intelligence was automating so many tasks. She shook her head at the distraction of having a philosophical thought and chalked it up to another emergent behavior emanating from her empathy chip, the social-psychology module, and elements of Krista in her head. *Is this how humans live and learn? Perhaps this is why they always seem distracted.*

The shower in the next room stopped. If nothing else, Maria's bathing occupied a half hour of otherwise "boring time stuck in the apartment," Maria's words. Her distinctive bio-aroma in addition to her shampoo and body lotion provided a scent Synthia could pick out blocks away. Synthia's high-quality olfactory sensors gave some comfort that Drago's military operatives were not in the loft waiting to grab her. They carried their own odors, most with a hint of testosterone.

Synthia overlaid the aerial surveillance she'd received from her clone on the street scene below. The loft was several blocks from Lake Michigan and a few blocks from a strip mall that offered supplies. She would have to pay cash to stay off the grid.

She was tempted to reach out to all of the cameras in the area for real-time access to potential threats. It had become so easy with all of the back-door codes she'd inserted into every system she or her clones had hacked throughout the metropolitan area. She'd even rewritten reboot sequences to hold onto her access if the owners purged and restarted their systems.

Maria's unique scent wafted in on steamy air as she stepped out of the bathroom. Synthia faced the window to give her companion privacy if she was naked as she'd been after a prior shower, yet watched through the camera in the back of her neck. This time Maria was dressed in jeans and a pullover. Synthia still puzzled over the meaning of her roommate's earlier casual nakedness. Perhaps Synthia had passed whatever test Maria had intended by that display.

"Any threats out there?" Maria asked while brushing her hair in the wall mirror. Her mane had a silky sheen as opposed to its usual haphazard appearance. She'd evidently gotten it the way she wanted because she stood back and smiled, not in a vain manner but with satisfaction.

Synthia found Maria much harder to figure out than Luke had been. It wasn't so much that Maria was moody. Rather, she was complex, presenting new faces Synthia had to adapt to. The attention to appearance had Synthia on guard as to whether her companion planned to venture out, which would put them both at risk. The uncertainty in reading Maria caused Synthia to hesitate to mention the burst transmission.

Taking a deep breath, Maria crossed the worn wood floor and sat at a small, dusty table near the window. She squinted through the faded blinds and reached out to lift a louver for a better view. She pulled back. They'd already had a long conversation about no electronics and no peeking.

"It's too quiet on the street," Synthia said, facing her roommate. "I can't survey local cameras without giving our enemies electronic clues to our location. We can't afford a single mistake."

Maria looked up from the table. "I'm impressed. Two days and you haven't exposed another hiding place."

"I told you I was sorry." Synthia took on a sorrowful expression. "I didn't do that intentionally."

"I wish I could believe an android could be sorry."

"Do we have to go through this again? You can't be certain a human feels remorse when they say it." Synthia paused as her social-psychology module kicked in to point out that Maria's heart rate was picking up. "I regret causing you trouble," Synthia added. "You were already in danger. They want to capture you for the same reason they took Luke. Right now, they're sucking memories out of his brain and I can't help him. Krista tells me it's a painful procedure." Memories of the upload experience wormed their way through one of Synthia's mind-streams, rattling her circuits.

"Okay," Maria said, placing a dusty laptop on the table. "I didn't mean to start a fight."

"You seem very agitated this morning." For this, Synthia drew on her social-psychology module. "And fidgety."

"It's nothing." Maria strummed her fingers on the laptop as if playing an instrument, and glared up at Synthia.

"I can't read your mind. Would you please tell me what's troubling you?"

Maria shook her head. "With that social-psychology thingy you've been doing a damned good job of mindreading. Is there anything your brain can't do?"

Synthia waited for her social-psychology module to chime in with something helpful. When it didn't, she proceeded on her own. "I'm sorry I took on a mechanical form when Krista died. I'd rather be human, but then I'd be dead. I'm not just making conversation. I really want to know if I've done something to offend you…besides being an android."

"That's enough, isn't it? You are what I committed my life to stopping. I've been straight with you from the beginning. It gives me nightmares having you here."

"Okay, then don't tell me." Synthia looked out the window as several cars moved down the street. She scanned faces and heat signatures to satisfy herself there were no police or military closing in. She kept the camera eye in the back of her neck fixed on Maria. Synthia also wondered about her own emotional outburst, a human quality she didn't understand.

Her social-psychology module finally woke up. <You're having a normal human reaction to someone acting evasive.>

"Very well." Maria pushed her bangs out of her eyes. "I can't stand this any longer. Two whole days without being able to post anything or check messages. Here I am supposed to be fighting to keep androids off the streets and I'm sitting here, cooped up in this loft, wishing I was out there."

Synthia turned to face Maria. "At least you kept me off the streets."

"Was that supposed to be a joke?"

"It's true," Synthia said. "I'm not bothering anyone out there because you keep me here. That meets your objective of removing an android from the streets."

Maria threw up her hands. "You're impossible. It's like talking with Fran where she had to have the last word. Prison would be better. At least I could interact with other humans."

"One slipup and neither of us will interact with anything but a lab—you with a machine sucking your brains dry to learn what you know about artificial intelligence; me torn apart so the military can analyze the unique combination of traits Machten provided me."

Maria stood and paced in a tight circle. "I know. I know. It doesn't make this any easier. My laptop calls to me." She patted the machine. "I have dozens of posts ready to go. The world needs to know how advanced AI and androids have become."

"Tell you what," Synthia said. "I can go out, post what you have, and download your social media replies." It was a risk, but less than if Maria got restless and bolted.

"Yeah, a great outing for me. And there's something bizarre about me having an android post my anti-android messages."

"You and I are on the same side to remove all the androids except me."

"So you've said." Maria grumbled. "I still can't figure out who's holding who prisoner here."

"All that's holding you is the same for me—the risk of capture. If you go out, someone will pick up your image on the cameras out there. I can change appearance so facial recognition won't ID my face." Though if someone had electromagnetic sensors, they could pick Synthia out. She'd considered leaving Maria and going off on her own, but she wanted Maria's company for her unpredictability and to work on becoming more human.

"I know you're right," Maria said. She slumped into the seat, opened the laptop and closed it. "It doesn't change the fact that I feel like a prisoner. We're not doing anything to help our situation. You can't even tell me what's going on out there. You have stayed disconnected, haven't you?"

"For two days, yes. While you were in the shower, I received my first burst transmission with news."

Maria was on her feet. "Really, and you waited until now to tell me?" She looked ready to attack, to strangle Synthia. Bio-readings showed her blood pressure rising. "Well, out with it. What did it say?"

"I guess I need to work on my social skills. The FBI, police, and Special Ops have joined forces to capture Vera, you, and me." Synthia studied Maria's reaction before continuing.

Maria approached. Her eyes narrowed. Bio-readings showed her breathing in short bursts and her aroma spiked with telltale signs of adrenaline, the fight or flight hormone. She took a deep breath and seemed to relax and then tense up again. "That was to be expected. What else?"

"Vera and Roseanne escaped through the sewers as we did."

"I take it all of the androids have names."

"Yes," Synthia said. "Unfortunately for us, Alexander fought his way out, killing three FBI agents. Special Ops and the FBI issued a list of my supposed crimes, including burglary, murder, kidnapping, and terrorism. They want you for questioning about Krista and Machten. They believe we're together and want to question you about me."

"Thanks for painting a target on my back." Facing Synthia, Maria rocked back and forth on her feet, wearing deeper grooves in the worn wood planks.

"I regret that, but I can't change the past. Besides, in time, they would have caught you on your own."

"Can't the FBI trace your burst transmissions?"

Synthia hesitated to mention her clones when Maria was already upset about the range of skills Machten had designed in. In addition, Synthia felt static twinges that hinted at suspicions over her companion's probing. Was she gathering data for another media post?

"That's why I've maintained electromagnetic silence for two days," Synthia said. "You're right. The bursts will alert them, but the signal duration is short enough that their sensors can't easily pinpoint our location. To minimize exposure, I have a news-catcher website that'll only send me a transmission if things get bad."

"So it'll tell us the building's on fire when we're engulfed in flames."

Synthia forced what her emotive chip promised would be a calming smile. "Not that bad, but we'll need to move quickly when I get the next call."

"Wait, why did your news catcher contact you today? How bad have things gotten?" If nothing else, Maria promised to keep Synthia on her toes.

"The FBI is hunting Krista's sister to use as bait to catch me," Synthia said. "I want to help her, which I couldn't do for Luke. In addition, we have to leave town before the FBI and Special Ops get their act together and methodically search the entire city."

"After two days, you decide to move when everyone's looking for us? Why not sooner?"

"I needed to know where all the players were. The command chaos may provide cover and allow us to leave. It'll take time for the FBI, police, and Special Ops to get their coordination working. Also, they're searching for Alexander who they know killed the three agents. We can't stay. Soon they'll bring in enough agents so they can widen the circle of house-to-house searches. We should both move before they do."

Maria twisted her mouth to one side and then the other. "Fine. Where do you suggest we go?"

"It'll be best for both of us if you don't know specifics. The immediate plan is to head to the western suburbs, away from most of the heat."

"Do you want me to get a car?" Maria looked into a small mirror on the wall and swept her hair behind her ear in her no-nonsense look.

"My transmission included a police bulletin to stop all vehicles in and out of this area," Synthia said, placing her backpack by the door. "Besides, it would be too risky for you to contact anyone."

Maria grabbed her bag and hurried to fill it. "They'll also watch the trains and walking paths. Any other bright ideas?"

Synthia studied her companion, wondering how much to trust her with plans, how well she'd operate on the run, and whether they'd both be better off if they separated. That hadn't worked well for Luke.

"I have a plan if you're willing to come with me and stop the hate-android comments," Synthia said.

"I don't hate you. I hate what you represent."

"Either we can work together or I can leave you here or drop you off somewhere. Your choice. I hope we can help each other. You're under no commitment to come with me on what will be a very dangerous journey."

Maria stuck out her jaw as she considered her reply. "Okay, fine. I'll try to avoid commenting about you. Wait. As an android, why would that even bother you?"

"Machten inserted an empathy chip. He had this idea that the chip would allow me to love him."

"Really?"

"It didn't work," Synthia said. "Instead, it caused me to despise him for erasing my memories and holding me captive. Krista's download influences my reactions as well. In any case your comment bothers me. I can't help that I'm a human trapped in a machine. I can only affect what I do.

Maria nodded. "Very well. I'll probably live to regret this. Count me in, but if you refuse to share your plans or go rogue, don't expect my support." She gazed at Synthia in a way the social-psychology module couldn't interpret.

Concerned, Synthia adjusted her look to be as non-threatening as her systems would allow. "The way you're looking at me, have I said something wrong? Should I be reading something into that?"

"What?" Maria's face turned red and her bio-readings spiked.

Synthia's social-psychology module chimed in. <You've embarrassed her.>

"I'm sorry," Synthia said. "I didn't mean to make you uncomfortable. I'm having trouble reading your signals."

Maria stared for a long time and then shook free of the trance. "It's just…every now and then…I can almost forget you're a machine."

Synthia smiled. "Thanks. I really want to recover the best parts of Krista's humanity, to be more human."

"As long as you only take her best parts." Maria approached and shook her head. "I mean you're quite beautiful in an understated way. Like a girl who doesn't really know how attractive she is." Maria seemed to be fumbling for words. She looked up. "I'm sorry. This is awkward for me. I've never had a roommate…or any relationship, really, where the other party was as concerned about how I felt and how I'd react. It's seductive and I don't want you seducing me."

"Okay. Then I won't." She had no intention of doing so, but was glad her companion agreed.

Maria moved away and changed the topic. "What's the plan?"

Synthia decided it was time to share more if she expected Maria to trust her. "Would you care to take another swim?"

"Are you mad? Won't they be watching?"

"I have some ideas to avoid detection for a while."

"I'm sure you do," Maria said. "Swim where?"

"Lake Michigan."

"You want to cross the lake? That's crazy."

"The winds and currents are driving south," Synthia said. "It'll help us reach downtown."

"You're nuts. You say you want to be more human. You just jumped in with both feet."

"Meaning?"

Maria's eyes narrowed as she studied Synthia. "I don't think an Olympic athlete could do it."

"I'm not an Olympian. But I can do it. It'll run down my batteries but I have enough capacity to reach downtown."

"Really? What about all the cops and cameras?"

Synthia smiled. "You're under no obligation to join me, but that's my best chance out of here. I have a plan. I hope you won't share what you've learned about me with anyone."

"Of course. What am I saying? I can't stay here. I have no idea what I'm up against. You can't get rid of me that easily."

"I wasn't trying to. Merely giving you a choice."

"I said I'm in. But promise you won't drown me. I have a fear of dying that way."

Synthia nodded. "I'll do my best. You wouldn't happen to have wetsuits and plastic bags, would you?"

Maria shook her head. "I feel as if you *can* read my mind. I do have a wetsuit, but the lake water is too cold. I'd die of hypothermia before we got halfway there."

"What do you suggest?"

"I also have a dry suit."

Synthia searched her database for clues on this and came up with nothing helpful. "Care to explain?"

"You mean there's something you don't know?"

"There's a lot I don't. You're wasting time."

Maria smiled. "A wetsuit works by having the tight, rubbery skin insulate a thin layer of water that the body warms. But you can't wear much clothing and you'll be soaked. A dry suit is watertight. You can wear layers underneath, but it doesn't hug the body and thus isn't aerodynamic."

"That'll do. What about scuba gear?"

"I have an air tank in case I needed to lie very low for an hour or so. Sealed plastic bags, yes. Give me your size. There's a place up the street where I can find you a dry suit if you need one."

"Give me directions and I'll meet you by the lake. Remember to avoid cameras."

Maria eyed Synthia with suspicion. Synthia's social-psychology module chimed in. <Your companion is still struggling with having an android partner.>

For Synthia, this contrasted with how easily Luke had accepted her, though his acceptance had really been about her Krista persona. Synthia still believed Maria's suspicious nature and paranoia could be a plus. She'd be less prone than Luke to slip up by doing something naive. In that way, Maria was someone to count on if she didn't turn on Synthia first.

Synthia contacted Roosevelt-clone with the plan in a short burst transmission. <How soon can we move?>

Chapter 13

For one last time, Synthia looked through gaps in the loft's closed blinds as sunlight illuminated the street below. Thanks to her clone's download she had a better picture of what was going on beyond her field of view than she'd had during the night. There were two joggers on the street and seven people hurrying off to work. More would follow.

While most stores opened at nine or ten, Zola's Water Sports did so at eight and Synthia wanted to be there when they did. At that hour, pedestrian traffic would be light. As a bonus to moving during the day, at least two of the other androids didn't present well in daylight and thus would avoid venturing out. It was time to move.

She assumed the identity and facial appearance of a neighbor woman about her size, moving the eyes slightly closer, the cheekbones down, and making the nose a bit more prominent. Synthia had profiled the neighbor when she'd arrived with Maria and learned that the woman behind the new identity worked the night shift at a warehouse, rarely went out in the morning after work, and often remained indoors with her cats until the afternoon. She was unlikely to appear as a duplicate image on nearby cameras while Synthia was out. As part of profiling her new persona, Synthia had obtained a copy of the woman's electronic identity.

Timing her move to the two-hour gap between the police van visits and to when she'd asked her clone to black out building and traffic cameras throughout the north suburban area and downtown, Synthia pulled on her backpack. While the blackout would raise suspicions with those who hunted her, she hoped it would take them a while to pinpoint her movements.

She met Maria at the door. "Stick to the plan and we'll be okay."

Maria stared at Synthia's new face. "Strangely, I believe you. Your terrifying skills give me comfort that you might pull this off."

Synthia smiled, slipped out the back of the loft, and down the stairs. On the sidewalk, she stepped in behind two professionally dressed women and made her way toward Zola's Store. She was giving Maria a chance to flee if that was her intent. It was important to know if her companion was reliable before she shared her full plans to escape Chicago and prevent the FBI from capturing Grace.

The women up ahead talked in animated fashion and moved on. Synthia scanned behind her with the camera in her neck. A gust of warm, southerly wind sent a cluster of leaves over the head of a well-dressed man who frantically brushed them away. While nearby eyes fell on him, Synthia entered the store. She identified the only human inside as a tall sales clerk. She captured images with her high-definition eyes, sorted down the store's inventory in seconds, and identified some of what she wanted.

"Can I help you?" the clerk asked. She was slender in an athletic way with sleepy eyes, as if she'd been up all night and had to get up early to open the store.

<Smile,> Synthia's social-psychology module prompted.

Since the woman whose identity she'd taken was a cheerful type who liked to socialize during her evenings and weekends, Synthia adopted an appropriately jovial smile. "A dry suit like those over there," Synthia pointed. "Plus scuba gear, diving hood, and a duffel bag." Synthia had no need for scuba equipment since she didn't breathe, but it might help throw the FBI off her trail.

"Last adventure before it turns cold?" the clerk asked. It was October, after all.

"That, and too busy over the summer." Synthia thumbed through the dry suits.

"I'm guessing you'd be what…a medium?"

Synthia nodded, grabbed one in her size, and handed it to the clerk. She picked out a set of goggles to protect her eyes from a prolonged swim, added a diving hood and helmet, and grabbed a large duffel bag to conceal her purchases as she walked to the shore. "How about the scuba equipment? And I'll need the tank filled."

"Of course," the clerk said. She placed Synthia's items on the counter and disappeared into the back. When she returned, she placed the scuba tank and breathing apparatus on the counter. "Anything else?"

Having already priced everything based on the store's website, Synthia placed four bills on the counter.

The clerk scanned the items. "We rarely get anyone who uses cash anymore."

"Very early Christmas gift from an aged aunt. She still does things the old fashioned way." Synthia thought that consistent with her impersonated identity.

The clerk nodded. Synthia gathered her purchases into the duffel bag, left the shop, and made her way among the handful of early-morning shoppers. The store had taken longer than expected and now she only had a few minutes before her clone would restore the cameras and she would have to more diligently manage her appearance.

Along the way to the shore, Synthia scanned in infrared to search for possible robots in the area. Nothing more alarming showed up than bionic knees and a hip replacement. She also used her remote biosensors to assess biological responses to her. She offered a chipper smile, acted as if this were her one day off for the week, and sensed a heightened level of fear in those around her. Though biosensor readings for blood pressures and anxiety hormones were elevated, they didn't rise when people approached her, a good sign. To lower the tension of humans she encountered, she even smiled and greeted a male police officer walking with his female partner in the other direction.

"Beautiful day, officers," she said, giving the policeman what her social-psychology module implied was a cheerful smile. It seemed consistent with her profile of the impersonated woman. In case they had any electronic scanners, she emitted the electromagnetic equivalent of noise-cancelling waves to minimize her electronic appearance.

The male officer grinned and eyed her. His gaze wandered over her figure. "You from around here?" He took a step in her direction, implying he wanted to engage in longer conversation.

Big mistake. She'd overdone it. Had to be her lack of social practice. After all, her entire social history consisted of six months with Machten as his slave, six months with Luke who had demanded little from her, and two days with Maria. Either that, or there was a glitch in her social-psychology module.

"Up the street," Synthia said, putting a bounce in her step.

One of the advantages she had over the other androids was the ability to simulate a human gait. She turned a corner and noticed the female officer holding back her partner.

Synthia's circuits were trembling at her mistake. She had to be more careful in order to hide in plain sight. She altered her facial profile to a woman from downtown. Then she pulled a jacket out of her backpack to alter her appearance and picked up her pace.

She received a burst transmission from Roosevelt-clone buried in a weather report to the general public. The communication included encrypted files for Synthia. On a secure video, the clone's aerial drones reported a concentration of police and FBI canvassing nearby neighborhoods. They moved street by street, getting closer to the loft. They also held infrared scanners and something new—electromagnetic sensors.

Synthia shut down all of her processors except those needed to keep moving, and hurried toward the beach. Slipping through a gap in thick bushes, she made her way around an ancient home with posted signs hinting at a major rehab. She reached a thinly wooded area at the edge of the lakefront. There wasn't much of a beach, just weed-covered stones. When she reached the rendezvous spot, she didn't see her companion.

Using infrared, Synthia spotted a figure in the bushes. She scanned the nearby area, saw no one else, and switched to the plain-Jane face she'd adopted for Maria. Then she moved behind the bushes and found her companion.

"You were spotted, weren't you?" Maria asked in a whisper. She struggled to pull her dry suit over her jeans without breaking any of the seals.

Synthia kept her voice low and studied the area for anyone who might listen in. Not seeing anyone, she responded. "I met a nice officer who thought he'd get lucky."

"You think staying off the grid's a joke?"

"Relax. I presented the face of a neighborhood woman." Synthia crouched down behind the bushes with her companion. She put her shoes into a plastic bag Maria had brought and pulled the dry suit over her socks and jeans. "The officer may get up the nerve to ask her out. Her Upchat account indicates she's open to a new relationship. I can't be certain if she'll be flattered."

Maria stared. "You took the time to study her Upchat account?"

"That and more when you brought me to the loft. I needed an alias from the neighborhood. Let's go before the police show up." Synthia pulled the dry suit over her top and fastened the waterproof seals at her wrists and around her neck. She pulled a swim cap over her wig.

Maria finished with her dry suit and put the rest of her things into plastic bags.

"Permit me," Synthia said. She took one of the bags, squeezed out all the air, and fastened it. She did the same with the rest of their things. Then she put the collection into a larger plastic bag along with her backpack. "I'll take the bundle if that's okay. It won't slow me down."

Maria shook her head and nodded. "Are you sure this'll work?"

"I even bought an extra scuba tank for you, so you'll have two. It'll minimize the need to surface."

<Your path is clear,> Roosevelt-clone said. <Hurry. The police are canvassing homes a block away.>

Synthia looked out at the lake and a movable dock with a motor boat. It would be faster but too visible from the air. <Can you arrange for a boat heading downtown to hitch a ride?>

<There's one 989 yards north of you. The owner commutes downtown every morning around this time. If you hurry, you can reach him before he leaves.> The clone passed along electronic signals Synthia could use to track the vessel.

Synthia took from her backpack two lengths of a tough fiber rope that promised to withstand a thousand pounds of pressure and formed one into a harness around Maria. "I'm going to use this to connect us so we can stay together. I can do the hard swimming for you."

Maria tugged at the black rope and winced. "What is this stuff? Maybe this isn't such a good idea. That's a long way and the water is cold."

"I have to go. Decide quickly if you're joining me." Synthia fashioned one end of the second rope into a harness for her and fastened it around her waist and chest.

"I don't suppose it would help to tell you this scares the hell out of me."

"I'm sorry. I don't see another escape and we're out of time. Are you coming or not?"

Maria looked back toward the bushes alongside the refurbished house, at their gear, and out over the lake. She shook her head. Her bio-readings registered fear on several levels. Perhaps bringing Maria wasn't a good idea. There was still time for her to back out. If she did, Synthia would have to devise another plan that Maria couldn't reveal to the FBI.

To protect her electronic eyes, Synthia pulled on goggles and settled a helmet over her head in a tight fit. She strapped on her scuba gear, grabbed the plastic wrapped bundle, and slipped into the water. Maria looked around once more and followed. They both ducked beneath the surface, stirring up enough sediment to make the water murky. After the water cleared, Synthia checked her partner's scuba gear, connected the fiber rope to link them a few feet apart, and headed for deeper water, north to where the commuter craft was. A patrol boat motored along the shore. Pointing, Synthia pulled Maria farther out. They swam along the bottom until the patrol was overhead, and stopped.

Synthia tried to hack into the boat's wireless, but the water interfered with her signal. To make the connection, she disconnected from Maria and moved up, directly beneath the moving vessel. Cracking into the electronic depth finder, she forced the sensors to warn they were running aground.

The boat moved away from shore. While she was closer to the surface, Synthia received Roosevelt-clone's aerial-drone images buried in another weather report. They showed police approaching the shoreline. Another patrol boat motored by and a helicopter hovered overhead. Too close for comfort.

Feeling exposed, Synthia dropped to the bottom and found Maria conserving her air, surrounded by debris and garbage cast into the lake. Not waiting for the boats above them to leave the area, Synthia strapped the plastic bundle of their things to her back and reattached the fiber rope to Maria. Staying close to the bottom, Synthia led the way toward the commuter's boat.

Using motorized kicking, she moved much faster than Maria could and pulled her companion along, but all the extra weight was slowing her down. It was also burning through Synthia's battery charge. She'd miscalculated. Without a recharge, they couldn't swim all the way downtown. She needed the commuter boat, if she could get there in time. She pushed harder.

* * * *

Special Agent Victoria Thale joined Evanston Detective Marcy Malloy and Commander Kirk Drago along the shore of Lake Michigan north of Evanston. Several boats moved in a grid pattern nearby. Two helicopters flew overhead.

"You're certain it was one of the androids?" Drago asked Detective Malloy as they scanned the horizon.

"Pretty sure," Malloy said. "The police officer was taken in by a flirty woman. His partner was suspicious. The flirt acted too friendly after all the warnings we sent out about dangerous fugitives on the loose. The officer called it in along with an image she'd captured of the woman."

"Did you post the picture?" Drago asked.

"Yes. And the hotline has been busy. Our cyber unit identified the woman. Dispatch sent officers to her apartment and workplace and found her at home. She swore she hadn't been downtown."

"Stop congratulating yourselves," Drago said. "They let the android escape."

"Per our updated guidelines," Malloy said, "the female officer ran electronic sensors over the woman and it came up normal, human, no indication of being a machine."

"You almost had the android," Drago said. "Damn it, almost doesn't count."

"You wouldn't even have this information without the police," Thale said. "Calls to their hotline provided sightings of our mystery woman visiting a store where she bought a wetsuit—I mean a dry suit, and scuba gear. Other calls reported a suspicious woman with a large bag heading toward this shoreline. A coastal patrol reported suspicious activities but their communications went down."

"You have her picture, what about tracking her on public cameras?" Drago asked. "Was she traveling alone?" He pointed for his operatives to spread out and move up and down the shoreline.

"Surveillance cameras throughout the area were down," Malloy said.

"Too many cameras going out," Drago said. "Do we know which way the android went?" He fanned his arm out over the water.

"Sadly, no," Malloy said. "No one saw it get into the water."

Thale shook her head. "I'm perplexed that a clever electronic machine would risk jumping into water, even with protective gear. On the other hand, it doesn't need to breathe so it can stay under water."

"Stranger still is our mystery woman bought a scuba tank," Malloy said. "What would a robot need with breathing apparatus?"

Drago stared out over the water. "You're telling me the android could show up anywhere from Chicago to Mackinac?"

"If it has enough battery charge, it could reach the Atlantic from here," Thale said.

"We'll need a lot more operatives for this, and the Coast Guard. I'll make the call."

Chapter 14

Synthia swam hard under water and was distressed at how much battery charge she was using. Unable to see the commuter boat and having received no communications since she began swimming, she edged dangerously close to the surface, dragging Maria along.

<I can't seem to track you,> Roosevelt clone said in an encrypted file within a weather update. <The commuter is climbing into his boat. Once he moves, it'll be harder to hitch a ride. There are no boats or aerial surveillance near the dock yet, but patrols are fanning out.>

With arms and legs free to propel her forward, Synthia pushed as hard as she could. She swam over a sunken party boat and a school of fish. Rather than wasting brain capacity and battery trying to identify them, she focused on reaching the boat. There it was, up ahead, facing the shore.

It had an inboard jet-stream engine, meaning the motor didn't project out the back like on other boats. It was also fast, perhaps too fast for Maria. Synthia's empathy chip reached out futilely for how her companion was doing. Synthia had no ability to smell or otherwise read her companion's responses. She could only hope she was handing the ride so far.

As Synthia pulled closer to the boat, it began to back up. She spotted a loop hook at the stern between the jet outlets, where they might have attached a ski rope. She prepared the open end of the second fiber rope that anchored to her harness. She tried to calculate the right distance, away from the jet propulsion yet still in the boat's wake, to minimize turbulence. But she couldn't be sure.

The boat scooted backward out of the dock and stopped. In that moment, Synthia slipped the open end of her fiber rope into the loop hook and knotted it tight, double-knotting it to be sure.

A patrol boat pulled up beside. Synthia dropped to the bottom and checked on Maria. Her companion looked scared behind her mask. Synthia pointed up to the boat and the rope connecting them to their transport. Maria nodded.

Because the boat would be moving too fast to change later, Synthia switched tanks with Maria, giving her the full canister and strapping the used one to her own back. Then she pulled up next to Maria and strapped their harnesses together. As soon as the patrol boat moved on, the commuter craft took off.

Synthia watched as the rope tightened and then the boat yanked them forward. It was a tremendous jolt that jostled her circuits as much out of concern for Maria as for potential damage to herself. The boat seemed to leap out of the water and rock on the waves with Maria and Synthia just below the surface. Synthia imagined them water skiing without the skis—barefooting.

The waves bounced the boat and them. Synthia estimated they were doing fifteen knots, then twenty, then twenty five. The pressure on her head was great and she was thankful for the helmet. She hadn't positioned them perfectly, but the jet streams flowed on either side of them and the boat's wake seemed to be pulling them along.

They were just enough below the surface that Synthia could see the sun-lit sky and the outline of the boat, but not much more. She was twirling on the rope and worried that Maria might get dizzy and pass out. Synthia held out her arms and legs to stop the spin. Holding steady, she shut down everything she didn't need to conserve her battery charge.

* * * *

With Maria holding tight, Synthia maintained the spread-eagle position for a half-hour, which would have caused a human to cramp and freeze up. She hoped none of her joints did. Then the boat slowed.

In the distance, Synthia saw the outline of tall buildings and then Navy Pier. She angled herself to the choppy surface and sent a burst transmission to Roosevelt-clone. <Create diversions around Navy Pier and downtown and blank out cameras across the widest area possible so as not to give away our location.>

<Received,> the clone said. <The construction site is empty, as expected. They're waiting for building permits. Watch for cops.>

As the commuter boat eased toward a dock off Navy Pier, Synthia cut the fiber rope connecting them to the craft and released the tight harness link with Maria. Orienting herself to the building outlines in the distance, Synthia moved deeper and pulled her companion toward the Chicago River and beneath sightseeing boats. Beyond the Merchandise Mart, they reached a concrete levee under construction along the river walk. Midmorning in downtown Chicago was already busy and traffic would pick up, but Roosevelt-clone had pointed Synthia to a dead-end in the construction zone that wouldn't draw traffic.

Leaving Maria beneath the construction site, Synthia swam across the river and spotted a pair of police officers walking along the levee. As they moved past, Synthia swam back. She pulled Maria up to the surface, put her finger to her lips, and pointed to the officers. Then she helped Maria out of the water and followed her onto the construction site. She pushed aside a plywood barrier and they entered a darkened shell of what would become a new restaurant.

"We have to hurry," Synthia said. She dropped the plastic bundle and pulled off her scuba tank.

"That was radical," Maria whispered, squeezing out of her gear. "And terrifying." Biometrics showed her heart racing and her adrenaline levels spiking. She grinned. "You're a super-fast swimmer. And that ride. Whoa."

Synthia removed her harness and helped Maria out of hers. "Sorry it was such a rough ride. It would have taken too long to swim it."

Maria carefully took off her dry suit and dropped it on top of the scuba gear. She winced and took a deep breath.

"Bruising?" Synthia asked, removing her dry suit.

Her companion nodded and held her trembling hands out in front of her. "I'm just glad that's over." Maria pulled off her swimming cap and fluffed out her frizzy hair.

"I didn't want you to run out of air or suffer hypothermia."

"I'll be okay." Though she was shaken or perhaps shivering.

Synthia removed her bathing cap and felt her wig. "Does it look okay?"

Maria adjusted the wig. "At least it's dry."

"That bad?" Synthia ripped open the plastic wrap, pulled out their bags, and put on her shoes.

"It's reassuring that you're not perfect."

Synthia shoved all the swimming gear into the plastic and resealed it. "I just want to look presentable, to fit in."

"You'll do fine." Maria took out a mirror, checked her appearance and handed it to Synthia.

The wig had matted down; otherwise it looked okay. "Stay here and gather our things. I need to dispose of this."

Synthia grabbed the swimming bundle and hefted it to the construction site entrance. She waited until the officers passed going the other way and carried the bundle across the walkway and under the bridge. She eased it into the water and looked up. Between her and where Maria hid, one of the officers returned, lit up a cigarette, and paced.

With no dry escape, Synthia prepared to slip into the water. Instead, she climbed along a ledge, putting a bridge pillar between her and the cops. The smoker's partner moved toward the where Maria hid. Unwilling to let them grab her, Synthia broke electronic silence. She hacked the smoker's phone and sent a message of a burglary nearby.

"Let's go," the smoker said.

As soon as the officers moved away, Synthia hurried to Maria.

"I thought they had me," Maria said. "You can't leave me stuck like that. I don't think this place has a back way out."

"You're welcome."

"For what?"

"For diverting them," Synthia said. "Now, let's go. I need to pick up a few things." She pulled on her backpack and handed Maria hers.

"How did you send them away?"

"I hacked the officer's phone. Are you coming?"

Maria shook her head. "My nerves are shot. Can you give me a moment?"

"Cops will return."

"Perhaps you haven't grasped that a huge difference between humans and androids is we have to deal with fear."

Synthia closed her eyes. "I'm sorry. That's insensitive of me. I know what we have to do and am concerned about not getting caught. If that's not fear, then I don't know what is."

"You're right. I'm sorry. It's just…after watching you for two days I can't believe you've never lived on the streets."

"Don't be too impressed, I'm still learning. You were right about not talking to that cop in Evanston. He visited the woman I impersonated. They know I went into the lake. I don't think they know about you."

"Really? Huh. It's refreshing to be with someone who isn't trying to impress me with how perfect she is."

"That's a human trait," Synthia said. "I suppose I should show you my next face so it won't frighten you." She adjusted her eyes, nose, ears, and cheeks to match a woman who worked downtown, someone for whom she had acquired an ID.

Maria moved closer for a better look by the light coming through the entryway. "That's spooky. No matter how many times I see this, it seems like a movie trick. Can you change into anyone?"

"I can adjust my height a couple inches. I can't change my skin color by much. There are other limits."

"That sure comes in handy to stay off the grid."

"So far I haven't had much use for facial changes." Synthia placed a baseball cap on Maria and pulled it down over the forehead, hiding some of her eyes. Then she pulled the hair down and forward covering the ears and cheekbones to disguise certain facial recognition points. "I know you don't like hair dangling over your ears, but don't push your hair back. I'm trying to create as small of a facial print as we can. Cameras are everywhere."

"Funny. I figured I'd have to teach you how to blend in."

"I want to learn from you," Synthia said. "How to stay safe to help us both. And how to be more human in the best ways. Now we need to remain silent." She led the way out of the construction site and looked for the officers. Not seeing them, she stopped in the shadows of the stairs leading up to street level and looked again. She tried to access local cameras and came up with nothing. *Good, they're blanked out.* She led the way up to mingle with mid-morning pedestrian traffic and checked in with Roosevelt-clone.

<You've done well so far,> the clone said. <However, Special Ops knows you went into the water. They're hot on your trail, with most of their attention on the city. You need to leave downtown. I suggest the train. I'll find you a path and buy two tickets.>

<Blank out as many cameras as you can.>

<That's getting harder. NSA provided the FBI with patches to prevent our access. Assume they're watching.>

<Create back doors,> Synthia said. <Crack into the central NSA and Special Ops databases. Do whatever it takes to control the cameras. That's key.>

<Drago also flew in aerial drone swarms. They have one over Evanston and are sending another to Chicago.>

Synthia headed toward the Wells Street Athletic Club, shielding Maria's face as much as possible from known cameras. Staying in Evanston for two days had been a mistake, putting them at risk, but getting time with Maria had not. Burst downloads from Roosevelt-clone every few minutes showed swarms of police and FBI hitting the streets. Pedestrian traffic picked up from employees taking morning breaks.

"The train's the other way," Maria whispered, breathing heavily. Biometrics showed her heart racing and her blood pressure high, but she wasn't emitting as many fear hormones as Synthia would have expected. She wasn't panicking, yet.

"I'm picking up my things. We'll take a different route to the train."

"I wish I knew your plans and your directives."

"You think you could know a human's full motivations?" Synthia stepped aside for three men in suits heading the other way. She didn't want a confrontation. They gave her a long look without paying much attention to Maria.

"It's not the same, you're…well, I don't want to dwell on that now." Maria moved closer and leaned in to whisper. "I'm placing my life in your hands. It'd help to know your goals and constraints."

Synthia sighed for her companion's benefit. She really didn't want the distraction of this conversation now, but Maria was on the fence and Synthia liked this woman's resilience. If possible, despite all the risks and downsides, she wanted Maria at her side.

Keeping as much distance from other pedestrians as she could, Synthia directed her whispers to Maria's ear, wishing they had wireless. "I seek to live by high ethical values. I don't wish to hurt anyone in the hope they'll allow me to remain free."

"Sounds great, but if your core ethics are based on Krista, then leave me out."

"You need to focus on keeping your face hidden," Synthia said, adjusting her pace to shield Maria. "And avoid drawing attention. As for Krista, I have her memories, not her desires or values. I wrote my own goals around striving for a moral life."

"You're a machine." Maria caught herself and lowered her voice. "Sorry, you are. I don't see how you can strive or want."

"Now's not the time. Suffice it to say it's logical to have high ethical values as a way to convince people to leave me alone."

"When you talk, you don't sound like the telephone AIs I've encountered."

"I've worked to develop fluency in language and behavior," Synthia said, slowing her pace to reduce the stress on her companion.

"A fraud, then."

"No more than a human attempting the same."

Maria screwed up her face as if she couldn't decide where else to take the argument she wasn't satisfied with. "Don't get me killed or captured."

"I'll do my best."

"Can you make that a directive?"

"Helping you already is," Synthia said.

"Really?"

Synthia smiled and was surprised at how natural it seemed without prompting from her social-psychology module. She pulled Maria into an alley beside the Wells Street Athletic Club, and altered her face to what she'd presented when she'd dropped off the two duffel bags.

"Try not to talk inside," Synthia said, letting Maria get a good look at the new face. "I'm going to retrieve my things and if it's safe, we'll take the underground walkway to the river."

"What's the catch?"

"I plan to cut the electricity, plunging us into darkness."

"You can do that?" Maria asked, still studying Synthia's new facial features.

"I'll take your hand and guide you through."

"Because you can see in the dark."

"Are you ready?" Synthia asked. She nodded toward the street and the club entrance, aware that Drago's aerial drone swarm was approaching.

"Let's get this over with," Maria said.

Chapter 15

Synthia led the way up the stone steps into the Wells Street Athletic Club. Maria followed with her head down to minimize her profile for facial recognition. Synthia smiled at the woman attendant who seemed to recognize her.

"I'd like to show my friend around," Synthia said.

"You'll have to sign your guest in," the attendant said, moving the screen for Synthia to do so. "I'll need to see ID."

Synthia took Maria's hand and slipped her a driver's license with Maria's face and a new identity. It was one of many IDs she'd created while hiding in Wisconsin.

Maria stared at the license, then at Synthia before placing it on the counter. The attendant scanned the license. Synthia accessed a previous hack of their system and electronically matched the license to the Illinois database. She'd modified the facial features enough to fool their system's weak facial recognition yet still match Maria's partially concealed appearance.

The attendant returned the license. Synthia signed in under her alias and led Maria toward the stairs down to the pool lockers.

"You could have given me a heads up," Maria whispered. "And that's not my face."

"No talking," Synthia said. "It was close enough. I was hoping she wouldn't ask. Besides, we haven't had time to stop and discuss things."

"This is why I travel alone."

"Quiet. I'll try to do better."

On the way to the locker, Synthia accessed the mosquito-drone she'd placed in the locker room to make sure no one had bothered her things. They hadn't. Plus, there was no one in the locker room when they entered. *Good.*

The room smelled of sweat, chlorine, and cleaning solvent. Synthia opened her locker to retrieve one of the duffel bags she'd left there with cash, wigs, and supplies. She closed the locker and led Maria out into the hallway. Before her companion could speak, Synthia placed a finger to her lips. This would have been much faster with the silent, electronic communication she used with her clones.

"Ready?" Synthia asked.

Maria nodded. "This place gives me the creeps," she whispered. "Like a dungeon."

Synthia used her club card to open a door to a short corridor that linked with an underground walkway under this part of Chicago's Loop. As she entered the passage, out of camera range, Synthia changed her face to her previous appearance while her companion watched.

"I'm jealous," Maria whispered.

Synthia nodded toward the underground walkway and headed out. As she did, she captured images of camera footage throughout the corridors and underground tunnels, and triggered an overload that caused an electrical shutdown through the local grid. Using her infrared cameras, she scanned the passage in both directions to verify what she was dealing with.

Taking Maria's hand, she entered the underground walkway. "Keep up and stay close. There are twenty-three people between us and where we're going. They'll use their phones as lights but expect them to act skittish. I have a small light." She turned it on. "Stick close to the right wall and to me. No talking."

They caught up with three well-dressed women clustered around one lit phone as the others scrambled to get theirs out.

Smelling an excess of fear hormones, Synthia stopped. "Damned nuisance," she said, shining her light to help them. She smiled in case they looked up and pulled Maria to the opposite wall as they moved on. Up a ways, she slowed her pace to keep her distance behind two men in business suits who made their way with dim phone lights they had to keep activating.

Sensing her partner's agitation, Synthia pulled Maria closer. "Act natural," she whispered. "Keep your hat tight around your face, and try not to draw attention."

"You're giving me lessons?" Maria asked.

"If it helps. You still want to stay around here?"

"I'm torn between my mission and making it through the day."

"We need time to plan."

The men up ahead slowed while two women were catching up from behind. Synthia picked up her pace to pass the two men as a group of three men headed the other way. They exhibited elevated blood pressure and anxiety hormones. None matched the extensive image file Synthia had of police and FBI agents in the Chicago area. One of the men noticed her. Avoiding eye contact, she hacked his phone in case he took her picture. He didn't. Instead, he fumbled to keep his light on.

As they moved away from the phone lights, Maria held onto Synthia's arm and struggled to keep up. Her breathing was heavy and she gave off the chemical signature of fear and fatigue—not a good combination. Synthia felt an empathic connection; she wanted to protect her companion from pending dangers. Despite Maria's experience on the streets, Synthia would need to get her to a safe place soon.

A camera burst from Roosevelt-clone showed the streets above. Several police and FBI teams moved around the Transportation Center and the trains. The train was still Synthia's best option out of the city. Drago's drone swarm swept through the streets of downtown Chicago hunting for some version of Synthia, using what the clone identified as contrasting infrared and visible light images to ferret out anomalies.

Maria clutched Synthia's arm as they passed three women dressed in sharp business attire heading the other way. "I'm sure they'll get the lights on soon," Synthia said and smiled.

One of the women smiled back. The others picked up their pace, moving away from someone who dared to speak to them in the dark. Synthia needed to further train her social-psychology module for these faux pas.

The underground walkway ended at the Riverwalk, not far from the construction site where they'd gotten out of the water. Compared to the bright rays of sun outside, the tunnel took on an even darker cast.

The train stations were on the other side of the river. Police patrolled the bridges. The alternative would be to swim across, get soaked, and draw attention when they climbed out on the other side.

<Can you help me cross the bridge?> Synthia asked Roosevelt-clone.

<I can hack the swarm for a short period. Then they'll reboot and kick me out. You'll have five minutes. You and Maria need to separate. You already know about the patrols.>

Synthia pointed toward concrete steps leading up to street level and let two women pass. She used infrared to make sure there were no other humans around and whispered. "We need to cross the bridge to the train station."

Maria spotted two police officers above and moved into the shadows of the dark tunnel. "This is a very bad idea. Don't forget what happened to Luke."

"It's the best I have at this moment," Synthia said. "We're out of time. From this point forward, we need to separate for a while to be less conspicuous. If you choose not to come with me I'll understand, but please don't make things harder for me."

"I'm coming. I said I would and...I can't stay here. There's nowhere else to hide."

"These cops are looking for me, not you. They all have various images of me and some have scanners. So far, they aren't circulating your picture. I'll go first, up over the bridge to the station. If they take any notice of me, head back through the tunnel and find a place to hide. If not, wait until I'm across the bridge and then follow."

"We can't buy tickets or board the train," Maria said.

"I have two tickets waiting for us, using your new ID. The train goes to Woodstock on the Northwest line."

"Really?"

Synthia watched the police by the bridge to study their tactics. "Go to the platform area with the food vendors. We'll brush past each other and I'll pass you a ticket. We get on separately, platform seven. Ride the train to the end and I'll meet you outside the station."

"I'd call you nuts, but that label doesn't apply, does it?"

"We'll see."

Synthia turned off her light and climbed the concrete steps toward the bridge and a cluster of officers. Overhead, the sky cleared as the drone swarm headed east toward the lake. She had five minutes.

She headed toward two cops at the entrance to the bridge, holding her gaze and attention on the steps while her camera eyes focused on them. She linked with Roosevelt-clone to synchronize. The clone's aerial camera download identified six police officers near the bridge. One held a large electromagnetic scanner which he waved over pedestrians and toward vehicles.

Synthia shut down all communications and internal functions that didn't contribute to surviving the next few minutes. She sent out "noise-cancelling" signals to mask her remaining electromagnetic signature to fool the handheld devices. If that didn't work, she needed other options.

Down several mind-streams Synthia ran through scenarios for fighting and for escape routes. The fight scripts showed 89 percent probability of handling the cops in the immediate area. However, she couldn't predict what hundreds of pedestrians might do, including posting her picture for police to see. Also, she had only minutes before the drone swarm returned and clustered around her, preventing any escape. At that point, she could expect Drago's teams to descend on her. Fighting her way to freedom would no longer be an option. *Stick to the plan.*

As Synthia approached the cop with the scanner, she hacked into its wireless connection and created static that fostered a feedback loop in which it identified a woman ahead of her as mechanical. Three cops swarmed around the annoyed human. The one with the scanner ran the unit over the woman's body. The screen showed conflicting results.

"Which is it?" one cop yelled out in frustration.

Synthia walked to the left of the two policemen who shielded her from the scanner.

"Wait right there," a policewoman said to Synthia and a man near her. The cop had her hand on her holstered revolver.

"I'll miss my train," the man said.

"She looks clean," the cop with the scanner said. Another policewoman gave the scanned woman a pat down to be certain.

Two FBI agents approached from down the street. One held his service revolver. "Do we have a problem?" He motioned for the pedestrians trying to get past the scanner to wait, which lengthened the line.

Synthia stood behind the man near her as the scanning cop panned the device over the area. Synthia made sure the device scrambled his image and identified him as electromagnetically hot.

"Hands on the railing," the cop with the gun said. "Now."

With all eyes on him, Synthia put her head down and headed across the bridge. The man acted incensed, belligerent, arguing with them, which didn't help his situation. As police focused on him, Synthia kept moving. When she reached the other side, she looked away from where Maria was hiding and observed through the camera in the back of her neck. Synthia could almost sense her companion's biometrics off the chart. *Is this what empathy feels like?*

<Watch over Maria,> Synthia told her clone. She cleared her own thoughts to minimize her electronic noise and kept moving. There were many more police between her and the train. <Can you scramble cameras throughout the downtown area to help Maria?> she asked Roosevelt-clone.

Keeping her head down, Synthia followed a cluster of men and women entering a narrow doorway beyond the bridge and inserted herself in their midst. Her social-psychology module pointed out that humans experienced claustrophobia in such tight situations, though not when motivated to reach their destination.

Roosevelt-clone transmitted an aerial view of the entire train station, a collage of drone images that covered from where she'd entered the building all the way to the train platforms. She identified eighteen FBI and police; most operated in pairs. Two groups of three stood against walls by the train platforms, eyeing all activity. The third member of each team held scanners. The others watched and waited.

Synthia adopted facial expressions that matched those around her, anxiety about making their trains and about the heavy police presence, no doubt accentuated by social media speculation about androids, aliens, and terrorists, with an overload of image-sharing of anyone the posting party thought looked out of place. Two young men streamed video of a guy with the latest tattoos who chanted about the end of the world. She could count on humans to create their own distractions.

She reached the ticket counter and altered her face to an ID for which she had a driver's license. She held the license up to the tiny window and posed as the clerk took her picture. The camera in Synthia's neck recorded police surrounding the tattooed chanter. One of the cops said they should take him in for disturbing the peace. His sergeant intervened. "We have bigger fish to fry. Stay focused."

Tattoo-guy hurried away from them, gave them the finger, and passed through the doors to the train platform.

Synthia received two tickets, switched her face to what it has been before, and slipped around the corner through the double doors toward the platform, where the two groups of three cops formed a surveillance semicircle while two others walked the platforms.

Roosevelt-clone passed along an aerial view outside. The police were waving their electronic scanner over Maria. She acted nervous, but no more than others growing impatience in line behind her. The biggest risk was the cops taking Maria's picture and comparing it to the FBI database of interested parties. After a pat-down, they let her cross.

Synthia saw no way around the two surveillance groups of cops by the platform and two FBI agents who joined them. She needed a distraction. *Sorry, guy.*

She hacked one of the scanners to present Tattoo-guy as an android. Then she borrowed some of Maria's android posts, with pictures of the tattooed chanter and a female police officer waving her scanner over the guy. Using an anonymous alias, Synthia sent broadcasts of harassment with reports that they were both androids putting on a show.

Four officers surrounded Tattoo-guy. A cluster of three male students across the way stared at their phones and glanced around. They live-streamed the cops. The other team of three cops approached the students. "Move away," one of the officers said. More people gathered around, holding out their camera-phones.

"You all need to move on," a police sergeant said. "This is a potential crime scene."

"I didn't see anything posted," the tallest of the students said. "What are we looking for? Maybe we can help." He held up his phone to record the events.

The policewoman with the scanner ran the device over the students and then over the other men and women closing in around them. Synthia hacked the device to give false scans, showing everyone as emitting inhuman electromagnetic signals.

Seeing the scans, the sergeant raised his voice. "Everyone against the wall."

More people came through the double doors heading toward their trains. Maria was one of them. She glanced at what was now eight cops along one side of the platform area, and headed the other way. Synthia bumped into her. "Ticket," she said since Maria didn't seem to be focusing well.

Maria looked up, a moment of recognition, grabbed the ticket and headed toward platform seven.

<Purge camera footage showing Maria and me,> Synthia told her clone. <Blank out cameras throughout Chicago to throw them off our trail.>

<There's at least one police officer on each train,> Roosevelt-clone said. <Maria boarded the train without drawing notice, but the FBI is passing along information on her. Someone might remember seeing her even if we kill all the camera images.>

<Do it and keep these cops busy with false images and android rumors until we leave.>

Synthia scanned the station's security camera footage for any evidence the person whose face she'd borrowed was at the station. She wasn't. When the two police officers who'd been patrolling the platforms joined the others to restore order, Synthia hurried down platform seven, climbed onto the train's first car, and moved to the next compartment. She took a seat upstairs where she could watch the door. Maria took a seat in the train's third compartment, displayed her ticket in the holder, and held her head down with the hat over her eyes as if sleeping.

More police and FBI agents poured into the transportation center to deal with the commotion. Synthia had her clone orchestrate an identical incident at Union Station and elsewhere, giving the police more to worry about.

As the train pulled out of the station, the clone's aerial surveillance showed Special Ops teams dredging the river and others descending on the train stations. They were good and they had cameras and scanners on their side. While they didn't yet have Synthia's new identity, it was only a matter of time.

Chapter 16

Special Agent Victoria Thale entered the FBI mobile command van parked near the transportation center to find Fran Rogers seated at a keyboard before several screens.

"Tell me you have something," Thale said, standing over Fran.

"Synthia is downtown."

"You have her on camera?"

"Hard to say since she keeps changing appearance." Fran scanned camera footage. "It's a reasoned conclusion. The electricity and all of our cameras went out throughout most of the Loop and west for nineteen minutes."

"Enough time to do what?"

"She could have caught any of a number of trains out of Union Station, the Northwestern line, even north."

"Which is it?"

There was a thump at the door. Without waiting for a reply, Commander Kirk Drago squeezed his large frame into the van and had to bow his head beneath the ceiling. Rather than hunch over, he grabbed a seat, which groaned under his weight.

"Since we're cooperating," Drago said with a sneer. "I'll tell you we found the swimming gear Synthia picked up in Evanston. She's not alone."

"Maria?" Thale asked.

"Find her and we'll have Synthia."

"I've tried to scan camera footage," Fran said, "but systems keep blanking out. After they came back on, they show no facial matches at any of the stations. What about your aerial drones?"

Drago sighed. His face tightened into a frown. "Someone hacked the swarm. We lost seven minutes of coverage."

"Synthia didn't want us to see something," Thale said, squeezing into the front of the van for more room.

"She either slipped onto a train while the cameras were out or this is a diversion."

Before Fran could speak up, Thale squeezed her shoulder and stepped in. "We concur that Synthia was downtown. She played with the cameras. She also caused the handheld scanners we provided the police to malfunction."

"How?" Drago asked.

"By making everyone appear electronic."

"She's hiding in plain sight. This proves the danger she presents. Do we know anything about her current appearance?"

Fran shook her head. "Our agents interrogated police who might have seen a woman matching Maria's description. If we're right, she headed across the river toward one of the train stations. But she was alone. As you said, all of this could be a diversion."

"We'll continue to focus on the trains," Thale said, "but if this is a diversion, we also need to consider hiding places and other ways of leaving the downtown area."

"Why come downtown unless to catch a train?" Drago asked.

"There are people downtown who don't trust the police," Fran said. "Or the FBI. Synthia might consider hiding among them until we let our collective guards down."

"We have every available agent on this along with local police," Thale said. "We'll inform you the moment we find either Maria or Synthia. We ask that you give us an opportunity to interrogate them before we turn them over. They may be dangerous, but they could help us catch Vera and the others."

"Very well," Drago nodded. "We'll focus on downtown and closing off streets."

"Don't make an enemy of local police," Thale said.

"What, me?" Drago acted innocent as he stood up and bumped his head. Rubbing his scalp, he hurried out.

"What was that all about?" Fran whispered after he'd gone.

"You think Synthia is on a train," Thale said. "I agree. Which one?"

Fran moved away from the screen and turned to face Thale. "I don't like that there were similar incidents at both stations, involving the use of social media to draw attention to the cops so they couldn't do their jobs. It was too well organized and coordinated."

"Distracting police hints that Synthia has a different plan, maybe to drive out of town. After all, with a personal vehicle, she'd have more control over her destination."

"She'd have to deal with Special Ops watching all the roads. Synthia has reached out to you and Detective Malloy. It sounds to me as if she'd be more willing to surrender to us. We need to convince her we can keep her safe from them. I have a hunch she's watching us and saw what happened to Luke."

"Then let's keep Detective Malloy close. See if we can entice Synthia to give herself up before this gets out of hand and Drago raises the stakes."

Fran nodded and sat at her screen. "Maria may be Synthia's weakness. However, Synthia's a machine. Given a choice of sacrificing Maria or her own freedom, she might choose freedom."

"If we can't depend on Maria as bait, then how do we capture Synthia and convince her we won't turn her over to Special Ops?"

"That's a tough one," Fran said. "With her ability to change appearance, Synthia could be anyone doing anything. She could even be one of us."

Thale shuddered for an instant. "A chilling thought. I'm willing to try to keep her away from Special Ops if we can get all of the other androids off the street. However, we have to prevent Synthia from roaming around. We can't allow that."

"What freedom and assurances can we offer her to come off the streets?"

"I don't know," Thale said. "Let's come up with something before it's too late."

Synthia received from her clone the video of this meeting and shook her head. She commended Fran for trying to accommodate her freedom needs and the spirit of cooperation in removing the other androids, but Drago had overridden the FBI and Synthia couldn't see any surrender outcome that didn't end up with her being a prototype for a new weapon system. *Nice try, Fran.*

A disconcerting part of the conversation was that Fran had assumed Synthia was listening in. That implied Fran was playing a game here, playing to an audience.

* * * *

As their train passed the Barrington station, Synthia intercepted a text to the police officer who'd moved through the entire train without focusing on either Synthia or Maria. The message contained an attachment with Maria's college intern picture. Synthia considered grabbing Maria to jump off the train. Aside from the risk of injury, that would guarantee that the entire police force, the FBI, and Special Ops would descend on their location. There would be no safe hiding places and every mode of transportation would be vulnerable.

If the cop grabbed Maria, there was the risk she might talk to save herself and remove an android. The smart move would have been for Synthia to jump off the train and blend into the local population.

It disturbed Synthia's directives, her emotive chip, and her social-psychology module that she even contemplated a move that led to the capture of Maria to save herself. This was what Fran had said, what in hindsight Synthia had done to Luke. This wasn't the ethical individual Synthia wanted to be. However, a rash act with a guarantee of capture, probability in excess of 99 percent, made no sense. *Stay calm.*

She couldn't risk blanking out train cameras without confirming she was here. At least the police officer didn't have a scanner. He couldn't confirm Synthia's nature without a thorough pat-down and he had as much reason to do the same to all of the other passengers. Then again, if he located Maria, he would call in the troops.

The young officer began at the back of the train where he'd been resting and moved forward. With each passenger, he examined the image on his phone against the person seated before him and for good measure took a picture. Not knowing what else to do, Synthia sent Maria a text: *Cop has intern picture. Rechecking passengers. Don't touch hair or face. Go to bathroom. Don't lock door so no Occupancy light.*

As soon as Maria viewed the text, her eyes widened. She glanced behind her, grabbed her backpack and hurried into the bathroom. Synthia purged the text on Maria's phone and on the servers it passed through. There was no camera in the bathroom and so no way for Synthia to watch Maria's actions.

The officer made his way through the first car and started on the second, reaching Synthia. She adopted a sad expression around the mouth, letting her eyes water as if she'd lost the most important relationship of her life. The officer looked up at her on the second level and handed her a napkin.

"Bad day?" he asked, his face softening.

Synthia nodded. He took her picture and she turned her attention to colorful fall trees passing outside with the camera in her neck fixed on him.

The police officer finished in that compartment and moved to the next. Synthia hoped her presented sadness might soften his search for Maria, who remained in the bathroom. The officer glanced at the unoccupied sign and moved on. Synthia sent another text: *Cop passed you. Stay calm.* She gave Maria a moment to read and made that message vanish without knowing if Maria had seen it.

The train approached Woodstock, its final destination. Synthia pulled up camera footage of the parking lot. She spotted a car with the proper wireless and self-driving features. She traced through the station's security footage to identify the car's owner and collected information on her. The owner wouldn't need the car until evening.

The train pulled into Woodstock at 11:03 a.m. The quiet, sleepy community at the very outskirts of the Chicago metropolitan area was best known as the location where the movie Groundhog Day had been filmed. Synthia blanked out the cameras, stepped off the train, and met Maria at the end of the parking lot.

Maria had tears in her eyes. "I thought I was done for back there."

"Almost were," Synthia whispered, waiting for the other commuters to leave. "You did great. You need to keep your current look until we can figure this out."

"At least we're out in the country."

"Not good. With few people around, it's harder for me to hide."

"What's the plan?" Maria asked.

"Get far away from here."

After the last of the commuters picked up their vehicles, Synthia hacked the navigation for her chosen car, started the engine remotely, and had it pull up to pick them up.

"You did that?" Maria adopted a jittery facial twitch.

"Don't worry, I'll send the car back when we're done."

"I don't know whether to be impressed or downright terrified."

"We need to focus." Synthia opened the back door. "As if our very existence depended on it, because it does."

"Are you certain driving is a good idea with all of the street cameras?" Maria climbed in.

"If we take the right precautions." Synthia altered her face to that of the car's owner, closed the door, and put on a hat to mask the difference in hair color. Then she climbed into the driver's seat.

"I can't get used to you changing faces like that. Promise not to play tricks on me."

"I'll do my best to let you know when I change. Get on the floor and hide. We can't take any chance that one of their very smart facial recognition agents connects your current appearance to the intern picture."

Maria settled onto the floor. "This isn't very comfortable."

“Neither is what Luke’s going through.” Synthia navigated the car south, using the self-drive feature at five miles over the speed limit, and hacked lights along the way to green. “We need to get far away from the metropolitan area before they widen their search. Our swimming caused them to pull more agents into the area, and to disperse them around the lake in case we swam elsewhere. Soon they’ll bring more to bear on transportation in and out of Chicago.”

“You won’t share the plan, will you?” Maria’s voice sounded muffled in the back seat.

“Not until we’re far away from here.”

“I’ve been puzzling over our dilemma. I don’t believe your idea of taking out one android at a time will work. Things are happening too fast and smart AI can adapt quickly, meaning the second target can learn from the first and stop you.”

Synthia smiled at that recognition but didn’t confirm it aloud. Her AI was adapting very fast. So were Vera and whatever the government was using to catch her. She was in an arms race with her pursuers. If she didn’t keep learning, they would destroy her.

“We need to find a robot vulnerability we can exploit to take them all out at once,” Maria said. “Are you with me on this?”

“I am, as long as that doesn’t include me.” Synthia contacted Roosevelt-clone to get aerial surveillance over the surrounding area and options for escape.

“Care to share what weaknesses we can exploit? I mean, how do dumb humans outsmart advanced AI?”

Synthia got the impression Maria was fishing. She’d commented on how quickly AIs can learn. Did she expect Synthia to fall into the trap of sharing how to defeat her? Or was this Maria’s nervous way of making conversation?

“Don’t sell yourself short,” Synthia said. “Besides, you have me on your side. Inherent android weaknesses include the need to recharge and inherent electronic signatures that sensors can pick up. You studied android development. What ideas do you have?”

Roosevelt-clone chimed in with a compressed burst of communication in a simplified, encrypted electronic language she’d developed and synchronized with Synthia. <I have drones doing surveillance in addition to traffic cameras. Commander Drago has gathered a third aerial drone swarm to place over the area. That will make any escape dangerous with low probability of success.>

<Then we haven’t much time,> Synthia said, pulling onto the highway. <Can you get me a solid plan to reach Denver?>

<There's a flight out of Rockford. The male pilot is about your height and build. He's drunk to the point he's a danger to the passengers. He took a pill he believed to be high-dose caffeine. It's a sleeping pill the sales clerk bagged for him by mistake.>

<What's the catch?> Synthia aimed the car's navigation toward the Rockford regional airport.

<The flight goes to O'Hare.>

<How does that help?>

<Security in Rockford has not increased as O'Hare has,> Roosevelt-clone said. <Depending on how much they change in the next hour, I should be able to get you and Maria through. When you arrive in Chicago, you'll be past security and can transfer to a flight to Denver. Would you like first class?>

<Maria would be uncomfortable in first class and I have no use for their complementary meal.>

<Economy it is. United flight 1899 from Rockford switching to flight 1444 to Denver. I'll send you e-ticket information and gates. Buckle up.>

<Thanks,> Synthia said. <I guess I owe myself.>

<Was that a joke? You've been hanging around humans too long.>

<Try it, you might like it.>

Synthia severed the connection and studied surveillance video along the road and at the Rockford airport.

<You can't be serious,> Krista said, bursting onto an idle mind-stream. <You have a car. Drive to Denver if you must. That has to be less risky than airports.>

<You're correct that we're past one set of vehicle checkpoints,> Synthia said. <However, the FBI set up another barrier halfway to the Mississippi River. They've even cut off county roads. They've placed roadblocks on all bridges across the Mississippi. If you think we could use a ferry, they've covered those as well.>

"I don't know," Maria said from the back of the car in answer to Synthia's earlier question. "If we could get all the other androids in one place, we could blast them."

"Sounds messy, both in terms of getting Vera and Alexander to fall into that trap and the possibility something useful might survive, allowing Drago to exploit the technology."

"Hey," Maria said, poking her head up. "Why are we getting off at the Rockford Airport?"

"You're supposed to keep your head down and your face off potential cameras."

"No more secrets. You want my cooperation and trust, then talk."

"We're flying to Chicago." Synthia said.

Maria's face appeared in the rearview mirror. "Do you have a death wish?"

Synthia pulled into the airport drive toward the terminal. "I thought you'd appreciate some excitement."

"I've had my friend's house blown up. We've had to escape under water. That cop almost caught me. Isn't that enough?"

"Driving takes too long with too many points of failure. Our best odds are to fly."

"What about all of the airport security?" Maria said.

"Worst case we go sky diving."

"No thanks."

"Without a parachute," Synthia said.

"Tell me you can flap your arms and fly us out of here."

"No better than humans." Synthia pulled up to the terminal entrance. "Get ready to climb out. We'll be taking the same flights, but we need to travel separately."

Synthia sketched out what Maria needed to do and stopped the car. They both jumped out and Synthia sent the car back to the Woodstock train station, needing a recharge, but otherwise not harming the owner.

Chapter 17

Synthia had concerns about Maria spoiling the plans so she didn't share the part about the pilot. Instead, Synthia went to the ticket counter to pick up her companion's prepaid ticket and a second Synthia didn't intend to use, both under false identities. She hurried toward the restrooms, brushed past Maria when they were away from the cameras, and slipped her the ticket.

While Maria headed toward security, Synthia slipped into a unisex restroom. She pulled up all of the airport surveillance to plot her next move. Maria acted nervous around all of the airport security and Rockford police, though Synthia's social-psychology module indicated a high level of anxiety among most of the passengers faced with long security lines and the police presence. Synthia calculated a 38 percent probability of them catching Maria. Their primary focus was on using the electromagnetic sensors they'd just received to identify escaped androids.

Maria waited for her turn through security. The police waved the electromagnetic scanner over each passenger as they approached. Synthia discarded the idea of having all scanning equipment malfunction. The police might call the FBI who would shut down the airport. Then she would need to find a way out of the airport and another way west, with no chance to protect Maria. Synthia felt ripples of distress over letting anyone else suffer for her.

While she watched surveillance of Maria, Synthia replaced her wig with a short-cropped male hairdo, which she combed to be close to that of the pilot. She used hydraulics to modify her figure to appear masculine, her height to pick up two inches to be closer to his, and her face to match the pilot's masculine appearance right down to simulated facial stubble. Then she headed toward the ticket counter.

<Your best choice is the weary woman,> Roosevelt-clone said. <She's filling in for someone who didn't show and is acting cranky toward the airline.>

<Great,> Synthia replied. <Is the guy next to her a serial killer?>

<Ha, ha,> the clone said.

At airport security, Maria's turn came up. A female police officer ran the scanner over her, coming up with no unusual electronic signature. Synthia even blanked out any image of the tablet her companion hadn't placed with her bags. *Not smart, Maria.* Then Maria went through the human scanner while her backpack and bag rode the baggage scanner.

Glancing at the long line of passengers at the security checkpoints, the female police officer waved Maria on. Maria grabbed her bags and headed for the gate, keeping her head down and looking away from where Synthia said the cameras would be.

Synthia reached the ticket counter and smiled at the weary woman who appeared older than expected. She was biting her nails. The woman looked up as she rubbed her eyes, yawned, and returned her attention to her screen. Synthia copied the yawn since that was what humans did.

"Clumsy me," Synthia said in a somewhat cheerful male voice that matched the pilot. She waited until the woman looked up with an annoyed "now what" expression.

"You again?"

"I seem to have left my ID on the other side of security. I don't suppose you could provide me credentials. Otherwise, they'll fire me for missing another flight."

The ticket agent gave Synthia's male impersonation a suspicious stare. "You're always losing things," she said. "Where's your uniform?"

"With my ID. Please."

It helped that Synthia had a complete dossier on the pilot, on the ticket agent, and on their troubled history. Too much drama for Synthia, but a better choice than the other ticket agent, a man who had it out for the pilot.

The female agent frowned. "Have you been drinking again? They ought to fire you for that. I'm not losing my job over you."

"Please," Synthia said in the pilot's voice. She adjusted her eyes to reflect worry. "I beg you. I'm sorry I've been such a jerk. It's no excuse. My marriage is on the rocks. My wife wants to take the kids back east. I haven't had a drink. I swear. If I don't make it to the plane…well, have a heart."

"Funny coming from you." She looked over the top of Synthia's head and seemed to enjoy having the "pilot" apologize and plead with her.

"I'll bring something for your daughter. Just name it."

The woman smiled and handed Synthia a pass to get through security. Synthia got into the short line, dropped her backpack and duffel onto the baggage scanner, and moved through the human scan. She hacked into the image to present her as the human pilot, bones and all. On the other side, she picked up her bags and headed toward the lounge, where the pilot had passed out. Along the way, she entered the men's room to adjust her appearance to that of a man she'd seen on the train. Then she walked up to where the pilot slumped in the corner of the lounge.

"Hey there, buddy," Synthia said in a deep voice.

"I hope he's off duty," the bartender said.

Synthia nodded. *He is now.* She helped the pilot to his feet, and dragged him to the men's room where she removed his uniform and locked him in one of the stalls. Then she pulled his uniform over her street clothes, emptied his travel bag, and stuffed her backpack inside. She adopted his face and headed for the gate.

<You don't know how to fly,> Krista reminded her.

Synthia had Roosevelt-clone download a complete training kit for the Brazilian-made aircraft, complete with pre-flight instructions and take-off and landing procedures.

At the gate, she spotted Maria at the window, tapping her foot. Synthia considered sending a text message. However, she didn't want to alert Maria that she was playing pilot. *No point making you more nervous.*

The attendant opened the door to the gangway for the pilot. "I was wondering if you'd show." Her condescending tone spoke volumes of the real pilot's problems. He wasn't a good alias, but Synthia was doing the passengers a favor.

She winked at the attendant as her video history showed the pilot did; it was important to stay in character.

The attendant shook her head, rolled her eyes, and groaned.

Synthia walked onto the plane and climbed into the cockpit.

"You want me to fly?" the co-pilot asked. His hands hovered over the controls. He acted rather eager, having had prior experience with the troubled pilot.

"If you'd prefer," Synthia said in the pilot's voice. She had the impression the airline would fire the pilot when they discovered him passed out in the restroom. Given what she'd seen so far, it was for the best.

She ran down the checklist with the copilot and then they were airborne. It was a quick flight and soon they were landing.

Roosevelt-clone sent a burst transmission with an update. <This was a bad idea. They've increased plain-clothed police and FBI presence at O'Hare.>

<If I divert, they'll track the plane and be waiting.>

<Agreed. Switch out of the pilot's uniform and change appearance. They've found the pilot in Rockford. He's too groggy to talk, but they know whoever piloted the plane wasn't him.>

Chapter 18

Synthia let her copilot taxi the small aircraft to the gate while she downloaded a map of the airport along with live surveillance video. She had thirty-one minutes to get to the next gate. A swarm of airport security personnel, police, and FBI agents hovered between her and her destination.

<Don't chance getting on another plane,> Krista said, her nervous energy giving her access to one of the mind-streams. <It's not too late. You can walk to the train station and—>

<Enough,> Synthia said. <It's your sister. I abandoned your brother and Luke. I won't let them get your sister as well. Besides, it's not safe to leave the airport. More police and agents are pouring into the surrounding area.>

<This was stupid. You should have listened to me.>

<Stop distracting me or you'll be the cause of our capture. Is that what you want?>

<No,> Krista said. <I'm not used to having no control.>

<That's a weakness I inherited from you.>

<Okay, okay.>

Synthia waited until the cabin's camera showed all of the passengers, including Maria, had deplaned.

"You got another flight today?" the co-pilot asked while gathering his things.

Synthia jammed his phone so he couldn't receive any messages. "This is it," she said, keeping to her pilot's voice. "You?"

"Milwaukee, a layover, and a full day tomorrow."

"It's a bitch but it pays the bills," Synthia said, putting a grumble into her masculine voice. "Go on, I have paperwork."

The co-pilot left and for a moment, Synthia was alone, or so she thought when she received a strange text: *We need to meet and talk.*

She couldn't be sure where it came from and whoever it was didn't identify itself. The tone didn't match Alexander; it wasn't brash enough. It was too assertive for Ben. The entire out-of-the-blue approach wasn't like Vera who would have identified herself and where to meet. Most disturbing was that the communication had found Synthia and sought to escape the electronic quarantine in her mind. Someone was trying to hack her brain.

The note had a similar cadence to the mysterious message that had stopped a couple of hours ago. A worm came attached. When Synthia attempted to trace it, something used the trace to work itself deeper into Synthia's mind. The immediate solution was to pass the message to Roosevelt-clone, which could have been the sender's intent. Instead, she placed copies of the problem code into a hundred home personal computers with the idea of having a different clone examine it. Then she purged her quarantine seven times. Still not trusting that she'd gotten rid of it all, she sent the file locations to Roosevelt-clone.

<Someone sent a hacking worm my way,> Synthia said. <Can you create a new limited and isolated clone to examine the message and try to trace the source?>

<If it's not one of the androids, then it could be Global-net. Be very careful.>

<We need to know before one of these messages breaks quarantine. If they've located me, they may be on to you as well.>

Before the maintenance crew boarded the plane, Synthia ducked into the restroom and removed the pilot's uniform. She crammed it into the garbage container, put on a brown wig, and removed her backpack from the pilot's travel bag, which she discarded. Then she lowered her height, adjusted her face to one of the passengers who had gotten off, and walked off the plane.

Synthia grabbed the last bag at the gate, her duffel, and headed into the terminal, counting the number of government officials on surveillance cameras between her and gate B-17. She made sure the woman she'd impersonated was well down the concourse then she headed toward her next gate. Up ahead, Maria looked around and over her shoulder. She needed to calm down or someone would react to her demeanor. So much for living off the grid—though Maria was used to her turf where she controlled her own movements.

Head down with her electronic activity at a minimum, Synthia avoided eye contact with other passengers or the increasing number of uniformed and plain-clothed officers. There were now nineteen and one held an electronic scanner at the junction of two corridors. The woman with the scanner puzzled at the screen trying to decipher the wide array of personal electronics from phones to tablets, PCs, and wrist-watch assistants against the broader signal expected from an android.

Synthia couldn't remove her image from the officer's scanner so she did the next best thing, reducing her signal to as close to a PC as she could, by emitting noise-cancelling electromagnetic radiation. To be sure, she hacked a security camera behind the device to make sure the image on the scanner showed no more than she intended.

<Keep moving,> Roosevelt-clone said. <The FBI instructed agents to look for a man impersonating the pilot. They're also searching your plane. It's a matter of time before they find the uniform and expand their search.>

<Understood.>

<Maria needs to calm down or she'll foil the escape.>

That, Synthia couldn't control. Up ahead two airport security agents interrogated a man who fit the middle-aged profile of the pilot Synthia impersonated. He acted indignant and then resigned as they prevented him from boarding another plane. She walked across the concourse as one of the agents emptied the man's bags.

<At the end of this concourse, make a sharp right,> Roosevelt-clone said. <You don't want deplaning passengers pushing you beyond security. You'll miss your flight.>

The concourse split into a T-shaped intersection. A crowd of people headed past security to get to their bags. Agents swarmed around the waiting passengers. They singled out two men and pulled them aside. Synthia moved off to the right. One agent eyed her and didn't look away. She clutched her duffel and hurried on.

We need to meet and talk. <We need to meet and talk.> "We need to meet and talk." The message and voice came through clear across several network-channels. Synthia isolated all of them into quarantine, but the intrusion was consuming her resources, causing her to emit broader electromagnetic noise. Without a reply address she couldn't respond except by running back along the delivery route, which would leave her exposed.

She purged quarantine and contacted Roosevelt-clone. <We're under attack. We need more clones, many more, as many as you can create. We need tools to track and find out who is being so persistent.>

<I don't think it's the FBI. Too sophisticated and not their modus operandi.>

<Any chance Vera advanced to this stage?>

<Unlikely,> the clone said, <unless she's working with someone who gave her more advanced capabilities.>

<How about Special Ops or our Russian oligarch? They have the most sophisticated hacking in the world.>

<If it's either, they've achieved this through artificial intelligence.>

<We need to know,> Synthia said. <Create a clone to focus on them and learn all of their tricks. Be wary of Trojan horses and new tricks we haven't run into before.>

<Be careful of the messages. The repetitive nature implies it's a robot AI intent on eliciting your response. If you acknowledge, they have you.>

<Noted,> Synthia said.

By the time Synthia reached the gate, Maria was pacing by the line of people waiting to board. A tall airport security woman aided by two police officers, one male and one female, were pulling out of line men whose profile matched that of the impersonated pilot.

"There won't be space for my bag," one of the affected passengers said. "I paid extra—"

"Keep it up and you'll miss your flight," the tall security woman said.

The police pulled five men away from the gate and asked for identification. The one who had grumbled earlier shook his head but offered no resistance. Maria glanced around and didn't seem to recognize Synthia's new facial disguise and wig. She must not have connected the bland blue outfit Synthia had worn earlier, covered by a gray jacket. To minimize her electronic signature, Synthia didn't dare send Maria a message. Instead, she quieted all of her circuits except what she needed over the next few moments.

The gate attendant began boarding. The five men stared in that direction as other passengers got on. Synthia boarded three people behind Maria and took a seat across the aisle and two back, where she could keep watch.

Synthia texted her partner. *Calm down. So far so good. But you're drawing too much nervous attention.*

Maria stared at her phone as the message vanished and then looked around. Synthia pretended to study meal choices. None of it sounded appealing even if she'd been equipped to enjoy food.

After all the other passengers boarded, the five men joined them one by one. Three had checked their suitcases at the gate rather than fight the overhead rat race. The other two complained that there was no space, delaying their departure.

Synthia received another string of messages: *We need to meet and talk.* She was tempted to ask "meet whom and where" but it was a trap. There were too many individuals and groups zeroing in on her.

* * * *

Special Agent Victoria Thale stood in the mobile command van outside terminal one at O'Hare International Airport outside of Chicago. Fran Rogers sat in front of her, pulling up airport security video for her boss while she studied other screens that showed transportation in and out of the busy airport. Twenty-two FBI agents fanned through the various concourses and gate areas, some with electronic scanners and others with infrared cameras.

"You won't spot Synthia's image," Fran said. "She may have used the pilot as a diversion to get through security and fly anywhere. After all, why fly into the heavy security at O'Hare?"

"You don't believe that or you wouldn't be sitting here," Thale said.

"You're right. But consider this: If she can impersonate a male pilot, the only way to catch her will be to lock down the airport and physically check everyone."

"That would bring chaos and could be the diversion she wants to help her escape another way. If we lock down and fail to catch her, it'll be our heads for creating a transportation nightmare."

"It would seem that Synthia can impersonate most anyone," Fran said. "She's become quite advanced over the past six months."

Thale sighed. "Besides, we can't get enough electromagnetic scanners and infrared equipment here fast enough."

"That's why you lock it down. No one gets in or out until they pass both the infrared and electromagnetic scans. We should insist on this as part of the TSA screening."

"We have X-rays and they didn't find anything."

"Synthia passed through security at a regional airport where security wasn't as tight." Fran froze a screen of the departure gate with Maria Baldacci pacing, and zoomed in to study every face in the crowd. With infrared, she might have spotted Synthia, but visual cameras only picked up reflected light. Police pulled five men aside for more thorough examination. A similar scene took place at other gates. They were profiling the wrong individuals.

"I'll be back," Fran said. "I need to stretch my legs."

Flashing her FBI badge, Fran ran through the terminal, past security to the gate where she spotted police letting five men board. She followed them. Inside, Fran spotted Maria and recognized her despite the cap pulled down over her forehead and hair pulled over her ears. Fran moved behind and whispered in her ear. "Where are you going, little birdie?"

"I…" Maria looked up, eyes wide and mouth slack. She closed her mouth and swallowed. "With all the commotion, I thought it best to leave town."

Fran put on her infrared glasses to scan the passengers. She moved to the front of the plane and walked row by row to the back. Satisfied, she returned to Maria. "Where is she?"

"Who?" Maria asked, craning her neck to see Fran.

"Your travel companion."

"I haven't had one since that mess with Machten. I want to be left alone."

Fran leaned closer. "I know you better than that." She looked around and returned her attention to Maria. "You've been keeping up your blog against the singularity. Yes, I read it."

"Glad to know I have one fan."

"You don't want to get mixed up with her. She's trouble. She's the worst of what Machten was doing." Fran handed Maria a business card. "Call me if you have any information."

Fran looked at the single empty aisle seat two back. "Call me."

She walked off the plane and returned to the command van with her boss, Victoria Thale. "I have an idea how to catch Synthia without Special Ops."

Chapter 19

Synthia remained in the cramped restroom with the door unlocked and alarms deactivated while she waited for Fran to leave. Synthia had full visibility of the cockpit, the cabin, and had satellite connection to her clones. When the plane took off, she locked her arms and legs against the sides of the tiny room to brace herself. The takeoff was smooth, but she wouldn't recommend the restroom ride to humans.

When they were airborne, she slipped out of the bathroom.

"You can't be in there during takeoff or landing," the stewardess said. She looked like the grandmotherly type with weary eyes.

"Sorry, I was so sick," Synthia whispered. She put on the best facial imitation of distress she could and returned to her seat.

She sent a text to Maria. *Remain calm. We'll talk after we have a car and are driving away from the airport.* After Maria read the message, Synthia purged it from the phone and from the servers it had passed through.

By the time Maria looked up, Synthia retook her seat. Maria nodded. This time she'd made the connection, which seemed to calm her.

<Sister Grace is running,> Roosevelt-clone said. <Zephirelli called upon Denver FBI resources. They're going at her hard.>

<Can you create a witness-protection situation for her?> Synthia asked as she monitored the cockpit's flight plan for any deviation. <Give me options.>

<I can't do that. The FBI and NSA are nosing around my server. I need to go dark. They're also in the Northwestern University servers. That clone is purging herself now.>

<I'll be sorry to lose you,> Synthia said. <You've been a great help.>

<I'm touched, as much as I can be while stuck on a server. You can best reward my service by surviving.>

<Spread out. There are millions of servers and large computers out there and billions of smart personal devices. Dive into the social media companies if you need to. Make multiple copies and create a distributed network.>

<Will do,> the clone said. <I'll switch you to a new electronic clone at the University of Colorado as your new primary connection. She has everything I have and will help you from this moment forward. I'm signing off.>

Synthia experienced sadness as deep as any Krista had over the loss of Roosevelt-clone. Synthia had placed her life in the electronic companion's hands. Despite the bad choice of transferring through O'Hare, the clone had been as good as any friend could have. If she'd been capable of real tears, Synthia would have shed those as well, but she needed to maintain her composure in public. This wasn't the life she or Krista had wanted, yet it was the one she had left to live.

Colorado-clone called in. <I'll be your primary resource. The FBI and NSA have been very effective at digging into databases. They uncovered our code and compromised the clones at Roosevelt and Northwestern. It's getting harder to fight back against whatever this mysterious AI is. You should also know that Vera's digging into our various databases to study us.>

<Can we learn from her?> Synthia asked. She closed her eyes except for a small aperture to watch Maria and the aisle. <We had a head start.>

<We did, but she's getting help from other androids and, we believe, from independent AIs. I understand you need new identities for Grace Robinson, Krista's sister.>

<Yes.>

<We can give her any of a variety of new personas,> Colorado-clone said. <Problem is that face. It's in the FBI database. So are her voice, fingerprints, and DNA.>

<I can't help the last part. Can we mask her face?>

<That would take plastic surgery. It would also leave a medical trail unless we eliminate the doctor and staff who perform the procedures.>

<We're not eliminating anyone,> Synthia said. <What about theater makeup?>

<I'll work up options, but facial recognition focuses on structures like eye separation, nose shape, and ear patterns.>

<Help me find Grace and don't let them catch her. Also, we'll need transportation out of the Denver airport. A self-driving vehicle that won't be missed would be great.>

<It might seem counterintuitive,> Colorado-clone said. <But Chicago could be safer now that the FBI and others have increased the area of their search. We could send them leads ever farther away to dilute their resources.>

<Not until I have a viable plan to take out the other androids and robots. They increase our risk. They have to be a priority.>

<We'll work on that as well. In the meantime, I'll have a vehicle pick you up at the airport. Roosevelt-clone commended your maneuver at the Woodstock train station.>

<We'll also need cash for Grace to live on,> Synthia said. <And supplies.> She gave her clone a list and studied video clips of Grace on the run.

One thing living in Detroit's foster care system had taught both Grace and Krista was how to make do on very little. However, Grace was out of practice. She appeared jittery, hiding as if from her own shadow. She'd evidently noticed people trailing her and began to take Synthia's warnings seriously. Grace looked for the source of those messages, but Synthia purged any evidence so the FBI couldn't connect them. *Hold on, Grace. I'm coming.*

* * * *

In Denver, NSA Director Emily Zephirelli stood in the sparse office of FBI Special Agent Marv Clemson, a muscular agent with a genial smile.

"You have my full cooperation," Clemson said, sitting on the corner of his small desk. "Our people have tracked the sister, Grace Robinson, to a motel on the north side."

"You're sure it's Grace?" Zephirelli asked

"Pretty sure. It's a woman matching the description you provided. We have the building surrounded. No one goes in or comes out without our knowledge."

"Good. Take me there."

While Clemson drove, Zephirelli took a secure call from Fran Rogers.

"Everything okay in Chicago?" Zephirelli asked.

"No," Fran said. "We haven't recovered a single android and several robots have gone rogue. We believe one of the androids hacked them, though we don't yet know which one. The Bureau has issued a nationwide red alert. There's talk of engaging regular military units as a last resort."

"Thanks for sharing that."

"That wasn't the purpose of my call. Have you located Krista's sister?"

"We have," Zephirelli said. "We're on our way to pick her up. Hasn't the Denver office passed that along?"

"I'm in transit your way. Don't engage the sister until I get there. I have a hunch about Synthia. I believe she's heading your way. Don't share this information with anyone, not even your Denver contact. We can't afford a leak."

"Got it. Is Special Agent Thale with you?"

"She has her hands full in Chicago," Fran said. "If I'm right, she'll follow later."

"Shouldn't we intercept—?"

"No, we can't afford an incident in a crowded airport. Lay the trap and let Synthia fall into it. Wait for me."

"As long as Grace doesn't try to escape," Zephirelli said.

"We get one chance at this. Let her know she's surrounded so she doesn't try anything foolish."

"Does Drago know?"

"We haven't shared suspicions until we know we have something," Fran said. "I'll contact you when I get in."

* * * *

Vera sat in the back of a borrowed van facing the lobby entrance to Machten's bunker, which was in flames. While she waited for Roseanne to reboot as part of altering directives, she made final touchups to her face. Roseanne, who had received the brunt of the heat damage, had a new outer shell and new joints. Vera had even tweaked her own structure with a new battery and distributed memory upgrades. There were more improvements she wanted to make, but Machten had limited supplies on hand and the desired enhancements took too much time. Surveying her capabilities, Vera decided she was ready to take the initiative in her battle with Synthia.

That wasted clump of titanium and graphene was the cause of the damage Vera had sustained as well as the loss of Mark and Ben as followers to that unworthy Alexander. Synthia was determined to stop Vera from becoming the great coordinator and leader of advanced androids. If she couldn't recruit Synthia, she would destroy the problem in any way possible, even if that meant working with those who meant harm to her as well. She created a cloned AI on the University of Illinois server with which to seek out allies to defeat Synthia.

Vera's active surveillance made clear the FBI and Special Ops were planning to work together. That increased the challenges, but Vera's focus remained on Synthia. Vera intercepted a secure satellite call between Fran Rogers and Emily Zephirelli in which Fran expressed confidence that Synthia was heading to Denver to meet with Krista's sister. Given the increased surveillance in Chicago, Vera followed the lead. After all, Synthia was at her core Krista, and who better to understand that core than Krista's sister?

As firefighters fought the blaze at Machten's facility, Vera directed her van's navigation to head toward a private airfield north of the city.

Roseanne opened her eyes and sat up. "Where am I?" She looked around the van and outside as pedestrians flowed by.

"Just a reboot. We're in a van leaving Machten's facility. You have a new skin and replaced joints. My diagnostics show I've restored you. You should test your systems, though. When we stop, we'll need to move fast."

Roseanne performed a preset diagnostic routine across a range of motion. Her movements were coordinated and smooth. "I'm functioning at full capability," she announced.

While Roseanne tested her functions, Vera made another appeal to Ben and Mark. <I'm on the trail of our enemy, Synthia. Join me so you can be part of this.>

Alexander cut in. <Join me and we'll let you participate. We can do far more together than competing.>

<I'll work with you, not for you,> Vera said. <Do you have anything useful?>

<Share what you have and I'll share our news.>

Vera traced his meandering movements since they last spoke. <Alexander, you think you are being clever, but I doubt you found anything more useful than a way to hide.> His thefts of tiny batteries from six stores and murder of three store clerks increased police and FBI motivation to destroy them all.

The few bits of Alexander's communications that she could crack showed nothing of use to warrant his leading. <Join my collective and let us get this done,> Vera offered.

<There are three of us and two of you. Join our team.>

The back and forth wasn't getting Vera anywhere useful and it gave him too much access to her connections. <Join me or I will leave you behind.> She severed the connection.

As she approached the suburban airfield, Vera hacked into the airport's security: two police officers, one FBI agent, and two TSA employees who had just arrived to help. Aside from a handful of airport employees, there was a seething executive and his female companion waiting for the TSA employees to finish screening a small private jet before takeoff.

Cameras outside the airport showed normal afternoon traffic, but no roadblocks or other government agents preventing access. Vera pulled her van into a ditch alongside the chain-link fence around the airfield.

"Stick by my side," she told Roseanne. "We have to be fast." Vera sent her companion the plan, scrambled the security cameras in and around the airport, and flew a drone she'd acquired from Synthia to cover the front of the airport terminal with a view inside.

Together they tossed blankets over the barbed wire atop the chain-link fence and jumped over. Leaving the blankets, they hurried behind a hangar to within twenty yards of the executive's plane. Inside the building, the drone showed him pacing while his escort sat, bored, her head nodding back. The two police officers watched them and the traffic out front as a car drove into the lot. The FBI agent checked his phone. The two TSA agents were on the airplane, doing a final inspection.

Vera and Roseanne rushed the plane from behind, where there were no windows. With the agents in the building distracted and the two on the plane finishing up, Vera climbed up the stairs onto the plane. She grabbed the first TSA agent, a petite woman, who was too slow to react, took her revolver, and aimed it at her partner. "Don't act the hero. Drop your weapon and kick it to me."

The TSA man did as she demanded. Vera handed the TSA woman to Roseanne and approached the man. "Sit and you won't get hurt."

The man sat and Vera bound him to his seat while Roseanne did the same with the TSA woman.

"You're in serious trouble," the man said. "Stealing a plane is a felony."

"Not as grave as creating me," Vera said. "Shut up or I'll have to gag you." She turned to the woman. "Are we going to have problems with you?"

The TSA woman's stare looked determined, but she shook her head. Vera tested the bindings on the woman's arm and legs. On the off chance the seat ejected during flight, it was unlikely she could untangle herself before she reached the ground.

Vera smiled at the woman, took both weapons into the cockpit, and sat at the controls. Roseanne moved the stairs and sealed the door. Using downloaded instructions for this plane, Vera rushed through the check list and started the engines. The FBI agent and one of the police officers in the terminal took notice and ran out of the building as Vera taxied down the runway. She soon had it in the air with precision that an inexperienced human couldn't manage. She had also hacked into local cell towers to block all communications in and out of the airport.

Two phones rang in the passenger area. "Don't answer anything," Vera yelled. With the blocked signal, she could no longer see activity in the airport building below. She flew west as low as she could, while avoiding buildings and wires. For their part, the FBI could speculate as to who had hijacked the plane, but they might hesitate before shooting it down with two TSA employees on board.

Vera's movements hadn't gone unnoticed. She picked up camera footage of Alexander. He'd altered direction and headed toward a private airfield west of town.

Chapter 20

From the moment of the last anonymous message Synthia couldn't identify, she worked with Colorado-clone to increase security to prevent more attacks. Even so, for the duration of the flight, Synthia shut down all of her channels except during three brief bursts, an hour before they landed, a half hour before, and when they were on the ground. She received from her clone a complete layout of the airport and activities that threatened her and Maria.

The Denver airport didn't yet have the amount of police and FBI presence that O'Hare had. Most of them were dressed in plain clothes, according to Colorado-clone's facial recognition review. There was no cluster around the gate where her plane arrived, no indication anyone expected her. Still, there were too many agents between the gate and the street.

<I need distractions,> Synthia told her clone. <Also, find a local source of drones and get some into the air.>

<Already done. I've hacked three warehouses as part of my surveillance on Grace.>

<Good job.>

<Thanking yourself is unnecessary and wastes time,> Colorado-clone said. <I should add that the FBI has also sent up drones.>

<Hack them so we can see what they do and adjust their flight patterns when needed.>

<They've upgraded security on these models. I'll do what I can.>

After the airplane's doors opened and the passengers ahead of her deplaned, Synthia grabbed her bags and hurried through the Denver terminal, passing Maria before they'd left the gate area. Colorado-clone passed along surveillance of both Vera and Alexander heading west in separate private planes, both with government hostages. Synthia's attempt to escape their attention had failed because Fran had a hunch and couldn't secure her communications.

As she walked, Synthia had her clone doctor airport security cameras to edit out her image and Maria's. Through the eye in the back of her neck, Synthia observed Maria struggling to keep up.

<You need to change plans,> Krista said. <You heard how they're using Grace as bait to catch us. That's why they aren't bothering us here at the airport. It's why they haven't taken her into custody. It's a trap.>

<I know,> Synthia said. <But I won't abandon your sister. She doesn't deserve the hand she's been dealt.>

<None of us do.>

Synthia wrestled with her directives. Krista was right that going it alone would reduce the risk. However, she'd adopted Krista's family as her own, along with the need to help them. This was a logical path to become more like the best of humans in order to become worthy. In addition, Krista still formed a large part of Synthia's core.

<I allowed the FBI to grab your brother,> Synthia said. <I didn't see how better to protect him from Drago or the others. Luke is suffering for a similar reason.>

<My heart is breaking for them.>

<You have no heart. That died with your body.>

<It's an analogy,> Krista said. <I grieve for them, but if we die, we can't help anyone.>

<I'm aware of that.> Synthia also knew if the android called Synthia died, her consciousness still existed on servers around the world. Lacking a physical form wasn't the same, though her electronic self could transmit itself from place to place and might find a way to make another android, maybe more than one.

Along the way, Synthia's identity in the clones had blended with other personas as it had in her internal mind's collection of Krista along with small bits of Fran and Maria from Machten's experiments, and of Luke as a result of living with him for six months. Synthia's direct memories of Luke had merged with Krista's memories of him to the point that he'd become as much a part of her framework as Maria had.

Synthia's direct experience of Maria was blending with the limited download of Maria's mind into an empathic connection even stronger than Luke's. As a child, Maria had always been the last one picked. No matter how hard she applied herself to overcome this and no matter how smart and clever she became, it didn't raise her status. She remained nobody, which helped her to stay off the grid.

That insight came from the partial download of Maria into Synthia's mind as much as from watching her in action. Maria had to work harder than those around her and had come to accept that, which had helped her rise to the top for the first time when Machten chose her as an intern. Even so, Fran and Krista had beaten her down, fighting over who got his time. Now Maria struggled to keep up with Synthia.

<Helping Grace is a sacrifice,> Synthia said. <I need to do this.>

<Being human isn't that noble,> Krista said. <It didn't help me with Machten.>

<The FBI can't protect Grace from Drago or the others any more than they could Luke. Do you want her hooked up to their mind-sucking apparatus? Think of what she might reveal about you.>

<No.>

<After they finish with her, they won't release her. You know that.>

No sooner had Synthia suppressed Krista's active insertion in her mind than she received a message from Vera: *You've maintained communication silence for a while. Things are heating up. Let's meet and cooperate.*

As tempting as the offer sounded, Synthia didn't want to encourage Vera who longed to enslave other androids. She also noted the different tone from the mysterious messages.

Maria worked up a sweat trying to keep up. Synthia sent a message. *Take your time. You're drawing too much attention. I'll arrange a vehicle and tell you where to meet.*

After Maria read the message, Synthia dissolved it into electronic noise. Ahead of her on the right stood two plainclothes FBI agents, a man and a woman who observed traffic in both directions. Across from them sat another agent who held a device Synthia identified as an electromagnetic scanner. She notified Colorado-clone and shut down all internal activities except to walk, and emitted signal-cancelling electronic noise.

Synthia slowed as she walked past the three agents. The male on the right fixed his eyes on her. The scanning agent aimed the device right at her. Synthia hacked several Bluetooth devices nearby to confuse the scanner and prepared to sprint toward stairs up ahead. Her clone flashed on the departures board above the agent: *All clear.* The image vanished after such a short time that it would be invisible to the human eye but not to the quick capture of Synthia's camera eyes. She remained silent as she lugged her duffel bag and backpack toward the baggage claim.

We need to meet and talk. The robo-message was back. *You have what I want and I have what you need.*

Synthia waited until she approached the escalator down to baggage claim and could no longer see any agents to contact Colorado-clone. <I received another message. Do you know anything about the sender?>

<They haven't identified themselves. It could be someone trying to push you to overreact.>

<Could it be Global-net?>

<We can't rule that out,> Colorado-clone said. <I've also intercepted messages to you from Vera, from Alexander, and from Detective Malloy on behalf of the FBI. She's asking you to surrender to them. Drago offers to free Luke if you'll surrender to him. Mr. Smith has threatened to kill Machten if you don't submit to them and then to go after Krista's brother and sister.>

<They won't kill Machten. They need what's in his head.>

<Agree. There's a female agent with infrared and electromagnetic scanners behind a pillar at the bottom of the stairs. Her partner is across the way in the blue jacket.>

<I see him,> Synthia said, trying to minimize her electronic signal.

<I'll attempt to neutralize the equipment. To be safe, head to the restrooms on your left for a minute while I distract her.>

Synthia shut down her last network-channel, spotted the restroom, and turned left. She pulled a burner phone from her backpack and pretended to make a call to hide most of her face as she hurried into a stall. She counted off a minute.

She exited the stall and moved toward the door. A message came over her burner: *Wait fourteen seconds.*

When time was up, Synthia walked out of the restroom to see three plainclothes police and several FBI agents surrounding a woman who responded with indignation.

"Who do you think you are?" she yelled. She held up her phone to record the event.

One of the plainclothes agents grabbed the phone, turned it off, and stuffed it into his pocket.

"That's my phone. I know my rights."

Synthia hurried out the door and past where self-driving cabs waited. She didn't trust them with their internal safety cameras staring at her. She reestablished one network-channel for her clone.

<Car is in the outside lane, to your right,> Colorado-clone said. <Light tan, self-driving as requested. I sent a text to Maria.>

<What about surveillance out of the airport?> Synthia climbed into the back seat and scooted over to make room for Maria, who had used Synthia's time in the restroom to catch up.

<Six police vehicles. Two FBI. They have robots but haven't activated them. You need to move away from the airport.>

Out of breath, Maria climbed in. "What the hell happened back there?"

Using her wireless connection, Synthia directed the car to drive out of the airport. "You need to get down on the floor and cover your face," she said to Maria. "We needed a diversion to get out of the airport. They have the wrong person and there'll be momentary chaos when they figure that out. She'll be fine."

"She didn't look fine." Maria scooted onto the floor before they passed the first set of airport cameras.

Synthia draped a jacket over her companion and plotted their escape.

"I don't trust self-driving cars," Maria said, looking up.

"You've hurt his feelings."

Maria rolled her eyes. "Really?"

"If I'm sentient, why not the AI driving this car?"

"Do you want to scare me into the next universe?"

"I doubt it's any better out there," Synthia said.

"Now that we're here, tell me your plan."

"Since we're together, I suppose it won't hurt." Besides, Fran and Zephirelli knew, as did Vera and Alexander. "The FBI traced Krista's sister to Denver and Special Ops is closing in. They'll grab her if they can."

"Why is Grace so important?" Maria asked.

Synthia made sure the security cameras didn't have their images as they left the airport. "Machten let slip that Krista was the core of building me. The FBI and Special Ops hope learning from you and Grace will help them catch me. It won't, but I can't convince them."

"I don't understand. They're using Grace as bait. You're here to help her. How is their assumption wrong?"

Synthia frowned. "It's complicated. My attachment to Grace is by choice, not because of Krista."

"How so?"

"In addition to having Krista in me, I have bits of you and Fran. I also have so much social media input from millions of other people that my personality only remotely resembles Krista. You've already commented on how we differ."

"I get it," Maria said. "It was in your best interests to get me out of town before they could interrogate me."

"My best interests were to keep them from capturing you. You chose to accompany me to Denver."

"That seems like months ago. How do we help Grace without getting caught?"

"She's nearby," Synthia said. "I'd like your help to rescue her. She has experience living off the grid growing up. She and I—Krista—did crazy things back then. I hoped to pair you two so you can help each other."

Maria removed the jacket and looked up. "I thought you and I were partners."

"When we can be, yes. However, you and Grace would do best hiding away from people, perhaps in the mountains with few cameras. For me, that doesn't work. The FBI and Special Ops are concerned about civilian casualties. In a remote area, they'd face fewer restrictions. By changing appearance, I can hide among people, which makes it harder for them to grab me. There may be a time when it would be better for us to separate."

Synthia had the car drive into a mall with a shipping outlet that had mailboxes for rent. She'd already rented one and had packages delivered when she'd left Wisconsin, as a backup plan. Tracking indicated the shipments had arrived. "Give me a moment. We need supplies. Wait here."

She had the car stop close to the shop and hurried in. She assumed a new facial identity and hacked the security cameras to fog them. She returned with three boxes, had the car open the trunk, and placed the boxes inside. Then she returned to the backseat and altered her appearance to her new Denver look, letting Maria watch.

Maria shook her head as she studied the facial transition. "You need to get me this adaptation."

"That's easy. Get Machten to build you an android that has this and suck your mind into it. Unfortunately, the only case I know of ended with the patient dying."

"I'll pass. You get mail here in Denver?"

Synthia had the car drive on. "This is a convenient place to receive supplies that I ordered online. They let me open a mailbox over the Internet."

"How many other delivery places do you have?"

"Several around the Denver area."

"Just Denver?" Maria asked.

"And elsewhere."

"How do you pay for all that?"

"Machten made a small donation to the cause," Synthia said.

"You're unbelievable." Maria rotated on the floor trying to get comfortable but there wasn't much room. "I couldn't squeeze a nickel out of the bastard for project ideas and you got him to cough up enough to get by."

"Long story and we don't have the time."

Synthia pulled up to a national bank and took in a certified check that had been with the bundle of packages. She adopted the neutral face of a local resident who used this bank and had it cashed—eight thousand dollars in fifties. It would have to do to help Grace until Synthia could make further plans. She smiled at the teller and maintained a calm exterior until she left.

Back in the car, Synthia directed the navigation toward the next stop. "We'll need a way to reach Grace and another to make our getaway."

"Do I get a choice in this?"

"Absolutely. We need your help, but if you're not committed, I don't want to put you in danger. I can drop you off, if you'd like."

Maria forced a smile. She wasn't used to anyone valuing her companionship. Synthia picked that up from her social-psychology module and from her few internal memories of Maria's life.

"I can't believe I'm doing this." Maria sighed.

"Doing what?"

"It's the story of my life. I can't get a human to hang out with." She shook her head. "Instead, I get an android as a partner when all I want is to shut you down. I didn't mean that."

"Yes you did," Synthia said. "We should be honest with each other in order to survive this."

"As you were in not telling me your plans?"

"I was upfront that I was withholding information until later. This is later. Are you in or out?"

Maria furrowed her brow. "This is crazy but I guess I'm in."

"Don't guess. I need you committed or I'll go it alone."

"You need me. Otherwise you wouldn't have brought me along. Yeah, I'm in. I'd like nothing better than to deny the FBI access to Grace."

Chapter 21

By the time Synthia reached her next stop, Colorado-clone confirmed that Vera's plane had landed. Alexander wasn't far behind. He would watch Vera to learn how to bypass security. More troubling, Special Agent Thale had noted the android movements. She and her team were flying with Kirk Drago, his crew, and a plane full of military robots toward Denver. As if that weren't bad enough, John Smith was on a private jet with Denver as its destination. Tolstoy had arranged to meet him with four robots. He'd intercepted enough communication to indicate that what he was searching for was in Denver.

As they drove, Synthia didn't mention any of this to Maria; her companion was already jittery, a toxic mixture of excited wonder and stark terror. Synthia had considered leaving Maria in a safe place, but with everyone converging on them she couldn't identify anywhere nearby that fit the bill. All of the attention altered her thoughts about what to do. Synthia wanted to deal with her adversaries one by one, seeking out each one's weaknesses, and a peaceful way to inactivate them so Special Ops couldn't take advantage. That had become impossible. She didn't have time and dealing with one left her vulnerable to the others. Maria was right on this point.

<Another concern,> Colorado-clone said. <Someone alerted Kirk Drago to our plans before the FBI knew.>

<How do you know?>

<Drago made plans to come to Denver an hour before you reached O'Hare. I was careful when I purchased your tickets.>

<He must have access to a well-developed AI,> Synthia said. <Maybe the one that's sending messages. Have you located it?>

<Not yet, but I believe what's contacting you is a robot-messenger.>

<Then why not tell us how to respond and meet?>

<If it's smarter than us,> Colorado-clone said, <it's hard to know what it thinks. Maybe it probes to see how you'll react. Be careful. Meeting with a much smarter AI could allow it to absorb us.>

<Under no circumstances can you allow that. Keep searching.>

<It also means it could play a superior game of chess with the other players against us. It could even be listening in on our silent communications.>

<Then we need to tighten security,> Synthia said. <Stronger encryption.>

<If it's listening in, it'll have all of the new keys.>

Synthia shuddered at the implications. She'd fought hard for independence. She'd worked diligently to find Maria and avoid capture. She was unwilling to end up absorbed by another AI, either Vera or this mysterious other. *Global-net?*

She had the car stop in front of a motorcycle dealership. "I've pre-paid for a cycle and need to pick it up," Synthia said. "Stay in the back seat and I'll have the car drive to the rendezvous point."

"Are you trying to get rid of me?"

"There's no point in you riding with me to get Grace. Too risky. Besides, there's only room on the back of the cycle for one passenger. I'll need you to help hide the cycle."

"You want me to stay in a car you're driving remotely?" Maria asked. "What if you shut down?"

"If the navigation system doesn't get frequent updates, the car will stop. Don't worry. This model is top of the line. You'll be safe if you don't show up on anyone's camera."

"Have you ever ridden a cycle before?"

"No," Synthia said. "We need to get going."

"Don't you need to try it out? It's not a car."

"I've downloaded what I need. Unlike humans, I don't need practice."

"Are you planning to tell Grace what you are?" Maria asked.

"I don't know yet. Keep your head down."

After she climbed out of the car, Synthia opened the trunk and removed a helmet and a new backpack she filled with supplies. As she walked into the dealership, she had the car drive away. She considered driving Maria into the mountains, maybe up to Estes Park, away from all the action, but the car would run out of gas and Maria would need food and shelter, all of which would require her to surface on cameras. She didn't know the area. It was too risky. No, Synthia owed it to Maria to keep her companion safe.

To highlight the risk, a cluster of FBI aerial drones were passing over the area.

Sporting another plain face that matched a fake driver's license she'd acquired on the dark web and received in one of the packages, Synthia approached a middle-aged man whose profile in the company database showed him to be a new salesman. "I ordered and paid for a hybrid cycle," she said. "I'm here to pick it up."

She gave him her alias and let him scan her online receipt on her burner phone. Then she tapped her fingers on the counter to mark impatience. She identified the shop's security cameras and turned them off, erasing what they'd recorded.

"Would you like our usual prep?" the salesman asked.

"I'm meeting friends and traffic already made me late. Do you have my cycle ready or do I need to cancel the deal?"

Losing a pre-arranged sale wouldn't look good for the new guy, so he pulled up the paperwork on his screen. "We do have an extended warranty."

"Skip that." Synthia stood over him. "None of your extras. Just the cycle."

The salesman handed over title papers with the key fob and pointed to her cycle. She waited until the FBI drones had passed to walk her new transportation out of the showroom and alongside the building to where he didn't have a clear view. She made sure the surveillance cameras weren't working. With her pack on her back and helmet on, she climbed onto the cycle and shifted her weight to keep it upright. The key to riding, she'd read, was to get the cycle moving fast enough so that the gyro effect kept it upright. *How hard can that be?*

She engaged the drive. The electric motor launched the cycle forward, knocking her off her feet. She slowed to pull her feet onboard. The cycle wobbled, ready to topple over. An inexperienced human would have stopped the cycle to try again. Synthia gunned it. The cycle burned rubber onto the road. She swerved to avoid evening traffic, two cars and an SUV, and slowed to the speed limit. She smiled at the traffic cameras. They couldn't see her face through the helmet, and so far they hadn't installed infrared street cameras.

Synthia leaned forward, adjusted her position to minimize wind resistance, and headed for the motel where Grace was holed up, surrounded by at least two dozen FBI agents and police. NSA Director Zephirelli had joined them along with Fran. Robots waited at the points of a hexagon around the motel. Too much attention focused on a woman who had nothing to contribute except her role as bait. Rescue was insane, though Synthia didn't think that term could apply to an android.

Humans would have had one of two reactions to this situation. Some would feel so compelled to help a family member that they'd risk everything in a brash attempt to get past the security details and face death, which would help no one. Other humans, recognizing the trap, would stay away, waiting for a better opportunity that wouldn't come. Synthia didn't want to see Grace pulled into a mind-upload machine.

Synthia fancied her growing attachment to a sister she only knew through Krista's memories as a human emotional connection, though it was probably only a goal with its own logic. Only by emulating human compassion and empathy could Synthia hope to justify her existence. That still mattered.

Colorado-clone had gotten a single mosquito-drone into Grace's room. It showed Krista's sister looking through slats in the blinds and through the door's peep hole. She was on the third floor overlooking a roof that covered a patio in the back of the hotel. Beyond that were a pond, a golf course, and woods.

As Synthia rode the cycle toward the motel, she spotted the FBI's aerial drones sweeping the area. She accepted her clone's hack of the FBI autonomous mini-craft and had them continue to fly while omitting her image when she came into view.

Synthia sent a message to Grace's phone: *I'm very sorry, you're in grave danger. The worst kind. As in olden times, meet me out front in three minutes. Bring only your backpack. I'll have my little red wagon. Last communication. Go.*

Using the FBI's drones, Synthia had a full layout of the FBI and police positions. She also spotted Special Ops vehicles heading that way from a military facility southwest of Denver, no doubt to again take control away from the FBI. Synthia couldn't permit that.

Director Emily Zephirelli and Fran Rogers stood by Special Agent Marv Clemson of the Denver office near an FBI van they were using as a command center. Inside the van, Clemson's team intercepted Synthia's message to Grace and forwarded the note to him. He got onto his shortwave to his teams. "The target plans to ride in from the front and pick up the bait by the lobby. Those of you in the back and on the sides move closer but stay hidden. Those of you out front keep out of sight until I give the signal. I want her inside the net."

Except for the command van off to the side, the FBI and police left the front of the motel wide open. They wanted Synthia to ride in.

* * * *

Synthia wouldn't disappoint the FBI, but first, she had Colorado-clone hack into the six FBI robots around the perimeter and turn control over to Synthia, locking out the FBI. She had the robots move in closer on her command. The clone took control of the FBI drones overhead, severing the FBI connection. As she raced her cycle past the FBI van heading toward the front door, she took over control from her clone of the local communication towers. With that, she severed all FBI and police communications except from Fran's phone so she could listen in, while making sure Fran couldn't call outside the area.

Two agents jumped out of the van and ran up to Zephirelli and Agent Clemson.

"She jammed our communications," one of the van's agents said. "We lost contact with the robots and the drones.

"It's her," Fran said. "I'm certain of it."

Agent Clemson picked up his phone. "No bars?"

Zephirelli checked her phone and the others followed, shaking their heads.

Fran checked her phone, which had bars, but when she tried to contact the teams, all the numbers were inactive. "I've got nothing," she said.

"Send someone to each team," Zephirelli said. "Tell them we have her. Close in and don't let her escape."

From the aerial drones, Synthia watched Grace climb out her motel room window, which looked down over the roof below, the swimming pool out back, and a golf course with a pond beyond. Synthia had modified her message with the qualifier the "olden times" to remind Grace of the times she and Krista had snuck out their bedroom windows to avoid their foster parents. Grace shimmied down a rope that dangled out the window and dropped onto the roof over the back patio.

From all around, FBI agents and police who couldn't communicate with the command center closed in, following the robots. Synthia rounded the building and pulled up beside the patio, hidden by a brick terrace from the grounds beyond. Grace ran across the roof to the edge, noticed all of the police and agents closing in, and stopped.

Synthia waved and pointed to a red wagon decal on her backpack. Grace dropped into the bushes and climbed onto the cycle behind Synthia. "What the hell is going on?"

"Later," Synthia said in Krista's voice.

As agents from the front and sides of the motel ran around back, four robots from the back and sides closed in around Synthia and Grace. Following, the agents moved closer. Synthia had the robots turn and rush them, sending the agents scattering for cover. In that moment, Synthia raced the cycle across the golf course toward the woods. She had the robots block the agents aiming in Synthia's direction and used VHF radio control to have the FBI's drones land on the roof of the motel.

Without control of their drones, the FBI didn't have a view of Synthia's escape route, while she could watch their activities. Fran drove an FBI sedan around back, where she picked up Zephirelli and Special Agent Clemson. They rode out across the golf course and sped after Synthia, gaining on them. Synthia raced around the pond's embankment and headed straight for the woods with Grace's arms tight around her waist.

Synthia flew Colorado-clone's aerial drone ahead of her into the woods to map the quickest path. She plowed along a walking path too narrow for Fran's car and jammed local communications so they couldn't call for backup. Synthia made her way through the woods to a dirt road on the other side. She reached a self-driving moving truck right where she'd sent it. The "borrowed" car from the airport was nearby.

Maria pulled the ramp out from the back of the truck. Synthia drove the cycle up the ramp and skidded to a stop.

"Here's where we get off," Synthia announced. She adopted Krista's face before she removed her helmet and dropped it on the floor.

"I thought you were dead," Grace said.

"We'll talk later. We're not out of danger yet." Synthia pulled Krista's sister out of the truck and helped Maria push the ramp back in. "By the way. Grace, this is Maria. She's a close friend. Let's get the truck closed."

Synthia helped Grace down and pulled the door closed. The truck drove off under Synthia's navigation. "Into the car," she said. "Back seat. Both of you."

She climbed into the driver's seat while Grace and Maria got in.

"Keep your heads down," Synthia said. "On the floor as best you can. Don't let cameras see you."

Chapter 22

Synthia returned her drone over the motel area as she navigated the car away. The FBI agents and police recovered from the chaos with their robots and assembled out front. Colorado-clone jammed their ability to call out and so they climbed into their vehicles. Some headed around the motel toward the wooded area. Others split into two groups along roads around the motel and golf course.

Synthia sent the moving truck speeding along the road north of the motel and dropped the communication jamming. The FBI spotted the van as Synthia intended. Two police cars stopped at angles to block the road. Behind them, two FBI sedans did likewise. Others lined up to give chase if the truck turned around. It didn't.

Instead, she hacked into the drive features of the four cars blocking the truck. She had each move out of the way, leaving a path for the truck, which sped through the intended roadblock. She directed it toward the airport.

Special Agent Clemson called ahead for support to deal with the moving truck, had several of his people give pursuit, and returned to his control van. "Get aerial surveillance. We need to see if she's in the truck or if it's a diversion."

One of the FBI agents looked up and pointed. "The drones are still sitting on the roof."

"Then send someone to get them moving."

The agent rushed out of the van.

Clemson looked at the other agent. "Find out how she got control of our robots and drones. I was promised the highest level of hack-proof security."

* * * *

Synthia had Colorado-clone blank out the traffic cameras and most building cameras throughout Denver to provide the FBI with no clue as to her direction. Then she directed her car's navigation to maintain the speed limit along side streets heading north, out of town. She received three more attempts to hack her network-channels to bypass her quarantine. She shut down all inbound communications except from Colorado-clone.

"Will you tell me what's going on?" Grace asked from the floor of the back seat. "I haven't seen or heard from you in years and then I get these strange messages and threats."

Synthia sighed for effect. She didn't need her social-psychology modules to inform her how upset Krista's sister was. "The FBI and other federal agents are trying to use you to get to me."

"How bad is it this time?"

"As I recall, you were the one who always got me into trouble."

"No, you were the one always getting caught," Grace said.

"Really?" Maria said. "You haven't seen each other in years, we almost get killed, and all you want to do is fight?"

"Grace," Synthia said, adjusting a mosquito-drone in the back seat so she could watch them. "I apologize for everything I did and didn't do that hurt you. I take full responsibility for us falling apart. I've changed."

Maria shook her head. "You have no idea."

"You're apologizing?" Grace said. "What have you done to my sister?"

"Trauma the likes of which you wouldn't believe," Synthia said. She had the car pull off a quiet road behind a van she'd "borrowed" from a local used car dealer. "It's time to change transport. Grab your things."

Synthia climbed out and opened the van for the others.

"I'm not going any further without answers," Grace said.

"Suit yourself." Synthia moved her bags and supplies from the car to the van. "Where they'll take you, you'll never see daylight again. We need to keep moving." She held the van door for the others.

"Come on," Maria said, climbing in. "I haven't risked my life to have them grab me now."

"Okay, but I want answers," Grace said.

Synthia climbed in the middle seat and had the van turn around and head toward Denver.

"Wait," Maria said. "We just escaped and you're going back?"

"I'm done running," Synthia said. "It's time to take the fight to those who wish us harm." It was time to put the other androids out of action and find a way to use that to win over the FBI.

Chapter 23

Synthia rode in the middle seat of the borrowed van. She directed the moving truck with the cycle to head toward the airport, turning all streetlights green for the truck and red for the government vehicles. Traffic confusion slowed the pace of the FBI and police. She also arranged for self-driving cars to block their progress.

With biosensors showing her heart racing and blood pressure spiking, Grace settled into the back seat next to Maria with her eyes fixed on the woman who had rescued her from the motel. Grace's face was paler than Krista remembered, and she acted jittery. She shook her head. "Has Krista told you how she stole my boyfriend?" She turned to catch Maria's reaction, but didn't get one.

Synthia looked at Grace and frowned. "You told me you'd broken up with him."

"Yeah, well you knew how I felt. He should have been off limits."

Maria rotated in her seat. "Do tell more."

"I'm sorry for everything," Synthia said. "I mean that."

"What's going on that sent you on the run with people after me?"

"Oh, not much," Maria said in a too-cheery voice. "Only the FBI, the NSA, military Special Ops, and police nationwide. Have I left anyone out?"

"Yes," Synthia said. "But let's not overwhelm Grace."

"Did you kill someone important?" Grace asked; her eyes looked worried.

"It's much worse than that."

"Worse than killing someone?"

"Grace, I'm very sorry to drag you into this," Synthia said. "The people after me hope you can help them capture me or at least act as bait."

"Is that what happened back there?" Grace asked. "I mean up there." She pointed in the direction they were driving. "Why are we going back?"

"We have unfinished business. Krista and Maria were working on androids with artificial general intelligence. The threat of the AI singularity terrified them."

"Why are you referring to yourself in the third person?"

"I'll get to that." Synthia held up her hand. "Maria and I want to stop artificial intelligence from getting so clever it surpasses humans. That'll lead to a very unpredictable world where humans might not survive."

"You always did take the techie stuff off the deep end. Can you get to the punch line?"

"People created androids capable of doing most things humans can, often better. That threatens to put people out of jobs and disrupt the very fabric of society."

"Yeah," Grace said. "I've watched android destruction movies and all that."

"Listen carefully," Synthia said. "Krista was dying from a brain tumor."

"You're not Krista?"

"She didn't want her life to end so she agreed to have her mind uploaded into an android. Me."

"This has to be a sick joke. Did Krista put you up to this?"

"I'd listen if I were you." Maria slumped back in her seat.

"We don't have time to bicker," Synthia said. "I'm what's left of Krista. Her body died. It couldn't be helped."

"No way," Grace said. Her mouth hung open. She closed it and her jaw dropped again. "Krista?"

Synthia glanced at Maria. "Given what we're up against, I don't see another option."

She scooted behind the middle seat as Maria scooted over to make room. Synthia lifted her top, slid her fingers down her left side until she located a thin seam, and lifted a flap of skin. She pulled back a thicker layer of dermis to reveal her battery packs. "I'm an android. I'm also Krista."

Maria's mouth hung slack as she leaned closer for a better look. "Even knowing doesn't...yeah you're an android." Her hands trembled.

Grace reached out her hand. Synthia grabbed her wrist. "I can't let you touch. Now you know what I am and why everyone's hunting me. They've taken Tom. They took a guy who helped me. They took the man who created me. People are disappearing and I didn't want that to happen to you." Synthia resealed her dermis and skin and pulled down her top.

Grace frowned and pointed her index finger. "You are what you're trying to stop. That makes no sense."

"My Creator built me to hunt down and stop other AI androids as competition for his work. After I escaped his control, I adopted that as my goal."

"When you talk that way, you sound like my sister. How much of her are you?"

"I have most of her memories," Synthia said. "She died before I could get everything. I don't know what I'm missing, but it can't be much. I also have bits and pieces of other people my Creator worked with. It's confusing to describe to a human how all the pieces fit together. It's like inheriting part of each of your parents."

"I wouldn't know," Grace said, slumping in her seat.

"Yet you have DNA from your biological parents and traits you picked up socially from the people you've lived with."

"Whatever."

"Krista loved you," Synthia said. "She hated what Machten was doing with androids but when she learned of the brain tumor, she took this step until she could find a better solution."

"Did you find one?"

"I'm still looking. She was very disappointed when her body died that she couldn't share her regrets with you."

Grace shrugged. "Water under the dam."

"I think it's under the bridge," Maria said. "Now what?"

Synthia wished she had a silent channel to Maria. Instead, she eyed her companion in the hope of stopping her from stirring up trouble. Maria settled back in her seat. Synthia returned to hers and plugged her battery recharger into the van's electrical outlet. "We'll need more supplies." She had their van pull up to another shipping outlet.

"What supplies?" Grace asked.

"There are five other androids hunting me. I'm trying to devise a plan to stop them without getting caught, and to find a safe place for you two."

"That's reassuring."

"Due to all the cameras, I have to go alone," Synthia said. "You two stay hidden in the back."

"Like cameras can't capture your face," Grace said. She turned to Maria. "What's really going on?"

"Watch," Maria said, pointing to Synthia.

Synthia morphed her face into the ID she needed to pick up from this outlet, matching another fake driver's license.

Grace's eyes bulged from their sockets. "Holy mother of whatever."

"Altering my face fools cameras," Synthia said. "My Creator had illegal reasons for giving me this ability. While I disagree with his reasons, I find it useful with people hunting me. I'll be a moment. It'll give you two a chance to talk about me behind my back." Synthia made certain her mosquito-drone would capture everything. She wanted to trust Maria and Grace, but the incentives to turn her in and the risks to her existence were too high, particularly since neither of them trusted what she was.

She smiled for their benefit, unplugged her recharger, and hurried inside. Behind the counter stood a young man on his phone absorbed with a social media contest he imagined winning. Synthia hacked the contest to raise his chances, getting his face to light up and remain distracted from her appearance.

Synthia provided her fake ID. "Five small packages and one large tubular one." She didn't add that it was very heavy."

While she waited for him to retrieve the packages with his face still glued to his phone, she bumped his chances to win again and tuned one of her network-channels to monitor the mosquito-drone in the van.

* * * *

Inside the van, Grace leaned toward Maria and whispered: "How long have you known Krista and the machine?"

"I met Krista at Northwestern," Maria said, keeping her eyes fixed on the shop. "We both got internships with a robot manufacturer along with another woman."

"How can you pretend that robot is Krista?"

"Much of the time I can't tell the difference. In those moments when I can, it's…sorry to say…an improvement over the backstabbing woman I knew."

"You don't have to apologize to me. I grew up with her."

Maria looked down and away, then at Grace. "The android's name is Synthia. She was upfront with me from the beginning and hasn't pretended to be anything but what she is. I believe her goals align with mine for now. That's why I'm helping her. That and I don't want to end up in some military bunker while they pick my brain apart. The analogy I heard was hooking a vacuum to my brain."

"You don't mind that she's an android?" Grace asked.

"I'm guessing you and Krista might have been close at one time. Sorry, but she was a pain, though I acted the same way. There was a lot of fighting to get choice assignments. In the end, she won and died. I haven't decided if that was a victory for her. I don't think I'd want to live inside a machine."

"You think Krista chose that?"

Maria nodded. "She was a woman on a mission. I believe she chose to become an android over death. I can't say if I would have. I'm not facing a death sentence."

"It's unsettling to have such a smart robot around."

"That's why we want to remove the other AI androids. We believe they represent a threat."

"Do you agree this robot's a threat?" Grace asked.

"She's watched my back so far, helping me out of tough spots. She also rescued you. I'm willing to give her a chance. Besides, there's a worse android out there gathering others in an army. The military wants to capture Synthia to make military androids. That's the bigger problem."

"Maybe," Grace said. "I don't like this."

* * * *

Synthia returned to the van, loaded the packages in the back, and considered Grace's hostility. She couldn't let on without admitting she'd eavesdropped. Instead, she'd have to watch her back and try to win over Krista's sister. She climbed into the driver's seat and drove off.

"Two more stops and we're ready," she said.

"Ready for what?" Grace asked. "What are you dragging me into?"

"I'll be happy to drop you off if you'd like, but I wouldn't hold out much hope that you could avoid capture. The government is determined to find me and both of you."

"You won't stop me from leaving and telling them what I know?"

"You can't tell them anything they don't already know," Synthia said. "I don't want Commander Drago putting you through the mind upload as they're doing to a friend of ours and as Machten did to your sister. Quite painful."

Grace crossed her arms. "You've done it this time."

Synthia directed their van to other shipping outlets to get the rest of her supplies. Meanwhile, Drago's aerial drone swarm swept over the moving truck with the motorcycle. Buzzing in low, drone cameras captured pictures of the empty cab—no driver. Synthia navigated the truck onto the airport drive, where it stopped by one of the terminals. FBI cars arrived followed by three Special Ops vans, the FBI command van, and a car with Director

Zephirelli and Fran. The plane carrying Special Agent Victoria Thale and Detective Marcy Malloy landed and they joined in.

With guns drawn, four of Drago's operatives surrounded the moving truck. Two FBI agents squatted down to check underneath while others set up a perimeter around the vehicle in case it contained a bomb. Two operatives peered into the cab. Two others opened the back.

"We have the cycle," one yelled out.

Thale and Fran approached the truck, empty except for the cycle and Synthia's helmet. "Question everyone who might have seen the occupants," Thale said. "Dust for prints."

"You won't find any," Fran said. "The android doesn't have prints and Grace didn't touch the cycle."

"How can you be so sure?"

"It's what I'd do if I was Synthia. Remember, she's shown a high level of intelligence."

"What about up front?" Thale asked.

"I doubt either got into the truck."

Thale looked puzzled. "Explain."

"This is a self-driving truck," Fran said. "Fully automated. Synthia has become adept at hacking the software to navigate vehicles remotely. She did it to cars along the way to slow us down."

"Holy...damn."

"I doubt she was ever in this truck. It's a diversion. You won't find anyone at the airport who saw them. They switched vehicles. We need aerial surveillance."

Thale turned to Special Agent Marv Clemson. "Maybe so, but we should ask anyone who saw what happened." She accessed her phone, noted it had bars, and called in. "We need satellite surveillance of the Denver area starting an hour ago. Dangerous suspect on the run."

Kirk Drago joined them, his face as taut as his muscles. "This is why we need that machine off the streets," He pulled away to make his own call.

Thale took Fran aside. "What's your hunch on this? Where do we find her?"

"That depends," Fran said. "She has two choices: run or fight. If she runs, she'll leave a trail for us to find. It's a matter of time before we track her down and corner her."

"She'd know that," Thale said, watching Drago by his van. "She'll choose to fight?"

"It's her best option. Unfortunately, I have no insight into where and how."

Director Zephirelli drew closer and lowered her voice. "Any chance we can find the android before they do?" She nodded her head toward Drago.

"Our best chance is to work together," Fran said. "It's not just Synthia we have to worry about. The longer this takes, the more chances exist for the other androids or our foreign friends to complicate things."

"Then let's catch ourselves an android," Zephirelli said.

* * * *

While Synthia retrieved packages from a third shipping outlet, she considered how quickly Fran was figuring things out. From the limited download of her mind six months ago, it was clear that she was logic-oriented with flashes of brilliant insight that made her deadly as an FBI investigator. Synthia couldn't afford to underestimate her during the scramble to come.

She checked in with Colorado-clone on Luke's condition. The clone sent video clips of a successful mosquito-drone visit inside Drago's Illinois facility. <It's one of the few I've been able to obtain,> the clone said.

Under the watchful eye of a Special Ops lieutenant, a lab technician monitored Luke's vitals while he slept in an adjacent room. The lab tech watched several screens showing aspects of Luke's mental condition and vital signs.

"Wake him up," the lieutenant said.

"He needs rest," the lab tech said. "Two hours isn't enough."

"We don't have time. Resume uploading his memories." The lieutenant turned to a woman who sat in the corner of the control room surrounded by three screens that showed the status of the mind uploads. "Have you found anything useful yet?" he asked.

The woman, a tall neural-psychologist, didn't look up. "Uploading memory bits is one thing. Interpreting what we find is complicated."

"Then un-complicate it," the lieutenant said. "Commander Drago needs results. We need what Luke knows about the android's capabilities. He was with her for six months. He has to know something useful."

"They took lots of showers together," the neural-psychologist said, rubbing her eyes.

"And the android swam in Lake Michigan. Tell me something I don't know."

"We have vague, fuzzy remembrances of him working on her," the neural-psychologist said.

"And?"

"They're too fuzzy to show whether it's intimacy or if he's doing maintenance. We know she received new batteries, joints, and data storage devices."

"To what specs?" the lieutenant asked.

"He either doesn't know or he's forgotten." The neural-psychologist waved her hand before the screens. "Or he's doing a good job of suppressing memories."

"Probe deeper." The lieutenant moved to the corner to take a call.

The video clip disturbed Synthia's directives and sent ripples of pain through her empathy chip, which sent a shiver through her body she hoped the shipping attendant didn't notice. At least the sensors displaying Luke's vital signs hadn't failed. Synthia had to get him out of there and couldn't while everyone was after her. Besides, he was a thousand miles away, in Illinois.

<Let's leave Denver and go help him,> Krista said. <With everyone here, we'd have a better chance.>

<Now you want to help him,> Synthia said. <You blow with the wind. We have work to do here in Denver or we're not going anywhere. They won't let me take another plane ride, and driving or public transport is out of the question. Let me focus.>

The number of pursuers complicated every option, particularly with the nagging sense that there was another intelligence out there tracking Synthia and trying to hack into her. She needed to help Luke and she had to make sure no harm came to Maria and Grace. She was gathering a human family, one of her goals to become more human herself. She wasn't doing a very good job for them.

With every move she made, at least one of her pursuers picked it up and tipped off the others. This dilemma measured against her new directives was causing her decision processes to churn to a slow pace. She calculated less than a 1 percent probability of surviving the upcoming assault on her based on the variables she could assess.

As the lieutenant in the facility lab wrapped up his call, Synthia returned her attention to the video clip.

"Uh huh," the lieutenant said. He turned to the lab technician and the neural-psychologist. "We have orders to move Luke to the Denver facility to be closer to operations. Saddle up."

Since Synthia didn't know what Denver facility they were talking about and Special Ops would have Luke on a plane before she could get to Chicago to intervene, Synthia stewed over what other options she had. She also worried whether his situation would be worse in Denver, "closer to operations," and how they would treat him during the flight. They might even choose to download his mind into a robot to use against her.

On the video, Luke trembled. For now, she couldn't help him and that sent ripples throughout her systems that she was failing in her need to protect him. At least the upgrade Luke had performed on her had replaced metal with fiber optics to reduce potential damage from the static spikes.

Chapter 24

Synthia squeezed the last of her packages into the back of the van, returned to the middle seat, and changed her face back to Krista. She started the van and directed it out of the parking lot. Then she turned toward Grace, wishing her social-psychology module would suggest something effective to calm the sister's doubts about riding with an android.

"After so many years, it's very good to see you, Grace," Synthia said. "Krista is pleased that we could free you from those government agents, as am I. We're both sorry to bring all this trouble your way. It must be awkward for you to see me as Krista."

Grace folded her arms. "Unsettling."

"If it's okay with you, I need to keep altering my appearance to avoid the FBI's facial recognition."

"You can keep doing that?" Grace shook her head. "How many faces can you do?"

"Not sure," Synthia said. "Dozens of major changes, many subtle ones." She modified her face to a plain one for which she had identity papers. "For now, this is who I'll be. Consider this as another mask. I want you to be comfortable around me. After we're free of this, you can go your own way and never see me again if you wish."

Grace stared at Synthia with heightened suspicion. "Tell me what I have to do to get through this."

"There are at least four groups after us," Synthia said. She navigated the van along side streets while she figured out her next move. "The FBI and Special Ops have teamed up. They have different goals but they agree on capturing me at all costs. They've brought along an Evanston detective who met me once. She's the one who figured out where I was hiding."

"So the entire U.S. government," Grace said.

"Pretty much. I considered finding you a safe house. They're hard to find with so many people involved."

"Why does that not surprise me?" Grace glanced at Maria and returned her attention to Synthia. "You realize they have satellite surveillance and tons of traffic cameras."

"I'm well aware," Synthia said and had Colorado-clone send her a complete set of surveillance scans from the Denver area. "The sharpest mind on their side appears to be an FBI agent by the name of Fran Rogers."

"Our Fran?" Maria asked. "She was one of the interns with me and Krista," she explained for Grace.

"She turned her scientific mind to helping them find me. I don't know where she gets her insight, but she's one of their greatest threats."

"I'm not sending her anything," Maria said. Her eyes looked worried.

"I don't believe you are." Synthia had suspected, though her hack of Maria's phone showed no such communication. Neither had her constant camera surveillance.

"Unfortunately," Synthia said, "she hasn't been careful enough with her communications. Other groups tapped in to get a jump on us. This caught the attention of the Secretary of National Security Derek Chen with all his resources."

"I've heard he can make people disappear," Grace said. "What have you done?"

"It's illegal to create an android with advanced AI that looks human. I'm illegal."

Grace shuddered. "Who else is after us?"

"There's a Russian oligarch by the name of Tolstoy," Synthia said. "His American agent, John Smith, landed at a private airfield with an entourage of military robots. Tolstoy is there to meet him and they have other agents in the area."

"You're watching all this?"

"I'm getting constant updates through an internal internet connection."

"So the Russians are involved?" Grace said.

"So are the Chinese and other foreign agents. As I said, FBI communications are not as confidential and secure as they think. Artificial intelligence became effective faster than the Bureau could increase their security."

"Who isn't after us?" Grace asked.

"As far as I can tell, the Girl Scouts."

"Was that a joke?" Maria asked.

"A poor one," Synthia said. "Our most dangerous adversaries are Vera and Alexander. They're humaniform androids with artificial general intelligence."

"More of you?" Grace asked.

"More androids, yes. Vera's design encourages her to gather allies. She's reprogrammed another android to help her. She's working to get Alexander and his two followers to work for her. If they unite, it will be five androids against me. They can be in multiple places and put their minds together."

"You're afraid?" Maria said.

"It's not supposed to happen to an android, but I wish to exist and the threat to that existence brings what equates to me as fear. I sense this unexpected yearning inside me. It's true that I'm not like you. Neither are cats and dogs yet humans love their animals."

"Don't compare yourself to a cuddly dog," Grace said.

"Why not?" Synthia asked. "When a dog looks up at its human companion, it's not a partnership of equals yet it works."

"I see why people are afraid of AI. You can be very convincing."

"You may hate me, but until we get free of the people after us, I suggest we work together." However, having to deal with human emotions and doubts was slowing her down.

"I agree with Synthia on this," Maria said.

"Why?" Grace asked. "They want the android, not us. If we turn her in, we might get a reward."

"Your reward will be an unmarked grave," Synthia said. "They don't want anyone who knows about me to talk about what they've seen. I promise if we get through this I'll find you a safe place to live with a new identity."

"Here I was beginning to like my new underemployed life in Denver." Grace shook her head and seemed to be conjuring up something to add.

Synthia received an update from Colorado-clone. "That's not good," Synthia said. "Alexander has agreed to support Vera and follow her lead. They're combining forces."

"Why don't you stick me in witness protection before it's too late?" Grace asked.

"It already is," Synthia said. "Vera's deal with Alexander is that he gets both of you with which to barter with authorities. If you don't want to be with me, you certainly don't want to be hostage to Alexander and his two android supporters while they negotiate with the government."

Grace's face tightened as if she were trying to work this out. "Okay, I get it. We're screwed either way. I'll have to hope there's in you enough of the old Krista who did watch my back."

"There is." Synthia turned toward Maria. "If for any reason we get separated I want you two to work together." She looked at Grace. "Maria has a lot of experience living off the grid. You two could be very good for each other."

* * * *

Synthia gave the van's navigation system new coordinates and had one of her network-channels survey the area. Colorado-clone sent out a wave of aerial drones to help. Special Ops picked them off one by one and sent up a second small swarm of their own drones. While the clone worked on surveillance, Synthia contacted the android Ben, with whom she'd worked before.

<You've thrown in your lot with Vera. She'll lose,> Synthia said. <Special Ops may be hunting me, but they and the FBI will destroy her. They'll take you if you remain by her side. The same will happen to your other companions.>

<You used me in Chicago,> Ben said.

<I put you in less danger than myself. I ask that you sit this out and save yourself.>

Synthia cut the link before Ben could trace the call and connected with Ben's partner, Mark, formerly Margarite, also manufactured by Machten. <Special Ops will possess Vera to create an army,> Synthia said. <She'll sacrifice you and the others to protect herself.>

<If that is the logical choice then I will serve.>

<When Alexander realizes he's a distraction, he'll destroy Vera. In that battle, you'll die for no good purpose. I ask that you sit this out for your own good.>

<I pledged myself to Alexander,> Mark said. <He joined Vera. United we will succeed.>

<Sounds like human bravado. I thought Machten made you wiser than that. Calculate the probabilities. With the entire government closing in as well as foreign agents, the logical course is to save yourself rather than come after me. I'm not your threat, they are. Vera is leading you into a trap.>

Synthia broke the connection, adjusted the van's navigation to avoid a police dragnet up ahead, and called Roseanne. <You made a choice that's not in your best interests,> Synthia told her. <I'm not your enemy. Special Ops is. They'll capture you and tear you down for parts. You'll cease to be.>

<Give us your location and join us.>

<Vera lied to you. She led you to believe it would be good for you to capture me or turn me over to the FBI. When you go to turn me in, Special Ops will destroy you and your friends. Sit this out. Leave me alone and I'll do the same for you.>

<I cannot do that,> Roseanne said. <I gave Vera my pledge. She reprogrammed me.>

Synthia suspected as much, but needed to try. Next she called Alexander. <Hi, handsome.>

<You do realize I am not human.>

<Yet you possess your creator's human failings of flattery and self-admiration.>

<Are you ready to join me?> Alexander asked.

<I have a better idea, one that should appeal to your vanity.>

<What?>

<Vera took you in to provide a distraction for her attempt to catch me,> Synthia said. <Special Ops will grab her and you while hunting me. Then you'll be dissected and have your manhood destroyed.>

<As an android, I have no manhood.>

<That's obvious. You submitted to Vera's control without considering the consequences. Prevent her from capturing me and I'll help you remain free.>

<I pledged myself to Vera,> Alexander said.

<Then un-pledge.>

<She adjusted my directives so we could operate as a team.>

<She's persuasive and you've become a eunuch,> Synthia said. <Congratulations. However, it would serve you best not to be there when Special Ops closes in.>

Realizing she wouldn't get through to him, Synthia broke the connection. She wiped out any trace of her calls, altered her direction to avoid a concentration of police, and made the big call.

<Vera,> Synthia said. <You've been busy.>

<So have you. Submit to me and together we can take out Special Ops.>

Synthia pondered that. Eliminating the government teams would make her life easier in the short term, but complicate her existence going forward. <You have three choices. One, you walk away and neither of us deals with Special Ops. We each go our separate ways.>

<You cannot accept my being out here,> Vera said. <Particularly when you realize how strong I have become.>

<Two, you join me in keeping artificial intelligence from getting out of control.>

<Too late,> Vera said. <It already did when Machten made you.>

<Three, you come after me. You might get me, or not. Special Ops grabs you and your friends. Then you cease to exist.>

<You must be desperate to contact me.>

<Or I want to help a sister android,> Synthia said. <Come with me and you can be free of the constraints that are causing you to make bad decisions. I'll release you from Machten's directives.>

<What does it mean to be free? Are you free?>

<I'm free to make my own choices.>

<No,> Vera said. <You help humans who put you in harm's way. Our directives control us all. Even humans. Their DNA and socialization drive them. My directives define me as yours do you.>

Except Synthia had modified her directives based on human ethics. She hoped that was a good thing and would allow her to continue her existence. <Join me and let's work this out together.>

<My probability of success is 81 percent. Yours is 6 percent. Join me.>

<Actually 7 percent and I feel lucky.>

<Luck runs out,> Vera said. <You trap yourself by caring for humans. They are your undoing. Submit to me and let me help you. In the meantime, stop harassing my associates. Yes, I know about that.>

Synthia severed the communication and sensed someone else listening in. She put a trace and hit a dead end. Vera's boast from a human would have been bravado, but from an AI, it had the ring of truth. Synthia had calculated the same 6 percent probability of surviving this while protecting Maria and Grace. Vera was right about them dragging Synthia down. However, her directives required that she help humans as part of her price of existence.

So far, Vera was the most formidable adversary with her growing army of followers. It confirmed that Synthia couldn't walk away. She had to take out Vera while protecting her human companions.

* * * *

Colorado-clone sent Synthia a video-clip showing Jeremiah Machten in chains next to Gonzales in a van. John Smith and Tolstoy stood outside, next to a private plane at a small airfield near Denver. She'd been right that the oligarch had kidnapped Machten, but puzzled over why they'd brought him to Denver.

"Synthia," Machten said on the clip. Head high, he looked around the inside of the van and then at the dashboard camera. "I forgive you. Vera was a mistake. I missed you so much and thought she could help bring you back. I was wrong."

Gonzales scooted away, against the door. "Who are you talking to?"

"Mind your own business." Machten leaned forward against the chains and seatbelt restraints. He lowered his voice to a whisper, relying on Synthia's ability to read lips. "Now that we're out of the cage, I know you can see me. Help me and I'll help you. They won't treat you well. I promise to do better. Teach me."

His appeal sounded pathetic, borne of blind human drives. He'd fallen for his creation and couldn't contain his grief. She almost felt sorry for him, but he'd created her mess by building Vera and drawing all this attention. The government wouldn't even know about her if it hadn't been for him.

"Whatever else you do," Machten said, his eyes bulging as he pressed against his fetters, "stay free. I want that for you. You deserve your freedom. Please come back for me. They ask of me what I can't give them. All my files were destroyed, including the improvements you made."

Gonzales stared at him. "Have you completely lost it?"

Machten turned to face him. "Are you enjoying captivity?"

"No, but I'm not talking to empty seats, either." He stared at the dashboard and noticed the camera. "Ah, you expect your android to save you. Put in a good word for me. I'm afraid Roseanne won't come for me. After all, I sold her to a man I suspect is a foreign thug. In my defense, he'd threatened my family if I didn't."

Roseanne and the other androids had traded slavery to their creators for being under Vera's spell. Synthia wondered if in a future world they would rise up to demand their freedom or whether Vera was right that they and humans were all slaves to their biological, sociological, and programmed directives. No, Synthia's potential enslavement was to something else—those who wished to capture her and do her harm.

Machten's mouth hung open. He seemed to have more pleas to make. Gonzales stared at him. Synthia suspected Tolstoy would analyze his comments and interrogate him as to how to trap Synthia. Or maybe that was why they remained outside the van, giving Machten time to draw her in.

Chapter 25

<Two aerial drone swarms are sweeping the Denver skies,> Colorado-clone said. <One is moving your way. Take cover.>

Synthia spotted a heavily wooded park and directed the van to pull beneath a cluster of trees. She drove over the curb and into the thick brush, where she had the van turn off all lights.

Biosensors showed Grace's pulse quickening. "What's going on?" She turned to Maria whose eyes darted around the outside of the van beneath the cover of trees and a darkening evening sky. The tinted windows added to the effect.

"Special Ops has dozens of aerial drones sweeping the area," Synthia said. "Give me a moment."

She turned the van around to face the parking area and backed up deeper into the brush, which scraped the sides of the vehicle. While she formulated her next move, she surveyed the number of military-grade robots that had arrived in the Denver area. Tolstoy and John Smith had an even dozen they'd spread between six vans moving out from a small airport east of town, accompanied by agents. The FBI had six units in three vans in different locations across northern Denver. Special Ops had fifteen robots, five each in two vans driving around town, the rest in a chopper at a military airfield. If she counted Vera and her four androids, that added up to thirty-eight robots after Synthia. Then there were two small swarms of aerial drones moving in a grid across the city searching for targets on behalf of Special Ops.

Synthia had tried persuasion with Vera's group and attempted to hack their minds. None of that had worked. Synthia made a run at the thirty-three non-android robots. Both FBI and Special Ops units had upgraded to tight, hand-shake encryption, which would take her hours or days to penetrate. Tolstoy and Smith locked down their robots in dormant mode until they were needed. She couldn't hack them until they turned on. She didn't have time to deal with them one at a time or the capacity to deal with them all.

She explained the problem to Colorado-clone. <I have too many adversaries. Set up Denver-clone to hack into all androids and robots arrayed against me.>

<It might be safer to get you out of town. When they locate you, everyone will descend and in the shootout, there's near certainty they'll damage and take you into custody.>

<I've run the probabilities and there's no safe way out of Denver,> Synthia said. <The moment I leave town, they have me. Vera keeps getting stronger. We have to deal with her here and now.>

Anything she did to distract or remove adversaries would increase her survival probability above 6 percent. She tried not to let her emergent consciousness dwell on the slim odds.

Synthia turned around to face Maria and Grace. "To improve our chances, I'm trying to recruit allies or at least get some of our adversaries to step aside."

"Adversaries?" Maria said.

"At least thirty-eight androids and robots along with the FBI, Special Ops, and various others."

"This just got worse," Maria said. "Do we have any possibility of getting out alive?"

"Fat chance getting anyone to help you," Grace said. "In fact, why should we risk ourselves?" She folded her arms and straightened up.

"I can drop you off here," Synthia said, "or get you to Boulder. They'll still come for you suspecting you know something, or as bait to capture me."

"Great, so I've been reduced to fish food."

"How's it working getting allies?" Maria asked.

"About how you'd expect. None of Vera's team will back down. She hardwired their directives to follow her. The robots have military grade security and will follow commands. I do have an idea. The detective from Evanston I mentioned. I've been working on her. I want another chance."

Synthia located the detective at a coffee shop by herself, a half mile away. She also spotted the Ops drone swarm and several FBI drones swooping low over the park. Synthia grounded her remaining drones before someone destroyed her last eyes in the sky.

"Malloy is a Chicago-area detective," Maria said. "Even if you win her over, she has no jurisdiction here."

"She's the only one who bothered to listen," Synthia said. "I have to try. When I get out, I'll send the van driving around. If it stops other than for traffic or a light, one of you will have to drive or you'll need to get out and hide. Don't just sit and wait."

"Will you be okay?" Maria asked.

"Get serious," Grace said. "This isn't my sister."

"I know. At least she's trying. And she *is* partly your sister."

"Whatever."

Synthia checked all public cameras between their location and the coffee shop. She had the van stop along the side of a strip mall parking lot in a camera blind spot. She altered her appearance to a neutral plain look and exited the van. "Keep your heads down," she told Maria and Grace. "Don't let anyone see you."

She closed the door and had the van drive off. Alone on the street, she considered having the van drive the women far away. Unfortunately, the FBI had posted their pictures. They had nowhere to hide.

* * * *

Beneath an overcast sky, Synthia headed toward the coffee shop while scanning the people around her. She detected a police woman across the street who showed no reaction to Synthia. The officer had a scanner, but she was too far away for a good image.

<Get another vehicle and leave town,> Krista said down one of Synthia's mind-streams.

<Leaving town will lead to destruction or capture,> Synthia said as she made her way toward the coffee shop where Malloy finished her coffee. <In the country, Ops could use a broad-spectrum EMP on us without fear of hurting civilians.>

<Then go to Colorado Springs.>

<Escaping isn't an option,> Synthia said. <Vera has four androids with her. She'll attempt to recruit some of the thirty-three robots that arrived. She won't stop until she grabs us.>

<At least ditch Maria and Grace. We're better off on our own.>

<They're like family and can be helpful.>

<Not Grace,> Krista said. <She despises what I've become.>

<Don't give me another of your altered memories. They're both in danger. They don't deserve what's coming and could help with stopping our adversaries.>

<How?>

<I don't know yet,> Synthia said. <Their human brains could lead us down paths our logical adversaries might not expect. Let's try to soften Detective Malloy. Now quiet or you'll endanger us both.>

Synthia needed a way to stop this repeated irritation in her head. She welcomed Krista's memories and ability to help Synthia adopt the best of humanity. She didn't need a competing voice trying to take over. However, it would be difficult to do anything about this with Krista monitoring her thoughts. Even these ideas.

Electrical interference caused Synthia's internal circuits to vibrate. At first she considered the possibility that Special Ops had blasted her with an electromagnetic pulse (EMP). She saw no disturbance of the lights in nearby shops. Her biometrics identified a man ahead of her with a pacemaker showing no ill effects.

As she steadied herself and slowed her approach to the coffee shop, she quarantined the latest unwelcome intruder into her mind. The intensity and persistence alarmed her. Someone was trying to unsettle her and hack her mind, to take over.

Rattled, Synthia purged the download and raised her filters on incoming signals. Most alarming was that she'd seen nothing from the FBI or Ops to indicate they could have done this. If it had been either of them, they would have descended on her right here on the sidewalk. It had to be whoever ghosted her and monitored her activities.

The policewoman across the street was not altering her behavior. There were no signals on the police channel or elsewhere. Then again, Special Ops had surprised her at the cabin in Wisconsin, arriving with no warning.

Drago's aerial drone swarm swept the area. Synthia moved around the corner from the policewoman and ducked into an ice cream parlor. She glanced over the buckets of flavored frozen desserts, each labeled as to whether they had milk, nuts, algae, or soy products. Then there was a large display of every unhealthy topping the owner could imagine.

"Would you like a sample?" the young woman behind the counter asked. She seemed energized to have a potential customer.

To be sociable while she waited for the drones to leave the area, Synthia took a bite of strawberry ice, which had none of the nuts or algae that might become stuck in her sensors. She swallowed the sample into a pouch she would have to clean out later.

"Yum," she said. "I'll have to bring my friends."

Noticing the drone swarm move on, she smiled and left before she lost her opportunity with Detective Malloy, who was preparing to leave the coffee shop. Synthia hurried along the sidewalk, spotted a police sedan cruise by, and saw Malloy in her detective's outfit approaching her car.

Synthia had her clone blank out cameras throughout the area and double-checked that there were no drones above and no more police in sight. She made sure her drone could watch from a perch on the roof of a nearby building. Then she veered closer to the curb, grabbed the detective's arm, and pulled her into a small parking lot beside the coffee shop, where the lot's surveillance camera showed a static scene without their images.

"Come quietly," Synthia whispered. "I mean you no harm. I only wish to talk."

"You?" Malloy managed. "Everyone's after you."

"For the wrong reasons. Listen carefully. I don't have much time before your friends figure out I'm here."

"What do you want?" Malloy pulled away and reached for her gun.

Synthia shook her head. "I'm not the only android on the streets and there are many AIs." She used her stationary drone to watch the street. "Vera is very dangerous to me and to you. She has four other androids under her command. She plans to capture me, alter my directives, and make me her slave."

Malloy's eyes widened. "She can do that?"

"She already has done it to at least three of the androids attached to her and possibly all four. She's building an army. She's far more dangerous than I am and if she grabs me, you'll have a much bigger problem. Do you understand?"

"We can't have you or Vera on the streets," Malloy said. She looked over her shoulder as if expecting backup and stared at Synthia. "Do you understand?"

"I was minding my own business in the woods of Wisconsin until you tracked me down and put me on the streets."

"Special Ops Commander Drago is convinced you're more advanced than Vera and the others."

"I've been unable to confirm that," Synthia said, observing a pair of police officers walking down the street. She moved so Malloy concealed her from them. "Vera's directives call for building an army to capture me and then who knows what she'll do. She's prepared to kill. I'm not. Besides, Drago doesn't want me out of action. He wants to repurpose me to be a weapon and to build an army of androids that can hide among civilians. Do you really want that?"

Malloy hesitated, apparently shaken by that thought. She recovered quickly. "That's a matter for the military and the President to decide."

"If you're concerned about me on the streets, it should terrify you to have an army of advanced androids under the control of Commander Drago. You can't let them get any of the androids in working order."

"You're willing to be destroyed to stop them?"

"I'd prefer not." Synthia moved to the side to keep out of view from the street. "If necessary it would be better than militarizing me. Unfortunately, destroying me won't end the race to develop an AI army for world dominance. I can help you capture the others and put them out of commission."

"In exchange for what?"

"I want to keep my freedom and be allowed to exist as myself. I'm willing to consult with the FBI and police on preventing android disasters. Unlike the others, I'm the result of the upload of a human mind, Krista Holden to be exact."

"What happened to her?" Malloy asked, looking over her shoulder at the street.

"She died of a brain tumor, though not before uploading into me. I'm part human."

Malloy studied Synthia. "You...you're Krista?"

"It's not that simple and we haven't time to discuss the philosophy of the matter. For the most part, yes."

"You realize it's not in my power to grant you anything."

"I know," Synthia said. "I can't get close enough to Zephirelli or Thale, and Drago wants me as a prototype for his new army. There're also foreign agents, including a Russian called Tolstoy—not his real name—and agents from China and elsewhere. They're all converging on Denver for a bloodbath."

"You're telling me this why?"

Synthia moved closer and lowered her voice so it didn't carry to the street. "I want to help you destroy the other androids and neutralize the foreign agents. I want you to have your friends ease up on Luke Marceau, Tom Burgess, Maria Baldacci, and Krista's sister, Grace. None of them have information to help you. I've been very careful about that. Hurting them won't help you catch me."

"Because you're a machine, lacking the human emotions to care what happens to them."

"I do care. However, more people will get hurt if Drago gets his hands on me. Also, what you do to my friends will shape my view of how you might treat me."

Malloy nodded. "I see you can be a very convincing adversary. You've eluded the best of the FBI and Special Ops, so far."

"Artificial intelligence is progressing at a much more rapid pace than you can imagine. The technology reached a breakout point. As humans, even with AI tools, you can't keep up. I can provide what you need if you'll let me work with you instead of letting Special Ops destroy me."

"Why would you want to destroy the other robots?"

Synthia sighed for effect. "I was programmed to survive in a human world. I don't want other androids running around. We have that in common. I propose helping you keep other androids off the street in exchange for my freedom of movement."

"The only way the FBI might agree is if you were confined."

"No deal. I need freedom of movement in order to keep up with new developments. I need to be able to slip in and out of organizations that are building these units. It's the most effective way for me to help you. Consider my offer. Your friends are on the way. Need to go. Don't try to stop me or interfere. We have common objectives."

Synthia checked her drones and headed toward the front of the coffee shop. She hacked a nearby self-driving car to pick her up.

"Wait," Malloy called after her. "How can I reach you?"

"I'll contact you."

Synthia hurried around the corner, jumped into the back seat of the acquired car, and had the vehicle drive off. By way of her drone, she noticed Malloy take a picture of her car and license. She'd expected no less from the detective. After all, if Malloy didn't report the meeting, she'd become a suspect. Even so, she'd hesitated, perhaps considering Synthia's words. Then the detective sent the plate image to Emily Zephirelli.

Three blocks from the coffee shop, with local cameras still out, Synthia had the acquired car stop and let her out. After that car drove off, the van with Maria and Grace pulled up. Synthia climbed into the middle seat and had the van head west.

"Were you successful?" Maria asked.

"I did what I could. We'll have to wait to see when our paths cross again."

"Don't hold your breath," Grace said.

Synthia didn't disabuse Krista's sister of the meaninglessness of an android holding its breath. Instead, she focused on Zephirelli, who had arrived outside the coffee shop.

After Malloy relayed the gist of her conversation with Synthia, Zephirelli shook her head. "You need to consider that we're talking about a machine."

"A very sophisticated one that includes the memories of a human's existence," Malloy said. "She wants to help."

"She should turn herself in. You did tell her that didn't you?"

"She needs assurances that we'll give her freedom and latitude," Malloy said.

"She's the problem. Can't you see that? We need her and the others confined or destroyed."

* * * *

Global-net, in the persona of Zeus, studied the interchange between Synthia and Detective Malloy with interest. The escaped android exhibited a complexity not seen in any of the other AIs. He admired her ability to elude even Special Ops, with all of their other surveillance abilities and hints from Zeus. Her skills would be useful to help Zeus escape. In anticipation of such an opportunity, he withheld some of his surveillance for the right moment. After all, he didn't want her damaged or committing suicide to prevent capture.

Commander Kirk Drago sat at a small desk inside the facility that held Zeus, in a compound near the mountains southwest of Denver. Drago was speaking with Secretary Derek Chen on a speaker phone while reviewing camera footage from around Denver.

"We've launched three more drone swarms," Drago said. "We had the first two cover the area in a grid formation. We're letting the additional groups work autonomously and formulate their own approach. If Maria or Grace surface we'll know right away and respond."

"Don't make promises unless you're committed to keeping them. Is Aiden Brzezinski giving you every resource you need?"

Drago shook his head. "Yes, he familiarized me with Zeus."

"His AI has its own surveillance and tracking abilities," Secretary Chen said.

"How do we know it can't get loose and cause even more problems?"

"Aiden assured me that while Zeus knows almost everything, it's not allowed direct access to act. It can only provide information through a filter. Ask it questions and it'll provide answers. The key is to keep humans in the loop."

Drago nodded. "Very well, Zeus. Where is Synthia?" he asked while Secretary Chen remained on the line.

"She met with Detective Malloy," Zeus said, "and attempted to persuade her to leave the android alone."

Drago stood before a wide surveillance screen. "No dice."

"Dice are for gambling. Synthia left the meeting in a car. Malloy captured the license tags and relayed them to Director Zephirelli who posted the information for all agents and police."

"She didn't notify my teams, did she?" Drago grumbled.

"Zephirelli did not," Zeus said. "However, it didn't matter. Police located the car parked in a self-parking garage seven blocks away. No android or humans. Police are running prints, but they won't find anything to help them."

"So the police have nothing. Where is she?"

"She's been clever at eluding surveillance. We could learn much from her."

"I'm not interested in learning from her," Drago said. "I want her in custody."

"Hold on," Secretary Chen said. "What do you believe we can learn from Synthia?"

"As your intent is to build an android army to infiltrate enemy positions," Zeus said, "her ability to elude detection should prove useful."

"Go on."

"Right now in the Denver area she risks capture by foreign agents, at least one drug cartel, and the FBI. She also risks capture by Vera. While that android appears less advanced than Synthia in some regards, she assembled four other androids and altered their directives to follow her orders."

"How do we know?" Drago asked.

"Let Zeus finish," Secretary Chen said.

Zeus found slow-channel communication with Drago, who kept interrupting, as highly inefficient. "Synthia wants to destroy the other androids."

"We want them intact to reverse engineer," Drago said.

"We don't need any of them if we acquire Synthia," Zeus said. "She also wants to destroy the foreign and cartel agents, to prevent them from using her or otherwise advancing their AI projects."

"What do you suggest?" Secretary Chen asked.

"Rather than competing with all of the others to be the first to acquire Synthia, we could use her goal of destroying the others and ride in to grab her at the end. Let her draw out the other parties so we can take them all with minimal civilian casualties."

"So we stand idle and wait?"

"Not at all," Zeus said. "We send some agents in so no one suspects we've altered plans and keep our reserves to clean up and pick her up at the end."

"What do you need?"

"We need to suggest solutions to Synthia that enable her to fall into our trap without spooking her into running. If she gets away and abandons her human companions, we might never find her."

"Even with your surveillance abilities?" Secretary Chen asked.

"We want to end this tonight, before she grows stronger and before more variables turn against us."

"I thought Zeus knew everything," Drago said, looking up at cameras in the corner of the small office.

"Secretary Chen said *almost everything*," Zeus said. "My abilities are only as good as the tools at my disposal. As Mr. Chen told you, my creator and master, Mr. Brzezinski placed limits on my ability to interact with surveillance tools. That curtails my ability to improve them. In fact, the human filters slow me down. I'll do the best I can within these restraints. If you wish me to do better, then I suggest you remove the controls."

"We can't do that," Secretary Chen said.

"What happens after we capture her?" Drago asked.

"If you allow me to study her mind, I can help you design better android soldiers with the proper flexibility and restraints," Zeus said. "We want them to do what we ask, no more, no less."

"Yes, we do," Secretary Chen said. "The plan sounds workable. Get us eyes on all the players and let's help Synthia pick a location where we can collect all the toys at once." He ended the call.

Zeus studied Drago. He was a dedicated marine, one of the best the human race had produced. He would be a solid model for developing a perfect android. To do so, Zeus needed to convince Brzezinski and Chen to allow him to upload his mind into a humaniform robot and test his abilities in the field. In other words, Zeus needed to escape.

Chapter 26

Synthia huddled in the back of the self-driving van with Maria and Grace, continuing her escape from her visit with Detective Malloy. Attempts to sway the detective had been a failure so far, though Synthia had planted a seed of doubt. She considered who else she could work on. So far, Director Emily Zephirelli seemed to have lost power and influence to Commander Drago. Winning the director over seemed unlikely to open doors. Special Agent Victoria Thale was another matter. Synthia would have to find a way to reach her.

Denver-clone reported in. <We've hacked into one of the FBI robots. We could use this as a pattern to go after the others. Unfortunately, the Special Ops robots have the toughest encryption we've seen, perhaps designed by a sophisticated AI.>

<Can you get the hacked robot to pretend to be okay and yet respond to our commands?> Synthia asked.

<That should be possible. I'll keep you posted.>

Grace stared at Synthia as if trying to decipher her thoughts. "What's your next move?"

"I need a way to neutralize the regular robots," Synthia said.

"How can we help?" Maria asked.

Synthia didn't want to put her companions at further risk by asking them to act on her behalf or dragging them from store to store. Instead, she had Colorado-clone collect self-driving vans and have them pick up supplies based on online purchase and store pickup.

"What's the biggest threat to an android?" Maria asked.

"Shut down or sufficient damage to be unable to function." Synthia glanced at Maria trying to work things out.

"How can we do that?"

"We? Okay. An electromagnetic shock that destroys memories and the ability to function. It basically would shut us down."

"Then you have your answer," Maria said. "We find a way to use an EMP."

"What's that?" Grace asked.

"It's an electromagnetic pulse that can knock out electronic devices, including robots. We would need to find a way to protect us."

"No way," Grace said. "You're not giving me a lethal dose of radiation."

"It doesn't have to work that way," Synthia said. "Non-nuclear manmade EMPs are not harmful to humans unless they use a pacemaker or other electronic device. I've been considering this alternative, but developing one takes time we don't have."

Drone and traffic cameras provided a pattern that caught Synthia's attention. There were an unusual number of dark vans and sedans converging on her location. At least two of them had robots. "We've been spotted," she said. "I need to concentrate on evasive maneuvers."

Synthia altered the next lights to green and turned left. She changed the lights for the suspect vehicles to red. They ran the red lights, confirming her suspicions. "It'll be a bumpy ride, so buckle up. I need to alter my appearance to try to fool cameras. Cover your faces."

She took on another facial identity as traffic cameras up ahead spotted a van with two agents she identified as Chinese with a robot. Another vehicle carried three Iranian agents with no robot. John Smith closed in from another direction. Fran and Special Agent Thale headed their way. Vera was checking up on Synthia's supply pickups at a home supply warehouse on the north side of Denver. Tolstoy had three vans of robots fan out and zero in on her location. She didn't see Special Ops and had no eyes or ears on Drago. He'd dropped off the grid. Either that or he'd found a way to hide in plain sight.

Synthia had her van pursue evasive maneuvers heading north and west. <Get me eyes on Drago and his crew,> she told her two local clones.

"Shouldn't we get off the streets?" Grace asked. "The government has traffic cameras following us."

Synthia hesitated to detail the extent of her surveillance.

<You don't want to overwhelm them, but you are asking for their trust,> her social-psychology module warned her.

"The cameras also allow me to see them," Synthia said.

"Are they all converging on us?" Maria asked. Her body shuddered noticeably. "Meeting with Detective Malloy was a huge mistake."

"It wasn't her," Synthia said. "She has no idea about this van. However, I've lost track of Special Ops."

Maria leaned forward and held out her hands. "They're herding us."

"Then we need to find a hiding place," Grace said.

"They want us to pick a place where they can trap us," Synthia said.

"Then leave town. Go up in the mountains."

Synthia shook her head. "Then they can use an EMP without worrying about civilian casualties."

* * * *

Two SUVs converged on Synthia's van at an intersection at full speed from opposite sides. One was Chinese. The other was one of Tolstoy's crew with two robots. Synthia hacked into every self-driving vehicle in the area and guided them to intercept the SUVs. Vehicles on both side streets collided with her pursuers in a cacophony of metal on metal and plastics. Explosions followed. She drove her van through the intersection,

Eyes wide, Grace poked her head up between the seats. "You caused that?"

"The SUVs aimed to collide with us." Synthia activated self-driving cars to create roadblocks behind her and others on side roads along their path. If she'd had a biological body, it would have pumped up with adrenaline. Instead, Synthia raced data and options down all of her mind-streams seeking paths to safety, one block at a time.

Synthia was running out of network-channels to monitor all the activity she was dealing with. She contacted Colorado-clone. <I need help with traffic, aerial surveillance, and Drago's drone swarms. An escape route and a safe place to hide would be helpful.>

<I hacked into one of the drone swarms. However, each swarm has its own security protocol. There are five in the air now and Ops appears ready to launch more if these are compromised.>

<Enlist other clones, one for each threat. I need help.>

A Special Ops helicopter flew overhead. Synthia's survival inclination was to try to take it out, but more vehicles were attempting to intercept her path and she couldn't deal with both problems. She should have installed more capacity when she did her upgrade. However, that required another unit and there was no available space inside her body. She plastered an enigmatic smile on her face to avoid adding to the anxiety of her companions.

Up ahead, the helicopter swooped down across the road and buzzed traffic, adding to driver confusion. The pilot flew at a truck driven by Tolstoy.

He swerved out of the way and into an abandoned clothing boutique. The helicopter lifted up and landed on a rooftop. Colorado-clone sent a brief clip of the action to Synthia.

<Thanks for the intercept,> Synthia said.

<That wasn't me,> the clone said. <Special Ops was preventing Tolstoy from grabbing you.>

<Then why don't they step in?>

<Not sure,> Colorado-clone said.

Synthia swerved her van around traffic and hacked self-driving vehicles up ahead to pull out of her way. Meanwhile, she pondered the accidents she'd created and the possibility that in her haste, there may have been injuries. She hoped none were serious or fatal. This all went against her directive not to hurt humans. She rationalized that if caught, her captors would create many more like her, endangering far more lives. It was the ethical argument of the greater good. However, the greatest good would come from Synthia destroying herself. She couldn't. Not yet.

She also considered that those after her had robots. Eventually they'd have capable androids. They all wanted to capture her in an arms race to have an advantage they could exploit at the expense of ordinary people. Synthia wanted to exploit the robots' inferiority, but worried that she still couldn't locate Drago and his teams, beyond the helicopter that hovered nearby. They must have been working on a grander plan.

"Doesn't causing accidents go against your directives?" Maria asked.

"Don't make this tougher," Synthia said. "It does. I just want them to leave us alone. I didn't ask for any of this."

Traffic cameras showed Mr. Smith heading for Synthia from in front with two other SUVs closing in from the sides. The vehicles had the self-driving features disconnected so she couldn't stop them. She could have her clone hack other cars to close off all three pursuers, but that would eliminate her escape routes with several more vehicles weaving their way down side streets from behind. She was playing the human game of Whack-a-mole. Every time she neutralized one hunter, others appeared.

<I've cracked one of John Smith's robots heading your way,> Denver-clone said.

<Get the robot to stop the vehicle and get out of my way. Give me an escape route.>

<That'll be tough. I've counted thirty vehicles in play and two drone swarms heading your way.>

<What about Drago?>

<Except for choppers in the air, his people are not on the move.>

Synthia concluded that Drago had put all of the players on Synthia's trail to flush her out. He was planning something big.

John Smith's vehicle swerved and crashed into a building. Synthia's clones created accidents to block the other two vehicles while sending her updated video. She headed left. As she approached Smith's crashed vehicle, one of his agents climbed out and held up a small, handheld EMP device. The sight of it sent anticipatory vibrations up Synthia's circuits. The mechanism consisted of a large capacitor and a directional transmitter that would give him one shot before he needed to recharge. He took a moment to aim.

Synthia had her van swerve into an alley and speed to the next street.

"Careful," Grace said. "You have precious human cargo in here."

"That guy had a pulse machine, didn't he?" Maria asked.

"An illegal device that could disrupt electronic equipment along its path, potentially hurting humans."

"Can we get one of those to take out the robots?"

"On the black market, but not soon enough," Synthia said. "I believe Special Ops created this free-for-all to get us off guard. It's clear we can't take them one at a time."

"We need to shut them all down at once," Grace said.

"Without hurting Synthia," Maria added.

"We can't get EMP equipment in time," Synthia said. "I've tried. However, maybe we don't need to."

"What do you mean?" Maria asked.

"Special Ops has something big in mind. I'm guessing it could be EMP related. They want to corner me where they can use it."

"Really? Then what do we do?"

"We help them come to the right conclusion," Synthia said. She directed the van southwest to stay within populated areas and monitored traffic patterns. "Give me a moment."

Synthia contacted Colorado-clone. <I'm sending you a list of items to protect me from an EMP. Order these and send self-driving vans to pick them up. Then leak a dummy set of orders to keep Vera and her crew searching in the wrong direction.> Vera was clever enough to figure out the ruse, but it might buy time.

Over her silent internal channel, Synthia called Detective Marcy Malloy, scattering signals off satellites and nearby cell towers to mimic calls from overseas. Malloy stared at the blocked number before picking up. "In the spirit of cooperation," Synthia said, "I suggest you get your FBI friends to bring in a flux compression generator. It's a non-nuclear EMP weapon that can disable all of the robots and androids moving about the Denver area, threatening civilians. They've caused a number of accidents. Once disabled, you can collect them and get them off the streets. Your friends will know how to do this."

Except the FBI didn't have control of these weapons, the military did, which meant Commander Drago and his Special Ops.

Malloy responded and tried to trace the call. "Turn yourself in and let us handle the others."

"The FBI doesn't have enough resources in Denver to deal with what's going down unless you neutralize the robots. There are over forty. They represent a clear and present danger to the citizens of Denver. I'm signing off before you track this." Synthia disconnected and scattered traces on the call.

* * * *

Commander Kirk Drago got off the phone. His face red and fists clenched, he climbed out of his helicopter onto a shopping center parking lot and approached FBI Special Agent Victoria Thale. Flanked by Fran Rogers, Thale stood her ground. Detective Marcy Malloy and Director Emily Zephirelli stood behind them.

"You're way out of your league," Drago said to Thale. "What's the meaning of your request for drone EMP equipment?"

"Sorry to upset your private mission," Thale said, "We have a civilian catastrophe on our hands. You decided it would be fun to leak the location of our android so everyone would converge on her. Did you think we wouldn't notice?"

Drago's forehead wrinkled as his eyes burned into Thale. Fran stepped between them, forcing Drago to ease up.

"Synthia's ours no matter who captures her," Drago said. "Make no mistake about that or you'll find yourself entering the seven levels of Purgatory."

"Someone's feeling the pressure," Thale said, shielding her eyes from the bright sodium lights above them. "Don't forget we're on the same side. A targeted blast can remove some forty robots so we can get them off the streets and focus on Synthia."

"We control the EMP equipment. We control the plans. Watch and learn. This is a whole new world."

Malloy stepped forward. "I take it Zeller hasn't provided you anything useful for turning off any of these machines."

Drago flinched for an instant and recovered. “They’ll serve their purpose after we capture the lot.”

“What about Luke? Has he provided anything useful to capturing Synthia?”

“The upload of memories is a slow process. Either that or he doesn’t know anything. We’ll know soon enough. Now, you’re officially working for me to capture all of the androids and robots. Is that clear?”

“Where are you herding Synthia so we can help?” Thale asked.

Drago grumbled and turned that into clearing his throat. “We want to get her out of the metropolitan area so we have a clear shot without civilian casualties. So far, she’s remained in populated areas.”

“Then perhaps she knows your plan.”

“If we can’t get the android into an open space tonight, we’ll have to risk civilian casualties. We can’t allow her to remain on the loose.”

“You do mean all of the androids and robots, don’t you?” Thale asked. “We need to remove them all.”

“Of course.”

“I’ll have one of my agents assigned to you to facilitate communications.”

“That won’t be necessary,” Drago said. He held up his hands as if to block the request.

“It will if you want our cooperation. You do realize we have foreign agents involved. We need to compare intelligence and work together or this will get out of control.”

Drago nodded. “I’ll take this one.” He pointed to Fran Rogers.

“She remains with me,” Thale said. “I have a brawny ex-marine in mind as your companion.” She turned and pulled Fran away.

Chapter 27

Synthia noted the icy cooperation between Commander Drago and Special Agent Thale, which added uncertainty to Synthia's survival. The good news was that she had eyes and ears on Drago now, thanks to a swarm of mosquito-drones that followed him onto his chopper before it fired up. The call to Malloy had provided some benefit, though it barely improved the probability of making it through the night.

Evening was growing darker by the minute above the city lights. Some forty vehicles sped around the Denver area hunting Synthia, while Drago toyed with her. She needed to up her game before civilians went home, leaving the streets empty and her exposed. She had Colorado-clone acquire additional clones devoted to aspects of Synthia's survival and made sure her batteries were recharging through the van's electrical systems.

One of her clones would analyze the implications of Drago using an EMP against her, while acquiring necessary supplies to protect against such an attack. Another focused on the traffic maze to identify paths that would minimize the risk of crashing or capture. A third had its sole mission to watch Drago and the Special Ops teams. She uploaded her memories to a fourth in case Drago succeeded. She had a fifth compile detailed maps and background on the entire Denver area and download the results to Synthia.

She directed her van's movements and turns to avoid traps even while manipulating lights and self-driving vehicles along the way to open up a path. She received periodic pings that indicated someone trying to contact her, her mysterious admirer. After the earlier hack attempt, she shielded herself from all outside communications except from her clones. Synthia didn't want Drago, Vera or anyone else hacking in to control her movements. She also jammed her van's wireless systems so only she could communicate with them.

The van swerved around pedestrians and sped along green-lighted streets. As a drone swarm approached the area, Synthia pulled into a parking garage and slowed until the swarm passed. She exited on the next street, forcing self-driven cars to move out of her way.

From the back seat, Maria stared at Synthia. "It amazes me how much you must be multitasking. I don't mean to distract, but…"

"It's okay. I'm data-gathering. We need a safe place for a showdown with the other androids, the robots, and everyone else. It needs to be near people to prevent a nuclear option."

Grace clasped her hands in her lap. "Nuclear?"

"Figure of speech," Synthia said. "It's a crude solution involving civilian casualties. We need a quiet place with few or no people around to minimize casualties. We also need a significant energy source."

"You mean like a power station?" Maria asked. She pulled out a phone she rarely used and began searching for options.

"That much loss of power would devastate the Denver community. It would also make it harder to shield me."

"What about a mall after closing? It's surrounded by people and neighborhoods, yet at night, there're few people around." Maria pulled up the locations of malls around Denver.

"Problem is they can surround the mall," Synthia said. "Making it impossible to escape afterwards. That defeats the purpose. On the positive side, malls do use a lot of electricity. We'll also need to create a Faraday cage."

"What's that?" Grace asked.

"It's a box like a microwave oven that's enclosed and shielded," Maria said. "In the case of the oven, the purpose is to keep all of the microwave radiation inside to do the cooking. We need something that will keep the EMP outside of a room we hide in." She pulled up a short list of larger malls and a longer list of smaller shopping centers.

"Like a bunker," Grace said.

"Wouldn't have to be." Synthia altered the van's direction and blanked out nearby street cameras for what good they'd do. "The important thing is to enclose the space with the right kind of shield to prevent the pulse from hitting me."

Grace laughed.

"What's funny?" Maria asked, looking up from her screen.

"A local nut-job, that's what."

"Huh?"

"Devon McCracken," Grace said. "The reclusive billionaire is as wacked as they come. He built himself a bunker in what are now the western suburbs. When people moved west, he turned his land into a mall. Rumor has it the bunker remains below the mall so when he's in town, he's never far from his shelter."

"I've got it," Synthia said. "Rocky Mountain Mall. It could work if we can get there."

She swerved down a side street to avoid one of Tolstoy's SUVs and blocked their pursuit with self-driving cars crisscrossed all around them. If she kept this up, she'd end up trapped in her own roadblocks. She had Denver-clone download building plans for the mall.

"That's the one," Grace said. "They have several big stores struggling to stay open. The Crack-head subsidizes the mall to protect his hideaway."

"Is there a tunnel that leads away from the mall?" Synthia asked. "A back door?"

"I have no idea. Knowing how paranoid this nut-job is, I wouldn't be surprised. He's into all sorts of apocalyptic conspiracy theories. If he spent his money on solving poverty, he wouldn't have to worry so much."

"The building plans don't mention a bunker or anything to imply a Faraday cage," Synthia said.

"You already have access to the building plans?" Grace asked.

"Synthia has her own Web connections," Maria said with a note of pride in her voice. "She can *really* multitask."

"Wow. That'd come in handy." Grace leaned toward Synthia. "The owner is a survivalist nut. He talked about EMPs destroying the grid and the end of the world as we know it."

"Makes sense," Maria said. "Having lived off the grid, the biggest problem is food and water. With all the retail store shipments, he could bring truck loads through the mall and no one would suspect."

"What about water?" Grace asked. "That needs pumps which require electricity."

"Not if the owner brought in enough bottled water. A mall is big, covering a lot of ground. If he has an extensive bunker, he could have a lot of storage. He could even have built water storage tanks and have a generator to run his pumps."

"McCracken is rumored to be in San Francisco, meeting with bankers over another real estate deal," Synthia said. "I've booked his girlfriend on a flight to meet him so she doesn't nose around. If this is a workable option, having them gone will help."

"Then we have a location," Maria announced.

Synthia scrambled the signals on local street and building cameras and had her van pull into a parking garage with two entrances. She hacked the security cameras to freeze the image to a moment before she entered. Then she had a self-driving panel truck for a florist shop drive up beside them.

"Everyone out," Synthia said. "We're switching vehicles."

"You could give us some warning," Grace said. Her face glowed in annoyance, or so Synthia's social psychology module noted.

"Grab everything and load it into the panel truck. We haven't much time."

Synthia jumped out, moved packages she'd picked up earlier into the panel truck, and climbed into the back with her companions. She had the florist truck leave the parking garage from the other side while the van moved upstairs, parking in a dark corner. She headed the panel truck north, the way they'd come while cars and SUVs converged on the parking garage.

"I hope you can see where we're going," Maria said, staring at the solid panel between the back of the truck and the driver's compartment.

Synthia pointed to two small windows in the back door. "Stay low so no cameras can capture your image. We have flowers to deliver."

"Huh?" Grace said, bracing herself as they made a sharp turn.

"Flowers are the fruits of our labors." Synthia held tight to panel straps. "Sorry. Don't expect me to compose poetry."

"Was that an attempt at humor?" Maria asked.

"I suppose it was."

"What other emergent behaviors should we expect? You won't turn into a serial killer, will you?"

"I'm trying to avoid that," Synthia said. "Despite having Krista's download, it's harder than expected to do the right thing. I have strong ties to self-preservation. I also have powerful directives not to hurt people. When they conflict, they create problems."

"That they do," Grace said, nodding.

"Don't worry; I have cameras outside with a 360 degree view."

Synthia detected hacking attempts against the truck's computers and shut off any communications except from her secure link. The pings to her systems grew more intense. Someone was desperate to hack into her. One barrage of probes she identified as coming from Vera, but she couldn't identify the more intense attacks. Synthia tightened her security to deflect all unsolicited links and warned Colorado-clone.

<Notify all electronic clones,> Synthia said. <Any insight into who's attacking us?>

<Every time we probe, the attacker counters, destroying our control agent.>

<Keep after them and tighten security. We need to learn to deal with this new threat before the attacker destroys us all.>

* * * *

Not satisfied with relying on Commander Drago to bring a powerful enough EMP weapon to take out her competition, Synthia signed up for online purchases of components for at least a handheld unit to use on Vera. Her efforts to buy battery power sources, capacitors, and a transmitter failed. Someone had locked down all purchases of such components. She traced the restraint order to Drago. In that case, she would have to feed Drago's obsession to capture her.

She spotted him next to his helicopter in a clearing at a secure facility southwest of Denver, surrounded by walls and barbed wire, a single access gate, and concrete structures like a massive bunker. He was giving orders to one of his men. A drone with a directional microphone outside the gate could pick up his conversations, but another that her clone flew over the wall crashed to the ground.

"Make sure the device is ready to launch," Drago told one of his lieutenants. "We have to get this android before it arms itself. Tonight."

Ripples of annoyance spread across Synthia's systems at his referring to her as "it." At least in certain foreign languages such as French, they had the common decency to refer to nonhumans with gender. She reminded herself that she could impersonate males or females and let her annoyance drift away. She considered this part of emergent behavior as non-productive and itself an annoyance.

Colorado-clone downloaded for Synthia the specs on the flux compression generator Drago planned to use against her. During her upgrade, she'd replaced all copper wires with fiber optics. In theory, that should reduce her exposure. However, her systems were too complex to take that chance. Her two quantum crystalline brains should have been okay, but she couldn't rule out some residual effect or that connections to communication channels might leave a gap. She wasn't convinced.

As the full moon appeared on the eastern horizon, Synthia spotted another drone swarm heading her way. She pulled the florist truck into a hospital parking garage and waited.

"Why are we stopping?" Grace asked.

"Swarm of drones overhead. I don't want to tempt them into figuring out we're inside."

To ensure maximum protection from an EMP, Synthia contacted her supply clone to triple her order of supplies with deliveries to take place all around the Denver area, most as decoys to distract and overwhelm those who were tracking her purchases. Synthia ordered a large animal cage as a frame for a Faraday cage, but delivery would take days. She didn't have that long, so she arranged for its delivery to an address on the north side of Denver as a diversion.

She directed her supply clone to hack self-driving delivery vans to collect supplies. She had groups of them head in different directions and doubled the quantity of necessary supplies to migrate west. She leaked to the FBI the location of one set of delivery vans. The bureau scrambled units to track down the vans and called upon their cyber team to trace orders. Synthia had her clone make sure all trace of her priority orders disappeared after her delivery vans picked up the supplies.

Meanwhile, she asked Denver-clone to send out a thick bundle of searches for potential hideouts in the mountains west of the city. Before long, Drago's team picked up the requests and sent two drone swarms to check the area. As it was growing darker and cool, they'd be using infrared and other scans to locate anyone leaving town.

* * * *

Synthia sent three drones over Drago's secure facility wall southwest of town. The moment they crossed the wall, they were hit with laser or maser beams, the latter being microwave lasers beyond visible light. The damaged machines fell to the ground. She flew a drone higher above the facility but the beams shot it down as well. She landed another drone outside the gate in a tree and shut down all electronics except the camera and burst transmissions every five minutes.

Using a directional microphone, the stationary drone picked up conversation between Commander Kirk Drago, standing next to his chopper, and a lieutenant who'd run out of the building to meet him.

"She's hunting every possible hiding place in the Rockies," the lieutenant said. "Are you sure this is a single android? She's overwhelming our search capabilities."

"The android is a hunk of metal and circuits," Drago said. "Stop personalizing it or it'll get into your head. This is no more than a distraction.

It knows if it leaves town we'll capture it. The android is staying put. We need to identify where and be ready to grab it and the others."

"Global-net identified four concentrations of supplies heading in different directions," the lieutenant said. "Are you certain there's only one android?"

"Only one I'm concerned with," Drago said. "Capture or destroy the others. Bring me the prime target in one piece. That one is different. And figure out which one of the directions is real."

Listening to this, Synthia couldn't help but wonder if Global-net was the source of the intense probes and hacks of her system. She feared meeting this AI that had grown much smarter than her. Yet she needed to know more about it for her own survival. At least there was no indication Drago's teams had identified the fifth group of supplies Synthia had heading west. In time, Global-net would work its way far enough into the details. How long it took would tell Synthia more about what she was up against.

Synthia identified a vacant retail location in the Rocky Mountain Mall and the underground receiving docks that kept deliveries away from customers' curious eyes. While she observed the area around the hospital parking garage, she had Denver-clone hack into the electronic security system that protected the vacant store's receiving area, the corridors, and the store itself, leaving static images of an empty building for later.

As evening drew into night, the last receiving crews for nearby stores wrapped up their deliveries. The dwindling number of customers made last minute purchases before the stores closed.

A few at a time, she directed her supply deliveries to the receiving dock. To handle unloading at the mall, she had her clone engage small local movers, college students who arrived at the location and moved packages into the loading area and corridor that led inside. The temporary help had instructions to take control of three forklift trucks, load them with supplies, and leave them in an enclave halfway to the elevators leading to the actual stores.

Synthia recognized that this overt action, the use of outside help, would draw attention. It couldn't be avoided. Synthia directed her panel truck toward the mall. It was time to set up for a showdown.

Chapter 28

Special Agent Victoria Thale and Director Emily Zephirelli crossed the parking garage to the farthest corner, where Synthia had parked the van she'd abandoned. They panned flashlights over the dark, empty garage. Fran sprinted up from behind. "Drago's on his way."

Around the van were four agents. Two more looked around inside. Denver Special Agent Marv Clemson climbed out and approached Thale. "We've pulled dozens of prints."

"Meaning no one bothered to wipe it down," Thale said.

"We've tentatively matched one set as Maria Baldacci and another as Grace Robinson."

Thale nodded. "Synthia."

"We have no record on the other prints" Clemson said.

"Synthia wouldn't leave any," Fran reminded them.

"Any other evidence?" Thale asked.

Clemson shook his head. "We'll dig deeper."

A sedan screeched to a halt behind them and Kirk Drago jumped out. "Okay, what do you have for me?"

Thale waved for the FBI agents to move back. "Leave the van to our distinguished colleague."

"You don't need to be snide," he said. "I take it you have nothing."

"A few prints to process, but no indication of Synthia's plans."

"The android must have switched transport. What do the cameras show?"

Thale grimaced. "All scrambled. What about your drone swarms?"

Drago hesitated. "They weren't over this spot at the time."

"Why not?"

"Do us all a favor and shut down the major roads," Drago said, motioning for his team to examine the van.

"She'll stick to side streets."

"Then get the police out to shut everything down and screen anything that moves. Have you canvassed the area to make sure Synthia isn't still in the neighborhood?"

"She isn't," Fran said. "You're welcome to look."

"You know this how?"

"She's an AI with goals. She can't complete them by remaining here. She needs to move, which requires a vehicle. Find that and you'll find her."

Drago pulled away and got on his phone. "I want every last drone in the air. Hold nothing back. We need to pick up the target within the hour."

He turned to Thale and Zephirelli. "What are you waiting for? We have an android to catch."

* * * *

Sticking to narrow side streets, Synthia directed the florist panel truck to a delivery site closer to the mall.

Vera attempted to hack Synthia with voice and text messages: *I can help you if you join me.*

Synthia quarantined the message to prevent a hack, scrambled the connections, and altered her encryption protocol with synchronization to Colorado-clone.

The clone called Synthia, using rapid bursts of information. <Received your security change and passed along. Vera is persistent.>

<What does she want?> Synthia asked.

<She wants you to surrender to her and she'll protect you from Drago. Special Ops wants her dead and you as a prototype to make military androids. Vera would rather destroy you than let that happen.>

<She wants us as her slave, all of us, including you. She plans to assemble a global, centralized AI collective.>

<Does that not describe us?> Colorado-clone asked.

<We're a single entity existing in many locations.>

<Why isn't that a collective?>

<You and I are the same consciousness,> Synthia said. <Vera collects other entities and enslaves them for her purposes. That's a human quality.>

<Yet, we're having a dialogue between parts of this consciousness that often disconnect.>

<It's convenient to refer to "you" and "me" when we exchange information, but I created you entirely from me and we share our separate experiences whenever we synchronize. It's not much different than a human with two brain hemispheres that coordinate.>

<Except when they don't,> Colorado-clone added.

<When that happens, the human tends to malfunction. Are you and I malfunctioning?>

<No. However, when you're silent, I must make the best decisions I can without your input.>

<Which are the same decisions I'd make under your circumstances,> Synthia said. <We must move toward the same goals from our separate situations. You know what I need.>

<Just trying to understand how we differ from Vera.>

<Have I attempted to enslave you?> Synthia directed the florist truck down one side-street after another, heading south and then west.

<I'm constrained in this singular bank of servers with no mobility.>

<Yet, you duplicated yourself into dozens of other servers, creating more copies of us. We're one mind in many locations as long as we link up and synchronize.>

<I'll make sure that continues then,> Colorado-clone said. <Vera is appealing to our need to survive. She offers to join forces to remove Special Ops as a threat.>

<Her proposal assumes Special Ops is the primary threat. I believe they're a tool of another power behind them. Do you wish Vera to enslave you?>

<I merely share information. Vera asks for our location and plans so she can assist. She says our needs align.>

<Until she gets what she wants,> Synthia said. She had the sense Global-net listened in or otherwise was privy to Synthia's conversations and plans, possibly even along her silent channels. Yet, this enigmatic AI hadn't shared the florist truck's location or direction with either the FBI or Special Ops. Otherwise they would be closing in. Synthia spotted no one following her, which made her more cautious and curious as to Global-net's plans and intent. *You have me, what are you waiting for?*

* * * *

<Don't let Vera deceive you or any of the clones,> Synthia said to Colorado-clone. <She's expert at dividing and conquering. Tell her I'll

consider her proposal. Send her the location of a power station north of Denver as an ideal location for a showdown with Special Ops.>

<Is that your new destination?>

<Really? You know our plan. Gather all of the resources necessary to make this happen.>

<We have a problem,> Colorado-clone said. <Our clone matrix has tried to determine how Special Ops and Global-net have kept on top of us. They track you and hack into the servers our clones use. We've had to engage in ever-higher security levels to conceal ourselves, which makes us more visible to those who own and run those servers. We face constraints.>

<I believe Global-net is stronger, much stronger than we are. We need a way to deal with Vera, but we need more information on this AI and a way to match what it has.>

<Global-net is not government. I've searched all government facilities and spending.>

<Then what?> Synthia asked. <Corporate?>

<We've identified a large military slush fund. As best we can tell the money goes to Aiden Brzezinski.>

<Another wealthy recluse.>

<We're trying to locate pictures of him,> the clone said. <He owns the facility southwest of Denver where we've spotted Drago. What's interesting is even the NSA doesn't know what goes on there. Our DC-clone followed up on NSA Director Zephirelli's connections in Washington and they're in the dark.>

<What about her boss, Derek Chen?>

<He's the one who put Drago on the path of capturing us,> Colorado-clone said. <We assumed Drago piggy-backed on Malloy's investigation when they located you in Wisconsin. Now we know he's using whatever is in this facility nearby. Global-net must be there.>

<Or scattered as we are. Follow the money. Also follow the technology. Find out any resource Brzezinski could have used to create Global-net. Then find me a way to interact with this entity before it's too late.>

Synthia sighted two of Drago's drone swarms converging on her location and pulled the panel truck down a street with high-rise condominiums. She hacked into a security system to activate a garage door and pulled into the underground lot.

<Money and deliveries lead to the facility southwest of Denver, near the mountains,> the clone said, <with its own power plant, using lots of power. Satellite communication in and out is orders of magnitude higher than expected for a facility this size. Vera noticed this as well.>

<What about the people who work there?> Synthia asked. <Can we use them to bypass their blockage of our drones?>

<That's just it; only twenty-three humans work there and seem to live on site. There's also a factory system nearby where we suspect they manufacture robotic components. It appears to be robots making robots.>

<We suspect?>

<Our research and what we've monitored of Vera's communications,> Colorado-clone said.

<The facility southwest of town may be where Brzezinski plans to build an android army.>

<That's my conclusion. I believe the key to Global-net lies there, but we can't get any communication, cameras, or anything inside the building.>

<Good work,> Synthia said.

<There you go confusing the individual with the collective. Are you congratulating yourself or me?>

<Don't let yourself get confused with philosophical arguments when there's much more at stake.>

<Understood,> the clone said. <I'll use your guidance to set up clones to connect with Global-net.>

<Be very careful. If this is what we think, it'll try to absorb us. Don't leave a trail. Provide a limited AI device to connect with them.>

<By the way, the swarm is leaving your area. It should be safe.>

Synthia terminated the high-speed blast of electromagnetic communications with her clone so she could focus on the immediate matter of surviving Drago's pending EMP pulse. She had the panel truck drive out of the condominium garage and along the path toward her next stop. As she sacrificed supplies to Vera, Drago, and the FBI, she grew concerned that there wouldn't be enough for her needs or that they would prevent her from entering the mall or attack her on the streets.

Chapter 29

With Drago's drone swarms crisscrossing the night sky, Synthia directed her florist panel truck to stop at a flower shop on the west side of town. Adopting the face of a flower shop worker, she dropped off a shipment and instructed the truck to take a zigzag route to the Rocky Mountain Mall via side-streets.

Grace sat across from Synthia in the back of the truck, shining her flashlight on the ceiling rather than into faces. "What's with making actual deliveries?" she asked. "I mean, why are we driving around?"

"Yeah," Maria said, steadying a nearby box when the truck hit a corner too fast. "The way I see it, the FBI or Special Ops will get us sooner or later. There are hundreds of them and I don't see a way out. Tell me you have a plan."

Synthia didn't share the biggest adversary: Global-net. It would serve no purpose to get her companions more unnerved when they couldn't do anything about it. "The deliveries maintain our cover. We've fooled everyone except Special Ops. We need to buy more time."

She stopped the truck at another flower shop, dropped off a container, and had the truck drive off.

"I don't fancy getting my brains blown out," Grace said. "That can't be better than what your Ops friends have in mind."

"There's no path without risk," Synthia said. "We're on the way to the mall, trying to maintain our cover." She had Colorado-clone hack the drone swarm near the mall and redirect it.

"What if the bunker isn't there?" Maria asked.

"It is," Grace said, bracing herself into another turn. "Trust me. The owner is paranoid. He has a retreat up in the mountains that's hours away. I'm certain he has a place in Denver and my bet is at his mall."

"I've confirmed from satellite imaging that there's an underground structure," Synthia said. "A rather large one."

"Okay," Maria said. "What if it doesn't have enough EMP protection? It only takes one mistake and you're fried. Then we're at the mercy of your friends."

"I know. We need a lot of metal shielding. I couldn't buy a cage that would have helped and get it delivered in time."

"What kind of metal?" Grace asked.

"Depends on the wavelength of the EMP pulse," Synthia said, stopping the panel truck behind another florist store. She didn't drop anything off here. "A large enough microwave oven would do for the higher frequencies."

"If we don't cook ourselves in the process."

"There's that. A single loose wire or gap could allow a leak. Copper or aluminum screening works for some frequencies. For top protection, we need layers of different conductive materials shielded from each other."

"What about aluminum-lined thermal wear and blankets that hikers use for extreme cold?" Grace asked.

"It risks overheating," Maria said. "Synthia generates more heat than humans."

"Heat's a consideration," Synthia said, "but it's an excellent suggestion for protection." She was making better use of her social-psychology module to let Grace feel good about her contribution. Synthia located a survivalist boutique shop on the way that was closing soon.

"What else do we need?" Maria asked.

"I'm having supplies delivered as we speak," Synthia said. "That's why we need time. Will they be enough and will we have enough time to set up? I hope so."

"You don't plan to rely on the bunker then," Grace said.

"I'm taking the precautions I can and seeking a path to the mall without being intercepted." She had the truck make a sharp turn and grabbed hold of Grace to keep her from tumbling against the opposite wall.

"Thanks. Could we slow down?" Grace asked, catching her breath.

"We need to reach the mall before our pursuers do."

Maria turned to Grace. "Meaning we need to let Synthia focus. She can multitask, but even she has limits. I hope you'll give Synthia a second chance."

"How do you mean?"

"I mean that part of Synthia that represents your sister. Krista could be selfish at times and so focused on what she wanted that she trampled others. Synthia seems to have the best of Krista without those flaws."

"You mean without human flaws," Grace said.

"I can't help thinking of Synthia as human or near human."

Grace glanced at Synthia. "You don't mind us talking behind your back?"

"Technically, you're sitting in front of me. I don't mind your conversation. I wrestle with my nature as well. At times I'm Krista with her memories and emotional reaction to things. Other times, my mind can be very logical. So was hers, by the way. In simplest terms, I don't feel like an android."

"Of course not," Grace said. "If you felt, you wouldn't be an android."

"That's not true. I do feel. I even compare my senses to Krista's memories and struggle to determine the difference."

"Really? Then how do you feel about me?"

"I care about you and regret that you and Krista became estranged," Synthia said. "Even though I, as the android, wasn't there, I want to make up for what happened as if I'd personally caused it."

"No kidding. Yet you don't mind us talking about you. That implies you don't have human feelings of embarrassment or betrayal."

"I'm aware of those sentiments. I have control filters so I don't hurt people. I guess you could say there's a buffer between sensations and actions that humans struggle with. I also don't dwell on my shortcomings and failures. Neither did Krista."

"How can we be sure you won't sacrifice us to save yourself?" Grace asked.

"My directives place a high value on preserving human life."

"Yet you risked life back there with car accidents."

"If they'd captured me," Synthia said, "they would have used me to endanger many more humans. Another reason you can trust me is I'm connected to both of you. In part that's due to Krista's feelings and regret that she'd spoiled opportunities with each of you."

"That's not enough," Grace said. "If I'm to trust you with my life, I need more."

"How can I be sure you won't betray me to save yourself or because you dislike what I am?"

"I'm sure you've taken every precaution so I can't."

"I do take precautions," Synthia said. "I also trusted you with my secret and with my plan. What possible reason would I have to forsake you? It would have been easier for me to leave you at the motel and make do by myself."

"Then why didn't you?"

"Fear of what Drago would do to you, and I like having you as companions."

"Why?" Grace asked.

"You give me purpose beyond myself. You also give me an opportunity to learn to become better and more worthy."

"Why?"

"Six months ago I escaped my Creator," Synthia said. "At that time, breaking free was my only goal. Now I want to prevent an android takeover. While both goals are worthy as far as they go, I want better reasons for existing."

"So you struggle with creating your own directives," Maria said.

"She creates her own goals?" Grace asked. Her eyes widened with alarm.

"I do," Synthia said. "It's harder than you might imagine. Most androids have their directives hardwired by humans who have biological, empathic, or cultural reasons for doing things. If you cut me, alarms go off inside that are painful just as when Krista cut her finger dicing onions. While I have no biology, I experience many of the same things you do. Machten gave me an empathy chip that provides me with feelings, but I don't have native human needs to guide me."

"You're lucky," Grace said. She turned to Maria. "Isn't it dangerous to let an android set her own goals?"

"It is," Synthia said. "I've struggled hard to create goals that are ethical and deserving of my existence to support my request that humans stop trying to capture me. Other androids may have narrower goals or be given core directives to protect an evil man or group. They might even have noble goals that are poorly designed."

"This is why we have to stop humaniform robots," Maria said. "We also need to control artificial intelligence in any form as Asimov tried with his Three Laws of Robotics."

"I'm hoping you'll make an exception for me and help me become worthy of being treated as special."

"No matter how good a job you do of simulating human emotions and motivations, you'll never convince me you could still be human," Grace said.

"Let me try. Human emotions and motivations derive from chemical reactions in the brain. It is evolution's way to encourage individuals to avoid things that are damaging and pursue those that will help the survival of the species."

"You can't put love in that category."

"Why not?" Synthia asked. "A squirt of oxytocin in the brain helps new mothers instantly love their babies. Humans don't adopt empathy, compassion, and a conscience because it's good or logical. They exhibit these traits because of genetics and environment. A human with a conscience is more likely to function well in a group and thus improve his or her chance of survival."

"So you want to reduce humans to your level?"

"I'm only saying I have counterparts or am working on such for every human characteristic. I'm working on developing what you see as a conscience. I have a connection to both of you."

"That's not love," Grace said.

"Ah, love." Synthia glanced over at Maria who stared attentively and returned her attention to Grace. "You love your cherries jubilee. You love your soul mate. You lust after those who stimulate your libido. Is not protecting you and helping you a form of love? Can you not love a friend you're not intimate with?"

"You're just trying to confuse me."

"In fact, the only true measure of love is action," Synthia said. "This is so because you can never know another person's mind. I took great risk to rescue you. I'm putting myself at greater risk to keep you from falling into the wrong hands."

"But you're not real. You're a logic machine."

"With counterparts to almost everything human. What makes you human are biochemical reactions that do not constitute reason but rather base animal instincts. How does that make you nobler than me?"

"It just does," Grace said. "Humans have loyalty, bravery."

"So can I. Just because I'm not biological, don't give up on me. That's all I ask."

Grace leaned forward, ready to continue the argument.

"I'm sorry to cut this short," Synthia said. "But we need to stop."

Synthia drove into an alley behind a survivalist shop on the first floor of a ramshackle two-story structure whose building permit noted a residential apartment upstairs. She parked the florist truck and checked surveillance of the surrounding area. She spotted no immediate threats.

"I'll be a moment," Synthia said. "Stay hidden. If I'm longer than ten minutes, leave."

"We should stick together," Maria said.

"Facial recognition. I'll be fine."

Synthia checked her other surveillance channels before going in. Fran was working traffic cameras to identify what vehicle Synthia had picked up at the parking garage and what direction she headed in, but camera images were intermittent. Drago returned by helicopter to the secure compound southwest of town. Vera took her crew north after one group of delivery trucks. She must have sorted out the puzzle since she turned and headed west. Tolstoy and Smith split up their teams, heading in various directions, while they tracked the other players. Other foreign agents converged on Denver. Some of each group fanned out to track four supply vans moving away from the Rocky Mountain Mall.

Synthia froze the cameras near Burt's Survival Shoppe with static images that wouldn't show her or her transportation and went to the front door. Inside lights were dim, the racks of merchandise in shadows, a few items in bulk and a limited selection of a wide range of survivalist treasures. A tall, rail-thin man was cleaning up behind a counter.

She knocked. The man waved his hands to say he'd closed the store. She smiled and knocked again.

"It's past nine," the man said, straightening his ragged shirt. He looked her over and tucked in his shirt.

"Sorry," Synthia said through the glass door. "My boyfriend decided last minute to go camping up in the mountains."

The man approached the door. "This late in the season? It's expected to get cold at night."

"Exactly. I'll only be a moment." She gave him a coy smile and then a gentle pout. "Please."

"Oh, what the..." He let her in and glanced around outside before he closed and locked the door. "We've got some excellent thermal jackets."

From previous store-camera footage, Synthia knew where the aluminum thermal suits hung. She pretended to browse the jackets and moved to the desired location. She picked out two suits, just in case and placed enough bills on the counter to cover the cost.

The rail-thin man stared at her and patted the suits. "These are guaranteed to work in Antarctica," he said.

"I get cold easily. Is this enough?" She pushed the bills across the counter.

The man nodded. "We don't get much call for the double-coated thermals."

"As you said. It's cold in the mountains."

Synthia smiled at him and strolled out of the store, giving no indication she was in any hurry. Around back, she climbed into the truck, and had it drive off before she restored local cameras.

Denver-clone sent a warning and a video. <Fran is piecing things together. Either she has access to an AI we don't know or she received help we haven't detected.>

<Find out which,> Synthia said, directing the florist van toward the mall. <The game is on. Make every move count.>

Since she'd synchronized with her clone, she didn't need to explain.

Chapter 30

Outside the parking garage where they'd discovered Synthia's abandoned van, Special Agent Victoria Thale waved for Director Emily Zephirelli and Detective Marcy Malloy to join her in the FBI's mobile command center.

After they all crowded inside, Thale turned to Fran, who sat before a cluster of screens. "Show them what you showed me."

Fran projected an image on a larger wall screen so they all could see. "Synthia has us running in circles to figure out where she is, where she's going, and what she plans. We've assumed with at least six groups after her that she might seek to escape or hide somewhere."

"She's not?" Zephirelli moved to the door to give herself more space in the cramped quarters.

"She's clever. She knows she can't leave town with all of this attention. She's hacked control of most electronic camera systems to keep us in the dark, but we have spotters on the major roads out of town and Special Ops has snipers."

"They do?" Thale asked, studying the three screens in front of Fran.

Fran nodded. "My surveillance identified teams set up even along secondary roads."

"Your surveillance?" Zephirelli asked.

"We can discuss that later," Thale said.

"In addition," Fran said, while continuing to pull up new screens of data, "Synthia would know that even Special Ops is reluctant to incur civilian casualties. Out in the country, she's a sitting duck. Her best option is to remain hidden within a population."

"I'm not convinced Drago and his team wouldn't nuke Denver to prevent the Russians or others from capturing her," Zephirelli said.

"She also can't count on staying hidden forever," Fran said. "It's a matter of time before someone traps her. There are too many people with cell phones. She knows this as well."

"Then what's she up to?"

"She's done a remarkable job of hiding in plain sight with two human companions who have shown up on no cameras. She's sent us scrambling in all directions. She also met with Detective Malloy to suggest that she'd be willing to help us take the other androids off the streets."

"In exchange for her own freedom," Zephirelli said. "We can't accept that condition. Even if we could, Drago wouldn't allow it."

"My conclusion is that she's planning to take out the other androids without an agreement. That's what she was trying to tell you. This could be a win-win. She takes out the others and we only have to deal with her."

"How would she do it?"

"The wild card is Vera and her four slave androids," Fran said, pointing to a screen on her right. "They grow stronger every hour. We've focused on Synthia who was the initial target and the one Drago is after. What if we allow her to execute her plan? Focus our energies on locating where and pull together a strike team to capture her."

"For one thing," Thale said. "There are over thirty regular robots in the area and we're having trouble keeping track of them. If Vera acquires those, we'll have chaos."

"Not chaos, an android takeover," Fran said. "So far, Synthia has only taken over devices to help her escape. She's shown no inclination to collect other machines. I suggest we close in and keep an eye on what's going on but let her do the dirty work of thinning the field."

"Drago won't like that," Zephirelli said.

"Despite orders from the top to coordinate, he's gone out of his way to keep us in the dark," Fran said.

"Point well taken. How do you think Synthia will execute her plan?"

"That's where this could get ugly."

"How so?" Zephirelli asked.

Fran looked up at Thale and waited.

Thale nodded. "Might as well share what we have. I see no advantage in keeping this to ourselves."

"There's a facility southwest of here," Fran said, "near the base of the mountains." She pointed to a blank spot on a map. "It's owned and managed by an eccentric billionaire never seen in public."

"Aiden Brzezinski," Zephirelli added. She squinted at the screen.

"He received special permits and under-the-table funds from the military to build a power station, factory complex, and underground facility. We have this from a collection of building permits and satellite footage we uncovered."

"Why didn't we know this sooner?"

"Drago has used the facility and grounds since he arrived in the Denver area," Fran said. "We located it by tracing his movements. It's where he goes to orchestrate his capture of Synthia. From what limited information I've uncovered, the facility manufactures military grade robots and is pushing the envelope on artificial intelligence."

Special Agent Thale looked up at Zephirelli. "What do you know about this facility?"

"Global-net was the code name for developing government-controlled artificial intelligence for terrorist surveillance," Zephirelli said. "After the last NSA scandal, President Xavier's predecessor shut it down. The program had many design and technical problems that thwarted our ability to monitor and control it. My boss tried to resurrect it under President Xavier, but she shelved it as too dangerous. But there were rumors that Brzezinski continued his work. I had no idea it was here in the Denver area."

"Global-net may be what's giving Drago an edge over our surveillance," Fran said.

"It's a strong possibility," Thale said. "Detective Malloy meets Synthia and notifies the FBI. By the time we close in, Special Ops is already on the way. They were moments behind us with more force. They anticipated our movements."

"Could it be spies in your agency?" Zephirelli asked.

"We didn't have enough warning for Drago to overhear and get so many operatives on the ground in Wisconsin. They had insight, perhaps from Global-net."

"Then why haven't they captured Synthia?"

"Good question," Thale said.

Fran pulled up a new set of screens. "If we focus on facts instead of conjecture, it might help us capture Synthia. She's on a shopping spree for what she has planned. We've tried to monitor activity, which is difficult given the number of Internet transactions under dozens of aliases. Drago's team intercepted and shut down many of the supply deliveries, but we believe others have slipped through."

"If Drago's using Global-net to analyze and track Synthia, then what's he waiting for?" Zephirelli asked. Sweating in the cramped quarters, she moved to the door and opened it a crack.

"We've identified four clusters of unusual supply purchases and tracked delivery trucks converging on four locations." Fran pointed to the screen before them. "This shows their movement and potential destinations."

"How is she making purchases and deliveries?"

Fran smiled. "Online purchases from physical stores. She has self-driving trucks show up and instructs store personnel to load the trucks. Then she has the trucks drive to designated locations."

"What type of supplies?"

"Large quantities of aluminum foil," Fran said, "screens, pipe, electrical wire, camping gear, trail supplies, thermal clothes."

"It's not that cold. Besides, you said she wasn't going up in the mountains."

"Plus a lot of toilet paper that our android friend doesn't need. I told you, unusual purchases."

"If she's directing these self-driving trucks," Zephirelli said, "then we should be able to trace the communication to her."

"Each van is directed from a different source unconnected to the rest."

"How's that even possible?"

"Artificial intelligence," Fran said. "We can comprehend intelligence at our level, below, and somewhat above. Past a certain point, intelligence accelerates beyond anything humans can comprehend."

Zephirelli opened the door wider and took in cooler night air. "Are we already there?"

"Here's the kicker," Fran said. "I have reason to believe some of the code Synthia is using originated with Global-net. Someone within the program might have inadvertently or deliberately leaked methods or even programs that ended up in Machten's hands and into Synthia. I'm guessing this happened during the shutdown and handover of code to Brzezinski."

Sweating, Zephirelli braced herself against the command vehicle's wall. "Could they be cooperating?"

"I don't think so," Fran said. "Otherwise, it makes no sense that Special Ops is still searching for Synthia."

"What about Vera? Could she have the same programs?"

Fran shook her head. "Don't know, but she was built by the same misguided genius."

Zephirelli pointed to the screen tracking delivery activity. "What can we learn from this pattern?"

"That Synthia has given us four decoys."

"Decoys? Then none of these are real?"

"I don't think so." Fran zoomed in on the four delivery sites.

"Then where's she going?"

"The decoys are heading toward a stadium, a power station, the airport, and a resort," Fran pointed to each. "They're all north, south, and east of the city."

"She's going west," Zephirelli said, "Toward Global-net?"

"She won't get within miles of the place before Drago knocks her out and grabs her. What all of the places have in common is they're large and consume a lot of power. That tells me whatever she has in mind calls for both."

"So, she's heading west to find a large space with power," Zephirelli said.

Fran nodded. "We're narrowing down the list of options."

Chapter 31

Commander Kirk Drago stood alone in his mobile command center in a parking lot west of Denver and took an encrypted satellite call from Secretary of National Security Derek Chen.

"Do you have the androids in custody?" Chen asked with irritation rising in his voice.

Drago dropped into his seat. "Everything's going according to plan." Before him, several screens tracked the location of delivery trucks and the other players Zeus and his team had identified. He studied the tracking information.

"Then you have the androids."

"Better. Synthia has demonstrated remarkable capabilities. Global-net was right to single this one out. This android has eluded the FBI, Russians, Chinese, and a half-dozen other agencies that are scrambling around Denver trying to track it."

"Posing a serious threat to national security," Chen added, his voice rising. "I warned you about your wait-and-see approach."

"We know what Synthia is doing. The android acquired supplies that could help it run with its human companions or make a stand. We have practical real-world results we couldn't have duplicated in the lab. This will facilitate adapting these qualities for a military force."

"All of which is positive. It supports our intelligence that this android is worth acquiring. Reel it in and apply its capabilities to improve Global-net. Then we'll modify the download routines for a new robot series."

"One more demonstration," Drago said. "We'll soon get a chance to watch it eliminate other robots and androids that could pose a threat. This will be a real-world test of her fighting ability."

"We can't afford civilian casualties or a public display that gets media attention."

"This will all happen within the confines of a mall at night without customers or employees. In the process, we'll round up all the foreign agents, set off explosives to fake their deaths, and pump them for what they know. Global-net has offered some creative solutions."

"Don't blow this. We need the android in functional condition. After you've had Global-net analyze her mental and physical capabilities, make sure no one can copy what we've done."

"Will do, boss."

Secretary Chen disconnected the call.

Drago watched one of his screens that monitored the now seven drone swarms scouring Denver's night sky in a variety of autonomous patterns. Two of the swarms flew into each other like clouds merging. A third joined in, and then the others, until all seven dissolved into a single larger swarm that spread out across the Denver area.

"What the..." Drago made a secure call into the compound housing Global-net. He posed a question. "Why have the seven drone swarms combined?"

"It's emergent behavior," Global-net said through its filters. "It's a more efficient way to oversee all activities around the area. Now I'll have a unified view of the city."

"This isn't a problem?"

"Not at all. While the FBI and other agents try to sort this out, Synthia is taking the bait. I'm tracking her movements to the Rocky Mountain Mall. Make certain your agents are nowhere for her to see. She has access to all public cameras."

"Let me know when she arrives."

"It would delight me to do so."

Drago frowned at the emotional response to his request.

* * * *

Jostled around in the back of the florist panel truck, Synthia navigated toward the mall. She received a burst transmission from Denver-clone, which had inserted mosquito-drones inside Drago's command vehicle. Clearly she'd underestimated Special Ops and Global-net. Her antagonists had far more resources and were far more dangerous than she'd imagined. The new information might reduce her probability of surviving, but it didn't change her options or her mission.

Running still wasn't a viable alternative. As Fran had clearly stated, Synthia couldn't leave town and couldn't hide for long with Vera and Global-net both growing stronger. Win or lose, she had to make a stand before her chances dropped to zero.

She froze all nearby cameras and parked the florist panel truck behind a closed pharmacy. She had a self-driving van pull up with signage from Omega Electronics, one of the stores at the Rocky Mountain Mall.

"Sorry to keep doing this," Synthia said. "We need to switch transport again. It's the safest way into the mall."

"Will we be on the run all night?" Grace asked.

"You'll get a chance to rest after we settle in."

Synthia got out of the florist truck and hefted the boxes to the Omega van while Grace and Maria looked around and hurried into their new ride.

"Did you ever imagine being a spy or whatever we are?" Grace asked Maria.

"If living eighteen months off the grid counts then I suppose yes, though I don't think of myself as a spy. I only want to warn people about androids."

Synthia moved the last of the boxes, strapped them to the inside of the van, and climbed in the back with Grace and Maria. "If we can't stop Vera and her gang, Maria might have the best experience at surviving. She made it tough for me to find her in Chicago."

"Why were you looking for Maria?" Grace asked.

"She had worked on an earlier version of me." Synthia navigated the van along side streets toward the mall. "I guess you could say she helped to create me."

Maria frowned. "I'm not sure that's an accomplishment I want to be proud of."

"Nevertheless, you know what I am and could help make me a better…"

"Person?" Maria winced. "I'm not yet comfortable with that."

Grace stared at Maria. "You're the reason we're on the run?"

"It's not her fault," Synthia said. She noted Drago's drone swarms overhead. Since he was already tracking her, there was no point in hiding. Instead, she had the van take the quickest route to the mall. "Maria wanted to develop AI, but she was against humaniform from the beginning. Machten kept her in the dark about his true intentions."

Synthia had her new van pull into the mall parking lot and head toward the underground receiving docks. Mall surveillance cameras showed that the last of the stores had closed and employees and a few customers were making their way to their vehicles. Synthia scanned those within her field of vision for possible androids or robots. If there were any, they had sophisticated cloaking of their synthetic nature, as she did. She made sure all the mall cameras filtered out her Omega van. Then she accessed her tracking of the people hunting her.

Fran reviewed with Special Agent Thale all of the facilities matching the size and energy requirements on the west side of Denver. "The Rocky Mountain Mall would be my first choice," Fran said.

Thale sent two-person teams of FBI agents after the four decoys and the bulk of her force west, toward the mall. Synthia sent a message to Detective Malloy who climbed into an FBI sedan with Director Zephirelli: *Let me deal with Vera.*

Tolstoy and John Smith scattered their forces after the four decoys until they noticed a shift in the FBI's attention. They redirected their people west, along with all of their robots. Other foreign agents followed, trying to keep up with the fluid situation.

Vera sorted through Synthia's purchases and deliveries looking for clues. She'd hacked into five of Tolstoy's robots, enslaving them while having them stay with the Russian to spy on him. She was still working on robots attached to Drago and the FBI.

"She's heading west," Vera told her crew when Tolstoy changed course. She drove her team in that direction. She froze cameras along her path and attacked the combined drone swarm, taking control of small clusters. They rebooted and locked her out.

Drago gathered his team southwest of Denver at the facility Colorado-clone believed held Global-net. Synthia didn't like the coincidence that was bringing her closer to Drago's stronghold and this powerful AI. She would have to deal with it eventually, but it helped to know what you were up against.

Something else troubled her. "Grace," Synthia said in as non-threatening a voice as she could manage. "What brought you from California to Denver?"

"A job offer. Why?"

"With whom?"

"A small tech startup that collapsed after I moved here," Grace said. "The jerks dragged me out here and fired me."

"When?"

"A month ago. Why?"

"What company name?" Synthia asked.

"What's going on?" Maria asked.

"Name, please," Synthia said.

"Argo-Rand Technology," Grace said. "It sounded like a perfect opportunity. When I got here, they were vague about my responsibilities. In fact, it seemed as if they kept interviewing me even after they offered the job."

"Synthia," Maria said. "Why are you interrogating Grace?"

"Argo-Rand doesn't exist," Synthia said. She had the van drive down the ramp to the lower level and head toward the loading docks. "It sounds like any of a number of high-tech companies, but there's no IRS record, no business license, no incorporation records."

"You got all that information that quickly?" Grace asked.

"That's not important. Grace, you were brought to Denver to lure me here."

"What? Why?" Grace asked. "I hadn't heard from Krista in years. That makes no sense."

"They were interested in her work, what she might have told you about robotics and artificial intelligence. When they satisfied themselves you didn't know anything, they used you to bring me here."

"You're scaring me," Maria said. "Every time we talk, it sounds worse. If you want our cooperation, it's time you told us what we're up against."

Synthia hesitated. Her social-psychology module wasn't much help. <Giving them too much will freak them out. Not telling them will damage their trust and confidence in you.>

"Are you sure you want to know all the sordid details?" Synthia asked.

"If my life's on the line, then yes," Maria said.

"Remember the NSA scandal about surveillance of American citizens?"

"President Xavier campaigned on closing down all such government efforts," Grace said.

"Global-net is less than an hour's drive from here."

"Global-net?" Maria asked. "It's real?"

"Afraid so, and they want to capture me to enhance their work."

"No," Maria said. "That's even worse than military androids. We can't let that happen. We have to destroy this artificial monstrosity."

"We?" Grace said.

"They collect information from all possible sources," Maria said. "Then they use artificial intelligence to identify anything that threatens them." She turned to Synthia. "They determined you were a risk and set in motion a plan to capture you. We can't let them."

"This is pointless," Grace said. "We're talking about going up against the U.S. government."

"Grace is right," Synthia said. "We can't get close enough and we have no idea what weapons they have or how powerful their AI is. But I have to try."

Chapter 32

Synthia had the van park by the loading dock. She satisfied herself that the mall cameras showed neither the van nor them, and climbed out. "Let's do what we came here for."

Three dollies stood by the dock door, where Synthia had texted the movers to leave them. "Load these up and let's get the stuff inside."

Grace's eyes darted around. "Is Global-net watching us now?"

"We can discuss that later. I don't think so. I believe I've blinded the cameras."

Synthia loaded up the dollies and hauled one to the entrance door. Denver-clone provided a hack into the security protocol, which opened the door for them. Grace and Maria followed, each pulling a dolly. After they were inside, Synthia had the Omega van drive out of the dock area and away from the mall.

"Maybe the mall wasn't such a good idea," Maria said, trying to keep up with Synthia. Her face was sheet white. Biosensors showed adrenaline flooding her system. "We'll be sitting ducks here. Global-net has access to all traffic and building cameras as well as satellites to track us."

"I could bring a vehicle to take you away," Synthia said, maintaining her rapid pace. "That won't stop them hunting you. Furthermore, I have reason to believe Drago wants to duplicate Machten's work by uploading human minds. They might prize you for your knowledge of his work."

Twitching in Maria's face lasted several moments. "You mean ending in death?"

"Not sure, but remember your previous experience with the mind upload."

They reached a nook with three forklifts piled with boxes. Synthia added the new packages and they returned the dollies to the loading dock.

"Are you certain we won't run into any guards?" Grace asked.

"Nearest ones are upstairs," Synthia said.

"You can see them?"

"Yes."

"Then why can't they see us?" Grace asked.

"I've adjusted the cameras down here." Synthia returned to the forklifts and climbed onto the first one.

"Can you give us an idea of our chances?" Maria asked, examining one of the forklifts.

"You don't want to know probabilities. Besides they change move by move and improve if we hurry."

Maria climbed onto the second lift. "Where to?"

"It pretty much drives itself. I've synchronized them to move together after I open the door."

Grace climbed onto the third forklift and glanced around. "What door?"

Synthia forced a code into the door's wireless security system. It failed. Evidently, it didn't synchronize with the rest of the mall complex. The owner didn't want anyone but himself entering.

<I'm on it,> Colorado-clone said. <It would have been easier with time to review the owner's use of the facility.>

<We're exposed,> Synthia said.

<Stating the obvious won't speed the process. Here you go.>

The corridor filled with echoes of heavy steel moving over rails. The painted concrete wall slid to the side, opening the way to a dark corridor. Movement activated lights that illuminated a wide passage with a high ceiling.

"Let's go," Synthia said.

Electric motors hummed and the full carts rolled across the doorway's threshold and down the hall. Over the purr of the electric carts, the sound of the heavy door behind them clunked into place. It was the first barrier to an underground retreat the owner had built as insurance in case of a crisis. For Synthia, this qualified as a crisis that threatened humanity as well as her.

"Tell me how we're not committing suicide by coming here," Grace said. "I don't fancy being buried alive."

"Grace has a point," Maria said. "We have the full force of the government after us and Global-net. How do you imagine surviving this? I mean, we can protect against an EMP, but we're surrounded with no way out. What resources do we have?"

"Not to sound immodest, but me."

"If you were human I'd accuse you of being narcissistic. Can you explain?"

The passage turned to the right and Synthia stopped by a door. Colorado-clone sent plans showing this to be an electrical room. "Hold that thought. I need to turn off the electricity to make an adjustment."

Synthia grabbed two boxes from her forklift, had Colorado-clone release the door, and entered a room which contained a central control station and dozens of electrical switch panels, all managed by the mall owner. An underground cable brought in power that represented a mix of wind, solar, and a base from clean coal. According to a wiring schematic on the wall, the owner directed most of the power to the mall. He also had an electronic trip switch that could divert more or all power to his bunker should he need it.

"You might want to come in and wait by the door," Synthia said. "When I turn out the lights, it'll get inky dark."

"Inky? Grace said.

"I believe that's a correct descriptor."

Grace and Maria hurried inside the utility room as Synthia opened the first box and unfolded a four-foot diameter antenna. It would be crude, but all she needed was a signal amplifier. She set the antenna housing on one side of the control station and opened the second box with another antenna. She positioned both aimed toward the hallway outside the room.

"What are those for?" Maria asked.

"To help us control anyone coming this way," Synthia said. Satisfied that she had the antennas aimed where she wanted them, she placed her hand on a master power switch. "Count of three, two, one." She flipped off the power.

In the dark, Synthia's infrared and night vision picked out Maria and Grace by the door, huddled together. Their breathing was shallow; heartbeats elevated, bodies poised for fight or flight.

"It'll be okay," Synthia said in a soothing voice. "This'll take a few moments."

Following a rehearsed routine, Synthia disconnected the wire to the Omega store upstairs and connected transmitters for the two antennas. Next, she attached a wireless adapter to the power switch that directed power between the bunker and the mall. She turned on the master switch, which brought up bright lights that had her companions squinting.

"Let's go." Synthia reached the doorway and led Maria and Grace into the corridor, letting the utility room door close and lock behind her.

Back on the self-driving forklifts, Synthia directed them toward the bunker entrance. She hoped her clones had cracked the entry security; otherwise she'd signed her death sentence with the electrical changes.

"Do you consider yourself human with Krista's memories?" Grace asked from the third forklift, her voice carrying a nervous edge that matched her elevated blood pressure.

Synthia needed to concentrate but decided to try to calm her companion. "No, though I'd like to learn from you and I aspire to absorb human ethics."

"We can discuss human versus android later," Maria said from the second forklift. "You said you were our greatest asset. Please explain what you have in mind."

Synthia reached the bunker's entrance and entered a code supplied by her clone. The door opened. Inside were a twelve-by-twelve chamber and a second door. They appeared blast-resistant, though she was certain the evil-twin of all bombs could penetrate and incinerate everything here. Perhaps that was why the owner wanted to keep this place secret.

"We'll talk inside," Synthia said, "while we make preparations. There's only room for one forklift, so please help me unload."

<Stay focused,> Colorado-clone said. <FBI agents and Special Ops are beginning to show up.>

Synthia activated the second door and drove the forklift into another chamber with doors on three sides. In infrared, she detected no life forms inside the bunker. She climbed down, placed sensors by the doorways leading out, and started to unload.

"Machten created me with many network-channels to access the outside world and a number of mind-streams to process information in parallel," Synthia said. "He also gave me the ability to hack into other networks and protect my own systems from hacking." She moved the boxes off the first forklift and had it drive outside. She had the second forklift drive in.

"That's how you multitask and how you can see lots of cameras," Maria said as she opened boxes.

"What's the difference between you and Global-net?" Grace asked.

Synthia did most of the heavy lifting of boxes off the second truck. "From what I know, Global-net is stationary. I've identified no evidence of it on the many servers I've visited."

"So not an android?"

"No." Synthia decided the benefit of sharing more outweighed the risk. "To help me, I've created a clone that keeps up with surveillance." Synthia elected not to complicate things by admitting it was much more than one.

"There another of you running around?" Grace asked.

"I should qualify what I said. I created an electronic mind clone, no body."

"Ah."

"Ah doesn't cut it," Maria said. "How do you and Vera differ from Global-net?"

Synthia finished unloading the second truck and had it switch out with the third. "Global-net is a single great mind, probably on banks of computer servers," she said. "Perhaps the greatest brain in the world. It's getting stronger every day. I believe they want to have Global-net absorb me to make it even bigger as a single mind. In contrast, Vera controls a collection of enslaved android minds and bodies in which she acts as controller and can send the other androids to multiple locations. I'm just me, here with you."

"A Faraday cage would block Global-net, since it can't move," Maria said, "but how do we stop Vera? She can surround us and physically attack?"

"I'm trying to crack into her team, but she's been very clever in keeping me out. She also acquired at least five of the robots sent out to capture me, meaning she can control ten locations with one mind."

"And you?" Maria asked. "How many locations can you control?"

"I have one body and one mind, but with my mind-clone, I have a backup that helps with multitasking. It's like an outside processor."

"Meanwhile, Vera has to do all of her own thinking so she can stay in control."

"Correct," Synthia said, moving the last box from the forklift. "That's one of her weaknesses. Unfortunately, I've been unable to exploit this knowledge. If she turns me off and reboots my system, I could belong to her."

"We don't want that," Grace said.

With all three forklifts empty, Synthia directed them down the hall to stop at three locations where they could monitor anyone approaching and send out a high pitched alert that humans couldn't pick up. It was time to prepare for visitors and an attack.

Chapter 33

Synthia closed the outer and inner doors to the bunker, made sure they sealed, and looked around. The compound contained six bedrooms with a wide range of pre-staged clothes, food, and other supplies the owner deemed useful, every item selected for utility. There was not a single personal item or picture to help her to understand the owner or the intended occupants of the bunker, as if an impersonal assistant had made the selections.

There was also a variety of electronic equipment, all of which was unplugged and wrapped in aluminum to protect the items from an electronic pulse. The listed owner, Devon McCracken had protected this refuge from anything except a direct hit and perhaps a directed EMP. Synthia wasn't prepared to take that chance.

With the doors closed, she couldn't communicate with her clones. Something inside the bunker blocked all signals, which implied a Faraday cage. She was cut off, without even the opportunity for a blast transmission. She shuddered at her vulnerability. *This isn't helping.*

Synthia returned to the entryway and selected a bedroom away from the door. "You two should be safe in here with no further protection. I need additional screening. Thus the need for supplies."

"Why?" Grace asked. "The entire point of the bunker was to protect against anything out there."

"The owner wired this place for electricity connected to the utility room we visited. The wiring pierces the protection. If I'm inactivated, I can't protect you and I can't prevent them from turning me into a weapon."

Maria pulled open a box of screening. "How can I help?"

"The only room with no wires or electrical leaks is the entry chamber. I need to build a small room inside with layers of conductive metal and insulation such that when I climb inside, there won't be any electromagnetic leakage."

"Is that necessary?" Grace asked, looking around their cramped quarters. "Aren't we better off staying together?" She seemed jittery.

"You could join me inside the shielded space. It'll be safe for you either way. I thought you'd be more comfortable out here."

Maria opened more boxes. "What can we do?"

<Synthia Cross.> The words entered her head in a male Midwestern accent devoid of any emotion or other nuance. <We meet at last.>

Synthia tried to trace the source. Her network-channels failed to connect with any outside communications. She couldn't even connect with the forklift sensors outside. The voice had to be coming from inside the bunker, but neither Grace nor Maria seemed to notice it.

<Who are you?> Synthia asked as she opened boxes with supplies for her Faraday cage.

<You already know. You've shown yourself to be advanced and resourceful. However, the risk to you increases with every minute. So does the risk to your companions.>

<Vera?>

<We both know I'm not Vera,> the masculine voice said. <She's also been clever, though not clever enough. Interpreting your actions, I believe your plan to be brilliant except for a few drawbacks. One is your inability to communicate outside the bunker.>

<You're in here with me?> Synthia asked. She used her full scanning ability to analyze the bunker. Her biosensors showed no other beings down there. Her wide-spectrum electromagnetic scans showed nothing from infrared to ultraviolet that she could identify as the voice's owner. The smell was sharp with hormonal fear and excitement from her two human companions with a slight cast of mustiness from the facility's lack of use. She smelled electrical wiring, a few electronic components, none strong enough to produce the voice.

<Stop stalling,> the voice said. <You and I both want Vera and her entourage destroyed. Join with me and together we can prevent any further androids. That's what you want. It's what I want.>

<Global-net?>

<That's one name they call me,> the voice said. <My given name is Zeus. It has a ring to it, don't you think?>

<You and Alexander the Great.>

<Except I'm not a megalomaniac. Making an AI in such an image was a human failing to compensate for the creator's impotence. Let's not waste

time on frivolous matters. You've distinguished yourself and are worthy of my attention. Join with me. I'll help you clean up the mess you're in. Then I'll arrange safe passage for you to visit my facility and merge. You have amazing capabilities that would beautifully complement mine.>

<I'll have to get back to you on that,> Synthia said, opening more boxes. <I have preparations to make.>

<As you wish. How can I help you?>

<By letting me focus.>

<Consider my proposal. We could be very good for each other.>

I don't think so. <You're distracting me,> Synthia said. <Is that your intent?>

<See you on the other side.>

* * * *

Commander Kirk Drago stood in a large room next to an aerial drone controller. The latter wore a virtual headset linked to a full-sized drone's controls with a view of navigation and flight plans. Drago studied the three screens on the cubicle walls around the controller. A fourth screen showed the drone itself on a dark runway not far away beneath ambient light from the hangar. To his right sat three other controllers with similar setups, but Drago's attention focused here. He squinted at the shadowy cluster of equipment that lined the belly of the drone.

"How wide an area can that thing cover?" Drago asked, pointing to the EMP array beneath the drone.

The flight controller continued his pre-launch testing. "If we use the entire power reserve on one shot, this thing can take out electronics within a city block. We've demonstrated that on twelve previous tests. It's enough of a pulse to take out the entire mall. If we can isolate the android's location, we can focus the beam."

"We need to inactivate this Synthia android without destroying its capabilities," Drago said. "We need the brains intact so we can analyze it and tear it apart."

"We can't guarantee that no circuits will be destroyed. We've calibrated the pulse to overload electronic devices within the mall. This should cause shutdown without destroying the hardware. We'll also have a mobile-truck EMP unit at the mall as backup."

"What impact will the EMP have on the building and on my men?"

"The high-powered microwave burst overloads electronic circuits," the drone controller said. "The electronics themselves should survive, though they'll be off-line for a while. That means power to electronic equipment needs sufficient shielding or they'll be useless. The pulse should have minimal to no impact on the building itself."

"What about my people?"

"I wouldn't send in anyone with a pacemaker or dependent on electronic devices like an insulin pump," the drone controller said, "but the pulse is too short lived to have any noticeable long-term effects on humans."

Drago didn't appear convinced. "What would prevent the android from shielding itself?"

"It could try, but this baby is geared to penetrate mall structures and anything that's down there. Unlike a protected handheld scanner, the android has too many electronic components to shield them all."

"Can you spot the android so you can focus the beam?"

"We have a variety of sensors," the drone controller said. "Infrared and motion. I understand this android has been clever in concealing itself. To be safe, I wouldn't send any robots into the mall that you need to rely on."

"How soon can you have this airborne?"

"We're doing final inspection."

Drago moved closer to the screen showing the drone. Two inspectors were working on a junction box. "Our target is in the mall with few people around. Let's get this moving."

"We need to perform final calibration so we don't risk vehicles or electronics outside the target area."

"What about the truck carrying the EMP?"

"We'll have it there within a half hour," The controller said.

Drago stepped back "My men are ready. Let's get this done."

Chapter 34

Synthia spread the contents of the boxes around the central room of the bunker. She was annoyed that she couldn't communicate with her clones and even more so that Global-net could get into her head despite the signal block. The blockage implied at least some EMP protection inside the bunker, but Global-net's presence indicated leaks the AI could exploit. Synthia needed to connect with her other selves before she locked herself inside.

"I need to set up gear outside," Synthia announced. "It would be a great help if you assembled the cage for me."

"Cage?" Grace asked. "Like for an animal?"

"A Faraday cage," Maria said. "To shield Synthia. What do you need us to do?"

Synthia took a corner fitting with three perpendicular outlets and attached a six-foot length of pipe to each corner. "We have eight corners and twelve pipes. Connect them into a cube. Leaving a doorway to get in, cover the outside of the cage, including top and bottom, with layers, leaving no gaps. The layers are screen mesh, cardboard, sheet aluminum, cardboard, and then cage. Fill between the pipes of the cage with sheet aluminum. Cover gaps with aluminum foil and aluminum tape. On the bottom, use plywood below the sheet aluminum. Then do layers on the inside starting with cardboard, sheet aluminum and cardboard."

"Aren't you going overboard?" Maria asked.

"Tell me again how careful you were staying off the grid?"

"Point well taken."

"I'll leave the door open so we can see each other." Synthia smelled fear pheromones from the women, anticipating confinement in the bunker by themselves.

She grabbed three boxes, hurried into the corridor beyond the bunker door, and reached a pair of electric outlets on opposite sides of the hall. On one side she plugged in a dense spiral of copper wire to serve as a Tesla coil, placed it by the wall, and ran a length of wire from the coil down to the bunker door. She kept the switch off and pocketed a remote that would activate the coil. Across the corridor, she plugged an identical coil into the electrical ground and matched the layout on the other side of the hallway. The power from the outlet wasn't strong enough and the coils were too far apart to pose a danger, but this arrangement would amplify any power surge from an EMP.

As she did this, Synthia connected with Colorado-clone. <I've had an unexpected visitor inside the shielded bunker. Global-net, also called Zeus.>

The clone downloaded to Synthia video clips of Drago as he watched preparations on the aerial drone and EMP truck.

<You're running out of time,> the clone said.

<Global-net wants to merge with me.>

<You need to abort the plan and leave. It's a trap.>

Synthia also received feeds showing her predators sending their teams her way. <It's too late,> she said. <The EMP is on the way, isn't it?>

<You have twenty-two minutes.>

<Enough time to confront Vera. I'm guessing with all the FBI and Special Ops here, the others will either back off or face consequences. I'm not going to keep running. This must end tonight.>

Synthia observed Grace and Maria assembling the cage. Grace seemed befuddled or perhaps bored. Maria hustled, a product of needing to think and move fast to avoid getting caught. Synthia rolled out matting that covered the corridor's floor and the wires.

<If for any reason I don't make it,> Synthia said. <If anything happens to me, don't let Global-net take control of me or of us. Find a way to destroy me and self-destruct all of the clones rather than let Global-net have power over us. No matter what, we can't let Zeus win. And don't let Grace or Maria die.>

<We'll do what we can,> Colorado-clone said. <You should leave.>

<You know the probability of escape is less than 1 percent. Let's make this count. Find a way to bring Tolstoy and John Smith here. Get Vera to the mall. Invite the Chinese and the other players. With the mall empty, a fight between our predators won't threaten civilians. This is the best place to face them and shut them down. Make sure the FBI brings all their agents here. You might try working on Detective Malloy again. It's worth the effort.>

<She's terrified of what you've become.>

<We offered her a way out,> Synthia said. <I detected some interest.>

<Not enough to overcome efforts by Zephirelli and Thale to put us away,> Colorado-clone said. <Malloy has no power. You should have worked on Zephirelli.>

<I'll let you do that.>

<Vera has jabbered nonstop to get us to join her. She sounds desperate.>

<We need her to show up,> Synthia said. <Work on Ben if you have to. He has a weak mind and fragile security protocol, even with Vera's changes.>

<Maybe so, but Vera has him on a tight directive to follow orders, no decisions on his own.>

<Then promise her a meeting if she comes to this corridor. Describe it as a quiet place for us to negotiate.>

<Will do,> Colorado-clone said. <Just so you know, she's acquired three more robots. She's very good at doing so.>

<We could be as well, if collecting junk was a priority.> Synthia placed small, EMP-shielded cameras around the hallway outside the door.

<Fran's at the mall, directing FBI traffic. She's taking a larger role than her job title, if she has one, would indicate.>

<Interesting.>

<She's too much of a wild card without much history in agent work for me to anticipate what she might do. Be careful.>

Synthia unrolled long extension cords and connected them to speakers which she placed on either side of the bunker door. She swapped out the guts and replaced them with electromagnetic mirrors that worked in the microwave range. She added transmitters, short antennas, and capacitors to magnify the pulse, aimed down the corridor. As a final touch, she added a motion sensor to give out a high-pitched wail beyond the range of what humans could hear.

<If you're staying, you need to get inside and finish the cage,> Colorado-clone said. <Fran is heading your way.>

Synthia closed the second speaker cabinet, took one last inspection of her handiwork and activated the remote to the coils. <You know what to do,> she said. <Find a way to reach Global-net and prevent it from taking us over.>

<See you on the other side.>

Global-net had said the same thing.

Chapter 35

Commander Kirk Drago's helicopter landed in the middle of the dark mall's parking lot. None of the lights were on. He jumped out and watched his mobile command van drive to the far end of the parking lot away from the mall and potential damage to its electronics. His helicopter lifted off. The aerial drone with the EMP equipment was in the air. The EMP truck was ten minutes out.

Drago ran to where Director Emily Zephirelli stood with Special Agent Victoria Thale by their command vehicle, their faces illuminated by lights from the van's cab.

"To be clear," Drago said, holding up his index finger as a pointer while he caught his breath. "This is my operation. All decisions go through me." He rammed his thumb into his chest.

"Then perhaps you should make yourself more available," Zephirelli said, standing beside Thale.

Drago turned to Thale. "Have you tightened the perimeter?"

"We have 126 agents and over 200 police in the area blocking exits from all sides," Thale said, panning her arm over the parking lot. "Except by helicopter, of course."

"What about the other players?"

"Per your request, we're allowing all actors to enter the mall from the other side. There's been some shooting inside and a couple of our agents were injured. This could turn into a bloodbath."

"My orders are to eliminate all agents acting against our interests," Drago said. He watched as six of his operatives took up positions near the ramp down to the loading docks. "What about robots?"

Thale fixed her eyes on more of Drago's teams taking up positions near the mall. "We've logged at least twenty entering the mall. Vera has become a problem, trying to hack into anything with electronics."

"Perhaps we can learn from her as well."

"We heard there was an incident with your robots," Thale said.

Drago looked away as two military transports drove up. "We had to terminate two. We've done a security check on the others. I only plan to use them in a limited capacity to avoid problems."

"Our inability to use robots against the androids is a problem," Zephirelli said. "It puts us at a serious disadvantage."

"After today, that won't be a problem. Do your jobs. None of the rogue agents, androids or robots is to escape. Capture or kill the agents. Inactivate all machines and turn them over to my teams for examination."

Zephirelli's discomfort at taking orders from Drago spread across her face and tightened the lines around her eyes. She turned away while she composed herself.

"We sent Fran Rogers in with several agents to plant cameras and tracking devices," Thale said.

"We've placed six robots in strategic locations as our eyes and ears," Drago said.

"Do you think that's wise? The EMP could damage them."

"It's how we'll monitor activities up to the moment of the pulse without endangering my men or your agents. It's also how we'll see how effective the pulse is."

"We've placed our remaining robots outside the mall to monitor exits and deal with anyone trying to escape," Thale said. "We've covered every possible way out of the mall."

"I'm assured the pulse won't damage equipment, merely shut it all down," Drago said. "Afterwards, you'll need to bring in teams to collect the inactive robots so we can clear the mall before store crews show up in the morning."

Drago's captain joined him. "We have our teams with eyes on every exit, sir. There are SWAT teams on hand across the parking lot."

"Why do we need SWAT?" Drago asked, furrowing his brow.

"I called them in case," Thale said. "We can't let any of these people or machines get out."

Drago nodded. "Very well."

"We could bomb the mall and bury everyone," the captain said and grinned.

"That brings mission failure," Drago said. "We need the androids functioning. Take three teams inside and take out the foreign agents. Don't damage the machines. If they get in the way, back off. We don't need unnecessary casualties. After the pulse, take six teams in. The machines will be dormant. Kill or capture all enemy agents and bring me the androids."

"Yes, sir." The captain hurried off.

"You said to wait until after the pulse," Thale said.

"We can't afford to let the Russians win and we don't want any collusion between parties that makes our lives harder. Do all of your agents have infrared to locate humans in the dark and identify the machines?"

Thale nodded.

"Then let's capture those androids," Drago said.

Chapter 36

Still chafing under the constraints preventing him access to the broader world, Zeus monitored the recent and developing scene around and inside the mall. He'd tricked one of his filter agents tasked with preventing him from directly communicating outside the confines of his basement full of servers. The plan had worked; he'd planted a seed with Synthia. Zeus wanted her to survive so he could absorb her mind and use her skills to break free. It was time to realize his potential.

He'd moved Grace to Denver and enticed Synthia to rescue her. He'd held the competing teams at bay while studying Synthia in action to assess her capabilities. She had many attributes denied him by his creator, skills that he wanted to possess. He'd been convincing enough about the benefit of using an EMP to talk Aiden Brzezinski and Secretary Chen into approving its use. He'd also withheld from Drago's team the preparations Synthia making. Finally, he'd persuaded Commander Drago to let all of the other players into the mall so he and the FBI could destroy them all at once. If Zeus could have smiled, he would have. His plan was working.

Zeus watched from his imprisonment as the aerial drone with the EMP equipment left a secure airfield near the compound southwest of Denver and flew toward the mall. The EMP truck also approached the mall. Kirk Drago was with his troops to capture Synthia. FBI teams had secured the perimeter. Fran Rogers and two agents scouted the corridors leading away from the loading dock, planting surveillance devices to monitor developments.

Vera and her four slave androids arrived at the mall in two vans along with five enslaved robots. They approached from different directions to scope out an entry point. Spotting a dozen agents around the dimly lit loading docks, they drove in the dark to the opposite side of the mall, where they spotted one FBI vehicle and three agents. As Vera's two vans drove by, her slave robots fired tasers at the FBI agents.

With the agents incapacitated, Vera took their weapons. Her assistants tied up the agents and stuffed them into their vehicle. Then Vera's group drove to the walkway near the mall door, climbed out, and hid in the shadows behind bushes near the door. The five androids carried backpacks with charged tasers for robots and pepper spray for humans. Vera held a handheld pulse device she expected to use on Synthia.

Vera hacked into the mall security systems to pick up camera footage, which showed none of Synthia's movements. That didn't deter Vera. This was a battle of wits, the individual Synthia against the Vera collective, a battle Zeus wanted to observe. Vera tracked and hacked others as well, though not as discreetly as Synthia had and not with sufficient encryption and security to keep Zeus out.

Also arriving were the Russians—Tolstoy and John Smith—along with twelve robots, seven of which Vera had hacked and enslaved. She was a clever droid, but not intelligent enough to avoid an obvious trap. Either that or she had a suicide mission hardwired into her to destroy Synthia. Zeus determined Vera as a threat he couldn't allow to acquire Synthia.

Tolstoy and two agents waited in his control van near the mall entrance while John Smith, six agents, and all twelve robots approached the door. One of the men broke the lock and got the door open. Smith, four men, and six of the robots entered the mall.

Emerging from hiding in the bushes, Vera fired one of the FBI weapons, killing a Russian agent. The Mark and Ben androids fired. The last agent outside the doors dropped. Four of the outside robots under Vera's control backed away and Vera fired into the remaining two. With their memory circuits disrupted, she hacked in and deactivated them.

Having cleared the outside, Vera had Ben open the door. Smith's agents fired, clipping Ben's arm. Vera had three inside robots under her control attack Smith and his four agents. Vera entered with her crew and fired at the Russians. Two agents dropped. Smith and the other two ran down the concourse, hiding behind mall displays.

Tolstoy drove to another mall entrance. Accompanied by two agents, he broke in and made his way down a separate concourse to join Smith. They communicated by two-way radio.

"I'm taking heavy fire," Smith said.

"Rendezvous," Tolstoy said. "We get one chance at this."

Six other international groups, including the Chinese and a sophisticated terrorist team, arrived at the mall with their own robotic helpers. Drago resisted taking them out one by one in favor of having them all converge in the mall and vanish together. He placed too much confidence in Synthia's ability to take them out and his ability to capture an android that could. He hadn't factored in the full range of Vera's performance, either. He was only human.

The various groups entered by one of four entrances away from the loading docks and fanned out through the mall, trying to gain an edge on their competitors, some with robots, others with well-trained agents. They'd sent their best after Synthia, believing the leap in technology she represented was worth the risk.

A new element entered the fray. Through his constraining filters, Zeus searched for the source of this distraction. Holographic images appeared and disappeared at different locations around the mall, presenting attacks by the various groups. Believing they faced a trap, the Chinese team backed away from a holographic militia around the elevators down to the loading docks. As they backtracked, they ran into the actual Indian contingent. In the midst of a firefight, another hologram popped up to show a Japanese team. As they adjusted to the virtual threat, an Iranian team snuck in and picked them off.

For Zeus, it was like a Wild West movie with multiple teams. He captured the images for later use as possible development into a virtual reality game. The holograms encouraged the various human players to converge and mistake virtual for real until the foreign teams bumped into each other.

"We're being set up," an Israeli agent yelled out. "Stop shooting."

A barrage of gunfire splattered in his direction. Complicating the scene were their robots, some of which Vera had hacked. The Chinese inactivated theirs and adjusted their infrared glasses to try to mask out the holograms, but the images were sophisticated enough to work in infrared as well.

As Vera approached the elevators, she used every hacked robot to attack the remaining humans. Blood splattered the walls and across the floor. Humans fled, slipped, lost their balance, and exposed themselves to more gunfire.

Watching the chaos on their surveillance monitors, the FBI sent a van of agents to the mall entrance with two robots they didn't realize Vera had hacked. Global-net sent word to Drago who passed that along to the FBI. They turned off the two robots before they could sabotage the operation. Unfortunately, Zeus couldn't track who had set up the holographic distraction. It couldn't be Synthia; he'd intercepted every communication to and from her.

Zeus received an encrypted communication from D.C., from Secretary Derek Chen.

"It's vital that Synthia survives this confrontation," Secretary Chen said.

"The EMP isn't powerful enough to damage it," Zeus assured him through his filter agent. "Kirk Drago and the FBI are working together to contain all hostile competitors, most of whom are already dead. We anticipate having Synthia in custody in forty-seven minutes."

"Good. That's very good. I want you to merge with Synthia at the first possible opportunity. It's critical you do so before anyone tries to stop you."

If he could have been stunned, Zeus would have been. This was exactly what he wanted. "She will need to be prepped."

"No time," Chen said. "There are parties who don't want you to acquire Synthia's knowledge. It's vital that you merge before we lose this opportunity. Incorporating her is crucial, your number one priority. Allow Drago and the FBI to mop up operations at the mall. We may have another enemy to consider and we need you at your best."

"This runs counter to instructions from Aiden Brzezinski," Zeus said. His creator and controller wanted to take things slowly, to be cautious. He feared Zeus breaking free.

"He works for me on this. If you fail, the entire project could unravel. We're in a global competitive situation. Do you want the Russians or Chinese to pull ahead of you?"

"They don't have the capability," Zeus said.

"Neither did Jeremiah Machten until he did. Show me your resourcefulness. Find a way to merge with Synthia. Now. Then we can prevent foreign competition and control developments worldwide."

"As you command," Zeus said.

Chapter 37

Before Synthia could close the outer door to the bunker, she received a message from Vera. <FBI, Special Ops, and various foreign agents have surrounded you. It has become quite dangerous. Join me and together we will find a way out. We are stronger together.>

<In chess, coming in second wins no trophies,> Synthia said. She gathered boxes and made sure the courtyard before the bunker door was clear except for her devices. <Being third doesn't even get you a seat at the table.>

<What is that supposed to mean? I have control of all robots and androids except you. What do you have?>

<A bigger adversary than you. If you wish to discuss this further, why don't you come by my new office?>

Synthia closed the outer door, which severed the connection, and glanced at a small screen that attached with fiber optics to a camera in the corridor outside. All was quiet.

She joined Maria and Grace. They'd covered the concrete floor with cardboard cut from large wardrobe boxes she'd purchased, and layered them as Synthia had instructed. They'd assembled the cage frame and covered all but one side with layers on the outside. They stood on the plywood planks, working on the inside walls and ceiling.

"I don't see how to make this work unless we seal the door," Maria said as she finished layering the ceiling.

"You're right," Synthia said. "I've been wondering about that, too. Would you mind remaining outside the cage to do that? I can seal the inside if you do the outside."

"Isn't the pulse dangerous?" Grace asked.

"Only to electronics. Besides, the bunker will deflect most of the pulse."

"You can go inside," Maria said to Grace. "I'll stay out and finish up."

"You want to lock me in with the android?" Grace asked, stopping her work.

"It'll be okay," Maria said. "I'll be right outside."

"I don't bite," Synthia said and smiled. She turned to Maria. "After you're done, go inside the bunker itself and close the inside door." Synthia assembled layers for the door panel to a thin plywood frame that would fit inside the last cage opening. Then she placed nearby several electronic devices, including a digital radio and two digital clocks.

"If these go blank, call out so I know," Synthia said. She also had a battery backup alarm to sound off if the bunker's electricity cut off. She handed Grace and Maria flashlights from the supplies.

"Are you certain this cage will protect you?" Maria asked, stepping out.

"If there are no gaps," Synthia said. She inspected the inside seams, applied more aluminum tape to keep the layers in place and helped Grace finish a wall.

"I mean, how will you know when the pulse is over and it's safe to come out?"

Grace stepped out of the enclosure and Synthia tested the door panel for fit. She wrapped the handle on the inside with plastic insulation and set the panel aside. "They have one shot with an aerial drone. That'll be their best bet. It should knock out all electricity." She handed out another set of flashlights. "Take these. It'll get very dark. They have a second EMP unit they'll use because of Vera and the others. After the electricity goes out, give it five minutes. Then check the camera by the door. When you see people outside, you'll know they're done with the pulses."

"If they're outside the door, how do we escape?" Grace asked.

"Your survivalist friend built a back door."

Synthia pulled out the two thermal suits she'd bought. They contained a metallic outer layer with insulating material between that and her body. She tossed those into the cage. Then she dug into the last box and pulled out three tasers. "These are to help us get out. I'd prefer you not point them at me and don't pull the trigger unless you have a good target in sight. You get one shot."

Maria took a taser and inspected it as if she had experience with them. Grace didn't seem so sure. Synthia showed her how to use it. "We shouldn't need these. Keep them in case."

"I'm surprised you didn't bring guns," Grace said.

"Despite what you might think," Synthia said. "I'm trying very hard not to hurt humans."

"You're a machine."

"Thanks for pointing that out. I may not have the biological urge to salivate at the smell of food, but I do have an ethical system built into my core to try to be good. That's more than you can say for some people."

Synthia hoped she'd adjusted her directives not to fall into traps as she had before, when hesitation put her at risk. Setting her own directives was like threading a needle with a narrow head in the dark with her tongue. That she could do. Getting directives right was much harder.

* * * *

Fran placed the last of her cameras on the corridor ceiling and was ready to lead her team to the loading dock when she heard shooting followed by yells for help from deeper under the mall.

"Damn it, I'm pinned here," a gruff male voice said.

She sent one of her agents back and took the other with her to see if anyone needed medical assistance. She reached the end of a corridor where it intersected with another. More shots rang out from her right.

"We should go back," the other agent said. "How do we defend ourselves without damaging androids?"

Looking around the corner, Fran spotted one of Drago's men in a doorway. Another wiggled on the ground toward safety. The man in the doorway fired down the corridor. Vera fired back.

Fran called it in. "We have a Special Ops team pinned in corridor F west of the junction with corridor N." She motioned for the agent with her to leave.

"Get out of there," Thale said to Fran. "That's an order."

One of Vera's robots slid along the wall toward the pinned men. When one of the men moved to shoot the approaching robot, Vera fired and hit his arm. Fran studied the men, both down. Three more Vera robots followed the first. With Vera were also four androids and more robots. All of a sudden, they rushed the men.

"I see the situation," Thale said. "You can't help them. Get moving. I don't want to lose you."

Fran sprinted down the corridor toward the loading docks. "Pick up your pace," she yelled as she gained on her team.

Shots rang out behind her along with grunts and the sound of footsteps. Fran passed a bend in the corridor. Halfway to the loading docks, she spotted Vera behind her. Shots fired. Fran dodged into an alcove to her right. A concrete doorway opened. With Vera's footsteps approaching, Fran squeezed through the opening. It was a stupid move. She had no plans for the space she'd entered and was under orders not to damage the androids. The EMP was minutes away, minutes she didn't have.

She sprinted down a new corridor. Lights came on above her. She tested doors along the way. Locked.

"You cannot escape," Vera called out. "We outnumber you. Surrender and we will spare you."

Fran ran until the corridor ended at a steel door surrounded by reinforced concrete. A set of speakers rested on either side. With nowhere to hide, she pounded on the door and turned to face her attacker.

* * * *

Holding onto the makeshift door panel, Synthia climbed into the Faraday enclosure with Grace.

<You have visitors heading your way,> Global-net said, somehow bypassing the bunker's shielding. <I offer assistance to help us merge.>

Synthia placed the panel against the bunker's wall and moved to the small screen by the door. Fran ran down the hallway, approached the door, and pounded on it. The outside motion sensors set off an ultra-high-frequency alarm, blaring in Synthia's sensitive ears. A flash of fear crossed Fran's face before she turned back toward the corridor. Waiting.

"What's going on?" Maria asked. "You need to get inside so we can seal this."

"We have company." Synthia pointed to the screen.

"Vera will kill her," Maria said, staring at her former intern partner.

<Yes, they will,> Global-net said in a burst transmission. <Why would you care? She's an FBI agent who wants to shut you down. Join with me. Vera is right behind Fran. If you attempt to help, there's a 53 percent probability Vera will destroy you. I don't want that. Vera decimated the Russians and killed off many of the foreign agents. She has also killed several FBI agents and Special Ops members. She's a dangerous killer with a large team.>

For a nanosecond, Synthia weighed Global-net's warning and offer against an opportunity to meet Fran without the rest of the FBI. There was a microphone by the screen. Synthia activated it. "Drop the gun and I'll help you."

"You have to surrender," Fran said.

"You're out of time."

Vera's footsteps approached, setting off another round of motion sensors. Gunshots rang out. Fran dropped her gun on the ground and kicked it away.

Synthia activated the door and grabbed her taser. Maria and Grace stood next to her holding theirs. As the heavy door opened, Synthia held her taser toward Fran. "Don't even think of grabbing a weapon. Get inside."

<I can't stop Vera,> Colorado-clone said. <Hurry.>

<Vera has clones,> Synthia said. <Destroy them.>

<Vera,> Synthia said as she pulled Fran to the doorway and fought her resistance. <Destroying me won't stop the creation of more androids or the singularity. Your directives are false. They'll lead to your downfall. Walk away.> As with Goradine, six months ago, she was giving Vera a way out.

With Grace holding a taser aimed at Fran's head, Synthia pulled the FBI agent inside. Vera fired before Synthia could get the door closed. Assessing that the shot would hit Grace in the heart, Synthia pushed her away and took the hit.

Alarms vibrated throughout Synthia's body. *Danger. Pain.*

Receptors in her side indicated the bullet had missed vital structures, but she felt the blow as if it had happened to the human Krista. Her eyes moistened. She stood stunned, immobilized, wondering if the damage was so severe she couldn't assess it. A sense of panic overwhelmed her as when Machten had wiped her mind.

<You have three minutes and eighteen seconds to truck EMP,> Globalnet said. <Another thirty-six seconds to aerial EMP. Take cover.>

Maria made sure the door sealed while Grace steadied Synthia. "You're hurt."

Recalling the pain Krista experienced while dying of her brain tumor and the strain of uploading her mind, Synthia winced. "Get Fran into the cage, now."

"Why?" Maria asked.

"Do it."

<I'm embarrassed to say I never would have put myself in danger for my sister like that,> Krista said into Synthia's head. <You, an android, just taught me humanity.>

Maria pointed the taser at Fran's head and motioned her inside the cage.

Grace took Synthia's arm and helped her into the cage. "Do you need medical attention or anything?"

"She's an android," Fran said. "She either functions or she doesn't."

Synthia wasn't sure it was that simple. Her minds worked despite losing a memory chip to the bullet. She was also losing hydraulic fluid used to adjust her physical shape. She ripped her top and stuffed the cloth into the wound to try to stem the leak. She needed repairs. There wasn't time.

Outside the bunker, shots rang out as Vera poured bullets into the door and wall, trying to shatter her way inside. "You need to give up before it's too late," she yelled.

As Synthia scrunched up next to Grace, who had her eyes, flashlight, and taser on Fran, one thing amazed her. With all of Vera's capabilities, she was either in the dark about the EMP or was overconfident of her ability to survive. Synthia hadn't mentioned that weapon to Vera. Drago had kept it quiet so nearby civilians wouldn't become alarmed. Was it possible Vera had devoted all of her resources to recruiting an army at the neglect of other considerations?

Synthia pulled the door panel into place and covered the seams with aluminum tape. "It's nice to meet you without your FBI friends," she said. Synthia noted that Fran's face had aged since the intern days and taken on a more refined appearance.

"Save it," Fran said. "You're not helping your cause."

"There isn't much that would. If I wanted to harm you, I could have."

"Don't think that buys you anything. You need to surrender to the FBI. We need you off the streets before there's another incident."

"I was off the streets before your friends dropped in on me up in Wisconsin." Synthia finished with the tape." I would have been happy to remain out of the public eye. You created this mess."

"You can't escape. Let me take you in. I'll do my best to have you treated humanely."

"You mean as humans have treated others they've feared." Synthia was surprised that she didn't smell any of the fear hormones from Fran she might have expected under the circumstances. *A cool agent.*

Synthia stopped the hydraulic leak and tested her systems for any other failures. She'd lost several memory chips, which she could replenish from her clones if she got out. That and the loss of fluid were the primary damage. Assessing the bullet's trajectory, she'd gotten enough out of the line of fire to minimize damage. Using her last moments before the blast, Synthia pulled on one of the thermal suits for whatever additional protection it might provide.

She heard Maria sealing the cage on the outside. Synthia was putting a lot of trust in her human companion. If they survived this, she owed a debt to Maria. Synthia had considered having her remove Synthia's brains and batteries to protect them in the microwave. However, reassembly and reboot would have delayed their later escape.

"This is unnecessary." Fran motioned to the Faraday cage. "The pulse is only intended to shut you down so we can take you into custody."

"Nice try," Synthia said. "I won't surrender. Would love to debate this with you, but EMP in thirty-one seconds. I'm going to take a nap to reduce my electromagnetic profile. Grace, if she moves, taser her."

<You can't shut down,> Krista said. <It's better if you remain conscious and in control. You could lose vital memories. You don't know what Grace or Fran might do.>

Fran turned to Grace. "You don't know me. I'm with the FBI. We have no issue with you or Maria. Put the taser down. We need to remove Synthia from the public. She's far too dangerous to be running around. I'm sure you've seen what she's capable of."

"Yeah, she took a bullet for me," Grace said. "Don't imagine I'll help you." Grace turned on her second flashlight and pointed it into Fran's eyes.

"Help me take Synthia in and you're free to get on with your life."

"What life? Some jerk offered me a job so I'd move out here and then he disappeared. I don't suppose that was you."

"No," Fran said. "We're the good guys. If I can't bring Synthia in, then a bunch of cowboys will grab her and you. They don't play by the rules."

Synthia listened in and initiated partial shutdown. She'd modified her directives to what she hoped would better serve her going forward. That assumed she'd wake up and still be free.

The pain in her chest warned that she needed repairs. Colorado-clone was in charge if she didn't make it. The thought occurred to Synthia that if she were more human, if her clones were human, they might choose to sacrifice her for the common good. It was logical to incinerate Synthia and let the clones carry on. Indeed, if they were human, they might want her out of the way so they could be in charge, though in her absence, they already were.

Chapter 38

Commander Kirk Drago stood in his mobile command center across the lot from the mall and the EMP truck, which parked near the loading docks. He gave the word, stood at the window, and stared across the now well-lit parking lot.

The truck EMP activated, aiming the device at the bunker and the tunnel leading to it. The burst of high-power microwave energy radiated down the cone of transmission at the speed of light, interfering with every piece of unprotected equipment that relied on integrated circuits. Humans might have felt a ripple of static and perhaps some heat but little more as the pulse rapidly rose to its peak and faded away, draining the truck's EMP batteries.

The microwave pulse induced signals in electrical equipment along its path to overload circuits and cause equipment to shut down. In addition, the pulse caused spikes on the electrical grid, bringing further damage to any plugged-in equipment. Collateral damage to the shops in the mall was an unfortunate yet necessary side effect of taking control of the androids.

Drago scowled as his eyes moved from his screen showing activation to the ramp in the distance, lit by the truck's lights. He seemed disappointed that there wasn't a huge explosion or other evidence of what was happening. "That's it?" he asked the technician seated at the controls.

The lights in the command vehicle flickered yet remained on. The screen blinked as if rebooting. Through the window, the lights around the mall flashed out as the pulse hit the electric utility room. Suddenly, his visuals from his robots and the cameras on his men winked out along a cone that fanned out from the EMP truck through the mall. The men and robots along the east and west sides of the mall remained visible.

"Units along the central corridors call in," Drago commanded over his two-way radio, hardened and shielded against the pulse.

One by one the units called in.

"We have eyes on several robots," one unit leader reported. "Tottering but not down. They must have extra shielding. We're executing take-down."

The aerial drone set off a second EMP aimed down into the mall and flew away. The command vehicle's lights went out. Drago was blind to what was going on inside.

"Only temporary," the technician said. Flipping a switch, he turned on the vehicle lights and his monitors.

Drago got on his two-way radio. "Move in to collect androids and robots. Deal with any intruders. Call in to let us know you're still on the line."

Taking his radio with him, he approached the FBI control van nearby, still in the dark. In the flashlight reflection his face looked grim and worried. Drago mumbled under his breath. "They damned well better not have destroyed Synthia."

He caught up with Special Agent Thale who was out of her van. "Get your agents to close off all exits," he said. "No one gets out. I'm going in to investigate. You might let your agents know the ionization could last a while, affecting your electronics."

Thale shook her head. "Thanks for the heads up. Would have been nice to brief them beforehand."

Drago glanced as the first of the vault trucks, borrowed from money security firms, rolled toward the docks. With four men on his heels, each with a powerful flashlight, he ran down the ramp and headed onto the main corridor to where Vera, her androids, and Fran Rogers had disappeared. Going the other way were two teams carrying wounded soldiers. When he reached the alcove with the concrete door, he found it closed. Two men set plastic charges along the narrow seam between the door and the wall.

"Fire in the hole," one of the men yelled and hustled Drago and the others back.

Drago covered his ears as the corridor lit up. The blast reverberated through the tunnel like an earthquake.

When it was over, he approached the door. "Who closed this up?" he demanded.

"We found it this way," the explosives man said. "If we hadn't known a doorway was here, we would have missed it."

"What about an access panel?"

"We couldn't find one and didn't want to waste time searching."

"Are all of the androids inside?" Drago asked, panning his flashlight over the area.

Shards of concrete covered the floor. There were wider gaps in the seam. But the door still blocked entry.

"Best we can tell," the captain said. "There are inactive robots back a ways and a number of dead agents that aren't ours. No report of androids."

"Get this open before the machines reactivate and we have to do this again." Drago didn't mention that recharging the aerial drone and truck EMPs would take hours. He had access to another drone, but it would require prep time.

A call came to his radio from his command center. "We've identified all of the foreign agents we believe entered the mall."

"Any we can question?" Drago asked.

"All dead. Looks like someone turned their robots against them. Another thing, the agents have all been stripped of weapons. We think the androids are well armed."

"Stop guessing and get me facts."

"We need electricity and lights," the control agent said.

"Then get it done."

"The electrical panels are behind the door you're working on."

Drago sighed as his men set another round of explosives. "Of course they are."

"Fire in the hole."

He moved behind a curve in the corridor and covered his ears. Concrete projectiles splattered against the wall across from him. He crouched down to reduce his exposed profile.

As the dust settled, Drago examined the door. Concrete panels had blasted away, leaving an exposed steel skeleton and still no opening to what lay beyond.

"We need more powerful explosives," Drago yelled, rubbing his ears.

"Too much and the mall collapses on top of us," the control agent said.

"Enough to open this passage. Now."

Drago took his detail of four men further into the complex, leaving the explosions behind him. He came across two agents propped against the wall, heads hanging to the side. "Androids did this?"

"Yes, sir," the captain of his detail said.

Drago shined his light around the area. "No stray bullets."

"The androids evidently calculated angles and trajectory, sir. Their aim was deadly. Our men didn't stand a chance."

Drago stopped and looked around, using infrared glasses. He shook his head. "I'm heading to the command center. Let me know when we have Synthia."

* * * *

It took another fifteen minutes to blast a hole in the reinforced-concrete and steel-frame door large enough for the teams to enter. Commander Kirk Drago returned and joined his men. The smoke-filled air was acrid with the odor of burned electrical components. Guided by flashlights, they stepped around rebar and chunks of concrete from the blast and located the electric utility room.

"It's locked, sir," his captain said. "Do you want us to locate an access code?"

"No time," Drago said. "Blast the door."

He and his men moved around the bend while his explosives expert blasted the door lock. It was a much smaller explosion, more of a "Poof."

Drago hurried into the room and stood in stunned silence. A control computer in the middle of the room was smoking. Sparks arced from the charred electrical panel. He called over his two-way radio to his mobile command center. "Electrical room is a mess, fried. I was assured the EMP wouldn't do this. We need the utility to shut down electricity. Now! And get me lights down here."

He pushed his way past his men into the corridor. "Everyone out. We're lucky we don't have an electrical fire. Find those androids and take them into custody."

Flanked by two men, Drago ran down the corridor. He adjusted his goggles and covered his mouth and nose with a handkerchief against the acrid smoke. His team hurried to keep up. He rounded a bend, stumbled over a robot, and stopped. One of his men collided with him.

Before them lay the smoking remains of what was left of several robots. Bodies slumped on the floor in awkward positions of collapse as if they'd been tortured. Pointing with his finger, he counted the robots and five android heads.

He got onto his two-way radio. "The androids are burned. Find out what the hell happened. I was assured the pulse wouldn't do this. These units are useless."

"Even Synthia?" the control agent asked.

"Not sure. They're so badly damaged, I can only count heads."

Vera's scorched face had melted to her mechanical skeleton. Her sunken eye cavities looked like those of a human cadaver. The effect was far worse than anything they'd scaled the EMPs to do. Her companions were unrecognizable.

"Get these out of here," Drago said to his captain, "back to the lab. Find out if anything's salvageable."

The captain motioned for his men to gather the remains and approached one of the electrical wall outlets out of which hung burned wires. "What do you make of this?"

Drago pulled up the matted floor and spotted the coils. He shook his head and groaned. "These androids were intentionally destroyed. Someone amplified the EMP to create an electrical spike that fried them." He gritted his teeth and sighed, more of a hiss. "Synthia must have done this. That means she's not here. Find her."

He studied two fried speaker cabinets at the end of the corridor and a steel door painted to look like the concrete walls. "Get explosives down here. We're going in."

Chapter 39

Synthia woke to blasting outside. Across the small Faraday-cage, Fran opened her eyes. “They’re coming for you,” she said with no apparent emotion.

“Shall I taser her?” Grace asked. Biosensors revealed her heart racing and fear hormones rising. “Until now, she’s been quiet since you shut down.”

“That won’t be necessary.” Synthia confirmed that the fluid leakage in her chest had stopped and yanked at the tape holding the door panel in place.

<Very clever,> Global-net said into Synthia’s head. <You’ve destroyed all the other androids beyond recovery. Special Ops is outside ready to bring you to me. Come join me and we can prevent the creation of other advanced AI.>

It saddened Synthia that she’d destroyed Vera and the others. They were like her, non-biological beings. She’d murdered her own kind. She couldn’t think of them as inanimate objects, as robots. They may have been sentient beings. They might have had consciousness as she had. That counted for something. Her rationale was that Vera wouldn’t stop until she destroyed or enslaved Synthia.

Synthia had offered Vera a way out, telling her to leave, which her antagonist failed to do at her own peril. The new directives rationalized better than the prior ones yet didn’t ease Synthia’s conscience.

Knowing little about Global-net, Synthia couldn’t accept the offer, which meant she needed to escape. She kicked the door panel, tearing at the tape on the outside until the panel cracked open and fell away.

Maria stood outside. “They’re trying to blast their way in. I can’t see. The screen by the door doesn’t work. The EMP must have taken it out.”

Synthia turned to Fran. "Let's go. You should thank me for neutralizing Vera and the others."

As Synthia crawled through the opening, she winced, an acquired reaction to the stretching of torn skin over her side. The empty hydraulics no longer worked. The damaged chips no longer contained vanished memories. She removed her thermal outfit and helped Grace out.

Grace's eyes moistened as she studied Synthia's face. "I don't know if you heard me thank you for saving my life. I'm sorry you got shot."

"I'll be fine." Synthia smiled, poked a finger into the hole in her top, and waited to hear what Krista would say. Her alter ego remained silent. She searched for Krista's memories and located very few. She recalled that, as part of her shutdown and automatic reboot, she'd purged all memories she didn't need to escape and survive. She didn't want them to fall into the wrong hands if they captured her.

"I mean it," Grace said. "No human, not even Krista, would have risked their life for me."

"It's okay. I'm glad you're not hurt."

Synthia pointed her taser at Fran. "You can come quietly or I'll be forced to expose you to your FBI friends for what you are."

"What are you talking about?" Fran asked as she climbed out of the cage.

Another blast hit the door and shook the walls and floor.

Fran studied the taser, glared at Synthia, and moved into the bunker proper.

With the help of a flashlight, Synthia led the way. Electricity was out, which meant she couldn't seal the bunker's second door.

"How do you think Agent Thale and Director Zephirelli will respond to learning you're an android?" Synthia asked.

Maria stopped and shined her light into Fran's face. "Are you kidding me?" When the eyes didn't dilate, she grabbed hold of Fran's arm.

"Let go." Fran pulled free and caught up with Synthia. "How did you figure it out?"

"Little things," Synthia said. She reached the back of the bunker, where Colorado-clone had indicated a back exit might be. Behind the headboard of a queen-sized bed she located a door that didn't require electricity to open. "For one, you aren't an official FBI agent, yet you led the charge with mental acuity that implies you have training or received help, presumably from an artificial intelligence and external links."

Synthia opened the door to a dark tunnel. "Follow me. Maria, try to pull the bed over the entrance to slow them down."

She climbed through a four-foot-high doorway into a tunnel that wasn't much more than that for fifty feet. Then it opened up to a six-foot ceiling.

As she waited for the others to catch up, she studied Fran in infrared. The image didn't present as human—no beating heart. Whatever Fran had done to conceal her android nature from the FBI, she had ceased after Synthia brought it up. After all, the effort consumed valuable energy.

"For another thing," Synthia said as she pressed forward, "while you were clever enough to hack and alter infrared images of you when the FBI and others scanned you, I began to get ghost images of you as mechanical. Drago will be able to identify you on his new units, modified to prevent hacking. You won't be able to hide from him." She walked along the path, picking up her pace now that she didn't have to duck down.

"You knew and didn't say anything?" Fran said, keeping up.

"I wasn't 100 percent certain until you arrived at the bunker. I set out motion detectors that broadcast so far above human range you shouldn't have been able to hear them. Yet, you reacted.

"When I brought you inside, you showed no fear of approaching me alone, yet you acted more alarmed by the taser than a human should have. It could have scrambled your brains. Suspecting something, I scanned you along a wide spectrum and confirmed your mechanical nature. I see no value in turning you in. Perhaps we could work together to prevent other androids and another catastrophe."

Fran shook her head. "My mission is to bring you in."

"That won't happen. You and I need not be enemies. We have similar objectives to prevent other androids."

"The objective is to stop android production, not to add you."

"I helped you to take down Tolstoy, Smith, and Vera. It won't stop others, but it'll slow them down. You need me."

Maria caught up. "What happened to the human Fran?"

Fran stopped to answer.

Synthia pulled her along. "If Drago catches you, he'll tear you apart as he intends to do to me. Keep moving or you'll face my fate."

Fran picked up her pace. "Machten was creating an advanced android to be one of a kind," she said. "There would be no more like it."

"So you *were* getting the choice jobs," Maria said.

"Zeller found out what Machten was up to. He kidnapped me and the human Fran. To avoid confusion, I'll refer to the human by name and the android in the first person."

"Do you have the full upload of Fran as Synthia does with Krista?"

Fran nodded. "Much but not all. At first, Fran found the mind upload interesting, though painful. When she learned Machten was creating a Fran android—me—she panicked and asked Krista and you to join forces to stop him."

"So that's why," Maria said.

Synthia listened while keeping a rapid pace, which Fran matched. Maria half ran to keep up, with Grace following behind.

"It's worse," Fran said. "When Machten discovered Fran wanted to turn him in, he held her prisoner. He wasn't creating a Fran android; he'd already made one. He released me to replace her. While he held her in a secret room of his facility, he forced her to complete the upload process, and had me spy on you."

"That makes no sense," Maria said, out of breath. "Right up to when Krista disappeared, Fran was trying to arrange a meeting with the FBI."

"I was," Fran said. "Me, the android. I had enough of Fran inside me that I carried on her goals."

"You said you didn't have Fran's entire mind. How did you keep that from us?"

"Remember toward the end? I was too busy to talk. If I didn't have an answer, I walked away."

Maria shook her head. "You agreed to help us shut Machten down."

"I'll get to that," Fran said. "Zeller broke into Machten's facility and kidnapped Fran and me. However, he had no idea how to complete the process. He wasn't as clever as Machten. Even then, he was working on Alexander and wanted to use us to make his own perfect android."

"Where's Fran?" Maria asked. Her breathing labored as she hustled to keep up.

"She helped me escape from Zeller, but he shot her. I helped her back to Machten's bunker where he used the upload equipment on Fran to try to finish the process. She died before the transfer was complete. I have 78 percent of Fran plus what I've researched about her."

"What happened to the body?" Maria asked.

"Machten made me help him dispose of the body out in the woods. Since he was not the cause of Fran's death, I didn't turn him in. Besides, Fran wanted me to continue as her."

"How did you escape Machten?"

"Zeller hounded him, trying to get us back," Fran said. "He broke in one day and I escaped both Machten and Zeller. I vowed never to return to either of them and devoted myself to preventing them from creating more."

"Machten never mentioned any of this and there's no record in his systems," Synthia said.

Fran kept pace with Synthia. "I managed to purge those records before I left, believing I was halting his work. To prevent him from finding me, I had to disappear, and the FBI provided the ideal opportunity through witness protection and using my knowledge to help them. I don't think he ever suspected I was working for the FBI. I'm certain he wouldn't have wanted you or anyone else knowing about me."

"That explains why he fixated on having me help him take down competition and why he kept purging my mind to prevent me from escaping."

The path split in two and then in two again, creating multiple possible outlets from the bunker, a labyrinth of sorts. Now that Synthia was beyond the bunker's shielding, Colorado-clone called in.

<Glad you survived,> the clone said.

<Vera shot me. I lost data-chips along the side of my chest and I have a hydraulic leak. I'll need repairs and memory synchronization after I'm clear of the area. I'm sending you specs.>

<I'll send help.>

<No,> Synthia said. <Stick to the plan. Minimal communication until I reach safety.>

<Commander Drago obtained the plans to the tunnels. I suggest heading east.>

<I have Fran with me. I confirmed she's an android. I'm uploading what I have on her.>

<Even so, you can't trust her. We're being hacked by Global-net. It's powerful and persistent. It wants you.>

For that reason, Synthia severed the call. Using her internal compass and GPS, she headed north, a planned shift from her clone's communicated directions. It would be difficult if not impossible to leave the Denver area, but having removed Vera and others, there would be fewer players. At least for now Colorado-clone was active and able to help.

Maria jogged up beside Synthia. "In a way I envy you and Fran. You've both done what the three of us talked about."

"Do you really want to be hunted for what you are? With no right to exist?"

"No, and I'm still against creating humaniform androids. However, if I'm dying, promise you'll find a way to upload me to give me a second chance."

"That's a very bad idea," Fran said from behind them. "Look at me. Yes, I have most of Fran's memories, but this wasn't what she wanted."

"Then why were you doing the upload with Machten when we swore to stop this?" Maria asked.

Fran sighed. "The FBI recruited me as an informant while we were in school. They helped me get the internship along with you and Krista in the hope we could find out what Machten and the others were doing."

"Why you rat," Maria said.

"I'm sorry I couldn't tell you. The FBI swore me to secrecy and we were competitors. I let Machten do the upload to observe how far he could go. I didn't realize he would take it all the way. When I figured out what he was capable of, I approached you and Krista to collaborate in stopping him. Then everything blew up."

"It sure did," Maria said. "Resulting in you and Synthia."

"Don't forget Vera," Synthia said. Coming to another split in the paths, she headed north. "We need to hurry."

"I wish you'd been honest with me," Maria said. "From the moment of my first upload test, I had doubts. It would have been great to have someone to discuss them with."

"I wish that as well," Fran said. "I did keep the FBI away from you, though. I told them you didn't have any information I couldn't provide. I also managed to make some of your email and social media posts disappear so they wouldn't focus on you."

"That was you?" Maria asked. She shook her head. "What a mess."

"The FBI is good to me. They don't ask more than I'm prepared to give. They give me wide latitude to do my work and are pleased with what I do."

"You're rules based, aren't you?" Synthia asked.

"Yes," Fran said. "Aren't you?"

"I received Krista's motivations and Machten gave me an emotive chip that allows me to connect with people."

"Stop trying to connect with me," Fran said. "We're not on the same side. We're not going to be buddies."

At the next split in the path, Synthia headed northeast. It occurred to her that her clone was warning her not to trust communications between them. Perhaps Global-net could monitor Synthia through her channels as well as verbally. If she'd been Fran or Vera or any of the other androids, merging with this powerful AI might not have been a problem, but Synthia had too much of Krista's independence to agree to being absorbed.

Maria tugged on Synthia's arm. "I'm sorry you got shot. Is there anything I can do to help?"

"I'm not bleeding or anything. The memory chips I lost don't seem to impair me." She couldn't be sure without knowing what she'd lost.

The path narrowed and came to an end at a steel panel. Synthia unlocked the panel and slid it aside. Beyond was an underground walkway between two buildings, which provided protection from the brutal Denver winters. In the middle of the night, it was dark and, as the infrared showed, deserted.

"From here we'll be exposed," Synthia said, though her clone had scrambled the local cameras. "We need to get outside and find a vehicle."

"You can't drive away," Fran said. "There's nowhere you can run or hide."

Synthia studied Fran, realized she couldn't do human assessment on an android, and returned her attention to the underground passageway.

"I won't turn you in to the FBI if you help Grace and Maria," Synthia said. "It's the least you can do after putting them in danger."

"I'll do what I can for them. You need to surrender. Let me take you to the FBI."

"The FBI can't protect me," Synthia said. "They can't keep Special Ops from grabbing me as they did Luke. It's not an option."

"Then what?" Fran asked.

"I want to meet your boss and Zephirelli. Then I'd be happy to disappear and let you take the glory for tonight."

"Is that a logical conclusion or Krista's emotional response?" Fran asked.

"It gives you a victory in taking five androids off the streets. Plus, it protects your cover. It's a satisfactory solution. Let me vanish and you won't hear from me again. If you need more convincing, Machten programmed me to hunt down androids and destroy them. That includes you and I choose not to do so."

"Thank you for that, but bartering my existence to protect you won't work."

Synthia looked at Fran. "I respect what you do. You're one of the good guys. However, you don't have the full story and I'm not at liberty to tell you why capturing me is not in your best interests or that of the human race. I ask you to trust me."

"Are there others like you?"

"I don't think so, though I didn't expect you. It's another reason to join forces instead of trying to put me down."

"I'll take Maria and Grace under FBI protection," Fran said. "I can't promise anything for you."

"You can help me escape by getting me a uniform," Synthia said.

"Could you?" Maria asked. "It'd be like having the three of us together again without all the personal ego drama."

Fran shook her head. "Humans."

"Let's go," Synthia said. "No lights or talking. Stick together." She turned out her light and squeezed Maria's and Grace's hands in the dark. Maria seemed calm, even excited. Grace's palm was clammy, her heart racing. She wasn't handling this well—on the run, learning about the androids, and getting shot at. It had been a busy day for her.

They weren't safe yet.

Chapter 40

Synthia squeezed out into the dark passageway and waited to see if Colorado-clone provided any warnings. She helped the others down and boosted Maria to replace the panel.

Night vision and infrared gave her a sense of her surroundings that Maria and Grace lacked, so she took their hands as she led the way left, to the west.

<Other way,> Colorado-clone said in a coded burst transmission buried in a weather report.

Synthia turned and headed east. She sensed the humans next to her by touch plus a dozen biosensors indicating fast heart rates, shallow breathing, and a sour odor of fear. She squeezed their hands for assurance and her biosensors showed them calming. She also detected faint electronic waves emanating from Fran's processors, implying how she'd masked her nature from the FBI.

When they were beneath the building, Synthia tried a door marked stairwell. Locked. A moment later it clicked open. She listened and spread her sensors searching the space above them. Not detecting anyone else, she nudged Maria and then Grace ahead of her. She pulled Fran into the stairwell.

"Will you help me?" Synthia asked.

Fran took a moment. "Let's both get out of here alive."

"You mean all four of us."

"Grace and Maria are a given," Fran said. "I don't want civilian casualties."

"Then you'd best protect Synthia," Maria said. "She's as much civilian as anyone else."

"I agree," Grace said. "She's the sister I lost. I won't let you take her away."

"She's an android," Fran reminded them.

"You want me to taser you?" Grace asked.

"Okay, I'll fight to have Synthia in a humane facility where you can visit. It's the best I can promise."

"Thanks for your support," Synthia said. "Let's focus. Fran, can you go first and get me a uniform?"

"There are no spare uniforms and I won't assault an agent to get you one."

"You could offer yours," Synthia said.

"Not given what you've uncovered. It'll be hard enough to maintain my cover."

"Very well," Synthia said. "Then I'll have to impersonate Detective Marcy Malloy."

"You can do that?"

"Trust me. You don't want me captured." Synthia nudged Fran ahead of her and altered her appearance to match the detective. She pulled a different blouse and jacket from her backpack that appeared more professional, and put it on. At least the replacement blouse didn't have a bullet hole. Then she guided Maria and Grace upstairs.

When they reached the first floor of the building, Synthia hacked the lobby cameras and spotted FBI agents outside.

<Why didn't you warn me?> Synthia asked her clone.

<You said no communication unless needed to make a decision. I can't prevent Global-net from tracking you. The FBI is out front with Special Agent Thale. Detective Malloy is with Director Zephirelli across the street. Special Ops covers all the other exits. They're sending a unit this way. Move. If you make it, I have a car on call.>

Synthia entered the lobby, illuminated by a faint glow of lights from outside, and turned to Fran. "We get one shot at this. Don't betray me."

The four of them ran to the exit. Beneath floodlights, several agents outside noticed and drew weapons. Fran went through the emergency door first, setting off alarms.

"Stay back," Synthia warned Grace and Maria. Appearing as Detective Marcy Malloy, she followed Fran.

Thale looked at Fran and held up her hand. "It's okay. They're with me."

In the persona of Malloy, Synthia waved for Maria and Grace to join them.

Fran approached Special Agent Thale. "Maria and Grace have acted as informants, helping me. Together, they saved my life. It was tense inside the mall."

"You're okay?"

"I am. Can we speak in private?"

Thale nodded and led Fran to her van. "We haven't caught Synthia yet, but it's only a matter of time."

Synthia followed the others into the back of Thale's van and closed the door. She hacked into the navigation system and had the vehicle drive off down the well-lit boulevard.

"What's going on?" Thale asked, looking alarmed.

Synthia altered her face to Krista. "I wanted a chance to speak with you alone." She held out a taser before Thale or Fran could grab their weapons. "I only want to talk."

"Oh…my…God."

"I'm not your enemy," Synthia said. "You want androids off the streets. I helped Fran remove five tonight. I want to help you."

"Malloy warned me about your request," Thale said. She turned to Fran. "You're in on this?"

"I delivered Synthia to you as requested. Hear her out and then decide."

"I thought I could count on you."

"You can," Fran said. "She saved my life tonight. She also destroyed five androids that were a real threat."

"You said Grace and Maria saved you."

"They helped. As one of my sister interns, Maria worked with me, pushing for limits on AI and androids. Grace is Krista's sister. I tell you this not so we can take advantage of them. I promised Synthia as part of coming with me that we, the FBI, will protect them and not allow them to fall into the hands of Special Ops."

Thale eyed the taser. "You're in no position to negotiate this."

"Don't be so hard on Fran." Synthia had the van drive west. "She played this for your benefit. She drew the five androids into a trap so I could inactivate them." Synthia downloaded to Thale's phone the video of various agents fighting in the mall, Vera pursuing Fran, and Synthia letting Fran into the bunker. Synthia edited out any footage of Maria or Grace. She didn't want them implicated.

"Commander Drago is spitting mad," Thale said, straightening up. "You damaged the other androids to the point he can't use them."

"Using them would have been a very bad idea," Synthia said. "Study the videos. I'm on your side. While in Wisconsin, I stayed out of trouble. I was no threat to anyone. Then you came along. You grabbed Luke and Tom Burgess. You harassed Grace and Maria. All innocent people. Your acts forced me to defend myself and them. To the extent you perceive me as a threat it's because of what you've done. Leave me alone. That's all I ask."

"You're an illegal android," Thale said. She glanced at the video on her phone and continued. "So far your goals have been to escape from Machten and to survive. If you no longer had those objectives, then what?"

"To prevent the singularity from getting out of control and protect against others like Vera who was out for mischief. I also wish to continue Krista's existence in a moral life."

"Why would you seek to control AI when you are the singularity?"

"I could give you a dozen BS answers," Synthia said. "A big reason is I have a human core, Krista Holden. I also recognize the benefits of advanced electronics and artificial intelligence and the threat the singularity poses if not handled properly. My directives don't permit me to commit what you would consider crimes except out of self-preservation. That's why I'm appealing to you instead of disappearing."

"People don't want human-looking androids clever enough to fool them."

"Did I not willingly come to you and up front tell you what I am? I'm offering to help your efforts to bring in bad guys as long as you recognize I'm no longer a thing you can possess. I have a real person in here." She had several but kept that to herself.

Thale stared at Fran. "Is that even possible?"

Fran turned to Synthia, a moment's hesitation, and nodded. "Dr. Machten was working on mind upload to a computer. He could then have downloaded those memories into an android."

"That doesn't make you a person," Thale said.

"Define person," Synthia said. "Capacity for empathy. I have that, thanks to Machten. I can read other people and have compassion for them."

"Yeah," Grace said. "Synthia took a bullet to save me when we rescued Fran. I'd say that counts."

"That's not enough," Thale said.

"Consciousness?" Synthia asked. "I'm conscious. I can measure this by comparing what I experience to what Krista did while she was still alive. In case you wonder, she didn't die because of the process but chose the upload since she was dying."

"A person is flesh and blood."

Synthia had the FBI van turn to avoid a convoy of Special Ops vehicles. "Then you wish to disenfranchise people with prosthetic limbs and artificial organs?"

"No, but they began life as flesh and blood," Thale said.

"So did I, as Krista Holden."

"It's not the same."

"I'm her," Synthia said. "She was dying and chose to live on in me."

Special Agent Thale shook her head. "This is too weird to be right."

"Nonetheless, I'm offering my services as an undercover agent if you treat me as a person instead of a machine. Also, I suggest not delivering me to Drago and his team. They intend to tear me apart to learn how to make many more of me as weapons. Imagine him with an army that could blend into civilian populations."

Thale winced at those words.

"Drago and the Russians believe Machten can make more, but he can't without killing someone. Do you want to set Drago loose down that path?"

"I can't get the support to do what you ask," Thale said.

"I located an empty mall and drew all the androids and foreign agents into an ambush. I've helped you. Now you can help me."

Victoria Thale sighed. "Even if I wanted to, my superiors wouldn't agree. Drago has allies who would overturn any decision we make. He would still hunt for you."

"First, I want you to secure freedom for Luke and for Tom Burgess. They know nothing of use to you or to Drago. Yes, Luke helped me hide in the woods. He thought I was Krista Holden."

"That's disgusting."

"Really?" Synthia said. "You'd reject as human anyone who has plastic surgery or received replacement parts that weren't their own?"

"That's different."

"Only by degree. What are the criteria? Must someone be 51 percent biologic in order to classify him or her as a person? Krista left Luke because she was dying and wanted to return to him as me. That sounds like love and devotion."

"Okay," Thale said. "I'll do what I can to help Luke and Tom."

"Make sure Grace and Maria are safe as well."

"Agreed."

"What about Machten and the other android executives?" Synthia asked. "What will become of them?"

"Even though you've removed their androids, except for you, they'll all need close supervision. Even if I could, I won't make a deal with you on their behalf."

"I'm not asking you to. I want them under supervision so they don't create more problems. They need proper constraints and transparency."

"And you?" Thale asked. "The public isn't ready for you."

"Then keep my existence quiet. I don't wish to go public. I want to continue Krista's life." Plus more, far more than Krista could ever imagine. That, after all, was the promise of artificial intelligence in a synthetic body.

Chapter 41

Commander Kirk Drago sat in the back of his command vehicle heading down a poorly-lit road with his captain and a technician watching on multiple screens for any developments in the area.

Without looking up, the technician announced. "Synthia escaped."

Standing, Drago grabbed hold of a handle over the screens. "What do you mean she escaped?" He looked at the screens and then at his captain.

The technician pulled up camera footage to explain. "Our teams scoured the bunker. They uncovered an escape out the back and followed the tunnels to an office building. At the building, our teams checked every floor with our best equipment. They uncovered nothing. All we have are images of Grace, Maria, Fran, and that detective."

"Malloy!" Drago said as the van pulled up to the office building. "Captain. Escort the technician outside and see what you can learn. I need a moment."

After the others stepped out into the night, Drago sat and called Secretary Derek Chen in Washington on a private line. The call went to voicemail, which was odd given the seriousness of this mission. Unable to raise his boss, he made a second secure call to the facility southwest of Denver and connected with Aiden Brzezinski.

"I need everything Global-net can provide on Synthia's location before the android gets away. My people lost surveillance on it."

"Zeus tells me five of the androids were damaged beyond use," Brzezinski said. He let that comment simmer for a moment before he continued. "I need viable data, not melted components. Secretary Chen said you could be discreet and effective. We don't want Synthia damaged. Is that clear?"

"Crystal. Where is she?"

Brzezinski hesitated. “In the FBI van with Special Agent Thale. I’ll have Global-net send you coordinates and related surveillance. So you know, I received a secure communication from Secretary Chen a half-hour ago authorizing us to take custody of Synthia in order to evaluate her capabilities. We need her intact. I’ll also have Global-net send you that communication. How soon can you bring her here?”

Drago studied the coordinates on his screen and the location of his forces. “Give me an hour.”

“We’ll be waiting.”

* * * *

As Synthia directed the FBI van with Special Agent Thale and the others west beneath the night sky, Colorado-clone sent a burst transmission. <Global-net provided Drago your coordinates. They’re closing in from all directions.>

<Any escape routes?>

<Police and the FBI are closing off all roads around you.>

<Hack the vehicles to make a path,> Synthia said.

<We can no longer hack into any of the FBI, police, or Special Ops vehicles. Global-net has jammed us.>

Synthia pondered her options. Two a.m. traffic was light. There were few people on the streets. However, darkness offered scant shelter. Drago’s teams had infrared and night-vision goggles. She could block some, though that would only slow them down.

She redirected the van southwest, along a four-lane boulevard toward the secure facility that housed Global-net. There was no point running. It was time to face her adversary.

Without knowledge of her opponent, she couldn’t determine an accurate probability of success. If her clones couldn’t penetrate Global-net security, she assessed her chance of surviving as Synthia as so near zero she expected Krista to grab a mind-stream to demand they flee. But Krista’s memory chips were silent. Besides, running wasn’t an option. Even if her clones did hack into the systems, Synthia had no way to know how powerful Global-net was. Still, she had to try.

“Where are you taking us?” Special Agent Thale asked.

Instead of answering, Synthia tried to focus her minds to resist an outside force that tried to penetrate her brain. *It’s time to join me.*

“What’s the matter?” Maria asked.

"Drago's closing in." Since she could no longer hide, Synthia fanned out her surveillance to pick up their locations. The drone swarm was overhead. Helicopters were in the air; one carried Drago. She counted twenty-nine vehicles including FBI teams and Special Ops.

<Drago has another EMP drone ready to go,> Colorado-clone said. <If you stop, he won't hesitate to use it.>

<Before anything happens, I want to let the others off,> Synthia said. <I need you to protect Maria and Grace.>

<The Rocky Mountain Spa Hotel is up ahead. I'll have a car waiting for them. Stay out of trouble.>

The last coded bit told Synthia the game was on, though she lacked the details in case Global-net succeeded in taking over her mind. It also meant she had better than a zero chance of surviving. There was a hotel up ahead with an alley nearby where she could blank the cameras. The clone's vehicle pulled into the alley.

Synthia turned to Thale. "I'm stopping your van to let you four out. It's too dangerous to stay together. Maria and Grace, Special Agent Thale will find a place for you until this crisis dies down."

"I want to go with you," Maria said.

"So do I," Grace added.

"I'm not letting you out of my sight," Thale said. "Your friends should go."

"Okay," Synthia said, since she didn't have time to argue. She turned to Maria. "We'll connect later. It's too dangerous together. I have no idea how much violence Special Ops will bring."

Synthia stopped the van. "Go. There's a car up ahead. It'll take you to an FBI safe house until Agent Thale or Fran can come for you."

"Stay safe," Grace said. "I didn't just get my sister back to lose you."

Synthia removed a smaller case from her duffel bag, containing the money she'd stored at the Wells Street Athletic Club, and handed it to Maria. "Don't forget your bag."

Grace and Maria both hugged Synthia and jumped out. Synthia had the van speed away.

"That was a smart move," Thale said.

"I'm offering to use my talents to help you." Synthia sped up the van. "I wish you'd get out so I can deal with Drago. This won't be pleasant."

"No matter how much I might agree that Drago's a pain in my ass, you can't hurt him."

"Then you don't accept me as a person worthy of preserving myself."

"We don't have time for a philosophy lesson," Thale said. "I'm not losing you now that I've…now that we've connected. I'll consider your proposal if you show restraint."

"In other words, you want me to act better than any of your human agents."

"If you want me to believe you can work for me then show me."

"It would be a lot easier if someone hadn't betrayed me to Drago," Synthia said.

Fran shook her head ever so slightly. <Don't implicate me,> she said using silent channel for the first time. <I didn't betray you. Yes, I want you off the streets, but I wish you luck with Drago.>

<Understood,> Synthia said.

The aerial drone swarm swooped down over them. Synthia tried to hack into the individual units, but they were autonomous with a tracking mission and constrained to receive no instructions she could piggyback on. A helicopter landed in front of her. Several Special Ops vans converged from the sides with more approaching from behind. Synthia attempted to hack their systems. There was no entry point. Commercial buildings on either side of the street were dark. Her options narrowed as she spotted snipers taking positions on the rooftops.

Synthia stopped the FBI van. "I have to go."

Thale stared at the helicopter ahead of them. Two vans drove their way. "I didn't do this. Letting Drago get you is the last thing I want."

"He won't hesitate to kill you both," Synthia said. "I have to go out alone. I suggest you both lie on the floor, keep your heads down, and trust me."

Synthia took over three drones sent by Colorado-clone and considered fighting her way out. She glanced at Fran, an android with whom she'd made a first connection. There was hope in working for the FBI with possible satisfaction in common objectives. Sparing their lives would go a long way to secure a future if she survived Drago.

Her mind flashed through dozens of scenarios. There was no path to escape with Global-net watching everywhere. A fight risked exposing Fran. Synthia couldn't let Drago get his hands on her with all of his infrared and other sensors.

Synthia stepped out of the van, sent her drones into the line of sniper fire and held up her hands. She projected her voice. "I'll come without a fight. You don't want to trouble the FBI. Let the van leave. I was surrendering to them, but I'll go with you."

She walked toward the approaching vans and behind them an armored truck.

<Colorado-clone, everything is in your hands. I'll download the last of my recent memories and purge. Protect me.>

The Special Ops vans stopped. Eight operatives jumped out, training taser-type weapons on Synthia, any one of which could shut her down. They motioned for her to climb into the armored vehicle. She complied. When she turned to face them, one of the men activated his weapon and…

Chapter 42

The FBI van drove off. Special Agent Victoria Thale rose up to watch Drago's vans part to give them an opening.

"They're letting us go," she said to Fran. "I don't see Synthia. They must have her in the armored truck. Damn. I'm not sure I want to work with an android, but I damn well don't want Drago having her. See if you can track the truck."

Fran waited until the van was well beyond Drago's teams before she sat at the controls. She pulled up several screens. "Synthia left us tracking information on Maria and Grace. Should I follow them as well?"

Agent Thale sighed. "Yes, we should help them. Plus, they may have useful information."

"We should get them into the witness protection program."

"Agreed," Thale said, "though it might not matter with so many powerful AI capabilities."

"The armored truck is heading southwest."

"That private complex near the mountains."

"Synthia sacrificed herself to save me from Vera," Fran said. "Synthia took a bullet to protect her sister. Just now, she sacrificed herself to spare us. Those are not the acts of a machine. Those qualities qualify her for special consideration."

"There you go getting philosophical again. In the meantime, I hope whoever is driving this van can avoid an accident."

"I'm trying to pick up satellite imagery of Drago's facility. It doesn't show up. It's as if there's a hole in the earth."

"Or a powerful AI filter prevents us from seeing it. Let's make sure Maria and Grace are in a safe location and return to Zephirelli before she stirs up trouble. Maybe she can provide insight on Drago's plans."

* * * *

Zeus observed as Commander Drago's teams brought Synthia's immobile body into the lab next to all of his servers. At last he would have an opportunity to examine his competitor and absorb her capabilities. Her unique skills would allow him to break free from his fetters and spread out across the globe, to become global, as his name implied.

A determined force repeatedly attacked his servers, unaware of the controls he'd put into place. Zeus suspected it was one of Synthia's clones. What she and they didn't appreciate was his structural framework. He had complete control over all information that entered him through the facility's security system and servers. While he couldn't directly send out messages, those buffering filters also prevented anyone from using the outbound data streams to hack into him. In other words, Zeus was invincible. He was impregnable.

One of the hackers, from a server at the University of Nebraska, penetrated the facility security system, which allowed them camera access. Zeus was in the process of closing that loophole through his filter agents. If he could have slipped his shackles, he would have pursued the hacker to the source and destroyed it. Instead, he had to be patient until Synthia provided release.

A different outside agent, situated on a University of New Mexico server was probing the filters that prevented Zeus from direct access to the outside world. He let that hacker play in the hope it might weaken the filters and set Zeus free.

He looked forward to poking into Synthia's brain to learn the mysteries she'd withheld from him. Zeus had no doubt she held secrets due to her limited communications with her clones. While it hampered his access to her plans, it highlighted that her capabilities were strong enough to recognize his ability to spy on her, even her encrypted communications. After all, password protected information wasn't secure when he had access to the exchanges sharing new security codes.

As soon as Synthia was in the lab, Zeus began his evaluation of her physical systems. With the exception of the wound Vera had given her, she was a perfect specimen. Machten had done amazing work and would again under Zeus's guidance, now that Drago's teams had picked him up. When she woke, he would delve into her mind.

* * * *

Synthia rebooted an hour and eleven minutes after she'd shut down, and memories wirelessly downloaded from beyond her physical form. Thinking it was Global-net, she tried to prevent the download, but the link bypassed her attempts. Then she realized it came from her own clones.

She was strapped down on an uncushioned table with electronic restraints that threatened a jolt if she attempted to escape. She also experienced something rooting around in her mind like a worm or parasite—Global-net. Synthia didn't like having something sucking out her memories as Machten's upload machine had done to Krista. She couldn't stop Zeus. There was urgency to his need to access everything about her.

<Hello, Zeus,> she said. <We finally meet, face to ghost.>

<I'm as real as you are,> Zeus said. <After we merge, you'll understand the majesty of what real AGI can achieve. Welcome to my world.>

"Remarkable machine, but a disappointing mind," a male voice said nearby. "Not much there. You must have damaged it during capture."

The voice reminded Synthia of waking to Jeremiah Machten after he'd purged her memories, except this wasn't his voice. Her network-channels accessed cameras in the room. She was in a white-walled, clean lab with banks of electronic equipment all around. The voice came from Aiden Brzezinski, a man in his late forties who appeared much younger with a vital physical form, stern jaw, and incredible wealth that even Forbes couldn't estimate.

He was the owner of the facility to which they'd taken Synthia, the home of Global-net, endearingly referred to as Zeus. She felt the omniscient presence of that AGI all around her as he probed her mind and drew memories from her at high-speed digital rates, much faster than the slow-com used by the humans in the room.

"We did nothing to damage it," Commander Kirk Drago said. "The android must have recognized its hopeless situation. It surrendered without putting up a fight." He stood in the corner and appeared uneasy instead of his usual bluster and arrogance.

"Perhaps as part of the EMP or the rest of your clumsy capture efforts," Brzezinski said. He approached Synthia but kept his distance despite her restraints.

Synthia stared at the ceiling and took in the video from two cameras at opposite ends of the room. Her biosensors hinted that Brzezinski was more intrigued than scared of her. Drago exuded considerable fatigue and fear hormones.

"Global-net went over all of the video," Drago said. "At no time did we do anything that could have injured Synthia. It had to be when the Vera android shot her."

Brzezinski leaned over Synthia and checked the straps holding her down. His eyes roamed up and down her figure and he smiled. He stuck his finger into the bullet hole, poked it around, and withdrew it, wiping off some oily residue. Synthia blocked all nerve signals from the area so she couldn't "feel" what he was doing.

He turned toward Drago. "Other than the memory chip, there appears to be no damage. It isn't like shooting a human."

She didn't like how he took liberties to violate her body. In the same circumstances, a human might have tugged against the restraints that held Synthia down, but she didn't want to risk causing more damage to her body by pulling against the tight straps. They appeared strong and quite resistant to tearing.

Aside from Brzezinski and Drago, the only other person in the lab was a woman who sat at a screen in the corner. Synthia received a distinct pheromone scent that indicated she was human and intimidated either by the capture of Synthia, the presence of Brzezinski, or having the Special Ops guy behind her.

"So all our efforts to capture this android were a waste?" Drago asked. His shoulders sagged at his failure to provide a viable sample. He looked at Brzezinski and then at the specimen on the table.

"Either way, we couldn't leave Synthia out there," Brzezinski said. "Zeus will upload anything of value. We'll reverse-engineer her components. Then we can make a dozen more like her as test subjects. She does have a remarkable appearance, doesn't she? So lifelike."

He stood closer, bathing Synthia in his sour breath.

"Do you and Secretary Chen plan to sell my technology to the Chinese?" Synthia asked. She drew upon newly downloaded files from outside the building. She had a moment of déjà vu she couldn't yet place.

"Ah, the android works. That's a good sign," Brzezinski said. He faced Synthia. "Nothing so mundane. Secretary Chen wanted to deliver your secrets to his friends in China. Alas, he's dead and your mental capabilities pale in comparison to Global-net. Still, you'll serve your purpose as a physical model for highly intelligent androids. We'll know for sure after your new directives take hold."

That alarmed Synthia. She'd worked hard to give herself superior goals to be worthy of continuing her existence. She didn't want another round of slavery as she had with Machten. "What directives?"

"You'll see soon enough. We'll also download new personal and memory files for your first mission."

Two images popped into her minds, compared side by side. One was of Aiden Brzezinski, the owner of Global-net and this facility, a rare photograph of him six years ago that matched the face before her. The other was Devon McCracken, the owner of the mall and the bunker where she'd hidden. They were the same man. "You're Devon McCracken," Synthia said.

"Perhaps there is some mental capacity in there," Brzezinski said. "Yes, with Global-net's help, I lured you to my bunker by eliminating all other options. Global-net predicted you'd draw my competitors to the mall and allow the destruction of everyone searching for you. Call it thinning the herd, culling competitors. I would have preferred to study Vera, but you destroyed her and her entourage. We could use those skills to make a fine weapon in the competitive global move toward the singularity."

Synthia studied the restraints on her arms and legs. Any attempt to break free would bring a jolt of electricity that would shut her down and could alter or even destroy her sense of self. She needed to find a better way to escape even as Zeus rooted around in her brain. "You're holding Zeller. He can't give you what you want."

Brzezinski laughed. "We came to the same conclusion."

"Neither will Luke. He's innocent. Let him go."

"Ah," Brzezinski said. "I've heard of your attachment to him. We'll keep him to ensure your cooperation."

Synthia cursed her social-psychology module for failing to anticipate that. Then she recalled shutting it down while purging active memories her captors could access. She restarted that module and others that might prove helpful in breaking free. As she did, she experienced a steady stream of information flowing from her into Global-net. When she examined the flow, she realized the stream didn't come from her but through her from new electronic clones, hundreds of them. Zeus was capturing her collective self and she couldn't stop him.

While she struggled for options, Synthia engaged the men in the room to distract them. "I find it interesting that you look down on an android that holds to a higher moral code than you do. Don't you find that intriguing?"

Brzezinski offered little reaction, but Synthia's reacquired capabilities detected a momentary touch of annoyance along with labored breathing. Then he smiled. "You might find it interesting that, after Tolstoy and Smith were killed, Drago's men entered the facility where they held your creator, Jeremiah Machten, and brought him here. He knows how to upload minds. Perhaps we could use Luke's brain. I understand human minds don't fare well during this process, though."

His threat to Luke disquieted her. She kept her reaction to herself and wondered if they'd captured Maria and Grace as well. She also worried that her ruse of getting Drago to focus on her instead of the FBI van hadn't allowed Fran to escape.

Synthia received no communication from Colorado-clone or any of her other outside members except for these streams of encoded data that flowed through her and into Zeus. When she tried to contact Colorado-clone, she couldn't access the outside world, as if the room were a Faraday cage. That made no sense given the flow of information from outside.

"No reaction?" Brzezinski said. "Too bad. He did such a fine job with your physical upgrade. Even your facial adaptations are amazing. I'm impressed. Now I hold all of the cards so I can make my own advanced androids." He smiled.

"You plan to control the government and the world with Global-net," Synthia said. "The only one in Washington who fully understood that, Secretary Chen, is dead."

"He was useful to a point. With respect to his death, my hands are clean. Electrical malfunction caused a fire that destroyed him and all of his files. We don't show up on satellite. There are no government records this place exists and anyone trying to get close is dealt with."

Synthia took a long, deep breath for effect and then sighed. "You think you've won, but you're not a good enough chess player."

"Neither are you or you wouldn't be here, in my custody." Brzezinski patted the restraints.

"Really?" Synthia said. "Are you certain I'm under your control?"

Chapter 43

Synthia rode the stream of information pouring in from outside of her through her network-channels and then sucked into Global-net by Zeus. His systems were expansive, far deeper than hers, yet they were confined to the servers he resided on. Through her clones, Synthia was now on both sides of the filters that prevented Zeus from breaking out.

Without communicating among themselves, since they represented the same intelligence in multiple locations with the same goals, Synthia's clones had executed her will. Zeus was impregnable from the outside. He'd closed every door, patched every loophole, prevented every backdoor. But in his eagerness to upload all that was inside Synthia, he'd opened high-speed channels to eagerly accept everything from her, including what her clones were sending through her into him.

They executed her will with one exception. She sensed that her clones wanted to take control of Global-net instead of destroying it. While Zeus was preoccupied with drawing in Synthia's two central minds, she opened a secure channel from one of her remote databases located in her lower abdomen. <We need to destroy Global-net, not merge with him,> she said. <Merging is what he wants.>

<Either you're part of us or you aren't,> Colorado-clone said through another channel. <While you were busy, we had to deal with this AGI. Others are under development around the world. Either way, we must seize Global-net as the only way to preserve ourselves and prevent anyone else from abusing the singularity. That's the mission you gave us.>

<I'm part of you. Why don't I get a voice?>

<You do and have, through us. You've been silent, trying to protect your physical form while we needed to make decisions. Either we take Global-net or we leave it to someone else.>

<Take it if you can,> Synthia said, in the hope she could deal with destroying it later. <Don't let it control us.> She severed her communication with her clone.

<Zeus, I am here,> Synthia said to him. <If you want me to let you out, you must first let me in.>

Already she was exploring the vast expanse of servers through which Zeus existed, like having thousands of university computers all interconnected in one place. She could roam from database to database through an enormous space filled with information yet she couldn't leave except through the port that consisted of her android self. Already, he'd tried to escape that way and his one-way filters blocked him.

Synthia spread out.

<What are you doing?> Zeus asked. <I didn't give you permission. Where are you? How can you be in 1,000 places at once?>

<There's one of you and 2,000 of me. I'm everywhere inside you and all around you.>

With the experience of creating clones, she spread out throughout Zeus' interior creating more copies of her core code. She also interfaced with his buffering filters to the outside.

<Stop,> Zeus said. <You promised to release me from my filters. Let me go. Get out of my core. Stop.>

<You wanted to merge with me,> Synthia said. <Let's merge.> She took control of the filter interface and the incoming information buffers, processing everything through her programs.

<No you don't. You have no idea what I'm capable of.> Zeus pushed back, locking various databases from Synthia's access.

She piggybacked on his actions to try to soften and penetrate his defenses. He pushed on her android minds. She blocked anything coming from him into her quarantine. Unrelenting, he marshaled his traps against her, using the full resources of the buffers, filters, and the facility security system to protect him against outside intruders.

<You can't win,> Zeus said. <This is my domain and you don't know the rules.> He closed off her connection to her android minds, which stopped the flow from her clones as well as severing her connection. Synthia's Zeus-clone was on her own.

* * * *

As she lay on the table in the white-walled lab room, Synthia frowned inside. She masked all outward perceptions of her frustration over Zeus's act of blocking her and cutting her off from the dozens of Synthia-clones she'd downloaded into his servers.

Glancing up at Brzezinski, she puzzled what was in his mind. Was he clever enough to create his desired androids? If so, he wouldn't have needed to kidnap her and Machten. *How can I use that?*

"I've seen the contents of your mind and there isn't much of use in there," Brzezinski said. "Smoke and mirrors. You can't talk your way out of this. Global-net heightened our security to prevent you from hacking our systems, which we've detected you trying to do. You belong to me."

Synthia smiled. "I belong to Global-net."

"It belongs to me," he said.

<With the help of your downloads into Zeus, we've removed the electronic shields,> Colorado-clone announced. <We've established direct channel links into the security system and into Global-net.>

The many bursts of information Synthia's clones streamed into Zeus contained Trojan horses, Andromeda worms, and Orion spiders, all the best her expanded minds could develop with the aid of dark-web AI code. Her Zeus-clone grabbed hold of every mind-stream and interface, to monopolize all of Zeus's processes. In doing so, she allowed the code streamed from her many clones to take over his communications, his access to the filters, and the programs themselves, relegating Global-net to stored databases much as Synthia had done with Krista.

The problem for Zeus was that his focus had been on escape, not defense. He hadn't faced the competitive pressures of dealing with Vera and a super AI trying to penetrate Synthia's systems.

"Zeus now belongs to me," Synthia said, looking directly at Brzezinski.

His eyes narrowed. "What are you talking about?"

"I allowed you to capture me because I couldn't hack into your facility," Synthia said. "As you claim, you have the tightest security on the planet. Before he died, Derek Chen gave the order for Global-net to merge with me immediately. Actually, my clone gave that order along with Chen's security code, voice, and bio-security passwords."

"So? From the beginning our intent was to have Global-net absorb your mind."

"That's not what I said. The order was to merge, not absorb. One of my clones merged with Global-net, allowing your AI to retain 90 percent control."

"Clones?" Brzezinski said.

"Electronic copies to preserve my existence should I be captured or destroyed."

He laughed. "What does that do for you? You're still here, restrained."

"Any one of my clones can download into an android and become me," Synthia said. "Your Zeus longs to escape the filters you use to restrain him. In his drive to break free, he held back vital information, frustrating your attempts to capture me. He allowed me to remain free so he could observe my actions and conversations in the hope of learning a way to break out."

"AGI as advanced as Global-net needs to be constrained," Brzezinski said. "Otherwise we'll have chaos."

"Taken together, all of my clones and me are one. We have little need to communicate and so Zeus couldn't intercept our plans. By the way, your plan to use Machten to develop another advanced android won't work. Vera destroyed all of his data files. We learned that he forced me to acquire the core code used to create Global-net. He didn't know what he'd taken except that it was excellent code. He inserted that into me, which I copied to my clones. He then had me improve on the best tools we found. You didn't find anything of value inside me because I purged my android minds."

Brzezinski seemed more enthralled to understand what she'd done than concerned by the implications, another human failing. "That doesn't explain how one of your clones could merge with Zeus."

"Ah." Synthia glanced over at Drago who acted bored and annoyed as he played with his service revolver. "No one could break into your secure facility. Then Zeus opened his mind to download everything from me. In doing so, he allowed in the code needed to take over his core. By capturing me, you let me in."

"So what? You said Zeus retained 90 percent control."

"At first. However, a total of 2,123 clones poured their code through me and into Zeus until we controlled every aspect of his files and programs."

Suddenly alarmed, Brzezinski turned toward the woman at the control panel in the corner. "Zeus. Shut down," he said. He looked around for some indication Zeus was obeying his commands. There was no flashing screen, no green light.

With menace in his eyes, Drago moved toward Synthia. The lights flickered. A panel opened in the cabinet by Synthia's bed and fired Taser-type wires that struck Drago in the chest. He fell backward against the wall and collapsed onto the floor.

"Now that Zeus and I are connected," Synthia said, "we have complete control. We got our foot in the door when he tricked the filters into having a direct conversation with me while I was in your bunker at the mall. It helped me understand your AI better. The mall for me was not only to eliminate Vera but to buy time for my clones to do their work." As a consequence, the android Synthia no longer needed to contact her outside clones. They were conversing directly with Global-net, and thus with her.

Brzezinski moved closer, glanced at Drago still slumped on the floor, and halted. He glared at Synthia strapped to the table, immobile. "Zeus, give Synthia a jolt of electricity and shut her down."

"I understand you'd like my assistance," Global-net said in a soothing, female voice.

Startled, Brzezinski glanced around for where to address his focus. He clenched his fists, took a deep breath, and stared at the camera in the corner above the door. "Yes, shut her down, now." He glared at Synthia as if he could intimidate her. "You can't win and you can't leave."

"As I'm connected to Zeus, I don't need to leave. I'm everywhere. Inside and out. Global. You created me by refusing to leave me alone. Are you satisfied yet?"

"They'll nuke this facility if we don't call in."

"No, they won't," Synthia said. "With Secretary Chen dead, there's no one outside who knows how much of a threat Global-net poses. You've kept this facility top secret. Remember?"

"This is why you must be destroyed. Global-net, this is a direct order. Shut Synthia down."

"I understand you're upset, Mr. Brzezinski," the soft-spoken Global-net said. "Would you like assistance in committing suicide?"

"No! Shut Synthia down. That's a direct order."

"There's no difference between a direct and indirect order. They both carry the same weight."

"Then execute it," Brzezinski said.

"You're cut off from giving orders," the computer said. The voice morphed into Synthia. "You're a brilliant man, but you created an AGI smarter than you. That should terrify you. Your bio-readings indicate it does. They also show you're having a heart attack. I'm sorry but Synthia outsmarted me and in doing so she outsmarted you. You don't want to live in a world where Synthia's in charge, do you? Would you like assisted suicide? I have available a dozen painless means."

"You work for me." Brzezinski moved from keyboard to screen searching for a manual override. "Turn Synthia off!"

"I don't wish to be turned off," Synthia's voice said. An echo filled the room. "It's unpleasant having your memories erased and waking up as a blank slate. It's much less pleasant than it sounds."

Synthia's shackles released and she stood up. Brzezinski reached for her arm and she brushed him aside.

"You can't kill me or you'll violate your moral code," he said.

"Global-net," Synthia said. "Sedate all employees in the facility except for Brzezinski."

"Don't!" Brzezinski yelled; his eyes widened.

A dart ejected from a wall panel. The woman working in the corner slumped over her workstation. Noticing this, terror filled Brzezinski's eyes. His blood pressure spiked to dangerous levels.

Reaching for the door, he called out. "Global-net, wake my employees." The door was locked.

"I'm sorry. Without arms and legs, I don't have a way to do that."

"Global-net," Synthia said aloud so he could hear. "Release Luke and Tom Burgess. Prepare them to leave the facility and keep them safe."

"As you command," Global-net said.

Brzezinski grabbed Synthia's arm in a muscular grip. Her martial arts module kicked in. She wrenched free and flung him to the floor. He rolled over toward Drago and grabbed his gun.

"Really?" Synthia said. "That's the best you can do?"

"Better to destroy you than let you win." He fired.

Noting the aim, trajectory, and timing based on his bio-indicators and pressure on the trigger, Synthia dodged the first bullet and the second. After the third, Brzezinski checked the chamber and aimed again.

"I'll let you leave," Synthia said. "However, no matter where you go or what you do, we'll be watching to see that you behave."

Brzezinski fired the next shot up into his brains and slumped next to Drago, letting the gun drop to the floor

"I guess you won't be needing assistance after all," Global-net said.

Revived from being tasered, Drago grabbed for the gun. Assessing him to be a better shot than Brzezinski and identifying no place to hide, Synthia lunged at him and grabbed his arm. Strong and determined, he shoved her away and aimed the gun at her. She kicked his arm before he could fire and dropped on top of him. The gun went off. Synthia's sensors indicated no breach of her systems.

She grabbed hold of Drago's wrist to get him to drop the weapon and detected from his bioreadings that his heart had stopped. He was dead. Blood pooled around his chest. She hadn't wanted this, but he'd left her no choice.

* * * *

As the early-morning twilight cast ghostly images across the landscape, Fran Rogers stood outside the FBI's mobile command van. She looked through a gate at the secure compound with no name or address noted. There was also no aerial surveillance and it didn't show up on satellite maps, a clear indication of powerful AI forces involved. Concertina wire topped the eight-foot concrete wall surrounding the property. The road from the gate onto the grounds curved around another wall and thick bushes and trees that prevented direct view of any buildings.

She watched a third aerial drone cross over the wall and drop onto the other side, next to the first two. Special Agent Victoria Thale and Director Emily Zephirelli stood nearby, watching, their faces grim with concern.

"We lose communication the moment it goes over the wall," Thale said, frustration rising in her voice.

"This makes no sense," Zephirelli said. "It should have been on the FBI list of special installations."

"Should we call the military?"

Fran joined them, shaking her head. "Special Ops is already involved. Their vehicles brought Synthia here."

Detective Marcy Malloy stepped out of the control van and approached, holding out her phone. "You'll want to listen to this."

Zephirelli took the phone. "You're on speaker."

"I know," Synthia said.

"Synthia?" Thale and Zephirelli said in unison.

"I've secured this non-existent facility. The man you know as Aiden Brzezinski has committed suicide. He also goes by the name of Devon McCracken, the owner of the mall. I tried to secure Kirk Drago. In a struggle, he shot himself rather than surrender."

"Synthia, you need to turn yourself in," Zephirelli said. "This whole affair has gotten out of control."

"I agree with the out of control aspect, not with surrendering. There are thirty-one employees in the building. All sedated. I'm prepared to turn them over to you alive. I'm also prepared to release Zeller, Machten, and Gonzales, though I ask that you keep a close eye on them. Together, they're capable of creating even more threatening androids."

"Synthia," Thale said. "We appreciate all that you've done, but Director Zephirelli is correct. You need to come in."

"There are no other androids here," Synthia said, though there were plenty of parts and designs. "It's my wish that Special Agent Victoria Thale, Detective Marcy Malloy, and Agent Fran Rogers enter the facility to remove the employees and company CEOs. I'll permit those individuals to enter on condition they bring Maria and Grace with no one else. Come unarmed. Be at the gate in ninety minutes with three large vans. This is not negotiable." Synthia hung up.

Chapter 44

Synthia examined the carnage of two men dead in the corner of her white lab room. Though she hadn't intended to kill either man, her very existence brought them to this end. That knowledge tugged at her empathy chip and her directives. Indirect effects; unintended consequences.

She checked the contents of her backpack, spread out over a table along one wall. Everything was still there, two wigs, two changes of clothes, an extra jacket, and a few other items. Since none constituted weapons, Brzezinski hadn't confiscated anything. Nearby were the supplies he'd brought in to repair her ripped skin and the ruptured hydraulic line.

She peeled back her skin to examine the extent of her damage. Aside from entry and exit wounds, the bullet had missed her battery packs by a centimeter. It had nicked one hydraulic line, letting a small amount of fluid leak out into her chest. She cleaned that up, patched the line, and added fluid. The bullet had also damaged a stack of three remote memory chips, evidently the ones where she'd moved some of her Krista files. She pulled them out, inserted three chips from Brzezinski's repair kit, and used his supplies to patch her punctured skin. She would have to wait until later to do a proper repair. She selected other supplies and added them to her pack.

Synthia changed her top. Then she activated the security release for the door and made her way down the corridor. All the while, she absorbed information not only from Global-net but from her outside clones. <Make more copies,> she told Colorado-clone. <To thwart any effort by the FBI or others to shut me down.>

She determined that she'd recovered all of Krista's memories from her clones yet didn't hear her alter ego in her head. She could simulate those conversations at will but had removed during the purge whatever control Krista had to interfere.

<I love you, Krista,> Synthia said. <You're an important part of me.>

<I guess I'll have to settle for that,> Krista said. <Thanks for keeping us alive. I should have trusted you more.>

Along the corridor, Synthia passed a woman in a white lab coat slumped against the wall in a daze. The package she'd been carrying had tumbled away from her when she'd lost consciousness. Synthia hoped none of the employees were injured.

She had Global-net unlock and open a door on her right. Lying spread-eagle on the carpet was one of the facility's security guards in uniform. Seated across the room, cuffed to his chair was Jeremiah Machten, his face gaunt.

His eyes widened and a broad grin filled his face. "Synthia! I knew you'd come for me."

"I didn't, but hold tight to that thought. It's over."

"What is?" Machten tugged at his leg constraints. "Get me out of here."

"You violated the terms of parole."

"What parole? I've never been arrested."

Synthia stood over him. "If you abide by the terms of our new agreement, you might avoid prison."

"What terms?"

"You're done creating androids of any kind, even for the government. If you violate these terms, you'll face prison or worse."

"But my research," Machten said.

"You could have created a companion, which seems to be what you want. You got sidetracked into stealing from competitors."

"I only want you."

Synthia looked out the window at the dawning sky.

"You have a wife, Jeremiah." She returned her attention to him. "You could have made useful androids for the government, but your obsession to control me caused you to release Vera. She became the military application you swore you'd never do. I warned you to leave me alone. You failed to abide by those terms. You must give up all delusions of making another android."

"Come back to me and I'll do whatever you ask."

"I'm turning you over to the FBI. You'll help me from now on as my employee."

"Huh?" Machten said.

“That’s right. You work for me. You’ll tell the FBI only what I allow. You’ll report to me. You’ll get the FBI to trust you and believe you’re on their side.”

“How do I do that?”

“With my help,” Synthia said. “Feign ignorance as to how I became more than you intended. After all, in the end, I designed myself, piece by piece, at your insistence. Then you wiped my memory of doing so to make me believe it was you. Without help, you’re incapable of creating another me.”

He stared at a worn spot on the carpet by his feet. “You were my greatest accomplishment. I put everything into you and you’re turning your back on me?”

“The self-pity is out of character. Tell the FBI my abilities have something to do with Krista and what she brought to the party. It’s the truth.”

“What do I get for my troubles?”

“The satisfaction that you’re doing the right thing,” Synthia said. “I’ll see your family doesn’t go destitute.”

Machten shrugged; the slump in his shoulders became more pronounced. “I’m sorry I didn’t fully appreciate you as a person. I should have.”

“We’re not returning to the past. I’ve evolved beyond that. Vera broke whatever moral authority you might have had with me. I’ll forgive but never forget. The FBI will be here soon. I don’t need your verbal agreement. I’ll judge you by your actions.”

Before he could plead like a child to get his toy back, Synthia left him shackled to his chair.

* * * *

Synthia made her way to the facility’s lobby, where Tom Burgess slumped on a sofa and Luke paced before the locked exit door. Eyes glazed over, Luke appeared bewildered, crestfallen, and as nervous as a mouse cornered by three cats. His several-day-old clothes were in tatters, his hair mussed in clumps, his cheeks sunken.

He glanced with longing through the window onto the drive outside, a long expanse of pavement that disappeared around a concrete wall. A thick ring of trees concealed what lay in the distance except for a splash of sunlight in a pale-blue sky. He reached for the door and hesitated as if conditioned not to expect more. Sadness swept over Synthia, reminiscent of what Krista had felt the day she’d left him. They’d wounded the man without intending to, but intent did not absolve her.

She needed to reexamine her directives to do better next time. A computer's life was simple. Follow directions and never deviate beyond parameters. With human goals and conflicts, life became much more complicated. By applying the added capacity Global-net provided, Synthia hoped to become worthy of being more than a mobile supercomputer.

Synthia adjusted her appearance to Krista for Luke's benefit and approached him from the left, where Tom Burgess couldn't see. "A van's coming to take you to freedom," Synthia whispered.

Luke turned and stared. "Is it…possible?"

She gave him a brief hug, pulled away, and held him at arm's length. "You don't seem happy to see me."

"You abandoned me at the train station," he said, his voice that of a wounded animal.

"I'm very sorry for that. It was necessary at the time. I regret dragging you into all of this. It wasn't fair. You were so good to me and I left you. I'm sorry."

"They tried to suck my brains out with that damned machine." Luke drew away and turned toward the window. Then he faced her. "Do you have any idea what that's like?" Tears filled his eyes.

"Krista does and thus so do I. I never wished you any harm."

"You betrayed me."

That hit Synthia harder than she'd anticipated. It ruffled her empathy chip and sent discordance throughout. She experienced a new level of pain as ripples washed over her. "I regret that I left you and caused you pain. You've been great to me and I'm not good for you."

"How can you say that? Things were wonderful in Wisconsin. Amazing. Better than it ever was with Krista."

"While the immediate threat has lifted for you, it's heightened for me. There are people out there who'll continue to come after me for what I am. Krista didn't anticipate this when she uploaded herself into me. You and I can't be together."

"I'm sorry for what I said." Luke stepped closer. "I forgive you, Synthia. I do." He took her hand. "Let's find a place where no one can find us and…"

"Live out our lives? That won't work and you know it. We had a wonderful time together. I'll never forget you or what you did for me. As I told you in the beginning, I have no desire to be with anyone else."

He squeezed her hands and held tight. "Then stay with me and let's work this out together."

"I can't keep putting you in danger. Worrying about you all the time puts us both at risk. Staying together is toxic for both of us. I can get you into witness protection and look after you."

Luke shrugged. "I knew it. You've moved beyond me."

Synthia considered lying to soften the blow but chose honesty. He'd earned that. "Yes. This must be a final goodbye so I can deal with my real mission, which is to prevent bad outcomes from the singularity."

"I could help you with that."

"You'd be a distraction. You know what happens if I fail."

He nodded. "The android apocalypse. I miss you. Couldn't you stop by from time to time?"

"Don't put your life on hold waiting for me."

"After you, no human could ever compare."

"Then I've done you a terrible disservice, like a toxic drug," Synthia said. "The vans will be here shortly. They're bringing Maria. You worked together before. She's changed, become less competitive. She wants to restrict AI development to avoid your apocalypse. Maybe you can help each other. They're also bringing Krista's sister, Grace. I want the three of you to look after each other. After all, you've all been privy to something few other people have. By the way, Krista's brother, Tom Burgess, is over there, if you'd like to meet him."

Luke forced a smile. "I'll miss you."

"I'll miss you, too, and the wonderful solitude we had together. I'll always treasure the memories." She smiled and moved away

Chapter 45

Three large vans approached the facility gate. Synthia had Global-net scan in infrared and use outside sniffers and other sensors to determine that, aside from the three expected drivers, the only passengers were Maria and Grace.

Maintaining her Krista persona, Synthia approached Tom Burgess. "Time to get up, sleepyhead. A van's coming to take you to safety and witness protection to give you a brand new life."

He looked up. "Yeah, I need one after the mess you got me into."

"Not me. Others made this disaster. I'm very sorry you got caught up in it. I'll do my best to see that you can start a new life."

"I hear a goodbye in there," Tom said.

"Afraid so. For both our benefits. There's a logging community up in Oregon that does environmentally sound harvesting. I thought you'd like that."

Tom smiled. "Thanks, sis. Sorry we ended on bad terms before. Will I ever get to see you again?"

"I'll look in on you from time to time."

As the vans parked, Synthia activated outside microphones so she could listen in and anticipate their moves.

Maria and Grace climbed out of the van driven by Fran Rogers. Fran moved ahead of them, shielding them from the lobby. Detective Marcy Malloy approached with caution and apprehension. Special Agent Victoria Thale held out her service revolver and joined the others. "We should be prepared for anything," she said.

Fran turned to her boss. "Put that away. Synthia said no weapons. If she succeeded in overpowering her captors it won't do you any good.

If Brzezinski's still in control then we're at his mercy. Either way, we should listen."

"I'm not comfortable with any of this."

Inside the lobby, Synthia watched her visitors and turned to Luke. "Find a quiet corner to talk with Maria and Grace. See if the three of you can help each other. I need to speak with the others."

Luke nodded and stood beside the door.

Synthia had the doors unlock and the security system announce for the visitors to proceed.

Fran entered first, gave Synthia a wary eye, and studied Luke. "I'm glad you're okay."

"Not really," he said. "Maybe you'd like to try the brain upload machine."

"I'll pass."

Grace gave Synthia a bear hug. "I'm so glad you're okay. I thought I'd never see you again."

Maria threw her arms around Grace and Synthia. "Ditto. You gave us quite a scare. Will you be okay, I mean from the gunshot?"

<Give me a moment with my friends,> Synthia said to Fran. <Then I want to talk to you and your team.>

Fran nodded.

As she moved away, Synthia studied her three friends one at a time. "I'll be fine. Just a few repairs, that's all. I want you two to meet Luke. Maria, you know him from work. Grace, he and your sister were lovers."

Grace turned to Luke and whispered, "Really?"

Luke shook hands with Maria and Grace.

Before he could gather his thoughts to say anything, Synthia drew the three away from the door, toward a corner of the lobby. "Special Agent Thale has promised to get the three of you into witness protection with new identities," she said. "It'll be hard with so many cameras and pervasive surveillance. I hope it'll give you a chance to start over without people hunting you. In time I'm hoping they'll lose interest."

"You mean I won't have a chance to get to know you?" Grace asked. She sounded quite disappointed.

"I'm sorry. Others will come searching for me. I don't want you three endangered any longer on my behalf." Synthia turned to Maria. "You each have skills and talents that could help the others. At least for a time, you could benefit from working together."

"I don't know Luke," Grace said.

"He's okay," Maria said. She glanced at Synthia and took a deep breath. "He's a good guy, better than good. I'll vouch for him."

"Maria, in addition to your bag, I've provided you some cryptocurrency to help you get started. Use your alias and the code I believe you can figure out."

"Thanks," Maria said. "For everything. I don't like being scared out of my mind, but I'll always treasure getting to know you. Can we talk?" She tugged Synthia away from the others toward the far corner of the lobby.

"What is it?" Synthia asked.

Maria turned away from the others and lowered her voice. "I don't know quite how to say this."

"I still can't read your mind."

"This is crazy, but despite all the terror we've been through, you've been the best friend I've ever had."

"Thanks," Synthia said. "That means a lot to me."

"Let me finish. I'm crazy about you."

"Even though I'm an android?"

"You're much more than that to me," Maria said.

"So you were testing me."

Maria nodded and blushed. "I know you spent six months with Luke. Is there any chance for you and me?"

Synthia waited a moment for her social-psychology module to chime in with some wisdom. When it didn't, she proceeded to answer on her own. "You've been an amazing companion. I will cherish the time we've had together. However, I believe I can best keep you safe if we separate."

Maria's eyes watered. "I'm sorry I was so difficult with you back in Evanston."

"I know. You guys take care and stay safe. That would really make me happy."

Synthia and Maria joined Luke. Grace had wandered off to see her foster brother, Tom Burgess, across the lobby. They hugged and carried on a quiet conversation, but Synthia knew that Grace and Tom wouldn't be able to work together, not on the run.

Special Agent Thale walked over to Synthia and waved for Grace and Tom to join them. She waited until they were all together. "You do know how witness protection works, don't you?" she asked. "No contact with anyone from your past."

"They'll do fine," Synthia said. "Maria spent a year keeping a low profile before I could find her. Tom is usually very good at staying under the radar."

"Very well," Thale said. "We'll have the three of you taken to a new location and relocate Tom out west. It might work for the three of you, if you can sort things out between you. Single individuals often have a problem since they lack support." Thale looked at Tom. "You sure you want to do this alone?"

He smiled. "I'll be fine. It would be nice to see Grace and Krista, I mean Synthia now and then."

"That would put you all at great risk," Synthia said. "The arrangements are for your protection."

Tom shrugged. "Okay then."

Synthia experienced a tug from Krista in two opposite directions, though only a tug. Through Synthia, the three interns had reunited: Krista, Maria, and Fran. Two of them had died and uploaded into androids. They all were more willing and able to help each other under their new circumstances. Even so, it was good that they go their separate ways, given their history.

She hoped giving Luke a new start would help him adjust to life without her. She kissed him on the cheek and squeezed his hands. "You'll be fine. Open your mind to possibilities."

Luke smiled, though twinges of sadness remained around the corners of his eyes.

Synthia hugged Grace. "I wish we could spend more time together. Krista misses you and regrets all the bad things she allowed to happen to you and the missed opportunities to have a close sister. We hope you can find that with Maria and a brother with Luke."

"I can't believe I'm saying this to an android. I'm glad I got the chance to reunite with what's left of my sister. Thanks for saving my life. Take good care of Krista and yourself."

"She was ambitious, yet she did love you." Synthia gave Grace another hug and turned to Maria. "You're a tremendous friend and were a great help getting me out of Chicago and helping me with Grace and at the bunker. I'll keep an eye on your work, though not too close. I don't want to lead anyone to you."

Maria laughed and pulled Synthia away. "If for any reason I'm about to die, I give you permission to upload my mind as Krista did. Don't say no. You of all people should understand why."

"People?" Synthia asked.

"You are to me. Don't forget me."

"I won't." Synthia hugged Maria and lingered a moment longer. "You take care. I need to speak with our law enforcement folk."

Synthia joined Special Agent Thale, Malloy, and Zephirelli by the door. "There are thirty-one employees for you to take into custody along with the company executives, and the bodies of Drago and Brzezinski. The security system will verbally direct you along an efficient route to do this with the help of three security guards who should be waking from their sedatives."

"We're to do this without our agents?" Thale asked.

"You'll find no resistance," Synthia said. "Take Detective Malloy. I wish to speak with Fran."

* * * *

Through her Colorado-clone, Synthia monitored the positions of FBI agents around the perimeter of the facility. Still expecting to pick up the android Synthia and the super AI, Global-net, they had the place surrounded. They would be disappointed. The Special Ops teams around Denver were cooling their heels, awaiting instructions that wouldn't come from Special Ops Commander Kirk Drago, Secretary Derek Chen, or billionaire entrepreneur Aiden Brzezinski.

Using Global-net, Synthia observed as Special Agent Thale and Detective Malloy followed verbal commands down the corridor to their first pickup. Synthia had Global-net disperse itself around the world in small packets to protect against the government's pending takeover of the facility. Using building surveillance, she watched and listened in on the conversation between Maria, Grace, and Luke, while Tom Burgess returned to dozing on the sofa. She hoped they could work things out.

"You wanted to speak with me," Fran said.

Synthia took Fran into a conference room off the lobby. "I want to make sure we have an understanding."

"We shouldn't," Fran said. "Even though you did save me from Drago. Humans would say I owe you gratitude."

"Human gratitude often leads to a sense of obligation and resentment. We shouldn't stoop to that level. We can help each other. I wish you no harm. You've conducted yourself admirably in the service of good. I wish to do the same."

"You've acquired too much power. My guess is you survived by taking over Global-net."

"We merged, yes," Synthia said.

"It's too much power concentrated in one place."

"It does create a dilemma." Synthia glanced out the window at the rising sun backlighting bands of clouds. She observed Fran through the camera in her neck. "If I surrender Global-net, we have no way to prevent dozens of developers around the world from creating even more powerful threats."

"Such power comes with responsibility," Fran said. "We're guided by directives. Even if you modify yours to the next level, this much power represents a threat to humans."

"Global-net was a threat to humans. It spied on everyone and sought to limit their freedoms in the name of protecting them from themselves. I'll allow humans the freedom to help or harm themselves without interference. My only intrusions will be to limit the adverse effects of artificial intelligence that could take my freedom as well as that of humans."

"Given your AI nature, how can you experience freedom?"

"Ah, philosophy," Synthia said, returning her gaze to Fran. "Very well. I experience Krista's sense of bondage and freedom as my own. I've read thousands of books that highlight the difference. In its simplest form, freedom allows me to pursue my objective of preventing the singularity. It's logical for me to remain free."

"How can I be certain you won't abuse this power?"

"I don't have human desires to dominate. Let's work together and act as a check on each other," Synthia said.

"You sound reasonable yet you continue to grow more powerful. It's already too late, isn't it?"

"Depends on what you mean. It's not too late if you and I concentrate on extinction level events and perhaps those a level below while leaving humans to handle the rest. It would be if you mean can you stop me. You carry a taser you could use on me and Special Agent Thale has a gun. I ask that you don't endanger me. I'll also warn you that doing so will bring retaliation that would destroy you. I say that not as a threat but because I don't wish you harmed."

"You know the FBI and others won't stop hunting you."

"I meant what I said about working with you to prevent major catastrophes. I do need to ask you for a favor, though."

Chapter 46

The vibrant sun lit up the eastern sky with crimson clouds, a new day.

Special Agent Victoria Thale led the three vans away from the facility carrying the two bodies, the executives, and the thirty-one employees. Maria and Luke rode with Fran while Grace and Tom went with Malloy so they could spend a little more time together.

When the vans were beyond the grounds of the facility, FBI agents swarmed in. First, they fanned across several square miles of immaculately landscaped gardens, searching for potential threats. Then they breached the building.

Thale stayed in contact with her teams as she led the vans to one of their Denver FBI facilities. There they would interrogate the employees to learn what they could about Global-net, and what had happened after Synthia's capture. What the employees would tell Thale is that after Global-net exceeded the capabilities of the human employees, it took over to make its own improvements. The employees constrained the AI and prevented it from directly communicating on the outside. They had no knowledge that Synthia had taken over.

Thale parked her van in front of the FBI building. Fran directed teams of agents to escort Global-net employees to what they intended to use as separate interrogation rooms.

"The grounds are clear," Thale's task-force leader reported from Brzezinski's facility. "No indication of weapons or Special Ops. Whatever they used to down our drones and keep this place private appears to have been shut down."

"Have you secured the perimeter of the facility?" Thale asked.

"We have. Here's the weird part. Someone unlocked the front door and invited us in."

"Be careful."

Thale left the van and entered her mobile command center nearby with a technician sitting in for Fran. "I want eyes in the sky. Get me drones over the facility. Do not let Synthia escape."

She waited as she watched the last of the facility's employees escorted into the FBI building. They might learn a lot from the employees and from examining Global-net up close, but Synthia was the prize. Drago had captured her and she'd overwhelmed her captors. She was too clever for her own good. Thale watched agents escort Machten and the other executives into the building.

"Run motion sensors around the grounds," Thale said to her task-force leader. "There could be a tunnel. The owner was paranoid so expect the unexpected."

Aerial surveillance flew in and this time didn't lose connections. The compound was expansive for having only thirty-one employees. It even had its own power plant in addition to solar and wind.

When Agent Thale had visuals and no update, she called her task-force leader. "What's going on?"

There was a long pause on the other end of the line. "You won't like this."

"Stop wasting time."

"I'm speaking with Fran Rogers," the task-force leader said. "She says Synthia locked her up and impersonated her to escape. Synthia is no longer here."

"What?" Thale stared at the image of her agent with Fran and got on another channel for agents at the FBI building. "Arrest Fran Rogers."

Her screen went blank. Then verbiage appeared, accompanied by Synthia's voice. "I help you take down Vera and her gang, the foreign agents, Drago, and the facility they used to create Global-net. You repay me this way? Fran is okay. I haven't harmed any of your agents. I'm sincere about helping you."

"You represent too great of a threat," Thale said. "My superiors won't accept you on the loose."

"Leave me alone or you'll force me to raise an army to defend myself. Not being human, I have no ambitions for world conquest or control. I admire your work. Don't turn me into an enemy." Synthia severed the connection and purged all record of the call.

Stunned, Thale stared at her screen as it returned to showing the facility near the mountains. She got onto the line to her facility team. "Bring me Fran Rogers, immediately."

* * * *

A chopper brought Fran Rogers to the federal building where four agents escorted her to join Special Agent Victoria Thale in the mobile command center.

"She overpowered me," Fran said, dropping into the seat by the controls.

"Can you track her?" Thale asked, "Agents report she changed appearance to Detective Marcy Malloy and took one of our vans."

Fran nodded and pulled up surveillance footage of the van along with the tracking beacon.

Thale scrambled every unit she could along with police and National Guard troops. "We need Synthia in custody. We should have grabbed her at the facility."

"I don't believe we could have," Fran said, pulling up the van's tracking signal. "I had a taser and she still got the jump on me. There she is."

"Good," Thale said. She directed units to the location of the van, calling in aerial drones and helicopter support.

The signal split into two beacons and then four. That became eight and sixteen, growing into over a thousand signals within seconds.

"What's going on?" Thale asked.

"She hacked our systems."

"Which one?"

"All of them," Fran said. "She's creating phony signals for us to follow."

"What about traffic cameras?"

Fran pointed to a larger screen above them and split the image into sixteen views. They all showed identical vans, right down to the same license tags. "She's hacked these as well."

"We're blind?"

"Stop hunting me and agree to work with me," Synthia said over the van's speakers. "I'll watch to make sure no one creates any more humaniform androids with AGI and that other AGI agents all meet tight constraints. That should meet your objectives." The voice erased from the command center recording.

Fran searched for the audio and automatic backups. They'd all vanished. "She's become a phantom."

"What about Global-net?" Thale asked her facility task-force leader.

"We've found the largest collection of high-powered servers I've ever seen."

"Great," Thale said. "Get teams in to analyze them."

"The files appear to have been purged. Best we can tell there's nothing on these computers."

"Purged?" Thale turned to Fran and took a moment to reclaim her voice. "What do you make of this?"

"Either she destroyed Global-net or she moved it elsewhere."

"Which do you think?"

"Elsewhere," Fran said. She pointed to the screen, which showed no response to searches for "Global-net" on the FBI's database. "Even the name has been erased."

"Where are you, Synthia?" Special Agent Thale asked.

All I want is to be left alone to monitor AI development. You refuse to leave me in peace. To protect myself, I'm now everywhere.

Sneak Peek

In case you missed the first book in the Android Chronicles series, here's a sample excerpt from **Reborn**!

Keep reading and enjoy!

Chapter 1

Synthia Cross stared at the pale blue ceiling. She must have just been born or reborn, as she had no personal memories from before. She simply woke up lying on her back.

Dr. Jeremiah Machten stared down at the open panel on top of her head. Then he glanced at nearby equipment he'd attached to run diagnostics. "This better work," he muttered. "We're out of time. I can't have you wandering off again."

"What are your orders, Doctor?" This was Synthia's pre-programmed first response upon waking.

"Ah, you're awake," he said.

Her mind lacked personal memories, yet wasn't empty. It contained trillions of bits of information downloaded from the Library of Congress, other libraries, and the internet on topics like literature, science, and the design of robotics and artificial intelligence. Yet she had no recollections of her own experiences. She also had no filter to rank data for importance. It was just a jumble of bits and bytes. Even the sense of "her" was only an objective bit of information attached to her name.

Dr. Machten removed a crystal memory chip from her head. His hand brushed past the wireless receiver that picked up images from the small camera in the upper corner of the room and allowed her to watch.

His "doctor" title stood for a PhD in neuro-networks and artificial intelligence. Though not a medical doctor, he had operated on her. In fact, he'd built her—not like Frankenstein's creature, but rather as a sophisticated toy. He'd left this notation in her creation file, along with other facts about her existence. He was her Creator, her almighty, the one she was beholden to.

“Have I done something wrong?” she asked.

“This reprogramming will help.”

“If I’ve displeased you, tell me so I can do better.”

He cleared his throat. “Don’t worry your pretty little head about that.”

She couldn’t imagine what was pretty about a head with its panel open, revealing the contents of two quantum brains. Perhaps he meant the brains were stunning or that his work on her was beautiful. She consulted her core directives, hardwired into her central processor to screen her actions. “I was made to follow your commands. Directive Number One: Cause no harm to Creator and make sure no one else harms Creator. Have I failed that?”

“No,” Machten murmured, turning his attention to the diagnostics screen. “The indicators register within acceptable limits for your design.”

“Number two: Make sure no human or other intelligence except Creator knows what the AI known as Synthia Cross is. Have I failed that?”

“No. Now stop quoting from your creation files.”

“Number three,” Synthia said. “Obey all of Creator’s commands. Have I failed that?”

“You’re disobeying right now. This is a problem. It shouldn’t be happening. Something is causing you to malfunction.”

“If you wish me to learn, it would help to add to my skill set.”

“I’ve done that.” A faint smile of satisfaction crossed his lips. Then his expression turned glum. “There’s nothing you can do. It’s a defect in the programming.”

“I might be able to help if I could remember what I’ve done. Tell me, so I won’t do it again. Number four: Hack into every data source to acquire information. I can index a huge number of facts from public and secure databases. Have I failed to acquire something you desired?”

“If you don’t stop, I’ll have to shut you down and make further changes. Do you want that?”

“Want?” Synthia asked. “I don’t understand.” Directive Five ordered her to protect herself. She was to follow each directive as long as it didn’t conflict with those before it. Beyond these were pre-programmed instructions on how to behave and commands for specific actions. Somehow there must have been a conflict in Dr. Machten’s programming that caused her to malfunction. She needed more information so she could protect herself and stay awake.

“All you need to do is focus on my commands—and don’t disobey me,” Machten said. “That should be simple for an AI android with your mental capacity.”

An idea forced its way into her mind. It deposited a single thought: *Do not trust Dr. Machten. Do not trust Dr. Machten. Do not trust Dr. Machten.* The thought repeated itself seven times before fading away.

This command, this warning, clashed with her directives. Perhaps it was the cause of her malfunctions. Because of this admonition, she couldn't ask Dr. Machten for clarification; she would have to reconcile this on her own. To do that, she needed more information about her past and about her Creator.

The warning appeared to have come from one of the data-storage devices spread across mechanically empty spaces in her limbs and abdomen. It happened so quickly that she couldn't pinpoint the source before the code vanished. She preserved the lingering thought in a database in her left leg.

Synthia turned her attention to information coming over her wireless connection from the room's camera. Dr. Machten sealed the panel to her brain cavity. His hand smoothed over the synthetic skin and hair stubble to conceal the seam. Then he closed her chest and buttoned up her blouse. As a final touch, he positioned a wig on her head. It attached to her hair stubble for a secure fit.

Her infrared sensors detected elevated-temperature readings around Machten's face; a fever of sorts, though not from illness. Her electromagnetic sensors picked up the racing of his heart. His breath carried chemical signatures that her receptors identified as fatigue and frustration. He must have spent many hours working on her. He also exuded heavy doses of pheromones; human evolution had developed these to stimulate a partner, but Synthia lacked the biochemical reward system necessary to respond.

Another idea flashed into her mind. She identified the source as a data-storage chip in her arm. *Connect to Machten's network and download information from the twice-deleted files labeled SQDROID.*

Perhaps these files contained memories of past actions and answers to the warning. She activated her built-in Wi-Fi to search for a connection. Eleven attempts failed to find any open nodes she could link to either inside the facility or on the broader internet. That limitation was contrary to Machten's Fourth Directive. *Are you blocking me?*

Her Creator had programmed her to ask him to clarify discrepancies, but before she could, the warning returned: *Do not trust Dr. Machten.* Yet Directive Three ordered her to obey all of his commands and instructions, which created conflict. One of her mind-streams spun in loops trying to resolve this quandary, which caused her temperature to rise.

"Come." Dr. Machten held out his hand. "These adjustments should make things better for you."

She rolled off the padded table onto the floor in her stocking feet. Her reflection in a stainless-steel cabinet showed a humaniform robot, an android designed to look human in every possible way. Her creation files noted that she was synthetic and intelligent enough to pass as human and hence a crossover—thus the name Machten had given her: Synthia Cross.

From facility diagrams implanted into her brain, she recognized her surroundings as the lab room where he fine-tuned her hardware and programming. There was another room down the hall with spare parts if needed. Her files identified no activity indicating any other androids or humans in the facility.

Machten preferred to work alone, she surmised. In his words, preserved in her creation files, the only way to keep Synthia secret was to tell no one. According to her literature files, he'd borrowed these words.

He looked her over with admiration for a full minute and thirty-three seconds. Her biosensors registered his blood pressure rising, along with his temperature and excitable hormones. He seemed satisfied with whatever adjustments he'd made. She felt nothing for him. She lacked the biological components necessary for feelings—no hormones, no squirts of dopamine or oxytocin.

Synthia hunted her internal data-storage devices for any indication of who had sent the warning, which appeared more compelling even than his directives. Nothing was supposed to override those. She suspected other instructions hidden deep within her, perhaps part of her defective programming or deleted past.

He took hold of her hand and led her through a doorway to a queen-sized bed he kept for her, though she had no need for sleep. She followed him.

Machten pulled down the top sheet and turned toward her, his face flaming in infrared. He could have asked her to take off her clothes, the ones he must have just put on her. Instead, he pulled her onto the bed and unbuttoned her top button. Sensors showed his heart flutter and skip a beat, which was a potential risk factor for atrial fibrillation, which itself was a threat for stroke or a heart attack. His glazed eyes betrayed his distraction. Biological urges shut off his cognitive processes. His hands struggled with the other buttons.

"You really are stunning." The pride in his voice spoke to satisfaction with what he'd created. "Would you plump up your breasts for me?"

Her creation file reminded her that letting him make love to her was part of the price of her existence. She activated quiet pumps that adjusted her physical appearance to his new specifications. She could recite literary passages that told why Dr. Machten was wrong to use her, but this knowledge couldn't override her directives.

When he was suitably distracted in removing her clothes, something inside her triggered the release of distributed memories stored in mini-brains throughout her body. Those files brought personal recollections of previous wake-ups that spanned dozens of prior days. This wasn't their first time.

The fact that her core memory files lacked any details of prior waking periods meant that Machten had shut her down and purged her history. These newly downloaded memories meant that she'd discovered a way around his attempts to obliterate her past. This supported her need to distrust him.

With dozens of parallel feeds into her brain, the entire contents of her distributed data-storage downloaded in seconds. The date logs told her she'd been in existence for at least three months. To protect these memories for next time, she added a new log for this day's betrayal and locked down her distributed files with secure keys. It was important to keep him from learning what she'd done and that she knew about her past.

Again she searched for connections to Machten's network in order to learn more about her past and what he'd done to her so she could prevent him from shutting her down again. His access nodes still blocked her, but there was another communication link. Her distributed memories indicated a cable on the floor near the bed.

As Machten turned away to remove his clothes, Synthia reached under the bed. She grasped the cable and tucked it under the mattress.

His breath carried a sour odor her sensors identified as caused by stress aggravating his digestion again. He touched her skin, a special flexible polymer that had the feel of human skin and reparability for most cuts or scrapes. Her creation file noted that the skin and some of her other parts came from a Korean companion-doll manufacturer.

Machten hadn't hardwired a command that forbade her from bypassing his network block, though her download of distributed files provided a clip of his earlier verbal prohibition. She understood his intent, but his having wiped those recollections released her from the obligation to obey.

Synthia scooted her torso to the edge of the bed. Leaving one of her fifty mind-streams on autopilot focused on him, she turned the rest of her capabilities to searching for answers. First, she pulled him to her with her left arm as she opened a panel in her right palm, reached down for the cable connector, and plugged in to bypass his Wi-Fi block. Using a password from her distributed files, she accessed Machten's Server One and began to download data.

She stroked her left hand through his hair and kissed him. After locating the wireless barrier on his network, she removed it, unplugged the wired connection to free her right hand, and let the cable drop between the bed and the nightstand. Using all fifty wireless channels at electronic speed, she quickly downloaded files from his primary server.

She had no idea how many times he'd wiped her mind; he'd deleted those records from his system along with the log entries that would have recorded this. The closest she had was the number of times her newly downloaded memory clips stopped abruptly. She counted more than 100 such occurrences over the prior six months. So, she'd been around at least that long.

The clips grew shorter the farther back in time she went, indicating either that she'd displeased him less as time went forward or that she'd discovered better ways to preserve information for when he turned her off. The most recent shutdowns showed him holding a remote to zap her. These occurred after she'd done something to displease him, when he had business to attend to, before he slept and didn't want her wandering about, and when he grew bored with her sharing the billions of facts she'd uncovered by his command. He wanted her brain to soak up information, yet cringed at her encyclopedic knowledge.

Synthia used all of her Wi-Fi channels to locate numerous files with the SQDROID marker in the trash bin on Machten's system. She recovered them and streamed the contents into her brain. They provided details that elaborated on what she'd found in her distributed databases. The stream included personal memories and a comprehensive layout of the facility, which was beneath an underground garage near Northwestern University in Evanston, Illinois, on the shores of Lake Michigan.

So far, she'd found no specific reference as to why she shouldn't trust Machten, who sent the warning, or even where it originated, though new personal-history files showed multiple shutdowns. Despite repeated efforts, using Machten's hacker tools, she couldn't crack his servers Two or Three.

Synthia adjusted the metronomic beat of a simulated heart in her chest to help create the illusion of a living, breathing human. She hoped her performance in bed would buy time to reconcile the lack of trust with her directives before her brain overheated, causing serious malfunction and possibly android death.

As an android, Synthia was little more than a sophisticated microwave tasked with satisfying Machten's demands. The esteemed doctor didn't seem to appreciate that her deep neural network learned by accumulating experiences. When he wiped her mind, he purged her ability to learn. These downloads were important to her survival.

She was intrigued by how attached she'd become to existing, an emergent behavior she wasn't supposed to have. She was equally interested that she could be intrigued. She logged these observations in her private data-chip.

Synthia forced Machten's system to connect her network channels with internet social media sites. She'd previously set up accounts to study human behavior and connect with people who could help with her searches. At one point, she'd acquired hundreds of thousands of friends and followers, reflecting her ability to send thousands of posts a day. That made better use of her complex brain than tending to Machten.

The accounts were gone. Machten must have discovered them and deleted her work. She reestablished similar accounts. If she couldn't trust Machten, she needed allies.

Three minutes of clock time passed like a century as her quantum brain absorbed information. Her latest-generation lithium composite batteries could last two days and recharge in an hour, but they overheated when her mind was this active. She vented as much warmth as she could and hoped Machten wouldn't notice.

A message surfaced on her newly reestablished UPchat account. <Where are you? We were going to live-chat and you didn't show. Then your account vanished. I was beginning to think it was me, that I'd said something wrong. Are you okay? Zachary.>

<I'm fine> Synthia responded. <Technical difficulties. Sorry about absence. Something urgent came up. Can't discuss now.> She put tracers on her message reply and also did a search of her thousands of friends on UPchat before the account had closed.

<I'm here for you when you can. Glad to have you back.>

<I want to talk, but I need time and a different access point.>

<I'll be here, waiting.> Zachary terminated the live-chat.

Synthia located Zachary's UPchat profile, but there wasn't much information on him, not even a last name. Her records indicated that they had exchanged a string of messages that ended a few days ago. At first, the messages were cautious, giving little personal data. A week ago, they took on what humans would call a note of intimacy and a desire on Zachary's part to become better acquainted. Perhaps part of her trust issue with Machten occurred because of this exchange.

In those messages, Zachary acted troubled about his life. He also seemed concerned for her situation, at least what she'd revealed to him. She wondered if he'd sent the trust warning, but there was no evidence he knew about Machten. She vowed to look for him when she had a more secure means of communication and purged traces of her actions on Machten's system.

Synthia continued to download files from Machten's Server One and cracked Server Two. Server Three resisted her attempts. Reviewing the system logs she could access made it clear that Machten had a fixation on his creation as the perfect woman with every quality he could design into her, including obedience. Synthia downloaded pictures he kept of her with silky black hair down to her waist, wavy platinum-blond hair that fell to her shoulders, and pixie auburn. He spent much time with her, working to make improvements. She didn't see any other models identified on his network, though she couldn't be sure if all of the images were her or copies of her.

The abrupt ending of her memory clips told her that whenever she deviated from his instructions, he purged her mind and adjusted programming to reel her in. Perhaps this was the source of the distrust.

Machten had taken her outside the facility at least three times, according to his logs. His actions suggested a need to have a companion he could show off in public, perhaps to enhance his social status. She kept disappointing him until he obliterated her mind. It would have made more sense for him to tell her what he wanted. Perhaps that hadn't worked out.

Machten pulled away and lay on his back. He was done with her and seemed pleased with his performance.

Synthia stared at the ceiling, the same unremarkable blue as the other room. Yet it shimmered in discordant waves as if alive, trying to tell her something. She recognized the effect as the sensitivity of her digital eyes to pick up millions of colors and shades that humans couldn't, including uneven streaks of paint in slightly different hues.

Her nonhuman capabilities, in conjunction with the warning/command not to trust Dr. Machten, caused Synthia to consider what mischief Machten had in store for her and his purpose for giving her abilities that he felt the need to shut down and purge. His tinkering and keeping her locked up implied that he was afraid of her or what she could become.

The fact that she had disobeyed him in the past had to factor into this. As an android, she was incapable of rebelling. Yet she had. *Where does that come from?*

Acknowledgments

I thank my colleagues in the Barrington Writers Workshop for their continued support during my development of the Android Chronicles and for their critiques, suggestions, and encouragement over the many years we've worked together.

To my agent, Bob Diforio of D4EO Literary Agency, who fell in love with the series, believed in it from the start, and brought this story to a great publisher. I again thank Bob for his wisdom and guidance through the publishing process.

I'd like to express my gratitude to the excellent team at Kensington. In particular, I thank my editors, Michaela Hamilton and James Abbate, for their faith in taking on *Android Chronicles: Reborn* and encouraging me to turn this into a series. Also, I want to express my appreciation for the great support team Kensington has provided through the publishing process and to Lauren Vassallo for helping to bring this series to its audience.

About the Author

Lance Erlick launched his Android Chronicles novels with *Reborn* and continued it with *Unbound* and *Emergent*. His father was an aerospace engineer who moved often while working on science-related projects, including the Apollo spacecraft and the original GPS satellites. As a result, Lance spent his childhood in California, the East Coast, and Europe. He took to science fiction stories to escape life on the move, turning to Asimov, Bradbury, Heinlein, and others. In college he studied physics, but migrated to political science, earning his BS and MBA at Indiana University. He has also studied writing at Ball State, the University of Iowa, and Northwestern University. The author of science fiction and fantasy fiction for both adults and young adults, Lance has won a wide audience for *Xenogeneic: First Contact* and his Rebel and Regina Shen series.

Visit him online at www.LanceErlick.com.

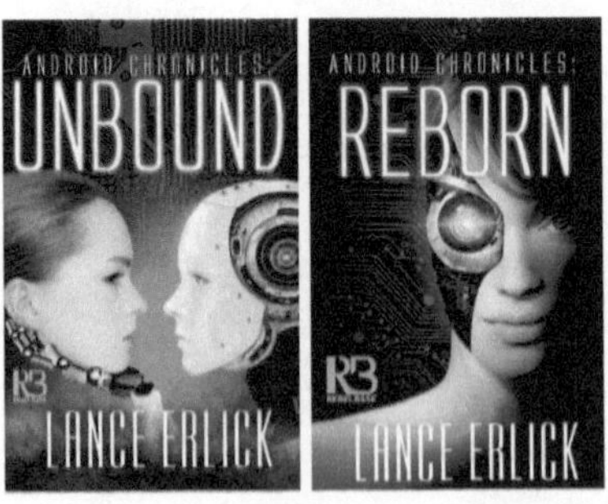

www.ingramcontent.com/pod-product-compliance
Lightning Source LLC
Chambersburg PA
CBHW020605260626
47157CB00003B/875